EMMA ST. CLAIR

Copyright © 2022 by Emma St. Clair

All rights reserved.

No part of this book may be reproduced in any form or by any electronic or mechanical means, including information storage and retrieval systems, without written permission from the author, except for the use of brief quotations in a book review. If you have questions and need to contact the author, please message emma@emmastclair.com.

Thank you to Stephanie of Alt19 Creative for this cover!

First, to Jo, a truly wonderful aunt. I miss you so much!

To Rob. I FINALLY finished the book. You're welcome. Same. Sandwiches. Jinx. Jinx again.

To Susan and George. Thanks for letting me crash in your guest house so I can write and be a hermit ... except for the wine on the back patio with y'all.

BUY-IN:
the minimum amount of money a player must spend to enter in a poker game

FIVE PERKS OF SMALL-TOWN LIVING

By Birdie Graham

NEW YORK, London, and L.A. may get a lot of well-deserved hype, but there's something to be said about small towns. Need convincing? Here are five perks of small-town living!

1. You won't be the weirdest person there. Small towns always seem to have a high concentration of strange, especially when compared to the population density. Maybe it's the woman who walks her pet cow on a leash or the man named Wolf who shouts marriage proposals from a moving vehicle. Whatever your level of weird, you're likely to find someone weirder in a small town.
2. Small-town gossip is the best. *People* magazine has

got nothing on a tiny town's grapevine. If someone so much as sneezes in the hardware store, you'll know about it. This also means you should watch where you sneeze …
3. The whole town is like family. This is a double-edged sword. On the one hand, you'll have a lot more support when you need it. On the other, you'll have a lot of family. Enough said.
4. You'll save on gas. In a small town, you might not even need a car. Acceptable alternative methods of transportation are on foot, bicycle, or horseback.
5. You can always go back to the city.

CHAPTER ONE

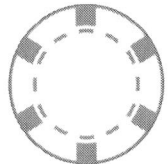

Pat

"You bought a what?"

The question comes out of me in something like a wheeze-snort. I set my coffee mug down, gripping the spotless kitchen counter with both hands, needing the stability.

My father repeats himself slowly, his eyes crinkling at the corners. "I bought a town."

That's what I *thought* he said. But buying a town sounds like something *I* might do. I'm the one in my family who gravitates toward highly impulsive decisions—often things I regret five minutes later.

"You, the most penny-pinching, responsible man I know, purchased a *town*?"

His grin grows wider and even more infuriating. "A *town*, Patrick. As in, a small city."

"I know what a town is. What I fail to understand is what possessed you to purchase one."

"I was searching through listings and came upon a very unique property."

I stare at the man who earned the nickname Think Tank on the football field for his combination of brains and brawn. The Tank part still holds up—I swear, he could still bench press me, and I'm no Thumbelina. But I'm starting to question if he may have lost some of the *Think*.

Tank is a rock. A practical, stubborn, no-nonsense stalwart of wise decisions. He doesn't have an impulsive bone in his body. He is the man who managed a successful pro ball career and then raised me, my two brothers, and my sister after my mom died.

I angle my head to the side, squinting at the man now sipping coffee as though this were a perfectly normal conversation to have. Dad's bright blue eyes still look clear and sharp. His dark hair isn't any more threaded with gray than it was yesterday. Outwardly, he *looks* like my dad, not an imposter or doppelganger. I don't believe in shape-shifters, so that's out.

I give myself a hard pinch on the arm. Nope—this isn't a dream.

And yet … here we are. Standing in his kitchen, discussing the fact that he PURCHASED A TOWN.

Narrowing my eyes, I ask, "Did you consult Consumer Report first?"

He rumbles out a laugh. "I did, but oddly enough, there was no section on townships."

I wait for the punchline, for one of my brothers to jump out and shout that I'm being punked. But Tank is serious, and the smug amusement on his face tells me he's enjoying my reaction. Maybe a little too much.

I blink. He blinks back, the corners of his mouth lifting. We are having a blink-off, and Tank is winning.

I rub my eyes, then drag a hand through my hair. "Dad, you can't just *Schitt's Creek* a town."

"Language, son."

I roll my eyes. Dad trained me and my siblings to steer clear of the three Ls: language, ladies, and the love of money. (For Harper, the ladies was probably replaced with something like lazy, lying, men.) Out of respect, we keep our language pretty clean, and Dad's relentless financial training turned us all into fiscally responsible adults.

As for the ladies ... well. As the old saying goes, two out of three ain't so bad. Over the years, Collin, James, and I were locked in a three-way tie for quickest turnover in the girlfriend department. Nowadays, Collin is too much of a workaholic to date, and James is practically a hermit. As for me, I want a romantic, true love, all-in marriage like my dad and mom. But seeing how I already met the perfect woman and, in typical Pat fashion, screwed it all up, I'm basically a monk.

"Catch up to the times, old man. *Schitt's Creek* is a show. You'd know that if you stopped protesting Netflix's price increase."

Tank grumbles, but thankfully doesn't launch into his tirade about Netflix and price gouging. Instead, he asks, "What kind of a show is named *Poop Creek?*"

I choke on my laughter. "It's got Eugene Levy in it. You love him."

"Is he the one with the eyebrows?"

"The very one. I'll let you Netflix it on my account."

"You should really stop *verbing* nouns. I'm not giving up my boycott based on moral principles for a show named after poop. Not even for Eugene Levy. What's it about?"

"A dad buys a town for his son as a joke, but the family ends up living there when they lose everything. Sound a little autobiographical?"

He chuckles. "Actually, yes. Considering I bought this town for *my* sons. Well, all of us, really. But especially you boys."

"Christmas is months away, and even if it were closer, none of us asked for a whole town in their stocking."

Tank shakes his head like he's disappointed in my lack of understanding. "It's for the *brewery*."

I shake my head. "James won't like it."

"James hasn't seen it."

"Unless it's a town somehow located within the Austin city limits, James won't be on board. And because you did this without even asking him, he'll say no on principle."

We may call the fledgling Dark Horse Brewery a family business, but it's my oldest brother James's *baby*. His idea, his award-winning brews. The rest of us are more like investors. Mostly the silent kind, since James doesn't love input.

He is notoriously control freaky about everything from the kinds of barrels he brews in to the farms used to source the hops. James is NOT going to be okay with Dad making a unilateral decision about location for the planned expansion.

Especially considering the fact that wherever this town is, it's not in *Austin*. First, my whole family lives here. Other than the few years Collin and I played pro football in various cities, we've all stuck close to home. I think losing Mom so young bonded us uniquely together. We're not just family, but best friends.

Second and maybe more importantly, Austin is a city filled with people ready to drop their cold, hard cash on fancy microbrews. The college kids, the foodie snobs, those busy keeping Austin weird, and even Gen X-ers still partying like it's literally 1999—they all like beer. Especially *good* beer. Custom stuff with fancy names and delicately layered flavors, which, it turns out, James is a genius at developing.

I'm honestly a little envious at how my older brothers have found ways to monetize their unique skill sets. James has Dark Horse, Collin has his gym for elite athletes (where Harper also works), and I have ... I don't even know what. My sparkling personality? My keen wit? My ability to binge several seasons of a TV show in a week?

I'm still trying to figure my life out at twenty-seven. I've yet to find something that holds my attention for more than a few months. Thankfully, because of a few years of pro ball salary and smart investments, I don't need to worry about finances. But it doesn't help scratch the itch of restlessness I've felt since my career ended.

"We can get James on board," Tank says.

I don't miss the *we*, like he already thinks I'm on Team Tank.

"The location isn't so far from Austin," he continues. "The town needs a little TLC, but once we fix it up—"

"Let me stop you right there." I hold up a hand. "The *town* needs TLC? Like, the whole town you bought?"

"It's a little past its glory days," Tank admits. "But nothing we can't fix up. I think it will be fun."

"Fun is taking a family trip to Cancun or a cruise to the Bahamas. Fun is an all-you-can eat brisket buffet. Fun is poker night. Fixing up a whole town does not sound like a good time."

Tank only grunts, crossing his arms and giving me a dark look. *Shut up, Patrick*, I tell myself, because I can tell that with every word coming out of my mouth, he's only getting more stubborn about this whole thing. But restraint is not in my wheelhouse.

"Let me get this straight," I say. "You bought a town to house the brewery, and you want us all to fix it up HGTV style?" Tank nods. "But you didn't think to ask us first?" He nods again, and I press the heels of my hands into my eyes. "I knew I shouldn't have watched all those renovation shows with you. Now they've got you thinking you can just up and Joanna Gaines a town."

"What did I say about nouns as verbs, son?"

I ignore him and pull out my phone to call in the reinforcements, aka my siblings. I'm not doing anyone any favors by running my big mouth.

Our dad has dug in his heels, and at this point, I think it may take all of us to pull the stubborn old mule off this idea. I open the group text with Collin, James, Harper, and her husband. Chase has a way of keeping us all calm. Or, at least, calm*er*. Our fistfights have decreased by at least seventeen percent since Chase joined the family.

Before I can type so much as a scared-face emoji or 9-1-1, Tank snatches the phone out of my hand. "Don't tell your brothers. Not yet."

"Give me my phone, Pops." When he slides it into the back pocket of his jeans, I groan. "This isn't the kind of decision you make alone. Or with just me. We're all involved here."

"I need you to see it first. That's why I asked you to come over."

"I thought you needed help moving furniture."

"It was a ruse," he says, looking far too pleased with himself.

"Clearly."

"I need *you*, Pat."

Being chosen should feel like an honor. Instead, it feels a little like my dad singled out the weakest member of the herd. I hate being thought of as the easy mark. Even if it's true. I'm less intense and serious than my siblings, but it doesn't make me a pushover. I'm the fun one. Not a dummy, not a weak link.

Except, maybe I am. Because already, curiosity is warring with my better judgment. I want to see the town in all its faded glory. But my brothers will murder me if I don't tell them. Especially James. And since he's the only one bigger than Tank, I tend to give his rage a wide berth.

"Tank."

"Patty."

Forget the African plains. We're at the OK Corral, hands on our holsters, waiting for someone to draw first.

"You'll understand when you see it," Dad says. "You're a man of vision, like me."

"Don't try to flatter me. It won't work."

Lie. It's already working, and based on his expression, he knows it.

Tank comes around the island and claps a big, meaty hand on my shoulder. "Just come and see it. The magic of the idea will get in here"—he taps his slightly graying temple—"and it won't let you go. Same as me."

"And then I'll help you convince the others? Is that what you think?"

"If you believe it, they'll believe it."

I smirk. "And if I believe it, they will come?"

He grins, picking up on my *Field of Dreams* reference. Tank is my movie buddy. Many nights, I find my way over here to veg out in front of the TV. Sometimes we're joined by my brothers or Harper and Chase. Mainly, it's me and Tank, watching and filing away quotes for later use.

Recently, those two nights a week have bled into more like five or six, sleeping in my childhood bedroom instead of in my latest apartment. I can't seem to find a place that feels like home, and this newest apartment is no exception. The lease isn't up for six months, but I'm already looking around. I've thought about moving back home with Tank, since I'm here so much.

I suddenly imagine me and Tank in the same spots on his couch ten, maybe even twenty years from now. Two lonely old dudes having movie nights and wasting away. It's a little too easy to imagine.

Maybe we do need a project, a new dream. But still. A whole town?

"You overestimate my power of persuasion, Pops. James is the one you need to convince. He's driving the Dark Horse train. And Collin is way too logical not to shoot a million holes in this idea. Having me agree with you won't help."

If my oldest brother wins the stubborn award in addition to the control freak ribbon of excellence, Collin would take the cup in practicality and cautious decision-making. Despite an excellent business plan and the still semi-famous status attached to our family name, Collin spent years planning and worrying before he opened his gym. Years.

"You're underselling yourself," Dad says. "You are the glue in this family."

"Me?" I glance around the kitchen dramatically, as though looking for someone else Tank could mean.

"You."

I'm practically preening under his praise and wish my face didn't display every one of my emotions like a Jumbotron in a stadium. Dad thinks I—Patrick, the one no one takes seriously, like, *ever*—am the glue? Well, shucks.

Then he has to go and ruin it.

"I also think," he says carefully, like a man picking his way across a room full of trip wires, "it would be good for you. Maybe provide some focus and clarity about your future. You've been in limbo too long, son."

This again. I can't say I don't understand his concern. I'm just tired of hearing about it, of being judged or joked about because I don't know what I want to do when I grow up.

Sure, I have a tendency to jump from idea to idea, excitement to excitement. I get bored. I get restless. I like change. Some of that may have to do with my ADHD, which was undiagnosed until this past year, but it's hard to say where my brain function ends and my personality begins. I'll figure something out I love doing. One day.

Could it be this? The idea is completely ridiculous, but it also sounds like a challenge.

With an evil grin, Tank pulls out a set of car keys, pauses for dramatic effect, then says, "I'll let you drive the Aston Martin."

Oh, he's good. *Real* good.

I've wanted to drive the Aston since the moment Tank drove it home. It was—towns aside—the biggest splurge he has ever made. He tried to tell us all about some great deal he found but no one missed the timing—he bought it the week after Harper's wedding. She is the baby of the family, Tank's baby, and so we all totally understood the car as his way of coping.

And how many *other* people have driven it these past six months? Not a one. I will be the first.

Tank's grin widens, like he knows he has me, which he does. In truth, it's only partly because of the Aston. I'll admit it—Tank sparked my curiosity about this town. There are so many questions, each of them breeding more questions like a couple of bunnies in my brain. I have to see what kind of town would inspire the Think Tank to buy it.

And what does that even mean—to buy a town? Do you get all the businesses and buildings? Or is it more of a batteries-not-included, assemble-at-your-own-risk kind of thing?

I chew my lip, willing my hands not to grab the keys. At least, not too quickly. I need to keep some semblance of my dignity about me.

Who am I kidding? I have less than a fluid ounce of dignity in my entire body. I snatch the keys and dart toward the door leading to the garage, like Tank might change his mind at any second. Because he might.

I don't know if it's because of Tank calling me the glue and saying I'm the one with vision, or maybe just the chance to drive the Aston, but excitement has me glowing from within. I'm like the Griswolds' lit-up house in *Christmas Vacation*—at least, before the fuses blow.

I slide in, loving the way the leather molds to my body like a caress. The engine doesn't roar to life so much as purr. I can sense her power and her need for speed. She's just a big, beautiful jungle cat, wanting me to play with her.

Happy to oblige.

Tank folds his big body into the passenger seat, adjusting it for leg room.

"Just so we understand each other, this little road trip doesn't mean I'm on board with your hare-brained scheme, Tank. I hope you at least asked for the return policy on towns."

"Don't worry," he says, buckling his seat belt. "I don't plan to *return to sender* it."

"If you're going to do the noun as a verb thing, there's an

art to it," I tell him, revving the engine a little just to hear her purr.

Tank waves a hand toward the Texas morning sun slanting over the driveway. "Come on, now. *Fast and Furious* this thing. But legally."

I groan. "You're not going to stop with this, are you?"

"Not until you realize how stupid it sounds to *verb* nouns."

"Well, then, let's *road trip* this thing, Pops. Where are we headed, anyway?"

He laughs. "That's right—I haven't mentioned the best part about the town yet."

"It comes with a pro football team and a whole bunch of gorgeous and single cheerleaders?"

He shoots me a dirty look. "No. The best part is the name. It's called Sheet Cake, Texas."

A strange sensation zips up my spine. One that leaves me uncharacteristically and uncomfortably silent.

"You have no response to that name? I thought you'd be tossing out jokes like candy from a parade."

Oh, I have a response: *No way is a town named after cake.*

But I don't say it now. I said it five years ago, to the prettiest girl I've ever laid eyes on. She told me she was from a town called Sheet Cake. I teasingly called her a liar, she dumped her drink on my head, and thus began the shortest, most intense, and the only *real* relationship in my life.

Lindy was the One, and I totally screwed it all up.

And out of all the towns in the state of Texas, my dad unknowingly bought hers.

CHAPTER TWO

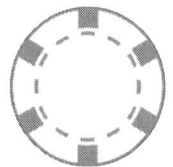

Lindy

I TRY NOT to stare at my lawyer, whose hands are neatly folded on her desk.

My lawyer. I have a lawyer, I think. *Does this mean I've finally arrived, or that I'm a complete failure?*

The jury's still out. Ha! Jury—get it? A perfect lawyer joke.

A few seconds into my brain's amateur comedy hour—which seems to be my response to panic—I realize Ashlee asked me a question. "I'm sorry—could you repeat that?"

Her deep brown eyes are sympathetic. "Do you want something to drink before we start? We have coffee, tea, or water."

I shake my head. "Just lay it on me."

Then I wince, because who says *lay it on me* to their lawyer? Or to anyone, really. Maybe it's partly due to my stress levels. But it's also because I'm more than a little star struck.

Ashlee Belle, better known to the world as Belle, is the biggest thing to come out of Sheet Cake. A supermodel heralded as the next Naomi Campbell, Ashlee hung up her runway heels when she hit thirty to attend Stanford Law. Two years ago, she moved home to star in her own version of a David and Goliath story. As a fairly young Black woman, she opened a law firm in direct opposition to Waters and Sons—the exclusively white male firm run by the richer-than-sin founding family.

I shouldn't say *exclusively* male. I think there are a few women working as administrative assistants. Maybe a paralegal or two? Billy Waters Jr., my giant mistake of an ex, works there with his father, Billy Sr., and almost every other male Waters. Which is why I called Ashlee when I suddenly found myself in a custody battle over my niece, Jo.

Ashlee and I have crossed paths before, but this is the first time we've had a face-to-face conversation. I need to stop being weird and fangirly and focus on the issue at hand.

Being a consummate professional, Ashlee ignores my awkwardness and gets right to it. "I've had a chance to look into your case. Your sister hired one of the best family attorneys in Austin. Given the fact that Rachel has completed a 90-day rehab program, attends weekly AA meetings, and is married to a wealthy tech investor with strong community ties, the courts may look favorably on reunification."

There are so many things to process. Rachel went to rehab? Rachel has the money to hire a decent lawyer? Rachel got *married*? That last one, for whatever reason, hits me hard. My baby sister is someone's *wife*.

For now, I'm going to skip right over what Ashlee said about *reunification*. I cannot imagine a world in which my sister, who abandoned her month-old daughter and did not so much as call once in five years, would get to be *reunified* with Jo.

Over my dead body.

I may not be her biological mother, but I am all mama bear when it comes to Jo.

"Rachel got married?" I ask.

"About six months ago, yes. Just before she entered rehab." Ashlee pushes a folder across the desk to me. "The information I gathered so far is in here, and I've hired a discreet private investigator to get more details."

I idly flip through the documents, which fill in the blanks of what Ashlee already said. Rachel checked into an upscale inpatient facility three days after her wedding. I guess rehab was her version of a honeymoon. Or maybe a wedding gift? I pause on a color photo of Rachel's license.

The last time I saw my sister was before Jo was born, just before Rachel ran away the second time. She was gaunt to the point of being skeletal, the skin below her eyes blooming purple like twin orchids. She twitched constantly, and her eyes couldn't stay focused on anything for longer than a few seconds.

The Rachel in this photograph is almost unrecognizable. No longer too thin, she instead looks like someone has attached her to a bike pump and inflated her unevenly. It's not that she looks heavy, more that the weight she carries in her face doesn't belong to her. Her hair is in a sensible bob, and she has pearls in her ears and around her neck. Four years my junior, Rachel looks at least ten years older than me.

I might not have recognized my sister at all if it weren't for her eyes. The green color matches mine and Jo's exactly, but the quality of them differs in a fundamental way. Flinty and sharp, they resemble some kind of gemstone cracked out of a rock in a deep, cold cave. I shiver at her smile, which looks calculating rather than happy. Or maybe I'm just projecting my memories of my sister into the photo.

"Why don't you tell me a bit more about your situation," Ashlee says.

I set the folder down on her desk, feeling the sudden need to sanitize my hands. Though Ashlee hasn't been back in town for many years, that's plenty of time to get all the dirt. Sheeters are very giving people when it comes to sharing secrets—unless it's a family recipe. And those, they take to the grave. Everything else is up for grabs on Neighborly.

The Neighborly is the app you'd get if you crossed Facebook with Reddit and restricted the users' geographical location to Sheet Cake. If it happens here, someone is talking about it on Neighborly within the half-hour. It's horrible and genius and it's totally addictive. Winnie, one of my two best friends, developed it. She's still getting the bugs out before trying to sell the whole thing to be used in cities across the country.

I raise an eyebrow at Ashlee. "You probably know my story as well as I do."

She smiles. "Small towns do have a way of keeping tabs, but I'd prefer to hear your version of events as well as anything pertinent to help your case."

I lean back in my chair. "Then I might need a coffee after all."

Ashlee opens a drawer and pulls out a bottle of whiskey. "Coffee with a kick?"

A shocked laugh bursts out of me. If it weren't official before, I kind of love my lawyer. "I've got to pick up Jo in a bit, so I better stick to caffeine. But you might need that drink."

Most of a coffee (me) and a whiskey (Ashlee) later, I finish my soap opera of a life story. "What do you think? Should we call Maury or Dr. Phil?" I brush my bangs out of my eyes and set my empty mug down on the desk.

"That's definitely some drama. I'm sorry for what you've been through," Ashlee says with a sad shake of her head.

The overview is that my sister started drinking and using drugs at thirteen, ran away at fourteen, came back, and left again at sixteen. She showed up on Mama's porch two years later with an infant. Rachel disappeared again almost as fast. I skipped my college graduation, gave up my post-college dreams, and moved back home to help Mama raise Jo. Then Mama was diagnosed with early onset dementia, which left me in charge of my niece and my mother.

"You're a writer, right?" When I nod, Ashlee gives me a kind smile. "Maybe you should think about a memoir."

I'm not sure if she's kidding or not, but the last thing I want to do is write my life story. Plus, I'm not that kind of writer. I had planned to be a travel writer, penning pieces focused around cultural geography and human interest. Thanks to a professor's recommendation, I landed the kind of lucky job no one gets right out of college writing for a magazine. It was a once-in-a-lifetime opportunity, but even that was worth giving up for Jo.

Now, I'm a freelancer, writing illustrious pieces of Buzzfeed journalism such as "The Hottest Leading Men in '80s Movies Ranked by Mustache" and "What *Jurassic World* Dinosaur You Are Based on Enneagram Type." It would be quite the leap to go to long-form, book content.

Even if I wanted to write it, no one wants the story of a twenty-seven-year-old woman scraping by in a small town while raising her niece. There is no action or adventure and definitely no romance. My two best friends, Winnie and Val, who aren't sidekicks so much as the other members of the Three Musketeers. As of right now, a happy ending is questionable.

What can I say? My pessimism ate my optimism for breakfast.

"I think I'd need to change the ending to sell it." I tap a finger on my chin. "Come to think of it, maybe I'd change the middle and the beginning too."

Ashlee laughs softly. "I've heard a lot of stories over the years. Each is unique, but they carry a few common threads. One of them is that we humans can either be very kind or very cruel to each other, as well as to ourselves."

Beautiful, whip-smart, and insightfully sensitive? Ashlee Belle really deserves better than our tiny, dying town.

I take a sip of my coffee, which has cooled considerably. How long was I talking? I really should have given Ashlee the short version of my story since I'm paying her by the hour. And her hours are not cheap.

"Do you think we could make a case for abandonment?" I ask, not wanting to mention the many google searches I've done on this subject the last few days. "Didn't Rachel essentially give up her parental rights when she left Jo?"

Seems logical to me. Leave your child for five years without so much as a phone call—BOOM. You have abdicated your throne of parenthood. Thanks for playing. Goodbye.

Ashlee's smile is tight. "Unfortunately, it's not automatic. There is a whole process to terminate parental rights. You are the sole managing conservator, correct?"

"Yes."

Ashlee takes a moment to weigh out her next words,

which makes worry start spreading through me like a fast-acting fungus. "Can I ask why you didn't ever file to adopt Jo?" She asks the question delicately, but all the tact in the world couldn't make it land softly.

"I should have," I tell her with a helpless shrug.

I wanted to—I still want to. The whole thing is just … complicated. When Mama started going downhill, I found and filed all the forms online to transfer the conservatorship to me, feeling like I deserved a merit badge on my vest of adulthood. But apparently, I should have taken things a few steps further to protect Jo. I never thought Rachel would seek custody.

There is not a chapter in any parenting book addressing my complex situation, so I had to wing it. I'm sure I've made and will continue to make a lot of mistakes. From the start, I had Jo call me Aunt Lindy. I was just a kid myself, only twenty-two, and the idea of being anyone's mom freaked me out. I never lied about Rachel and Jo knows as much as a brilliant and precocious five-year-old has any business knowing.

She may not call me Mom, but Jo is like a daughter to me. She is *everything*. Something shifted deep inside me the very first moment I held her. She stared up at me, clutching my pinky in her tiny fist, and that was it. As far as I'm concerned, Jo has been mine since that moment, just as I've been hers.

"Without support or good counsel, the process can be overwhelming," Ashlee says.

And expensive, though that's not the reason I never took that final step. Honestly, I'm not exactly sure why I started hyperventilating every time I considered officially filing to adopt Jo.

My old therapist had some suggestions. Namely that after

everything I've been through, I have commitment issues. It would be shocking if I didn't. My dad left right after Rachel was born and died a few years later in a car wreck. Rachel left again and again. Mama may not have had a choice, but in a way, her dementia means she left me too.

And then there's Pat, the man I loved. He didn't just leave. He left after running over my heart with a steamroller while throwing confetti to celebrate his accomplishment.

So, yeah, I have some underlying commitment issues. The adoption process felt overwhelming in more ways than one. And I never thought Jo would go anywhere. She's my happy little barnacle, and I'm the cheerful but worn tugboat carrying her along.

I should have been more responsible. I should have taken more agency and action. But I really thought I was doing my best. Clearly, my best needed some work.

Ashlee leans forward, putting her elbows on the desk. "Is there any chance your sister has legitimately changed? Could Rachel have turned things around? Could she be a good parent to Jo?"

If I had a dollar for every time I asked myself that kind of question about Rachel when we were growing up, I'd have a nice, cushy savings account. But Rachel only ever managed to pull herself together for brief periods. She would show up drunk to school, get arrested, or not come home at night. When she ran away, she took any cash she could get her hands on, plus Mama's credit and debit cards too.

I wish I could unsee the tears rolling down Mama's cheeks as she called hospitals and police stations, searching for a selfish girl who didn't want to be found. I picture Rachel's cold, green eyes again.

"I know change is possible," I say carefully. "But I gave up hope a long time ago. Rachel has done this too many times.

She had the best reason ever to get help when Jo was born. A daughter. Not even Jo was enough. Now?" I shake my head. "I have a very hard time believing it. Especially considering she still hasn't ever tried to contact me or Jo. It's not like she doesn't know where we live. I know it sounds awful, but I can't allow myself to hope."

"It doesn't sound awful. I have people in my life who suffered from addiction. It's a hard cycle to step out of."

That's true, but Rachel had issues long before the substance abuse. Mama said my little sister came out of the womb fighting like a cat stuffed in a burlap sack. She railed against everyone but especially me. It's like she was jealous I was born first, as though it gave me some unfair advantage. Rachel spent most of her energy trying to beat me in a race I was never running.

This whole thing with Jo doesn't feel like a healthy woman trying to reunify with her child. It's more like a power grab. If Rachel really had changed, she could have come to me. She had years to reach out, to do anything. I can only imagine what this will do to Jo.

My stomach feels like it's been shoved inside a trash compactor. "What can I expect with this hearing?"

Ashlee stares at me for a moment, as though measuring me up. I try to sit a little straighter, wondering suddenly when the last time I washed my bra was. Ashlee seems like the kind of woman who would wash her bras regularly. She probably never wears them until the armpit area turns a weird gray color and the underwire pokes out.

"It's unlikely they'll make a decision at this first hearing. They will probably do evaluations on both you and Rachel. We'll present the best possible case for you being the best fit for Jo."

Desperation is rising like a starving hyena, all wild-eyed

and panting, searching for any scrap of meat on a bone. "What can I do? I need specifics. What do they look for?"

This is how I operate. Give me a task, and I'll get it done. This is how I've survived the past five years essentially as a single parent. I've held it together so far, and I'll keep holding my little world together at the seams.

"I know you're working, but it would be good to be involved in Jo's school. Maybe volunteering or helping the PTO?"

A shudder passes through me. As much as I can, I avoid what I call the PTO Mafia, a tiny legion of women in athleisure-wear who coordinate—aka emotionally manipulate and browbeat—parent volunteers.

"I can do that." I'll hate it, but I can do it.

"The court will want to see a stable home life," Ashlee says.

"I'm stable. Super stable." My awkward, high-pitched laugh does anything but bolster this claim.

She continues, ignoring my weird laughter. For this, I am grateful.

"They'll look at your living situation."

"I have a house."

It's the one I grew up in, which is falling apart, but still standing. And fifty percent of the toilets actually work! (Which means exactly one working toilet, if anyone is counting.) Based on the uncomfortable look Ashlee is giving me, she knows the general state of my home.

"They like to see job security."

"I have a steady job." Steady-ish. Freelance can be up and down, honestly, but I have a few sites that pay well and don't turn any of my posts down now. "And I'm an active member of the community."

Mostly the Ladies Literary and Libation Society, a semi-secret and highly exclusive not-quite-book-club Ashlee and I are both members of. It's not quite Fight Club where we can't talk about its existence, but neither is it the kind of organization I would put on an official form.

"I don't like to sugar-coat things," Ashlee says, which is never a good start to a sentence. "Despite her history, Rachel has some advantages you do not. Her financial position is more secure."

I wait, because it's clear Ashlee has more to say. She doesn't shift her gaze, though it is rife with apology.

"As much as I hate to say this—being married will work in Rachel's favor. Coupled with the fact she's Jo's biological mother, this may hold sway with the courts."

These words hit me like a bowling ball to the gut. People sometimes treat being single as though it's a preventable condition, like a sunburn. I wish snagging a good man were as easy as waltzing into one of those candy stores with all the bins, scooping out exactly what I want, and then walking away with a perfect combination of exactly what I want.

Dating these days, especially while raising a five-year-old alone, is not as simple as swiping in whatever direction you're supposed to swipe on some app. Especially in a small town. Even if there were more guys to choose from here in Sheet Cake, Pat ruined me for other men. Or all men.

My dance card is empty. Wolf Waters, who jokingly proposes to me once a week, is my only prospect. Considering he's Billy's younger brother, it's a hard pass. Though I do applaud Wolf for being the only Waters to break the privileged, pretentious vibe the rest of his family wears like a crest. Wolf—whose real name is Walter—seems sweet, even if he gives off doomsday prepper vibes. He lives in his own underground bunker on a big piece of property where he runs

Backwoods Bar, the semi-legal drinking hole Sheeters frequent.

I stand, ready to be done with this conversation, this topic, this whole day. Unsure whether I should shake Ashlee's hand, I go into weird mode again and curtsy, giving her an elaborate wave.

Ashlee's kind smile only makes me feel worse. "I promise you, Lindy—I will do everything I can."

But will it be enough? I swallow down that question.

"Thank you." And because I'm not done being awkward, I add, "I'll be in touch if I find a spare husband by the side of the road."

Yep, I made that terrible joke. Before Ashlee can respond, I bolt through the door and almost run into Kim, Ashlee's assistant. She steps back, her brassy highlights glinting.

"Sorry! I was just going to see if you needed more coffee," she says, holding up the coffee pot in one hand. "What's that about you finding a husband?"

Kim graduated a few years behind me. She seems friendly but has that slightly too-eager-to-please thing going on. Not to mention she's got a bloodhound's nose for gossip.

"A husband? You must have misheard. I was definitely not talking about trying to find a husband. Though I've always wanted one of those husband pillows. Do you know the ones I'm talking about?"

From Kim's blank look, she does not.

"They're big and puffy, with arms you can sort of snuggle with—you know what? Never mind. Have a super awesome day."

I force a laugh, then practically run out of the office before I can say or do anything else tragically embarrassing.

CHAPTER THREE

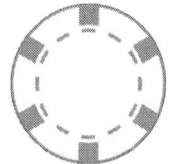

Pat

ON THE FORTY-ISH minute trek to Sheet Cake, I alternate between driving too fast and draggingly slow. One moment, my thoughts are racing and my foot turns to lead. The next, my mind snags on a memory and I'm a sloth. Apparently, I'm slothing right now because Tank glances over at me.

"Are you part of a funeral procession?" he asks. "Are we in an invisible school zone? I told you to slow down a minute ago, but I didn't mean like a snail. Pick up the pace, son."

"Right. Sorry. Is it hot in here?" I punch the A/C higher, then roll down my window.

On any other day, Tank would notice my jittery, nervous behavior and force me with the power of his fatherly gaze to tell him why I'm freaking out. I'm grateful he seems wholly distracted by the need to play tour guide. It's like he walked up to one of those brochure racks in a hotel lobby and mainlined every single bit of information on Sheet Cake. If there's a pop quiz at the end, I will most definitely fail.

"As I was saying, the town used to be a hub for grain, though its real claim to fame is the annual Sheet Cake Festival."

"Obviously."

"It's been going on for a hundred years and is the third largest food-based festival in Texas," Tank continues.

"Mm-hm. Food is good."

While he drones on about train routes and other inane details, my mind spins back in Lindy's direction. What are the odds my dad would buy her town?

Maybe it's a sign.

It's NOT a sign. Of all the things it could be, it is not a sign. More like a cosmic coincidence, the universe's joke at my expense. Lindy doesn't even live there. She is in Europe somewhere or a tropical island, maybe a remote village halfway across the world. Not in Sheet Cake.

But the optimist in me is unflappably optimistic. He keeps coming back with *maybes* and *what ifs*.

"Are you feeling okay?" Tank asks. "You're flushed."

"I'm just excited."

This is not a lie. I am excited, even if I have no reason to be, since Lindy doesn't live here. *Get that through your thick skull, Patty. Lindy isn't here.*

I know this because I came to Sheet Cake looking for her. After my career-ending injury sent me home to Austin, I drove this same route. The only Darcy residence Google knew about was a tiny, rundown farmhouse on the outskirts of town. I met Lindy's mom, a sweet, round woman who shared Lindy's green eyes and bright smile. She told me Lindy hadn't been home in ages.

"I'm sorry. She's never mentioned you," she said when I told her my name.

I must have looked as crushed as I felt, because Mrs. Darcy served me up coffee and a slice of homemade buttermilk pie. We ate together on the wraparound porch in a comfortable, if a little melancholy, silence.

When the pie was done and my plate scraped clean—I only refrained from licking it because *manners*—I wished her well and drove home.

If I cried all the way there, I left no witnesses to the fact. I thought it would bring me closure, but Lindy has always felt like a door that just won't stay closed.

"There she blows." Tank points to a large sign beside the road that reads, *Howdy and Welcome to Sheet Cake, Texas: Home of the Annual Sheet Cake Festival*. We round a bend, and a water tower comes into view. It looks a bit worse for wear and is rusted over in places, but the giant painting of a chocolate sheet cake on the side is pristine. So is the name of the town, written out in a sky-blue script.

"The color is called Sheet Cake Blue," Tank says, a note of pride in his voice. "A local artist developed it, and the city trademarked it."

Sheet Cake Blue is more than a color. It's my current mood.

We are suddenly in the midst of an area that looks shiny and new, almost like it's been plunked here fully formed after being purchased at a Costco. The speed limit slows to forty-five, then thirty-five, with stoplights and gas stations and fast food joints. There are a few newer planned communities with homes sprouting up like brick mushrooms, and strip centers with the normal Texas trifecta: donut shops, tanning salons, and Mexican restaurants.

"There's the high school," Tank says, continuing his A-plus narration of things about which I do not care. "Their football team won state last year in their division."

I glance over to see an older, two-story brick building with a web of trailers expanding out and out and out. The football stadium, naturally, looks shiny and new—Texas priorities!

Lindy went to school there.

The baser part of my mind has slapped a cheerleading uniform on Lindy, and I give myself a mental smack for checking out her legs.

Did she date any football players?

It shouldn't spark jealousy to imagine Lindy dating other guys before we even met. I mean, I hardly can stake a claim. And yet I'm ready to go back in time and break some jock's hands for touching my girl.

A few minutes later, we move from the new part of town to what reminds me of the start of a post-apocalyptic movie. Weeds sprout up between massive cracks in the sidewalks, and a blinking stop sign hangs at an angle. There might as well be a barbed-wire fence between the part of Sheet Cake we just left and the one we're entering.

"And what area of town, exactly, did you purchase?" I'm afraid I already know the answer.

We bump over a train track, and Dad winces as the bottom of the Aston scrapes concrete. I see the actual town square just ahead of us.

A little TLC—is that what Tank said? This town needs a set of defibrillator paddles.

"I own everything from the tracks onward," Tank says, infusing his voice with bright cheer. "Welcome to the historic town of Sheet Cake, property of yours truly! Park anywhere you like."

He's not joking, because all of the street parking is available. ALL of it. I could probably leave the Aston in the middle of this intersection, and it wouldn't matter. But I pull into a space and get out of the car, meeting Tank on the nearest sidewalk. He smiles broadly.

Does he see something different than I do? Because what I see is a ghost town. Historic Sheet Cake is more like an empty pan with a few stale crumbs.

Tank throws a heavy arm over my shoulder. "Let me show you around."

The grand tour of the town itself could be done right from this spot on the sidewalk, but I humor Tank and follow him. I'm sure in its heyday, whenever that was, this place was gorgeous. Most buildings have wide balconies on the second and third floors with wrought iron railings—except for a few places where they've fallen off, sitting on the sidewalk, ready to be slapped with a loitering ticket.

"Check this out!" Dad stretches an arm out toward the square in the center of town.

Where charm once was, now there is only knee-high grass and overgrown flower beds surrounding a white gazebo that's falling over. I can see the appeal—if I'm imagining the *after* photo, not … this. It's like the abandoned film set for *Hart of Dixie* and *Gilmore Girls* and *Sweet Magnolias* all wrapped up in one.

And DO NOT JUDGE ME for knowing all those shows. I am a man comfortable with his love of small-town drama with a heavy pour of romance.

I squint, trying to imagine what this place would take to fix up. I could totally imagine living in a renovated, loft-style apartment above one of the storefronts. It could be kind of cool, if the town weren't so dead.

The only signs of life are at the end of one block, where there's a white-columned municipal building next to a library. Both are open, according to Tank, though I've yet to see a single person entering or exiting either. And I've been looking. Because that dumb, optimistic part of me keeps hoping I'll see Lindy coming around a corner.

"Do you get to be mayor?" I deadpan.

"There's already a mayor," Tank says. "He's the one who sold me the place."

Is that something mayors can even do? All of this is so bizarre.

"I may not be mayor, but I do own all these businesses—"

I stare around us. *WHAT businesses?*

"—and properties. Everything you see here. See those grain elevators and the warehouse? That's where I thought Dark Horse could make its home."

He points to the end of a street where I can see hulking metal buildings that look a lot like—

"The Silos in Waco," I say, shaking my head. "I was kidding about Joanna Gainesing the place. Have you OD'd on *The Fixer Upper?*"

Dad laughs, the sound echoing on the empty street. "You can be the Chip to my Joanna."

I stare. "I cannot begin to tell you the number of things wrong with that statement. Except for the part where I get to be Chip. I like that man."

"Of course you do. He's like your long-lost brother." Tank puts his hands on his hips. "Anyway—what do you think?"

I have a lot of thoughts, and they're all scrambling around in my brain like eggs in a pan. Lindy is taking up a lot of real estate, but I'm trying to give this idea a chance. I'm scared to ask Tank how much he paid for this town. It would take far more than a seasoned pair of HGTV house-flippers to revitalize it. I can recognize the potential, but through a haze of dollar signs.

It's impractical, but I have to admit, I'm intrigued. Maybe even excited.

What would Lindy think about me moving here and fixing up her town? Would I be able to spend time here without feeling haunted by her ghost and the ghost of my mistakes? Does she ever come back to visit her mom?

"Let's discuss over food," Tank suggests.

"Is there food to be had here?"

"You'll see." Tank walks away from me, and I follow on the heels of his worn cowboy boots.

We head down the one side of a street we haven't crossed yet. A moment later, I see a neon *Open* sign flashing red and blue in a wide glass window.

Well, what do you know? There *is* a business open in Sheet Cake. A business. Singular. *One*.

A bell jangles as Dad opens the door. I smell the diner before I get a good look. Bacon, pancakes, strong coffee. And is that … salsa? The scent is half classic greasy spoon and half Tex-Mex, and I am here for it. My stomach immediately roars awake, pleased by this new development.

"Simmer down," I tell my growling midsection, following Dad to red vinyl stools at a linoleum counter. A short woman with sharp brown eyes and a flower in her white hair slaps down two menus, grinning like she's in on a secret we'll soon find out.

"Hello, hola, good morning," she says with a slight accent, her smile stretching wider. "Coffee?"

"Yes, ma'am."

"*Ma'am*," the woman says, clucking her tongue. "No, no, no. Call me Mari, short for Marisol."

She already has our two mugs and pours quickly, setting a bowl of creamers out between us.

"Thank you, Mari," Dad says, tipping his head.

She beams before darting away through the swinging kitchen door.

"You're doing it again," I tell him. "That Sam Elliot thing."

"What Sam Elliot thing?"

"Your voice gets deeper and your accent gets thicker. Give you a mustache and a gun and we're in *Tombstone*."

"I am not and will never be a mustache man."

"Too bad. I think you could rock a serious stache, Pops."

"That'll be the day."

I'm thankful for the easy banter. It settles my mind, which is like a highway full of speeding cars. I'm thinking of Lindy; I'm thinking of ideas for the town. And now, I'm thinking of food as I peruse the menu. I want to order a sample platter of it all.

Mari returns with ice waters. "Have you decided?"

"I think we have," Dad says.

He tries to order the senior plate, which leads to teasing and giggling as Mari tells him he's not old enough.

"I'm wise beyond my years."

"Fifty-six is young. Many good years ahead of you. I'll serve you the plate," Mari says with a note of scolding through her smile, "but you pay full price."

"That'll have to do," Dad says, winking, and I mouth *Sam Elliot*.

The man could charm a basket full of Diamondback rattlesnakes, but he never actually flirts with *intention*. Never with women who would be actual contenders. My siblings and I are split on whether we'd like to see Dad date again. James is against it, like he's against all relationships. Harper is more hesitant, and Collin is undecided. I'm squarely on Team Give Love a Chance. It's been years since Mom died. It would be weird, but my dad is a catch, and he's been alone long enough. But he's never shown an ounce of real interest in anyone.

I order a waffle platter and the migas plate, which makes Mari raise her brows. I pat my stomach. "Gotta nourish the food baby."

With a laugh, Mari retreats back to the kitchen, and Dad and I are alone. Mostly alone, I realize as I spin on my stool to examine the room. At the back booth, a dark-haired girl colors with an impressive intensity. She catches me looking and gives me a grin which reveals a dimple in one cheek. I give her a little finger wave that I hope is friendly, not creepy, and she goes back to coloring, her crooked braids dragging over the paper.

Tank turns to me. "Do you see it, Pat? Can you feel the magic of this place? Do you see what it could be?" He rubs his arms like he's trying to wipe away goose bumps.

"Pops, this place has charm, sure. But you and I and the guys—we aren't Chip and Joanna Gaines. Nowhere close. We don't have the fame to carry a project like this. The Grahams are not the Kardashians."

We never were that big of a deal, but the Graham name used to mean something. Tank was the most famous of all of us—he played for longer than me or Collin and made appearances on ESPN. But it's been a *while*. I stopped being famous the minute I got injured and stopped dating models and actresses. Collin kept his head down and focused solely on the game, so the only press he got was about him being a part of the Graham football legacy. We are old news.

"I didn't expect you of all people to be the Negative Nellie."

"I'm just trying to be a realist here. This is the worst possible location for Dark Horse. We're too far from Austin, not near anything else significant on the map, and you'd need other businesses to repopulate this town. We're not talking about one project but ten. Maybe twenty. I don't know if we have the manpower or money."

This is the kind of investment Dad always warned us away from. Now he's running headlong into it, trying to drag us too. Everything I've said is true, but I also still have a hum of excitement in my bones. But I don't want Tank getting too hopeful yet. This is a giant decision, and I still feel like it needs to be made with the whole family.

We sip coffee in silence for a few minutes, and Mari returns, balancing our plates.

"One senior plate at regular price, one waffle platter, and one migas plate for the bottomless pit."

"More like the bottomless Pat," Tank says, chuckling.

"Good one, Dad."

When I take a bite of my migas, my eyes almost roll back in my head at the taste. Maybe I'll make my decision about this town one bite at a time.

"You look like you're having some kind of life-altering experience over there," Tank says.

"I might be. For all its foodie ways, Austin can't beat this. Try a bite."

Dad takes a forkful of my migas and practically groans at the taste. "I'm not usually big on Mexican food in the morning, but that's spectacular." He wipes a dribble of salsa off his chin.

Mari pats Dad on the shoulder as she walks back by. "Can I get you two anything else?"

"A little more coffee?" Dad asks, and Mari fills our mugs. "Everything is delicious."

Mari looks pleased as she disappears into the kitchen again. Tank and I wolf down our food in relative silence, which gives me too much space to think about Lindy and the colossal mistakes I wish I could unmake.

The thing was—it never should have gotten serious between us. I knew the draft was coming and didn't want to go into my pro career attached, while Lindy planned to travel the world. Our relationship was supposed to be fun and casual. We even made rules, which seems like the most ridiculous thing now, especially considering they didn't do a lick of good keeping me from falling in love with her.

The closer it came to saying goodbye, the more I panicked about leaving her. Honestly, I wasn't sure I could do it.

So stupid, twenty-two-year-old Pat ripped the bandage off. I thought our goodbye would be easier if we didn't have to say it. I told myself I was doing us both a favor. Instead of meeting Lindy as planned on our last night together, I changed my plane ticket and flew out early.

I didn't call. I didn't text. I just … left.

If I had access to a T.A.R.D.I.S., I would go back and punch myself in the face. Repeatedly. But as any good Whovian knows, you don't mess with your own timeline.

And did my grand bandage-ripping plan work? No. No, it did not.

I was a mess. A hot, hot mess.

A month into my new life, I broke and called Lindy from some awful club, feeling guilty, lonely, and miserable. I wanted to apologize. I wanted to tell her I made a huge mistake, not just leaving without saying goodbye but leaving at all. I needed her forgiveness, needed to explain, needed her voice to make my head feel clear again. Nothing felt right after I left her. Nothing.

Instead, I got a chipper Lindy on the phone. She didn't seem fazed by the end of us. I barely got a word in as she told me how much she loved traveling alone, *being* alone. She made it clear she was happy without me.

Then: click. She was gone.

What followed that phone call was a string of deeper misery and even worse decisions. Like my quickie Vegas marriage to a lingerie model, which my family and I pretend never happened. Padma and I got it annulled almost immediately, so it technically didn't happen.

Shattering my ankle was probably the best thing for me, as it ended my streak of self-destructive behavior. Being back home and around my family grounded me, but the ache of losing Lindy never faded. I just got better at pretending I'm not living with a perpetually broken heart.

At this point, Lindy can't be as large as she looms in my memory. I've probably fictionalized her, idolized her. She can't be as beautiful, as electric, as important as the memory lingering in my head. Even thinking about her now has my pulse doing some kind of ninja warrior course through my veins.

Mari brings the check, and I excuse myself to the bathroom to wash off my syrup-sticky hands. On the way back, I can't stop myself from pausing by the little girl. She glances up at me with green eyes that remind me way too much of my very favorite green eyes in the world.

"You're not a Sheeter," she says.

I bark out a laugh. "I'm not *what*, now?"

"A Sheeter. It's what locals call themselves. At least the ones in old Sheet Cake. New Sheet Cake is a whole different town."

"Sheeters?"

"Yup. It was that or Cakers. I personally would have gone with Caketonians." She props her elbow on the table and rests her chin on her hand. "I'm sure the town founders had a lively debate before settling on it. Anyway, the point is—you're not local."

Her voice is clear and strong, filled with a poise and a vocabulary that belies her age. She looks no older than five or six, by my best guess. She's adorable and precocious and I could talk to her all day. There's just something about her I can't quite pinpoint, like a word stuck on the tip of my tongue or the hazy part of a dream hanging on the edge of my consciousness.

If I were living a different life—one in which I'd married my dream girl instead of losing her—I could see myself with a whole herd of children, ones with green eyes just like this.

"Seeing as how we aren't Sheeters, shouldn't you be concerned about stranger danger?" I tease.

"I'm Jo. Just J-O. Now we're not strangers." Jo smiles and exchanges her gray colored pencil for bright pink. "Anyway, Mari has a shotgun behind the counter. And Big Mo—he's the cook—keeps his knives extra sharp. I feel pretty safe."

I glance over at Tank, who is watching me with quiet amusement. He must not have heard the comment about the weapons.

"I'm just giving you a hard time," Jo says. "Though Mari does have a shotgun."

I clear my throat. "Good to know. Is Mari your mom? Or … grandma?"

Jo's pencil pushes so hard against the paper it's about to make a hole right through the middle. "I don't have a mom. Or a dad. Mari is kind of like my grandma. And I have the best aunt in the world."

Well, now I feel like the biggest jerk in the world. I look up to find Tank giving me a dirty look and Mari giving me a worse one. This is, and has always been, my problem. I do and say things with no thought as to the consequences. Until those consequences smack me in the face.

"I bet your aunt is amazing. What are you coloring?"

Jo holds up her book, showing me the cover. I can only stare. It's a *Jaws* coloring book. The cover is a cartoon version of the iconic movie poster, thankfully with dark waves blurring the details of the nude woman swimming above the shark's open mouth.

"I just finished reading the novel," she says. "Chief Brody is my favorite, but I also love Quint. I like to think the shark just needed a friend."

I have no response to this. Literally, none.

Jaws is one of my favorite movies—it's as much about the relationships as it is about a killer shark. But I've never read the novel. And this little girl did? Shouldn't she be into, like, board books or something? I can't help but be impressed. And maybe a little unnerved.

"Are you coming, son?" Dad gives me a look that says I need to stop overstepping boundaries.

"Yep."

Before I can walk away, Jo tears out the page and holds it out with a dimpled smile. "I'm not done, but it's close enough. Keep it."

I take the page, looking down to see a pastel-hued version of the scene where the shark pops up behind Chief Brody, just before the iconic line, "You're gonna need a bigger boat." Jo has used the black pencil to tilt the shark's mouth into a sharp-toothed smile, and she's drawn and colored white and yellow daisies around his neck. It manages to be terrifyingly adorable.

Feeling oddly moved, I thank her and join Tank at the door.

"You know," he says, a teasing glint in his eyes. "You could always settle down and have one of your own."

If only. Too bad the one woman I could see myself marrying is half a world away and has probably forgotten all about me.

I have one boot out the door when I hear a voice behind me. A voice I would know anywhere. *Her* voice.

I'm hit with a rush of adrenaline, the likes of which I haven't felt since the last pass I caught on the field. My heart slams sideways in my chest. My hairline prickles and sweat begins to form on my lower back.

Slowly, I turn. And just like I've conjured her into being with all my thoughts, there is Lindy.

CHAPTER FOUR

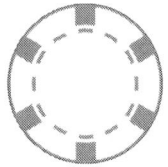

Pat

"Jo," Lindy says, "where did you get this coloring book?"

My gaze is guided by the melodic tones of a voice I never thought I'd hear again. And there she is. Lindy Darcy, looking somehow both unchanged and different. I was wrong about idolizing her memory. She is more than I remember—*more* beautiful, *more* alluring, *more* of a draw to some primal and real part of me.

Her dark hair hangs wild around her face, framing delicate cheekbones and a mouth that carries a gut-punch of kissing memories. I swear, for a moment, I feel the ghost of her on my lips, tasting of strawberry lip gloss and mint, a combination that would work nowhere else.

The long fringe of her bangs is new, and though they look good on her, something about them, or maybe it's the slumped set of her shoulders, makes Lindy look as though she's hiding. There is a sadness to her I can feel in a palpable way, and my stomach twists with it. A tidal wave of protectiveness crashes over me. I want to curl Lindy to my chest until she doesn't look so ... so ...

Sad? Lonely? Maybe ... defeated?

There was a time I swore to this woman I'd do anything I could to keep a smile on her face. The weight of my broken promises threatens to make my knees buckle.

My eyes travel over her face and down to strong shoulders and long, lean arms. My gaze catches on her lime green fingernail polish, which is so ... Lindy. Brash and bright and fun. Her legs are bare underneath her black cotton dress, and she has on cowboy boots almost as worn as my own.

My heart has come dislodged from its normal location inside my chest and is careening around behind my ribs, loose and excitable as a live wire.

"Aunty Val gave it to me," Jo says.

Lindy, who still hasn't noticed me in the doorway, makes a frustrated noise. "Well, your Aunty Val and I are going to have words."

"*Lindy.*"

When her name leaves my lips, it's on an exhale, an adoring sigh. It's pitiful—that's what it is. And I don't even care. I couldn't hold myself back right now if I tried. And why try? Before me is the woman I thought I lost. I'd give anything for another chance.

When she sees me, a muscle in her cheek jumps and her shoulders stiffen. Not the reaction I would hope for, but then, I didn't expect her to run across the room and throw herself in my arms. Even if I wish she would.

Our eyes lock, and my heart reacts like a bomb going off

inside one of those containment vessels—an explosion of catastrophic proportions hidden completely inside me. Because on the outside, I'm still frozen.

Lindy's green eyes flash with shock, then spin through a kaleidoscope of emotions, finally landing on something I can't name. I'm not sure what she sees on my face, but I probably look like a cartoon character with hearts for eyes and a tongue rolling out like a red carpet.

I am a man released out into daylight after being locked in a storm cellar for years. I'm blinking and blinded by the sudden exposure to the sun.

I move toward Lindy before I can stop myself. When I'm a few feet away, her hand jerks up.

"Don't," she whispers, and I stop where I am, fighting every urge in my body to move closer. Her eyes fall to the paper in my hand, the one Jo colored for me, and another unreadable expression passes over her face like a cloud. Jo glances between us, her brow furrowed.

"Is he my daddy?"

Jo's question, asked in that same no-nonsense voice she used to tell me about Jaws needing a friend, rips through me. I know Lindy must be the best aunt in the world Jo mentioned. I'm not her father, but a surge of protectiveness rises in my chest.

"No. He isn't." Lindy's voice softens as she brushes a stray lock of Jo's dark hair away from her face. I can hardly make out Lindy's words, but I do, and they're painfully raw. "Remember? Your mama didn't know who your daddy was."

"Okay."

Jo nods, and my heart cracks a little at the way she simply accepts this. It makes me want to find whoever her daddy is and give him a hearty shake.

"Then, who is he?" Jo asks, pointing to me.

Without so much as another glance my way, Lindy dismisses me with a firm, cool voice. "He's no one. Not anymore."

Well, I need to change THAT. Now that I've found Lindy, and she's *here*, my wheels are already turning. They're a bit squeaky, but still.

"Then why are you upset with him?" Jo asks. "Your chest always gets splotchy and your ears get pink when you're upset."

Lindy's hand rises to her collarbone, like she wants to hide the color rising there. And it's definitely rising. "I'm not upset."

"I think he's nice," Jo continues as though Lindy didn't answer. "I gave him my favorite picture."

Lindy's eyes go to the paper in my hand again, and she sighs. "Pack your things, Jo."

I lick my lips. "Lindy—"

"You can't be here," she says, not looking at my face.

I clear my throat, but still sound hoarse, and way too needy. "Could we just—"

"No. We can't. I ... can't."

"But why are you here?" I ask.

"Why are *you*?"

"My dad and I stopped in for lunch." That's not the full answer, but the whole story is a little too complicated. Based on the way she's responding right now, I probably need to ease her into the idea of Tank buying her hometown.

Mari appears through the swinging kitchen door. She looks at me, then at Lindy.

"Everything okay out here, mija?"

"Yes," I say, just as Lindy says, "Not even a little bit."

Mari nods, winding up a dish towel in her hands as she approaches me. "We're closed."

"It's almost lunchtime." I plant my feet.

Mari snaps her dish towel at me. "*Closed.*"

"Ouch!"

I start moving toward the door as Mari shoos me on, the towel snapping on my arms, my back, my hip. She is a fierce little lion tamer with a whip. *Snap!*

"Lindy, please!"

I see the corner of Lindy's lip lift when Mari's dish towel snaps on my arm. That hint of a smile plants a seed of hope. I always did make her laugh. I could again—I *know* I could.

I only need a chance. I need to find out why she's here, why she looks so sad, and how I can fix it.

I'm going to fix it for her. For her and Jo. I'm going to fix ALL the things. I just need—

Snap!

"Ow! Mari—I thought you liked me!"

"That's before I knew who you were." The towel connects with my thigh and I take another step back.

The door to the kitchen swings open and a man I'm guessing is Big Mo ducks through the doorway. He has bright eyes, rich umber skin, and a dark beard hanging down his chest, fitted with a hair net.

"Need a hand?" he asks, eyeing me.

"I've got it. Just uno necio—a little pest." Mari practically shoves me out on the sidewalk. I hear the metallic clack of the lock turning. Then she snaps the blinds shut one by one until the view inside is obscured.

Tank stands with his arms crossed a few feet away, one brow lifted. "Took you a minute. Did you get some food to go?"

"Uh, no." I lick my lips and rub my arm, where the worst

of the towel whippings left a red mark. I'm still seeing that little twitch of a smile on Lindy's lips. Those beautiful, kissable lips.

Tank pats me on the shoulder, and I jump. "Well?"

"What?"

"Are you going to help me convince your brothers?" Tank asks.

Oh, right—the brewery. The whole reason I'm here. Or the reason I *was* here.

I clap him on the shoulder before heading for the Aston, careful to keep Jo's drawing from getting bent.

"Are you kidding? This place is coal just waiting for someone to squeeze a diamond out of it." I relish the look of shock on his face.

"Are you serious?"

"Deadly. Now, come on, Pops." I unlock the doors and climb behind the driver's seat. "Let's discuss how to convince the rest of our family. Most especially James."

Tank's grin is too big for his face as he climbs into the passenger seat. "I knew once you saw it, you'd see the magic."

I did see magic—just not the kind he thinks. The enchantment is all about Lindy. I am no less under her spell than I was years ago. If anything, it has strengthened with time.

That said, I'm not sure if fixing up the town or somehow earning a second chance with Lindy is the more daunting task. I have a feeling the town is going to be a piece of cake, comparatively. No pun intended.

As I start down one of the country roads, Tank squints through the windshield. "You're going the wrong way."

"I've got one more stop we need to make before heading back to Austin."

"What else is out here?"

Nothing much—only the woman I think might be the love of my life. The one who just had me chased out of the diner like a dog.

Which I probably deserved, and then some. But I plan on fixing that, on making amends beginning today and every day after that. As long as it takes, starting with a sincere apology that's long overdue.

CHAPTER FIVE

Lindy

"YOU LOOK like you just saw a ghost," Jo tells me, her green eyes seeing, as usual, far too much.

I FEEL like I've seen a ghost. My heart is a shivering, hollowed-out husk and my hands are shaking. "I don't believe in ghosts, Jojo."

Whether I believe in them or not, I *did* just see a ghost. A Class IV entity, according to the Ghostbusters classification system, which I know about thanks to an article I wrote on real-life hauntings as classified by the Ghostbuster's system.

The particular ghost who just appeared in Mari's diner—Patrick Graham—has haunted me for years. Until today, he's done so in memory, not in person. And if I see him again before I have time to recover, I will fall completely apart.

"Grab your colors. We need to go."

And *quickly*, before Pat bursts through the window or

climbs down the ventilation system above the stove in the back. He's persistent—when he wants to be—and harder to kill than a cockroach. He's the kind of man who will squeeze through the smallest bit of wiggle room I give him, despite locked doors and closed-off hearts.

My stomach is fluttering with a horde of resurrected butterflies. They are still blinking awake, flitting blindly around in my stomach and trying to get their bearings after so many years.

It's the Pat effect. Which is why we need to leave NOW. I cannot have Pat. Or butterflies. Nope.

Anger is far more productive and much safer. I can channel all the feelings Pat woke up into a pure, white-hot rage. The resurrected butterflies can be an avenging zombie horde. That's a much better use for them.

With a last glance at the door, I pull Jo into the kitchen. "I have to pee," she says, bouncing from foot to foot.

Big Mo nods toward the cramped stairway leading to his apartment above the diner. "Use mine, little Jo."

He gives Jo a warm smile. Setting down her pencil case, she darts for the stairs. Big Mo is one of Jo's favorite people, which makes him one of my favorite people. He also makes a mean breakfast burrito.

I count the thuds of Jo's footsteps as she runs up the stairs. Sometimes when I'm stressed or overwhelmed, counting things helps calm me. Trees in a yard, cars passing by, number of times I overuse the words *so* and *that* in my articles.

The number of times I think about Pat in a day, or an hour.

The last number is embarrassingly high. Even after so many years. Even after he gave me every reason NOT to think about him. Now, after actually seeing him, not thinking about him will be impossible.

My Days-without-Thinking-of-Pat sign needs to be updated. It has been ZERO days since I thought about Patrick Graham.

I lean against the metal prep counter, trying to focus on the familiar scent of chopped cilantro and the pop of grease from whatever Big Mo is frying for the impending lunch rush. The familiarity of this kitchen does little to unknot the tension coiled inside me.

When Mari envelops me in a hug, there is a dangerous moment where her softness almost—ALMOST—loosens up a tear or two. I clutch her tighter, inhaling the scent of her hair.

I just have to hold it together for like seven more hours. Then, Jo will be asleep, and I can close my door, hide in the back of my closet, and sob or scream as loudly as I want. Jo asked me once why I had so many long coats when the weather doesn't get that cold. I didn't explain to her how well they muffle sound.

"He looks even more handsome in person than in pictures," Mari says, jerking me back into the moment.

I wish it weren't true. Pat has always been more handsome in person, though he's certainly photogenic too. A two-dimensional picture can't capture his personality or his charm. He also somehow managed to look better now than he did five years ago, in that infuriating way men have of aging well.

I pull away, clutching the strap of my purse. "Yeah, well. Him being handsome wasn't the problem."

"You were both so young," Mari says. "Maybe the time has come to let the troll go under the bridge?"

Mari moved here from Costa Rica fifteen years ago when

Val's mom took off. It was the same summer Winnie's mom died of cancer. Worst summer break ever! Mari's English is almost perfect, but her idioms ... not so much. She told Val recently that she needed to stop dating so many losers and find a man who would sweep her feet off.

Based on context here, I think she means water under the bridge, not trolls.

But I'm not planning to let the troll under my bridge sweep my feet off anytime soon. While it might sound easy from the outside to just forgive Pat, it's more complicated than that. My hurt is a deep, deep current running through me. What's more—I lied to him, and he doesn't even know yet. With what's happening with Jo right now, my complicated relationship with Pat is the last thing I need on my mind.

"We'll see," I tell Mari.

She only hums at this. "You think he's still out there? I need to open for lunch. He seems like the persistent type."

I scoff. "Not as persistent as you'd think."

Pat is a regular old Harry Houdini, slipping out of relationships like a pair of shiny handcuffs. He left me easily enough. Then he had a quickie Vegas marriage (which ended almost as fast) and a string of very public relationships and breakups until his career-ending injury. Since then, he's been almost a ghost online—NOT that I have online alerts set up for his name or anything—but I think I've got a pretty good read on his character.

Mari tilts her head. "I can't decide if you're more afraid he'll come after you, or afraid he won't."

You and me, both.

I DO want Pat to come after me, if only so I can say no to his stupid, handsome face. Yet there is a voice inside me growing louder that doesn't want to say no at all. For years, I allowed myself to daydream about Pat coming to find me, apologizing and declaring his undying love for me.

And now, here he is. Just an hour after I joked about finding a husband on the side of the road. Not that Pat is husband material in ANY universe, but it feels almost like I conjured him out of thin air. It's way too coincidental that he was right here in Mari's diner at the precise moment I came to pick up Jo.

"Any update on Jo's situation?" Mari asks.

Great—from one subject I don't want to talk about to another.

I shrug. "The hearing is in a few weeks. Ashlee will do her best."

But it looks pretty bleak.

Mari touches my arm. "You know I'm happy to help whenever you need me. You aren't alone."

I nod, the emotion swelling too thickly in my throat to allow a response. Normally, Val is the one with enough emotions for the whole town of Sheet Cake. Happy, sad, angry, enthusiastic—whatever Val feels, she feels it big. Today, apparently, I'm the one with all the feelings.

The thing is—I *feel* alone, because I *am* alone.

There is support all around me, but it feels just out of reach, even with Mari standing right here offering. Mari was my mama's best friend—or, *is* my mom's best friend. It's really hard to know sometimes how to discuss my mama's relationships with her dementia—but Mari isn't a replacement for my mama.

"Thank you." That's about all I can get out right now. "Don't tell Val about this, okay? She'll tell Winnie, and I'd rather tell them both myself."

"By tonight?" Mari asks.

I want to groan but manage to hold it back. With all the

events of the morning, I haven't even thought about the LLLS meeting tonight.

"Sure."

I'll *try* to tell Winnie and Val before the meeting. And if not, there's always tomorrow. Or next week. I can only hope news of Pat and Tank didn't hit Neighborly yet. Thankfully, the diner was empty, and Big Mo is the last person who would say a word.

Mari boops me on the nose. And I let her, because it's Mari, and she's the absolute best. Even when her kindness makes me more emotionally melty than I want to be. If I could, I would keep my emotions like a cinder block—firm, cool, and completely unyielding.

Mari's eyes narrow on me again. "I see that look on your face. Why don't you—"

"Whatever you're going to say, I don't want to hear it. Not today."

Mari chuckles as Jo's feet begin pounding down the stairs. "Are you sure? I was going to say, why don't you have a taco? They cure many of life's problems."

There might not be enough tacos in the world for all my problems. But I'm never one to turn down free food.

"I'll take half a dozen chicken tacos to go with a pint of tomatillo sauce."

FROM THE NEIGHBORLY APP

Subject: Regulation hotties spotted on main street!!!

The_Real_Shell-E
Saw these two guys today and WHOA. Definitely not Sheeters. I took a photo from the back but they looked just as good from the front. See pic! *fire emoji*

DeltaDeltaDelta
Duuuuuude. What time was this? Think they're still there?

BagelBytes
Can we please halt the objectification of men or women?

Vanz
U forgot animals

BagelBytes

Didn't think it needed to be said. Also, it's not cool to post pics of people without permission.

The_Real_Shell-E
It's not like I posted their faces. No need to get all salty.

BagelBytes
So ... butts are okay?

DeltaDeltaDelta
Is that even a question? Butts are AWESOME! Especially those butts.

Neighborly Mod
The comments on this thread have been closed due to inappropriate content and/or bullying. The photo has also been removed due to privacy violations. See our Community Guidelines if you have any questions.
Please remember to be kind and above all, Neighborly!

CHAPTER SIX

Lindy

"Are you sure that wasn't my daddy?" Jo asks as my car makes its way down the road leading to the tiny house where I've lived almost my whole life. The one I moved back to despite swearing I'd never live in this town again.

I swerve gently to avoid a pothole, and Jo giggles. The road needs to be maintained, but it's nothing compared to how disastrous my driveway is. Who knew you needed to continually add gravel to a gravel driveway? Not I. Just another joy of home ownership! Since I haven't added gravel, the heavy rains we've had the last few summers resulted in potholes the size of baby pools. When it rains hard, that's exactly what they become. I let Jo put on her bathing suit and play in them just last month when it was a little warmer.

"I'm sure, baby."

"I'm not a baby," Jo says, starting one of my favorite games, one I hope she'll never outgrow.

"I'm sure, potato."

She giggles, and the sound eases something loose in my chest. "I'm not a potato."

"I'm sure, pancake."

"I'm not a food!" she says through giggles.

"Fine. Chickadee?"

"Better."

"Bear cub?"

"Yes! Bear cub."

Of course bear cub is the way to go. Great whites aren't her only fascination this month. All apex predators are on the menu. Before apex predators, Jo was into baking.

I preferred conversations about icing versus frosting. (Confession: I'm still not sure of the difference, but Jo could tell me.) She was disappointed I never learned to bake aside from boxed cake mix, which I can make with the best of them.

"How do you know that man isn't my daddy?"

"Why do you think he is?"

And why is she so obsessed with this line of questioning, which only makes me wonder what kind of father figure Pat would be. Because I have a sneaking suspicion he'd be amazing—IF he stuck around long enough.

"Because you look mad at him," Jo says. "And I know you're mad at my mama and daddy."

Gah! Can a day go by where this girl doesn't have the power to punch me in the gut with her questions and observations? For a five-year-old, Jo is intensely curious and exceptionally bright. She started reading at age three—yes, THREE—which only intensified her tendency to talk like a miniature adult. I thought reading that early was a myth, kind of like when people say their kids decided one day to start using the toilet all on their own. (I still maintain those people are lying. Potty training isn't for punks.) Anyway, she has the ability to pick up on way more than a normal five-year-old.

Like the fact that I'm mad at her mom and dad, whoever he might be.

I've done my best to shield Jo from the ugliest parts of her past, and I try not to disparage Rachel. It's a very fine line to walk when I want to be honest and also protect Jo's tender, growing heart. I thought she'd freak out when I told her about the upcoming hearing, but Jo only shrugged and said, "No one would let someone so irresponsible as Rachel raise a child."

I agree. But her nonchalant reply broke me a little. Also, based on my conversation with Ashlee today, it isn't true.

I draw in a deep breath, letting it fill my lungs, mentally feeling them expand. I imagine the oxygen molecules attaching to my blood and circulating through my body, spreading calm. As our crooked mailbox comes into view, I count the fence posts stretching ahead.

"Sometimes I am mad at your mama and daddy. They don't know what they're missing because you are the best bear cub around." She giggles, and I continue. "I know the man in the diner is not your daddy because he never met your mama."

"But he knew you?"

"Yeah, bear cub. A long time ago, he did."

I can almost hear Jo turning this knowledge over in her mind, a shiny rock to study. "And he left you like mama left me?"

No, not exactly like that. And there's the rub.

My throat constricts, and I press a hand to my chest. But

it's like trying to plug up a crack in a dam with only your fingers.

"He left me, but not like your mama. And I left him in a way," I admit, feeling the truth of the words burn like whiskey in my throat. "People sometimes hurt each other, even when they don't mean to."

"Why?"

"I don't know, Jojo. We just do."

As I turn into the driveway, Jo pipes up from the back seat. "Well, he's not leaving now."

That's the moment I see a fancy sports car stuck in a pothole that's really more of a sinkhole. It's definitely not coming out without a tow truck. Or a forklift.

And on our front porch: the man I can't seem to escape today.

Pat should NOT look right at home sitting on the sagging front steps of our little farmhouse. It's not fair. The traitor dogs should be chasing him off the property. Instead, Amber licks his face with effusive yellow lab love while Beast, the heavily overweight terrier mix, is perched on Pat's knees, looking ready to make that lap his permanent new home.

I'm so distracted I forget about one of the last potholes and the car bumps over it so hard, my head almost hits the ceiling.

"Whoa!" Jo giggles as I pull the car to a stop. I hear the zip of her seatbelt.

"Jo—hang on a sec!"

But she's off and running through the yard toward the trespasser. Pat gets to his feet, scooping up Beast under one arm like a furry football.

When Pat beams down at Jo, I want to hate him for the way this starts to defrost my frozen heart. I melt completely into a puddle when he crouches down to her eye level as she starts talking, her mouth moving a mile a minute and her arms waving. She has already stuck herself to him like a postage stamp. Which only makes me angrier.

He can't just show up here, ingratiating himself with the dogs and winning over Jo. It'll be worse—for them, not for me, because I'm FINE—when he leaves. And he *will* leave.

Pat's eyes flick to me as I slam my door. Beast wiggles out of his arms and bounds my way. He nudges my ankles, looking for scratches, but Pat is sucking up all my focus.

His slightly crooked, *aw shucks* smile and those warm espresso eyes beg to take away the rest of my resistance. *Just forgive me*, they seem to say. *You know you want to.* I know how this works, because he disabled my resistance back in college, when I agreed to date him *casually*.

How did casual dating turn out? Right—me, here alone, nursing a broken heart for all these years. And, according to the zombie butterflies stirring to life again in my stomach, still harboring feelings that just won't die.

"Hey, Lindybird."

The way he uses my nickname, one only he ever used, makes an invisible fist close around my rib cage, tightening until I can hardly breathe.

"Why are you here? *How* are you here?" I snap.

Pat stands up to his full height, and Jo clears her throat, giving me a look intended to tell me how rude I'm being. There is a time and a place for being rude, and this is one of them. I cannot let Pat awaken old feelings and reopen old wounds.

Though, honestly, it's too late on both counts.

The feelings: awake. Like, ten espressos on an empty stomach, awake. The wounds: open. As open as a 7-11, which neither opens at seven nor closes at eleven.

Before Pat can answer me, another man comes around the

side of the house, a slight limp to his gait. I don't need to have met Pat's dad to know him on sight. Not only because he's famous, but because I can see Pat in the crinkle of his smiling eyes and the upturned tilt of his mouth. It's a snapshot of Pat years down the road, and I wish I could say it doesn't work in Pat's favor.

"Hey, there. I'm Tank." Smiling, he holds out his hand to shake mine.

Up close, he's bigger than Pat, which is saying something. Tank is, well—I can see why he earned the nickname. I hesitate, then put my hand in his. It's warm and firm. "Hello."

This moment is surreal. Not only because Pat shouldn't be here—not on my porch, not in my town, not in my life at all—but because it breaks the rules.

When Pat and I met, our paths were already starting to diverge. Pat was a shoo-in for the NFL draft, and I had secured a position as a travel writer thanks to connections from one of my professors. There was no future for us, only a *right then*. I knew better. You shouldn't start dating someone your first semester of college, because you're all still figuring stuff out. You don't start dating someone your last semester of college because you don't want to derail your plans.

Pat and I threw that wisdom out the window, convincing ourselves we could just have fun. To keep things casual, we established the rules: no meeting families, no sharing friend groups. We didn't say I love you. And ... we didn't have sex.

I'm sure most people wouldn't believe that, especially given the reputation of collegiate athletes, but it's true. Everyone talks as though women are the only ones who might form an emotional bond getting physical, like men are just dissociated sex robots or something. But Pat wanted— and even suggested—this rule, which honestly made me like him even more. Here was this big, sexy football player, famous on campus and on the cusp of going pro, respecting this unexpected boundary.

And I will say this—if you date a man as passionate and attractive as Pat and *aren't* sleeping together, you will get a seminar-level education in the fine art of making out.

Stop thinking about making out with Pat while shaking hands with his dad.

"Sorry," I say, taking back my hand and smoothing down my dress, suddenly nervous.

"I'm really happy to finally meet you." Tank's smile grows.

Finally? I glance at Pat, who is rubbing the back of his neck and scuffing his cowboy boot in the dirt. *What did he say about me? And when?*

"I'm Lindy. And this is Jo. My niece."

Tank strides over to Jo and crouches down the same way Pat did. He holds out his big hand and Jo's tiny one disappears in it. She grins, clearly loving all this adult attention. I'm trying my very hardest not to love it too.

This is how it would be, a little voice whispers in my head. *This is how it could be.*

I slam a mental door on that idea and attach a large padlock to it, tossing the key down a mineshaft. Those kinds of thoughts have no business in my mind.

"Is that your car?" Jo asks, pointing up the drive. "Looks like you got stuck."

Tank stands and glowers at Pat, but I can see the teasing in his expression. "Yes, that's my car. Someone was driving a little bit too fast and didn't see the pothole. I think we might have broken an axle."

My stomach sinks when I realize it's Tank's car, not Pat's. I don't recognize the make or model, which assures me it's expensive. I didn't feel so bad thinking it was Pat, because he deserves to break his fancy car in a pothole for showing up here unannounced. But if it's his dad's …

"I'm so sorry," I say in a rush. "The driveway is a mess if you don't know where the potholes are. Can I—should I—"

I'm not sure what to offer, considering I can't afford to do anything at all. Not to fix the driveway or his car, not to get a tow truck. Sweat prickles along my hairline.

Tank holds up a hand, smiling gently. "Hey, it's okay. I've got AAA, and a tow truck is on the way. It's fine. My son will be covering the damages. Right, Patty?"

Jo laughs. "Your name is Patty?"

Pat grimaces. "My name is Patrick. Most people call me Pat."

"But you can call him Patty," I tell Jo. "He really likes that nickname."

"He *loves* that nickname, right, Patty?" Tank throws an arm around Pat, then winks at me. I love him for it.

When Pat doesn't answer right away, Tank squeezes him. It's comical how Pat—not a small man by any means—is dwarfed by his father. The obvious closeness between the two men makes me ache. My father was never in my life, not even my earliest memories. Even after he died, I never missed him, specifically, but I long for *this*. My breath hitches, and I clear my throat to dislodge the sticky emotion there.

You have family, I remind myself. *You have Jo. Mari and Val. Winnie and her brother, Chevy. Big Mo. And so many other people in this town who have given you support these past five years.*

And yet, the display I see in front of me, as Pat playfully shoves Tank, whose booming laugh makes even my grinchy heart smile—*this*, I don't have.

"Can we get you something to drink?" Jo asks, so easily offering the hospitality I should have thought of. "We have water, sweet tea, and those fizzy flavored waters." She wrinkles her nose at that one, making Pat chuckle.

"I think we'd do just fine with water," Tank says. "And then, how would you like to show me around? I thought I saw a barn."

"I'll show you the barn. Two waters, coming right up!" Jo bounds up the steps, making sure to hop over the one with the gaping hole in the center.

The door slams behind her, screen flapping from where Beast ran through it months ago to chase a squirrel. I'm suddenly and intensely embarrassed, remembering what terrible shape my house is in and how it must look to them.

Pat and Tank are probably both used to luxurious homes, or at least ones without massive holes in the driveway, a porch ready to detach from the house any minute, and knee-high weeds instead of grass in the yard. There's more white paint chipping off the exterior than on the wood at this point.

"Is that okay if Jo shows me around?" Tank asks. "I have a feeling you two have things you need to talk about."

Pat shifts uncomfortably but doesn't say anything. I wonder if this is the longest stretch of quiet he's ever maintained in his life.

The last thing I want is to dissect our past. We don't need a postmortem on this relationship because it's DEAD. Or, undead, if I'm going by the zombie butterflies.

Still, I need to tell Pat in no uncertain terms there is no future here. If I don't slam the door firmly this time, he's going to stick his boot in the crack and wedge the door back open, like he's clearly trying to do right now.

My mission, should I choose to accept it: make Patrick Graham flee. For good this time. Then kill all the undead insects swooping in my belly.

"It's fine," I say. "Just watch out for snakes and broken boards." Tank's eyes, the same dark brown as Pat's, go wide at the mention of snakes. "I think we got all the snakes out, but sometimes they come back once they've nested somewhere. Jo knows what places to avoid. You'll be fine."

Jo flies back through the front door, almost plowing into Amber, who has gone to sleep on the middle of the porch. Jo passes out two bottles of water, then grabs Tank by the hand. It's hilarious to watch her drag the giant man behind her. Beast bounds after them.

As they disappear around the corner of the house, I hear him ask, "Your Aunt Lindy said you knew where to avoid the snakes?"

"Don't worry," Jo says, her voice fading. "Snakes are friendly, and I'll keep you safe!"

It's all suddenly too much. Without meeting Pat's eyes, I sink down on the top porch step. Amber's tail thumps but she doesn't get up. I give her a quick scratch behind the ears, needing the touch to ground me.

"May I?" Pat asks, using the toe of his boot to gesture to the spot beside me.

"Might as well," I answer. "I'm not likely to get rid of you otherwise."

He sits down, and I'm hit with the scent of him. I asked Pat once what cologne he wore, because I was obsessed with it. He gave me the name of some generic store brand body wash and deodorant. In a moment of weakness years later, I bought both. But something in Pat's skin or his essence must combine with the scent in the products, because on their own, they did nothing for me.

Except make me cry.

Now, that same combination of product plus Pat makes my

hands tremble. I'm fighting the urge to grab him by the shirt and kiss him. I may be a messy tangle of emotions, but the desire for physical connection with Pat is very *uncomplicated*. I remember exactly how his mouth fit perfectly to mine, the heat of his body, and the way it felt to be wrapped up in his strong arms.

"You have a chicken," Pat says, and I glance over to see Elvis strutting around the porch.

"A rooster, actually."

This makes Pat smile, and I don't like it when he smiles. Mostly because I like it way too much.

"He's on your porch."

I shrug. "Some people have house elves. We have a porch rooster." Pat laughs, and I mentally kick myself for being playful. But it's hard to stop. Even now, with good reason to be hurt and angry, Pat makes me … light. He always had that effect, like when I was with him, we existed somewhere above the normal plane of living. "Elvis thinks he's a house cat. He's always trying to sneak inside."

"Elvis." Pat shakes his head and holds out a hand to the rooster, who gives him a heavy dose of avian side-eye before stalking away.

Smart rooster. Get away while you still can!

Pat shifts, and his thigh brushes mine. Even encased in jeans, I'm aware of his muscles, pushing the fabric to its limit. I always loved the way his legs and butt hardly fit into pants. Once, we went dancing at some country bar in Austin, and the back of his pants ripped all the way up the seam when he did some kind of ridiculous dance move.

Being this close to Pat requires an exercise in the most careful restraint. I could easily be persuaded to channel all my hurt and anger into a passionate, deliciously angry make out session.

Would that be so wrong? Some angry kissing before I kick him off my property?

Yes. Yes, it would.

I edge away from him, which takes me closer to the hole in the porch step. It's kind of a toss-up between Pat and the splintered wood, but I think I'm safest with the broken step.

I clench my hands into tight fists, letting them hang between my knees. "So, you're here. In my town, at my house, no less. How do you know where I live?"

Pat clears his throat and raps his knuckle on the porch. "I've been here before, actually."

My head whips toward him, which is a mistake. We're still sitting too close, our faces only a foot or so apart. I lean way back, looking awkward and obviously comical, based on the amusement glinting in his eyes.

"When? When did you come here?"

"Must have been about two-and-a-half years ago. Right after my injury, when I came back to Texas. Your mama didn't tell you I was here?"

Of course—Mama was still here.

Little black dots eclipse my vision. Though I've never passed out before, I'm immediately aware that's what's happening.

I wrote an article recently on old-timey words making a comeback, which is the only explanation I can give for what I say just before I start to collapse: "I'm swooning."

Everything tilts and goes dark. I'm foggy, but slightly aware, like I'm in a strange dream. One in which strong arms cradle me.

Warm hands position my body across something soft and warm. A lap. Pat's lap.

I have some sensation in my limbs, though I cannot move or respond. I'm not sure how I even would respond to Pat murmuring, "I've got you. I've got you now, Lindybird."

If I had all my faculties, I'd find a stick in the yard and beat Pat off with it. Instead, I'm helpless, a rag doll being curled against him. It's nice here, especially as my conscious mind slips away for seconds or minutes or hours. There is no time here, which means there is no past. No mistakes to atone for.

Just as I'm wishing I could float in timelessness, I begin to come back to myself, feeling a prickling sensation like the pins and needles after your foot has fallen asleep. Something brushes against my cheek—did Pat just kiss me? I try to tell him to get off me, and all that comes out is a mumbling groan.

"That's my girl. Come on back to me, darlin'."

As I come into full awareness, I'm embarrassed to realize my head is burrowed deep into Pat's broad chest. My fingers grip his shirt. I've untucked the whole front of it, revealing a tanned and toned stomach I definitely shouldn't be ogling. This is not the time to count Pat's abs.

"Let me go, you big oaf," I grumble.

Pat only chuckles, and there's a tenderness to the sound as he brushes my hair back from my cheek. "As soon as I'm sure you're not going to *swoon* on me again. I thought that word was only reserved for romance novels."

I *did* say swoon, didn't I? I am a complete and total mess. I'd like to crawl into a hole and emerge in a different decade, Rip Van Winkle style. I don't think I ate this morning, and the tacos Mari sent home with me are still in the car. Come to think of it, I'm not sure when the last time I ate was. The combination of hunger and emotional overwhelm seems to have short-circuited my brain.

"Are you okay?"

"I'm fine." I manage to sit up completely, though I'm still slightly dizzy. When I try to pull myself off Pat's lap, he circles his arms around me protectively.

"Relax," he says.

I can't. Not with his scent invading my senses and the familiar feel of him surrounding me. It's like I've been transported right back to the days where I spent as much time as I could just like this—greedy for his touch, knowing there was an expiration date on how long I'd have to rest securely in the space of his arms.

It's that idea of an end date, remembering with painful clarity how much it hurt to let Pat go, which enables me to pull back. "I mean it. Let me go, Patrick."

He opens his arms reluctantly, and I scoot back, careful still to avoid the hole in the stairs. I lean against the railing, putting my feet out in front of me to keep him at bay. I've lost a boot, which Pat retrieves from the sidewalk and slides on to my foot with an ease and intimacy that makes my breath catch. He doesn't remove his hand right away, letting his hand brush my knee. I don't have the physical or mental strength right now to fight him off, but he pulls back, then hands me his water bottle.

I hesitate before putting it to my lips, telling myself I am not allowed to think about his lips on this same bottle. It almost works.

"As I was saying, I came here looking for you," Pat says. "You weren't here, but I had a lovely visit with your mama. She told me you'd been gone a long time. She gave me a piece of pie and sent me on my way."

Pat came here. For me. It's what I always wanted, what I secretly hoped for. Seeing him in the diner today was a shock, but at the same time, I played through the scenario so many times in my mind that it was familiar. Like I had expected Pat to show up here someday. Which, I guess he did. Twice now.

I close my eyes. It must have been just before I had to put Mama in a home, one I can only afford because Lynn Louise, the woman who owns it, gives us a hefty discount. Jo and I were probably at the store or at the library for story time, maybe at a park. I bet Mama had no recollection of Jo even existing, or of me living here. Maybe that day, she was thinking I was in college still. I'll never know.

"Did she ... pass?" Pat asks, his brown eyes slowly moving up to meet mine.

I give him a tight smile. "No. She has early onset dementia. I had to put her in a facility, Sheet Cake Acres. It was getting dangerous to have her here. I couldn't leave her by herself."

Pat reaches out and squeezes my knee. When I don't tell him to stop—even though I should—his fingers trace a path down to the edge of my boot and back up. For a big brute of a man, he's painfully gentle. His touch sends all kinds of electric sensations up my body in ways that make me feel ashamed, given our current conversation. Nothing like getting all hot and bothered when discussing your mama's health issues.

Plus, I know better. I let this man hurt me once before. I won't trade my good sense for the man's touch. I pull my legs toward me and out of reach. A group of crows—a murder, in technical terms—flies overhead and I count them again as they disappear. A lone crow stays behind to watch the drama unfold from the branches of the dead oak tree. I really need to have that tree removed when I can afford it. I'll add it to the ever-growing list.

"I'm so sorry," Pat says.

His eyes flick to the side of the house, where Tank disappeared with Jo a few minutes ago, then back to me. The compassion in them makes me want to cry. Though we didn't talk much about our families (again, see the rules), I know he lost his mama young. I could tell the few times he mentioned her how much he loved her.

"Is that when you had to start caring for Jo?" he asks.

Oh, boy. Best pull all the lies out of the darkness and lay them all out in the sun to be examined.

I take a shaky breath. "I've been taking care of Jo since she was a month old. My sister abandoned her the week you left."

Pat's face shifts as he realizes what the timing means. "But that time I called," he says slowly. "You said you were in Europe."

I nod slowly. "I did say that."

The memory of his phone call is painfully etched inside my skull. I had not been in Europe. I'd been standing at the kitchen sink, washing bottles, the sour smell of formula mixing with the bright clean lemon of dish soap. When my phone rang, I was so exhausted, I didn't even look at the caller ID.

I heard Pat's voice, and I almost dropped my phone in the sink.

He'd been at a club or bar—I could hardly hear him over the thumping bass and sound of voices. I didn't know why he was calling when he couldn't have been bothered to so much as text me the night he ditched me without saying goodbye.

"I just wanted to catch up!" he said, practically shouting into the phone. "How are you, Lindybird?"

He wants to catch up? How am I?

In the window above the sink, I caught sight of myself. Lank hair, falling out of the same ponytail I'd worn for days. I had dark shadows under my eyes and hollows in my cheeks.

The stained shirt I wore had spit-up in so many places it seemed silly to wash it and change into something clean. That had been the week the dryer broke.

It's still broken. And so am I.

Before I could find words, I heard another woman saying Pat's name, asking him to buy her another drink. Her voice was clear enough for me to know she was *right there*, probably pressed against him, her lips near his ear and—

I snapped. Lie after lie poured from my mouth about cities I'd seen, places I'd stayed, how wonderful it was being free and unattached. Tears poured down my face to match the lies streaming out. Lying was a way to shove Pat out of my life and slam the door behind him. I couldn't have him calling me up when he wanted, breaking my heart all over again.

And then I heard Jo stirring through the baby monitor on the counter. I told Pat I had to go and hung up without waiting for a response. I went up to feed Jo, diving back into what had become my routine, hoping to forget about the man I'd loved.

Now, as understanding washes over Pat, I can see him fighting to contain his hurt and anger. I expect an explosion, but he holds it all behind the tightness of his jaw, the pinch of his forehead.

Pat has changed, or maybe he's simply matured. Restraint was never his strong suit. What he felt bubbled out of him like an underground spring, unrestrained and uncontained.

"Did you *ever* go to Europe?" he asks.

"Raising a kid and taking care of Mama changed all my plans." It changed *me*. Sometimes I think for the better, but it's really hard to say.

"I wondered why I could never find your articles. I

scoured the internet for your byline in every travel journal and website out there."

He did?

I can't let that detail soften me toward him, but it turns something in me, like the statement is a tiny brass key.

"I still write, just under another name. And not about travel, obviously."

A ragged breath escapes him, and though his muscles bunch like he's about to run, he doesn't. "So, when I called, you were here?"

"Right inside the house." I tilt my head toward the door. "I've been here ever since a few days after you left without saying goodbye. Remember that?"

I hate the way I wear bitterness like a too-small thrift store coat. But I won't allow myself to feel bad for stating a fact. I may owe him an apology for lying, but what I need right now is not reconciliation. I need him to *go*.

I need to launch all the ammo at him I can, driving him off my emotional—and actual—property. My feelings for Pat are like a sticker-burr on a pair of wool socks. But it shouldn't be too hard to get him off my porch. The man was easy enough to shake off the first time.

Except, maybe not. He came looking for me.

The idea rattles me. What if I'd been here that day? What if I had come home to find him sitting with Mama? What if I hadn't lied in the first place but told him about Jo? What if—*nope*. I can't play this game. It's way too dangerous.

Then there's the fact that Pat hasn't apologized for ditching me. I still feel the sting of it, lemon squeezed over the raw wound in my heart.

"And you're not … with anyone?" Pat asks. When I glare, he holds up both hands. "I know I don't have the right to ask."

"You definitely don't."

I don't want to tell him. I'm *not* going to tell him. I refuse to—

"I'm not seeing anyone," I find myself saying, as though my treacherous tongue is now under the control of those zombie butterflies. "I did date a little."

Total exaggeration. I went out exactly once with Billy Waters, the guy I'd dated all through high school. He was even more entitled and awful as an adult than he'd been as a teenager. I'm not sure why this surprised me. The man is lucky he still has hands after the way he tried to put them all over me.

I can't help but enjoy the flash of jealousy in Pat's eyes. *How does that feel, Patty? Now, imagine if my dating life was the one splashed all over every tabloid and every popular website.*

"Lindy, I know that my words are just words. They're too little and too late. But I am so sorry for leaving the way I did. I thought—I thought it would be easier to leave without having to say goodbye. For both of us." He flinches. "It sounds so stupid, but I *was* stupid back then. I knew the moment I got on the plane how big of a mistake it was. When I called, I wanted to tell you the truth—that I fell in love with you, Lindy."

He fell in—NOPE. We are going to pretend he never said that statement. It is categorically false and therefore does not exist.

I cut him off. "You called me from a club. There were women calling your name. If you called to tell me you loved me, that is the least convincing way I can think of."

I expect him to try and defend himself. It's a little disappointing when he doesn't.

I keep going. "Let's not forget the fact you got married to Padma less than a month after that call."

Padma is the underwear model's actual name. In my

head, she's Booby McUnderpants. In real life, I'm sure she's a very lovely person and was one of only dozens of famous women Pat was linked to. But the one that hurt the most was Padma.

I was destroyed when Pat left. I was devastated when I heard he got married. Val and Winnie practically had to force me to eat for a week.

"You and I had all these rules keeping us from getting serious, to keep us casual, but you married someone else so quickly. What am I supposed to think about that?"

"We got the marriage annulled," he says.

I throw my hands up. "The annulment doesn't take away the fact that it happened. You stood before a judge or witnesses or an Elvis impersonator or whomever and said vows. I never even got to meet your family, to hang with your friends. To—" I can't say the last part.

"I wanted it to be you."

His voice is quiet and measured, yet its impact hits like a wrecking ball. I just want this moment, this conversation, this pain to be over. Give me a dentist's drill every day of the year over this conversation. Throw in an OB-GYN visit too. Heck—I'll take both at the same time over dredging up this painful past.

"You left me." I know he already apologized for it, but I'm still processing. Because his words simply do not compute.

"Biggest regret of my life," Pat says. "And I have a lot of regrets, believe me." He pauses, his jaw working before he speaks again. "If you had told me the truth when I called, I would have come."

"Do you really think I could have asked you to come to this nowhere town and help raise a child with me? Would you have traded late nights at parties for late nights with a newborn? Drinks for diapers?"

"I would have."

I stare at him. And dang it if his deep brown eyes look sincere.

It's all too much. His apology, his confession, this whole conversation. My head is feeling dangerously swoony again.

"You sounded so happy with your life," Pat says. "Like everything was going so well without me. I called to apologize, but you didn't even sound like you cared."

"I did care. Too much." *And I won't make that mistake again.*

"But I'd like to try now. If you'll let me. Lindy, I am so sorry for hurting you. For leaving you without saying goodbye. For not being here when you were struggling. Tell me it's not too late," Pat says, and if I had to describe his tone, I'd say he's begging. I like it a little too much. "Please, Lindy —forgive me. Let me try to make things right. Let me show you I've changed. Let me have another chance. *Please.*"

No, no, and no. As much as I love the reformed bad boy in romance novels, I am not ready for one in my own life. Especially not with all the other emotional turmoil I'm already dealing with. I cannot possibly spare the emotional bandwidth for a relationship right now. Especially not one with a cargo plane full of baggage. But I can't seem to make myself tell Pat no. The tiny, one-syllable word refuses to leave my mouth.

Pat looks like he's about to say more, but I spot a tow truck turning down my drive, plumes of dust rising in clouds behind it.

I jump to my feet. "Catching up has been lovely. Apology accepted. And it looks like your ride is here."

"Lindy—"

Before he can say anything more, there is a shrill shriek the likes of which I've never heard before.

And then Tank comes running around the side of the

house. Jo follows a moment later, holding a small brown snake. It's barely big enough to hang over the sides of her hands.

"Don't worry, Mr. Tank! It's not venomous," she calls. "It's a rough earth snake. They eat earthworms, not people."

But Tank is still running. If I didn't feel like my heart was just dragged across a cheese grater, I might laugh.

Instead, I climb down the steps and meet Jo. "Better let the snake go, Jojo. I don't think Tank cares what species he is."

Jo sighs heavily, then sets the snake down in the grass. "Fine." It takes a moment for the reptile to disentangle himself from her fingers. In seconds, it disappears in the grass. I wish the human walking up behind me would disappear as quickly.

"Bye, snake," Jo says solemnly.

"Let me guess," Pat says, standing next to Jo with his hands shoved deep in his pockets. "Snakes are like sharks—they just need a friend?"

Jo grins. "Exactly."

Pat glances at me, then away. "I better go collect Tank. He's more scared of snakes than Indiana Jones. Bye, Jo."

He offers her a smile and a fist bump, then starts up the driveway, where the tow truck has stopped near the broken-down sports car.

I'm disgusted to find myself torn watching Pat walk away. He may have wrecked me today, but that doesn't mean I can't appreciate his backside in jeans.

I want him gone, but I also want to take him inside and tie him to the old wooden rocker so he can't leave ever again.

I want to tell him yes, I forgive him.

I want to give him—to give *us*—a second chance.

"Hey!" I call. Pat turns, blinking in surprise. "What kind of pie?"

His brow furrows. "What?"

"What kind of pie did my mama give you?"

He squints, the sun is gorgeous slanting over his cheeks. "Buttermilk."

I nod. "That was her best recipe."

CHAPTER SEVEN

Pat

"THOSE THINGS ARE DISGUSTING," Chase says, wrinkling his nose as I pass cigars around the poker table on Tank's back patio. "Even unlit. You know that, right?"

"I know no such thing. Besides, we aren't even smoking them," I tell him. "And you're family now. As a brother, you will take this cigar and *not* smoke it. Thank you."

It's poker night, a tradition we've kept for years as often as we can. Usually, once a month, but sometimes more if the stars and our schedules align. Harper is in the house with her and Chase's dogs, watching a movie. She happens to hate poker, though I suspect if she played, she'd have the only poker face to rival Collin's.

"Then why have cigars at all?" Chase asks.

But he takes the cigar I hand him. "Why protest when we aren't smoking them?"

"Why have them when we aren't smoking them?"

"It's just the feel of it," Collin says, dragging the cigar underneath his nose.

"Thank you!" I gesture to the most responsible of my brothers. He tips the cigar my way, and Chase rolls his eyes.

"Well, I'm smoking it," James says.

When all of us, including Tank, glare at him, he sighs. The no-smoking rule on poker nights came into effect this year after Harper, the lone XX chromosome holder and most influential member of our family, found out she's on the autism spectrum and also has sensory processing disorder. She had always complained about the cigar smell, and we had teasingly ignored her, like the brutes we are. When we realized we were being actual brutes, we immediately banished cigars from poker nights.

"Later," James amends. "I'll smoke it at home."

Chase, for being a peacemaker, can't seem to let this one go. "I just don't get *why*—"

Tank clears his throat. "Can we move on, boys?"

Dad is not so much trying to rescue me as he is trying to deflect the question. He and I agreed on the drive home not to talk about Sheet Cake until we'd played a decent number of hands. The news would go down better after everyone was in a good mood.

As to why the cigars—they were an impulse buy at the gas station. I saw them sitting right by the register and had to have them. My insides are hosting their own ticker tape parade in honor of seeing Lindy again. I can't help feeling like celebrating, even if not everything today was a win.

Definitely not the damage to the Aston. And more importantly, not the conversation with Lindy. I want to think of it as a start, like a nice, friendly comma after an introductory clause. But I'm pretty sure she saw it as a period at the end of a sentence—the last sentence just before the words THE END.

I have a lot of hard feelings: guilt, regret, and even anger. Not necessarily directed at Lindy, because I understand why she lied to me. I am hurt. But I'm also hopeful. Maybe she didn't say she forgave me. Maybe she didn't say yes to giving me a second chance. But she didn't say no, and I'll hold on to that.

I still can't believe she's been right up the road, all this time. She's *still* right up the road—forty-two minutes—and it has taken every bit of willpower I have to not drive back right now. I could set up camp on her front porch with Elvis the rooster. But I need a plan. I can't just fire myself off like a cannon, not when she seems so fragile. She's a shell of herself, a strong survivor to be sure, but a little like a cardboard cutout of the woman I knew.

My feelings for Lindy haven't faded a bit. Honestly, with the way they slammed into me the moment I heard her voice, I'd say they've only strengthened with time.

Yeah, I know. It sounds ridiculous. You can't fall MORE in love with someone from a distance when you aren't even talking. And yet … that's exactly how this feels.

I clamp the unlit cigar between my teeth and spread my arms wide, giving Tank a wink. "We're celebrating life, fellas. Life and love and family and the future. Now, who's dealing first?"

"You can't just buy a town." Collin stares pointedly at Tank.

"Except I *did* buy a town." Dad is in full-on defense mode. His chair is pushed back from the table, his arms are crossed over his chest, and his jaw is set.

I'm laying low, a little terrified now that the moment's here. So far, Tank has said nothing about my involvement, and I have half a mind to tuck tail and run. But I don't do that anymore. I am a reformed runner. I'll be the man who stays. Who finishes. Who commits. Starting now.

"Let's focus on some of the details." Chase's tone is neutral and friendly. "I mean, what's the legality there? How does purchasing a town work?"

Too bad there's no room for Switzerland at this table. Even Chase's peaceful demeanor is not going to diffuse the emotions. We're a bunch of nuclear reactors reaching critical levels.

So far, Collin is pelting Tank with questions, while James is fuming silently. Quiet isn't necessarily good when it comes to my oldest and broodiest brother. I can see the tension gathering like a storm in James's eyes.

I discreetly try to get Harper's attention in the house. Her attention is fixed on the TV, and she completely misses my laser beam eyes and the telepathic messages I'm trying to send her way. Brutus, curled up in her lap like he's a teacup chihuahua not a boxer, sees me but clearly can't read my desperation. Or he doesn't care.

"It's not so complicated," Tank says. "I own all the land in the town proper. All the leasing agreements for the businesses on site have been signed over to me. Other than city hall and the library, which are property of the state."

"Are you planning to move there?" Chase asks. He glances around. "And, uh, sell this place?"

Admittedly, I hadn't thought this far in advance, and the thought of Dad selling the house where we all grew up, the house where Mom lived—it makes my stomach plummet.

I guess there's a lot I didn't think about. Once I saw Lindy, I stopped thinking at all. I'm already all in on this plan, my figurative stack of chips pushed to the center of the table. I chew on the inside of my cheek, watching Tank.

"I'm not selling this house. We"—he swallows thickly at the reference to Mom—"paid cash, and the value is more than double. I'm hanging on to it."

He doesn't say anything about sentimental reasons, but he doesn't need to. We get it.

A large bit of tension eases from the patio. I don't think any of us are ready for THAT change. Buy a town—not a great idea, but we can deal. Sell the house where we lived with Mom? Nope.

Tank leans forward, elbows on the table. His winning hand is still spread out in front of him, a full house. It seems a little ironic. Or maybe like reverse irony? Depends on what happens next, I guess.

Harper *finally* looks up, and I give her wild eyes and a look I hope says, *Get your hiney out here, honey*. She walks out with Brutus and Smoky just as Dad says, "I do plan to relocate there eventually. And hopefully not alone. I did this for us," Tank says, rapping his knuckles on the table. The fan squeaking overhead is the only sound.

"How is you buying a town for *us*?" Collin asks.

I clench my hands into fists under the table, because I feel it coming, the way electricity crackles through the air before a storm.

"I think it's the perfect location for us to open the brewery."

And there it is, folks. Tank dropped the bomb.

For a good five seconds, no one speaks. No one moves. Only Smoky, Harper and Chase's almost full-grown puppy, seems unaffected, chewing idly on his own paw, then moving on to chase his tail.

"Dad, this isn't like you," Harper says. "No offense, but this sounds like a Pat move—risky and impulsive."

"Hey!" I protest, but everyone ignores me.

"Maybe it's time I take more risks," Tank says.

"Speaking of Pat …" Collin swivels to face me. "You've been awful quiet."

His words draw all the attention on the patio to little ol' me. I've been letting the argument happen around me until just now. I kinda thought they might not have noticed me. But I'm never quiet. Talking would have been less obvious.

"Yeah," James adds, and I don't like that his first words in a long while are directed my way. "Why has your big mouth been shut?"

Before I can formulate some kind of answer or locate a Get Out of Jail Free card, Tank drives up in a double-decker bus and throws me under it.

"Pat went with me to see the town today. He's totally on board."

James drops his bottle, which shatters on the flagstone patio, and all that building tension explodes with the subtlety of a dirty bomb.

Chase grabs Smoky to keep him from stepping on the glass, while Harper darts inside for the broom. I'm sputtering, trying to think of some defense, like *I didn't say I was TOTALLY on board*, while Collin and James start shouting over each other.

"I knew you were too quiet!" Collin points his cigar accusingly at me.

James practically rattles the nearby windows. "I can't believe you both went behind my back! You can't make those kinds of decisions about Dark Horse without consulting me!"

See! I knew that's how he'd feel.

I glare at Dad, forgetting for a moment that he's my only

ally. Or WAS. He doesn't take too kindly to my look, and stands up, pushing back from the table.

"We can discuss this at a time when you've all had a chance to cool down. I love you all, and I think you'll see how this could be great for our family. For all of us."

With that, Dad walks into the house. We can all hear the sound of his bedroom door slamming from out here.

And then there was one person to blame.

James shakes his head in disgust. "I can't believe you. Dad—well, that I can sort of understand. He's old."

"Not *that* old," Chase says, then holds up his hands when we all shoot him a look.

"He's right, though," Collin says. "They're both to blame."

"I'm not the one who bought a town!" I argue.

"You just kept it a secret and colluded with Dad about it." Harper finishes sweeping up the glass. She levels a judgmental glare at me before she dumps the contents of the dustpan in the trash.

I mean, I can't argue with her point. And when Harper's against me, I've gone and stepped in it.

"Fine. Yeah, I knew. It's not like Tank told me he planned to do this or gave me a big heads-up. I found out today, just like the rest of you."

"Not *quite* like the rest of us," Collin says, still pointing his cigar at me. "You went there. You've known for hours. You sat there, laughing and joking like things were normal. Is that why you bought these cigars?"

"No," I tell him, but my voice doesn't even convince me. I'm not lying—just hiding the bigger reason I'm on board. I'm not sure dropping the Lindy news on them right now is the best option. I'm thankful Tank didn't reveal that too.

"I'm out of here," James says, pushing back from the table and striding toward the gate.

"Jamie," Harper calls. She's the only one who can get away with calling him that, and she only does so when she needs the big guns. Tonight, she needs more like a cannon.

James pauses, one hand on the gate. He doesn't turn around but inclines his head the slightest bit.

"Take some time," my oh-so-wise sister says. "Then let's hear Dad out. Maybe Pat too. Maybe."

I throw my hands up. "How am I the big bad guy here when Tank is the one who did the purchasing and the planning?"

"I probably wouldn't say anything more if I were you," Chase mutters under his breath, shrugging when Harper narrows her eyes at him.

"James?" Harper calls again.

He grunts a response, which translates to, *Caveman mad at family. Me go brood in cave. Maybe forgive later.*

Then, he's gone.

"Why didn't you tell us?" Collin asks, as soon as we hear the throaty purr of James's motorcycle roaring down the street.

"Tank stole my phone."

Harper shoots a pointed glare at the device in question, sitting next to me on the table.

"He stole it while we went there," I clarify.

"I still can't believe you *went* there." Collin stands up, pacing near the edge of the pool, dragging his hands through his hair until it stands on end.

Then he's definitely not going to believe who I *saw* there. One of the rules Lindy and I had about our so-called casual relationship was no family members. No meeting them, no talking about them. Which was a challenge considering how close my family is.

After phonecallpocalypse, where Lindy told me what I now know were lies about how happy she was, I was crushed. Like, stuffed inside of one of those car compactor things CRUSHED.

And though my family may not have known her name or exactly what happened, everyone knew that someone broke my heart. My impulsivity hit all new highs. Or lows, depending on how you look at it. I made stupid decisions, like marrying Padma and getting involved with women who I knew were only interested in my fame. I spiraled from there into not caring about anything, which is not the same as my typical devil-may-care cheerful optimism.

I didn't care about football. My health, mental or physical. My money. My contract. My future.

Why did any of it matter without HER?

My brothers began referring to Lindy as The Woman, like Irene Adler in the BBC *Sherlock* adaptation. I tried defending her, telling my brothers it was my fault. But they still put one hundred percent of the blame on The Woman. Maybe more like ninety percent. Because I kept telling them I screwed it up and, well, it's not like I had a good track record before that with relationships.

I definitely can't tell my family the reason I'm on board with Tank's proposal is The Woman. They will lose their ever-loving minds. They'll flunk this idea based on me. I'll have to keep this under wraps as long as I can. Which, given my inability to keep a secret, probably won't be long.

Harper raises one brow, and that look has the power to make me feel like I've been instantly mummified. I'm now a withered and shriveled and dusty old skeleton. "That's really your excuse?" she asks. "Tank took your phone?"

"It was more like a half-kidnapping. I was under duress."

"How does that work, exactly?" Chase is grinning. "Duct tape? Did he slip something in your drink and tie you up in the back of his SUV?"

"I wouldn't put any of that past him. But no." I sigh, running a hand over my face and mumbling the answer.

"What was that?" Harper said.

"Dad let me drive the Aston."

They all groan.

"Such a low price for your loyalty," Collin laments.

"Shut up. You'd have done the same thing."

"No. I would have gotten behind the wheel in the Aston and driven straight to one of you to talk some sense into the old man."

Why didn't I think of that?

Oh. Right. Because Tank filled my head with nonsense about me being the glue and the one with vision. Then he mentioned Sheet Cake, I thought of Lindy, and I was kind of a goner.

"What do you think about his idea, Patty?" Harper asks, and the fact that she's asking my opinion stuns all of us into silence again.

I examine the cigar in my hands, slip off the paper band, a little loose from the humidity, and put it on my finger. My pinky, because my ring finger is too big. Premature though it may be, I'm thinking about Lindy, wearing my ring and a white dress.

And I thought Tank had lost brain cells buying a town. Joke's on me! I'm Tweedledum to his Tweedledee.

"Are you still with us, Patty?" Collin asks.

"Yep."

At least half of me is. Because I left the rest in Sheet Cake. I'm crumpled up in Lindy's pocket like a forgotten receipt or a bit of dryer lint. But I don't plan to stay that way. I don't have a strategy YET, but I've already got ideas popping up in my mind like moles needing to be whacked with a toy hammer.

"So," Harper urges, "what are your thoughts?"

Even Smoky and Brutus seem to be watching me like I'm wearing a shirt made of bacon or something. I consider how I can answer this honestly, but also without revealing anything about Lindy.

"I thought Tank was joking at first. Then I thought he had a vitamin or brain cell deficiency. The jury's out on that." I rock back in my chair a little, staring down at the chips and cards strewn around the wooden table. "But ... I'll confess, something about the idea intrigues me."

"Would this *town*"—Collin says the word like he's talking about cow patties—"even work for Dark Horse? I mean, if James is willing to consider it with a level head."

I scratch my chin. "It would be ... a project."

"The potential brewery location is a project? Like, the building is run down?" Harper asks.

I find myself giggling. Not chuckling. Giggling. Of all the stupid nervous tics to have, mine is one shared with little girls.

"No," I say through my giggles. "The whole place is a project. It's basically a ghost town. *The Walking Dead* without the zombies. Or without people fighting the zombies."

Collin sits heavily back down at the table and tosses his cigar at me. It beans me in the forehead and falls to the ground. Harper snatches it up before Smoky can eat it. He is a canine garbage disposal with zero standards. He's eaten— or tried to eat—socks, magazines, couch cushions, and doors. Yes—he ate his way through part of a door. Chase renovated their house before he and Harper got married.

Then he had to keep fixing it up because of the destructive pooch.

"What is he *thinking*?" Collin asks.

"He's been watching too much HGTV," I answer. "That and his baby girl went and got married."

"Don't blame me," Harper says. "What are *you* thinking?"

That's a loaded question. I'm thinking about how to win back my woman, but no way am I telling them that yet.

I choose my words carefully. "That it sounds like a viable option. Viable-ish. And I don't have a job or focus right now. Why not hop on board?"

I don't know how to read Harper's stare, but it's definitely the kind that comes before something I won't want to hear. "What happens if it fails?"

"Who says it will? And if it does, I'll just move on." I shrug. "What? Why are you looking at me like that?"

"I just don't want to see you going dark again," Harper says.

"Going dark? Doesn't sound like me." I pull at the collar of my shirt. "What is it y'all always say—I'm a big ball of sunshine?"

"You usually are," Harper says. "But when you're not, that's when you go dark. Which can actually be something that goes along with ADHD and—"

I hold up a hand. "That's enough of the therapy session. I'm fine. Let's swing this focus back to Tank and his big idea."

Harper is the reason I even got tested for ADHD. I got this niggling feeling when she talked to our family about her diagnosis, a feeling like I had questions that needed answers. But the answers I got would have helped me more as I struggled in classrooms for years. As an adult, I don't really see it affecting much of my life, and there's no need to psychoanalyze everything or attach my behaviors and actions to the label. It definitely doesn't apply to *this*.

"I've got a thought." Chase leans forward, glancing between the three of us before taking Harper's hand.

"Just one thought?" Harper teases.

He smiles. "Maybe a few. Your dad has been kind of floating for a while. He has you guys, and don't get me wrong, your family is amazing. But he hasn't had anything that's uniquely *his*. Not since I've known you."

This observation rankles a bit coming from Chase. But he's not an outsider since we basically adopted him when he and Harper first became friends. Often, he has insight into our family we can't see because we're too close. It's only *slightly* irritating. It would be more irritating if he was wrong.

Chase shrugs. "Maybe taking on this project is his way of finding his own thing."

"Yeah, but it's still a family thing," Collin says, shaking his head. "He bought the town for the brewery, which is something he's doing with *all* of us."

"Sure," Chase says easily. He's not arguing exactly, but he's also not backing down. "It's for the family, but it's his idea, his initiative, his contribution."

"What are you saying?" Collin asks, a little too antagonistically, earning him a dark look from Harper. He lightens his tone. "Sorry. I mean, what do you think we should do about this?"

"I don't know," Chase says. "But I'd say go easy on him. Open up your mind to the possibility."

"Is that what you did?" Collin asks, swinging his gaze to meet mine. "You *opened up your mind*?"

I ignore his sarcasm. "Maybe I did. And I could really see Tank's vision." I also saw Lindy, but again, I'm keeping that to myself.

"Maybe you could see it because you don't have a full-time job," Collin says. "Or a business. Or more on your social calendar than movie nights with Tank."

I'm not going to give into his needling. "Think what you want. I'm just giving my opinion. And my movie nights with Tank are an enviable social engagement."

Collin sighs. "Where is this town he bought?"

I start giggling again. Collin huffs out an annoyed breath, while Chase looks amused. Harper rolls her eyes.

"Forty minutes or so away," I answer. "It's ... it's ..."

The giggles take over, shifting into tear-inducing, gut-cramping laughter. I have to scoot back from the table and bend over, holding my stomach. Smoky, trying to fix whatever's wrong with me, bounds over and puts his tongue in my ear.

"Spit it out, Patty," Collin says.

I pet Smoky, wipe the tears from my eyes and look from Collin to Chase to Harper. "Drum roll, please." None of them oblige so I start drumming on my thigh until they all look ready to toss me in the pool. "Tank purchased a town called ... Sheet Cake, Texas."

Chase, who didn't grow up in Texas like the rest of us, looks as though his eyes are going to bug out of his head. The thing about living in this state is you just expect ... strange.

Not all strange the way Austin is strange—which it totally is, like weird, hippy artist strange—but Texans do things that are bigger and often quirkier than other places. And then we fully commit. If there's a town named after a classic cake recipe—the Texas sheet cake—of course it's *here*. And proud of it!

"They have a festival, don't they?" Harper asks, tilting her head.

"It's their claim to fame," I answer.

And not THAT much weirder than the Alligator Festival in Anahuac Texas, where they ring a bell every time someone traps a gator. Or the Poteet Strawberry Festival, Irving's Zestfest, or the Wurstfest in New Braunfels.

Have I been to a disproportionate number of these festivals? Yep. But never The Sheet Cake Festival. I suspect that's about to change.

"So, the town can't be totally dead," Chase says.

"Just mostly dead." I refrain from making a *Princess Bride* joke because Collin anticipates it and gives me a look like *Just try it and see what happens*.

"We could ask Thayden to look at whatever paperwork he signed. Maybe he could find an escape clause," Chase says.

Thayden has become the go-to lawyer for us after marrying Harper's friend Delilah. This makes him one degree from family. I honestly feel a little embarrassed how much business we're sending his way. I mean, not that we're all in legal trouble. But it seems like every other day, someone is like, "better call Thayden" or "Thayden will handle it."

I'm not sure if he's glad or sad he met us. His bank account is probably happy.

"Patrick," Collin says. "Could you really see this working?"

Ah, the million-dollar question.

I scoot back in my chair, gazing off at the velvety night sky as I picture the main drag of Sheet Cake. The quaint architecture and the empty—but charming—streets. The diner and Mari's best-ever migas. I can picture myself on one of the balconies, looking down to the end of the street toward the silos, where lights have been strung up outside. I hear the faint strains of live music playing.

I'm not alone. My arm is slung over a thin set of shoulders—too thin—but I'm working on that by feeding her good food and keeping her well slept. Her chestnut hair tickles my neck as the wind blows and the scent of strawberry lip gloss and mint is like a drug hitting my system.

Inside the loft apartment sleeps a little girl who may not be mine by blood, but whom I love just as deeply.

"Pat? Come on, man. What do you think?" Collin asks.

"Yeah," I say after a long pause, "I could see it."

And it's so close, so real, so powerful I can almost taste it.

CHAPTER EIGHT

Lindy

THE LIBRARY IS USUALLY one of my happy places. The building looks essentially like every historic library in a movie: high ceilings and tall shelves crammed with books, rich wood floors, and a curved staircase leading up to the second floor. For the Ladies Literary and Libation Society meetings, it's lit solely by candles—electric, because libraries and real candles don't mix.

Val has told me more than once she finds the library after-hours creepy, but I think it's amazing. Jo and I discussed moving in after she read *From the Mixed-Up Files of Mrs. Basil E. Frankweiler*. We won't. Probably.

But tonight, not even the library's ambiance can work a miracle on my mood. I feel like the heroine in an old cartoon, tied down to a set of tracks just waiting for the train to run me over.

"Are you okay, kiddo?" Val asks, giving my knee a squeeze.

My friends and I have our own corner, next to the glass case of historic photos, when our town was glorious and hopeful. It's like the little kids' table at a holiday meal. We don't mind, since we can make snarky, whispered comments and the other ladies, most of whom predate us by at least a decade, can pretend they don't hear.

"Fine," I say, giving her the best version of a smile I can manage.

Val isn't buying it but knows me well enough not to press me. Which is good. Because one good push is all it will take to have me spilling the news about Pat showing up today. And I am not ready to have this conversation, even if I promised Mari I'd tell my best friends.

I will. I *will*. But I can already guess how they'll react—Val feeling like it's fate, and Winnie wanting to know where Pat is now so she can give him several pieces of her mind. Before I can sort through their opinions, I need to know how *I* feel. And right now, that's just overwhelmed and confused.

From my other side, Winnie eyes me, like her keen gaze has the power to see my thoughts. We not-so-jokingly call her the scalpel, both because of her keen insight and her aversion to anything but honesty. With Val's soft questioning and Winnie's sharp eyes, it's hard to keep this secret. Especially when sandwiched between my two best friends.

I'm the perpetual middle of us, the medium setting in almost every way. My boring brown hair lands between Val's black and Winnie's golden; my olive skin is in the middle of Winnie's pale cream and the rich sepia Val shares with Mari. Val runs full-tilt in terms of her words and her emotions, while Winnie is like a tight fist of control, wrapped up in snark. I am—you guessed it!—right in the middle.

I also fit somewhere between the two of them style-wise with what I call Texas casual chic. My usual uniform is cowboy boots paired with simple dresses or jeans. The forest-green Dickey's coveralls Val has on tonight are one of her fashion staples, with multiple layers of paint across the knees and splatters on the chest. On most women, this utilitarian-artist look might not work, but not even coveralls can hide Val's curves.

Meanwhile, Winnie dresses like she climbed right out of a 1950s pin-up calendar. The more covered-up variety of pin-up, to be clear. She is the epitome of sexy without showing a lot of skin. Tonight, she has on cropped, black pants and a soft cream button-down shirt, tied at the waist. She has the sleeves rolled up to her elbows, showing just a hint of her tattoos, which are real works of art covering her upper arms and shoulders. Val designed most of them. The high ponytail with a silky pink ribbon and her black-framed glasses complete Winnie's look, which she's been consistently rocking since eighth grade.

At a glance, we might look like the unlikeliest of friends, but we've been inseparable since we were in middle school, barring the college years where we went our separate ways. Our friendship survived somehow via text and three-way video calls. None of us planned to end up back in Sheet Cake being with Val and Winnie makes being home bearable.

Except when I'm keeping a monumental bit of information from them.

Ashlee arrives just moments before the meeting starts, rushing inside with a wooden tray and tea set. I wonder if she spikes her tea with whiskey too. My lawyer has traded her conservative navy suit for cutoffs and a silky white T-shirt. If every eye in the library isn't watching her long legs as she strides across the room, I'll donate one of my kidneys to a stranger tomorrow.

She gives me a small smile as she settles in next to Kitty Bishop, whose daughter Deedee is babysitting Jo tonight. Kitty has three teenage girls, so it's hard to remember that she and Ashlee are around the same age, mid-thirties. They're like a tale of two cities, small-town style—one of them stayed and started having babies immediately while the other got the heck out to start a career.

"I wanna be Ashlee when I grow up," Val whispers.

"We should be so lucky," I respond.

"She's gonna mop up the floor with Rachel," Winnie says, and I know she means it to be reassuring. But I'd rather not think about the hearing. And as complicated as my feelings toward Rachel are, I don't like thinking about this as a competition. That comes too dangerously close to thinking Jo as the prize, not a person—and that's exactly the way Rachel operates.

I am saved from having to respond when Lynn Louise bangs her gavel. The town librarian perches on the circulation desk like a queen, despite her bare feet, the worn sundress she wears like a uniform, and the white pouf of hair atop her head. She frequently pulls pens from her coif, and I swear, once I saw her retrieve a key from its depths. It's the hairdo equivalent of Mary Poppins' bag.

"Let us call to order this meeting of the Ladies Literary and Libations Society," Lynn Louise calls, with another bang of the gavel for effect.

"Order is served," we echo back before lifting our various libations in the air.

Everything from moonshine to herbal tea is represented in our group. Val and Winnie clink shot glasses and toss back what smells like tequila.

Big Mo, the only man allowed into the Ladies Literary and Libations Society, sips a root beer. Judge Judie—yep, like the famous one except with an -ie—pulls a silver flask from her overalls, probably filled with her family's famous moonshine. Ashlee sips herbal tea from a china cup, Kitty drinks wine from a mason jar, and the half-dozen or so other members all have their own unique drinks of choice.

Here at the LLLS, we are serious about our libations, less so about our literary, and just plain willy-nilly with punctuation. I've been arguing in every meeting for the two years I've been a member that either *Ladies* needs an apostrophe, or we need commas after both *Ladies* and *Literary*. No one seems to care about this punctuation issue.

But they *do* care about this dying town, which is why we meet in the closed library once a month for what falls somewhere between a town hall meeting and a formal gossip session with about twenty of the town's key women, plus Big Mo. The LLLS may not have the public sway of city council, but this room full of powerful women holds this town together.

And we do it all without the presence of a single Waters. The women in that family are as awful as the men—snobby, entitled, and, I suspect, soulless. Billy's cousin, Spring, was in my grade and made it her personal mission to shun me, Val, and Winnie. I can almost forgive her, considering her parents named her *Spring Waters*, but a ridiculous name is no excuse for bad behavior.

I sip my Americano, a rare indulgence I allowed myself on the way here. I need the caffeine because I've got work to do when I get home. Insightful online journalism waits for no man, and my article on books with the best kissing scenes needs to be done by morning. To be completely honest, I may have over-researched.

But right now, the idea of kissing takes my mind straight to the man who showed up unannounced and rocked my little world today. The last thing my world needs is to be rocked any more than it already is. Right now, my only focus needs to be Jo.

Lynn Louise bangs the gavel again. It was a recent gift from Judge Judie, and the pounding in my head would prefer for Lynn Louise to be less enthusiastic about it.

"Let us take another sip—"

"Or swig!" someone calls. A few people laugh.

"Or swig," Lynn Louise says with a smile, "then get to serious business."

Val and Winnie switch to water. None of us are big drinkers. Me, because of Rachel. Winnie, because she's a lightweight. And Val because she says it's no fun drinking alone. We start with talk of the Sheet Cake Festival. This year, Maddie Nguyen, the town veterinarian, is the mistress of ceremonies, which basically means she'll be working a second job without getting paid for the coming months. She only moved here a year ago just after old doc Butts (yep, his real name) passed away. I'm not sure Maddie realized what she was getting into, but the overwhelm on her face tells me it's starting to sink in.

"Let's move on with the business of the feral hogs," Lynn Louise says, reading from a yellow legal pad.

I stifle a yawn. Destructive and potentially dangerous as the hogs might be, I don't have enough brain function to devote to porcine problems at the moment. I've got a very large human problem occupying my thoughts. Plus, just the presence of Amber and Beast keeps the hogs from tearing up my fields.

"Kitty, can you and Clark do some hog hunting this week?" Lynn Louise asks.

"Yes ma'am."

Anyone looking into this room might expect Big Mo to be the one you'd ask about hog hunting, not the mom who has three of the most well-mannered girls in the county. But Kitty and her husband, Tim, both hunt, and the girls all had rifles before they had driving permits. Big Mo is the one asked to do things like take in stray kittens who need to be bottle-fed. Which has happened a surprising number of times. The feral cats are almost as big a problem as the feral hogs.

"Next order of business." Lynn raises her eyebrows then holds the legal pad a little closer to her face. "Some non-Sheeters were spotted in town today."

Mari catches my eye and purses her lips. And THIS is why I should have talked to Winnie and Val *before* the meeting.

Lynn Louise trades out her legal pad for her phone, squinting at the screen. "According to this post on Neighborly, they wandered around town square and ate at Mari's."

Stupid Neighborly! When it comes to keeping secrets, the app is worse than a California grapevine during harvest season.

Val nudges me, ducking her head to whisper. "Weren't you at Mari's earlier to pick up Jo?"

I silently bargain with my face. *If you don't blush*, I promise, *I'll start actually moisturizing and, okay, fine, washing you on the daily.*

I'm not sure if it fully works, but Val doesn't say anything about me blushing. I make a mental note to stop on the way home tonight to grab some face wash and moisturizer to thank my skin for complying. Make that tomorrow, as nothing will still be open in Sheet Cake when we're done besides Backwoods Bar. Wolf sells about anything there, but I'm pretty sure he draws the line at beauty products.

"Yep."

"Did you see these guys?" Val presses.

Not a thing. Just a ghost of the future I once dreamed of. A man so handsome, so winsome, and so troublesome that I've struggled to catch my breath and slow my heart rate the rest of the day.

"They are apparently *investors*," Judge Judie says with a sniff. Despite the fact that our town could use some investors, the LLLS—and most of the population of Old Sheet Cake—are firmly against non-Sheeters meddling in our affairs.

Wait—*investors?*

My heart tears off like a dog at a hunt as Pat's appearance in Sheet Cake suddenly clicks into place. Hopefully, Pat and Tank realized with a brief look down Main Street how useless it is. It would probably be easier to sell tickets to the town proper as a ghost town than revive the crumbling buildings. Mari's is the only thing open down here that's not publicly funded.

"We've scared off investors before," Eula Martin says. She's scary enough to do the job on her own. With her tight white bun, intense makeup, and pointy red nails, she channels a storybook witch to a T. Her Victorian-style cottage near town, with its scrollwork and detailed trim, even looks like a gingerbread house. To complete the terrifying persona, she has a whole room full of realistic dolls with unblinking eyes. According to gossip, they have real human hair.

As kids, we used to hold our breath when we rode our bikes past her house.

"I'm sure it won't be a problem," Lynn Louise says. "We'll keep an eye out. If anyone hears anything, let us know."

Big Mo won't look my way, but Mari sure is. Now I'm not just bargaining with my cheeks not to blush but my armpits not to sweat. I silently wish for some topic—any topic—to get us off the subject of the mysterious non-Sheeters.

More wild boars, please! Or a traffic cycle that's too short—that one caused a thirty-minute debate at our last meeting. I'm even happy to talk about whether or not the Daylight Donuts Shop is slowly poisoning the town. Eula Martin swears up and down they've been using cleaning spray on the inside of the glass case while the donuts are still inside.

But no, apparently the one topic I want to avoid is not so easy to escape.

Lynn Louise squints down at her phone again. "Oh! Looks like there's a new post on Neighborly, identifying them."

I consider bolting for the door but decide to sit here and accept my fate. Which is going to be the ire and wrath of my two best friends.

"The older one is Theodore Graham, better known as Think Tank. He's retired, but he was a household name back in the day. His son, Patrick, played for Pittsburgh. They're from Austin, apparently." Lynn Louise sniffs. The only thing worse than being from Austin is being from new Sheet Cake.

Val's elbow finds my ribs, and Winnie tugs at my sleeve. I feel their stares lasering into me and pretend I am impervious. Meanwhile, I study my coffee mug, where the remnants of a clearance price tag cling to the side. I pick at the sticky rectangle, hating how it just won't go away. If I weren't feeling so stressed out and panicked, I'm sure I'd see a metaphor there.

"Isn't that the feller you used to date, Lindy?" Eula Martin says, and all eyes in the room swivel to me.

Before I can formulate an answer, Winnie jumps in to save me. "I think Mayor Whitehead left town!"

Thank you, Winnie.

"When's the last time you saw him?" Lynn Louise asks.

"Four days ago." Winnie is the mayor's secretary.

You couldn't pay me enough to work for the man, who is about as smarmy as the Waters family. But jobs here in Sheet Cake are scarce, and Winnie has a mountain of student loans. And until her accountant boyfriend, Dale, proposes or she sells her app, she's pretty much stuck working for the mayor.

"He was behaving strangely. More so than usual," Winnie adds.

"Strangely how?" Judge Judie asks.

Winnie rolls her empty shot glass between her fingers and grimaces. "He gave me a tip. The money kind, not the advice kind. Not that I wanted either one," she adds in a low mutter that makes me and Val snort.

I'm not going to ask Winnie *where* the mayor left her the tip. If I had to guess, the lecherous old jerk tried to put it down her shirt. Though if he had, I think Winnie would have slugged him. Despite her petite size, she can pack a punch. During college, she played roller derby, if that says anything about the amount of fight in her.

That's what happens when your dad names you Winchester after his favorite rifle. Her older brother goes by Chevy, short for Chevrolet, their dad's favorite car. In a twist of irony, Chevy drives a Ford. Their mom used to joke if she had one more kid, he or she would have been named ESPN.

Judge Judie's lip curls, clearly disgusted with the mayor, not Winnie. "You're his secretary, not a waitress."

"There's a number written on the bill," Winnie says. "I think it's a phone number."

Winnie pulls a twenty out of her wallet. Hopping up, she passes it to Judge Judie, who passes it to Lynn Louise and then gives it to Ashlee.

"Did you try calling this number?" Lynn Louise asks.

Winnie snorts. "Not a chance."

"Smart girl," Judge Judie says.

Ashlee pulls out her phone. "I'll call with it on speaker. Winnie, would you mind being the one to talk to him?"

"If I *have* to," Winnie says, getting to her feet again.

I give her an encouraging pat on the back as she gets up. Val smacks one side of her butt like a teammate wishing her a good game. Winnie barely even notices, cracking her neck like she's preparing for battle.

The phone rings twice, and then the mayor's obnoxious voice booms through the speaker. "Doll face! Is that you?"

Winnie bares her teeth. The only reason Mayor Whitehead keeps getting elected is that no one cares enough to run against him. That, and the Waters family backs his campaigns. The Waters aren't just loaded; they're oil-money loaded and as slick as oil too.

"My name is Winnie, *sir*."

"Sure, sure. Are you finally ready to join me in my tropical paradise?"

The silence in the room intensifies, and confused glances abound. *Tropical paradise?*

"You still there, doll face?"

Winnie shifts on her feet. "Again, it's Winnie. And I'm here."

Mayor Whitehead laughs. "I'd rather you be *here*, sweetcakes. I've saved a place for you. Right in my lap."

Ew! The faces in the room mirror my disgust, and Big Mo looks like he'd happily be set loose on the man. Winnie's expression turns hard, and Ashlee touches her arm, shaking her head as though to calm her. Winnie takes a few deep breaths before speaking again.

"Where are you?" Winnie's voice is strained with the

effort of being cordial. "What tropical paradise would that be?"

"My new place," the mayor says. "Nothing but sun and sand and surf. I can't share the details, but I'll happily send you a plane ticket. Then, I guess, the secret will be out."

Winnie's cheeks have flushed from pink to red and her hands are in tight fists in front of her. "When will you be back?"

"Oh, I'm not coming back to that miserable little town."

I may not have ever planned to end up living in Sheet Cake again, but even I take offense to his words. And what about his wife? Winnie seems to be on that same track.

"What about Mrs. Whitehead? Your wife?"

Another chuckle. "She's off at some knitting convention. It'll be quite the surprise when she gets back home and finds out I'm gone and have left divorce papers ready to be served as well. I sold the town for a little nest egg."

At this, several people at once seem to forget we're trying to be silent, because there are multiple people yelling at once.

"You sold the town?"

"He *owned* the town?"

"You can't sell a TOWN!"

Lynn Louise starts banging her gavel, and the room goes silent in a hurry. Not quickly enough. Ashlee shakes her head. "He hung up."

Winnie returns to us. "I feel like I need to bleach my brain and my ears."

Val practically throws herself over my body to give Winnie a hug. "You did good, Winnie. That guy is such slime."

"Total slime," I agree.

"The slime slugs leave behind," Winnie says with a shudder.

"But it sounds like he's gone now," I say.

Val returns to her normal spot. "Good riddance."

"Except for the whole part where he's my boss. Do I even have a job if the mayor is gone?" Winnie asks.

It's a solid question. One of many being voiced all around us.

"Can he do that? Can he sell the town?" Lynn Louise asks no one in particular. Judge Judie shrugs, and we all turn to Ashlee.

Her face is grim. "I can do some digging. It shouldn't be hard to find a paper trail of this size. I didn't even know the mayor—*former* mayor?—owned it. Or that any one citizen did. I'm guessing the fact that he's saying he's somewhere tropical means there was a sale, and he got paid. Whether he committed some kind of fraud—that I'm not sure of. I just know I didn't broker any deal."

"You think the Waters Firm would help with this?" Judge Judie asks, looking skeptical.

It doesn't really make sense for them to sabotage the town. They'd more likely buy it themselves. The Waters are Sheeters through and through. Billy Senior's great granny had the prize-winning sheet cake recipe at the festival for years. I don't think this was quite what they had in mind when they supported the mayor's campaign.

"Not really," Ashlee says. "Though they have the money to do it. I don't know what the going rate for a town is, but I'm guessing six to maybe seven figures."

It's hard to imagine our falling-apart and mostly empty town proper going for that much.

"Who would want to buy Sheet Cake, much less have the money to—" Lynn Louise starts to ask, then stops, as the whole room seems to come to an understanding at once about who might have the money to buy our town.

Pro athletes would. Like the two pro athlete *investors* who were in town today.

All deals and bets with my cheeks about blushing are off. My face, my neck, and even my ears are burning. If my educated guess is correct, then Pat and his dad aren't just interested investors.

They're the new town owners.

CHAPTER NINE

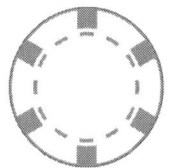

Pat

I CAN'T STOP THINKING about three things. Well, one person, one place, and one idea. So, basically, nouns. I can't stop thinking about NOUNS.

The *person* I'm thinking about is Lindy. Thinking is a vast understatement for what I'm doing. Obsessing. Dreaming. Mentally and emotionally imploding. Planning. Hoping.

The *place* on my mind is about as obvious: a dying little town named after a cake. I've almost driven back there four times in the last few days. Now that I know where Lindy is, I just want to be there.

The *idea* is how I can possibly win her back. So far, I'm coming up empty on this front, which is why I haven't returned to Sheet Cake. Yet. I can't go in guns blazing. Now that I know more about what the past five years have been like for Lindy, I know she's going to need a gentle hand. I have a lot of mistakes and time to make up for.

What I need is a good, solid action verb to get me started. To untie the veritable tangle of complicated knots in my head and heart. I was never a Boy Scout or a sailor, so I'm not good at knots. I'm just fumbling around, getting more and more frustrated with every passing second. Add in the fact that our family is still mostly at odds over Tank's decision to buy Sheet Cake, and I'm all tied up.

To ease some of my frustration and face the conflict head-on, I've joined James in his garage gym, which is also his workshop. In addition to crafting beer, James is a carpenter. He makes tables, benches, and other artistic wood pieces. I'm not sure if he was just extra blessed with the gene pool or if he simply channeled his rage into skills. Either way, the man is blessed. And full of rage.

Based on the way he seems to be punishing me with this workout, much of that rage is directed my way. He's hardly done more than grunt at me this whole time. I guess he's still angry about Dad's purchase and my collusion.

"Why are you humming John Mayer?" James asks, his nostrils flaring.

I didn't realize I was. I'm not sure whether he looks furious because he's lifting a stupid amount of weight or because of my musical taste, but I'm betting it's the latter. My oldest and surliest brother has hardly broken a sweat even though he's got just about every plate on this bar for his deadlifts.

Show-off.

"Don't be a Mayer-hater. The man's got mad skills."

"Mad skills? The early 2000s called. They want their lingo back."

"Har, har." While I do believe in John Mayer's musical

and lyrical ability (despite his personal unlikability), the reason I'm humming "Daughters" is because of Jo. Meeting her stirred up all kinds of extra feelings, protective feelings. Without a better term for it, *fatherly* feelings.

And yes, I'm aware this is putting like fifty carts ahead of one horse. Story of my life.

I've already framed the *Jaws* picture, which is riding shotgun in my truck, waiting for its forever home. I don't want to hang it in my apartment, which has seemed more hauntingly empty than normal this week. Seeing the picture makes me think of Jo, which makes me think of Lindy, which makes me all the more eager to get out of here. Tank and I at least are on the same page and decided to start renovating two loft spaces downtown above what we hope will be businesses. I threw a little extra cash to the contractors to finish mine first, and fast. They started demo already, and I'm itching to see.

Collin is asking actual questions now, not just launching attacks. Harper and Chase are neutral positive. Now, we just need to get my grumpiest, most stubborn brother on board.

Speaking of the grump, James drops the bar on the padded floor by the weight bench and wipes the sweat off his brow. "Need me to take off some of that weight for you, Patty?"

He's challenging me. But I *love* challenges.

"Nope. I'm fine. Deadlifts, no problem." But when I lean over and try to pull the bar up, I can't get it more than six inches off the ground. "Okay, maybe a little weight adjustment."

With a satisfied grin, James quickly slides off everything but the smallest plate. "That should be better for you, *little* brother."

If making fun of me smooths out his surliness, fine. It's

still a challenge to get through a set. Not that I'm going to admit it and feed James's ridiculous ego.

As my muscles protest, I remind myself of the end goal of this workout. It's twofold. I'd like to soften James up on the idea of Sheet Cake. That's the big one.

The other one is a little more superficial. Though Lindy isn't just into my looks, no woman turns down a good set of abs. This is about as far as I've gotten in terms of plans to win Lindy back.

Step one: Get my hot bod back.

Step two: Show off aforementioned hot bod by strategic losing of shirt. Repeat as necessary.

Step three: Show her I've changed.

Step four: Do whatever it takes to restore the sparkle in her eyes.

The first two steps are the easiest and probably the least instrumental in actually making a difference. I've hurt Lindy deeply, and with everything else she's been through, I can understand her resistance to me, even after my apology.

Even in our gut-wrenching conversation, I swear I could feel the same tension, the same tug, the same pull between us there always was. And I'm clinging to that with all the strength I can muster.

"Any word from Thayden?" James asks.

I try not to look shocked he's bringing up anything related to Dad buying Sheet Cake. "Yes. Despite being up to his eyeballs in paperwork, Thayden says the contract is solid. No take-backsies."

When I video chatted with Thayden to explain what paperwork I was sending him and why, his face was priceless. His laughter probably could have been heard all the way in Sheet Cake. "I'm so glad I met your family," he said, and I wasn't sure whether to be more honored or insulted.

"I guess you're done ignoring the fact Tank bought a town for your brewery?"

James practically growls as he shoves the plates back onto the bar and starts another aggressive set of deadlifts. "It's kind of hard to ignore."

"Don't throw your back out, brother."

"I'm fine," he grunts.

"You seem fine."

He drops the bar and puts his hands on his hips. His eyes narrow into judgy slits as he studies my face. I mirror his position, and we stare at each other like this for a few long minutes. It reminds me of the blink-off Tank and I had the day he told me about Sheet Cake. James has no clue exactly how much he's like a grumpier version of our dad. And I'm not about to tell James this.

Not today, anyway. I'll save it for a time when I really need to get under his skin.

"What was he thinking?" James asks, finally breaking the tension. He shakes his head. "I'm still trying to wrap my head around such a *smart* man making such a *stupid* decision."

I can't help but bristle, though I take a slow breath to keep my emotions in check.

Look at me! The picture of cool, calm, and restrained. Call me Ice. Not to be confused with any of the rappers—Ice Cube, Ice-T, or Vanilla Ice. Just Ice.

My voice is calm when I speak. "Dad was thinking about *us*, James. About family. He was thinking about creating a legacy and a future. I could see this as a valid option for Dark Horse."

"Yeah? You think so?" James crosses his arms and lifts one eyebrow almost lazily. But there's nothing lazy or low-key about the move. It's intense and intentionally slow.

Predatory. It makes my stomach twist, because I know this look, and it's never the start of anything good.

Oh, boy. I stepped in it now.

James's eyebrow goes up a minuscule amount. "Or is there perhaps some *other* reason you're into this ridiculous plan?"

He can't know about Lindy. He can't. Dad wouldn't have told him. Not after I begged him not to on the ride home. James doesn't know.

And yet ... James *looks* like he knows. His expression is a dead ringer for Dad's look the time he found out I was the one who put itching powder in Collin's underwear drawer and was trying to get me to confess.

But ... it's a bluff, right? Because James cannot possibly know.

He knows.

He can't know!

He looks like he knows!

I ignore the way I'm starting to sweat in places that weren't sweating even when I was lifting the bar. I won't cave. I'm not going to break. James doesn't know about Lindy. No one does. Only Tank, and I swore him to secrecy, at least for now.

A bead of sweat drips down the side of my nose, and I want nothing more than to brush it away. But if I move, I'm going to totally lose it. I'll start giggling, and then James will know for sure I'm hiding something.

I've almost made it out of the danger zone when James says, "It's sad to see you letting a woman cloud your judgment again."

"Tank promised he wouldn't say anything!"

My mouth clamps shut as I take in the smug look on James's irritating face. He *didn't* know. But he does now.

I stepped right into one of my brother's traps. Now I'm dangling by my legs, suspended upside down from a tree, while he circles me, smirking.

Okay, maybe I'm still standing in the garage, but there was definitely a trap, and he's absolutely smirking.

"Are you serious? That worked? I can't believe that worked. I'm an idiot!" I shout.

James smiles. "I won't argue the point. Who is she?"

I turn away, kicking my water bottle, which doesn't make me feel the slightest bit better. It skitters out the open garage door and halfway down the driveway where Chase picks it up.

Because this night wouldn't be complete without Chase and Collin showing up unannounced right at this opportune moment. Fabulous. Now I'm going to have to tell those two about Lindy as well.

"Not Padma again?"

I make a disgusted face. "No."

Padma might be an underwear model, but she was boring as heck and far more interested in selfies and social media than she ever was interested in me. Oh, and she married me to try and get a green card. That also happened.

"What are we talking about?" Collin asks as he and Chase step into the garage. "And why are y'all working out here when I *own a gym*. An actual gym. Pat—did you go and get a girlfriend?"

"No." *I only wish.*

"A woman is the reason he's so on board with Tank's plan," James says. "I'm trying to get details."

"A woman?" Chase says, grinning.

"Not just any woman," I say.

And now I've gone and done it. With hardly any pressure applied, I went and confessed it all. I would be the worst spy ever. They would come near me with a set of pliers or a sharp blade and I'd be singing like a whole cage full of canaries.

"THE woman?" James and Collin say in unison. It would be comical if they didn't look so irritated.

There aren't any more water bottles to kick but I sure want to kick something right now. This is not how I wanted the information getting out.

"Uh, guys?" Chase rubs his neck, looking between us. "What woman?"

"THE WOMAN," James and Collin answer.

"The Woman is the one who messed our little brother up nice and good," Collin says, trying to ruffle my hair with his fingers. I slap him away. "She's his Irene Adler."

"She most certainly is not," I say. "Not even the Irene Adler from the movies, who was arguably better than the BBC version."

"Both versions broke Sherlock's heart," James adds. "As women always do. As this woman did to you."

I roll my eyes. "That's not what happened. It was my fault. I totally messed things up between us. Me. Not her."

"She broke your heart," James says. "You played like crap, partied too much, and ended your football career prematurely."

"I got injured! Like, two years after we broke up!"

"Because your head wasn't in the game!" James yells, and I don't know how we went from him being mad about the town to him being mad about Lindy. If I wanted to make forward progress, I've instead taken a few giant leaps backward.

"You had your shot in the pros and you blew it," James continues. "All for some woman. And now you're blowing it again."

I get some of his anger, though it's directed in the wrong

place. James never got to play pro, which is highly unfair because he had the most potential of any of us. His career-ending injury came in the form of a blown-out knee playing college ball. Some knee injuries you can come back from. His was not one of those.

I glare at them both with all the fire I can muster. "Her name is Lindy," I say. "And my injury wasn't because of her. Our breakup was more complicated. I just never explained it all to you idiots. Because this is how you act."

Chase raises a hand. "I'm not acting like an idiot."

"Shut up!" James, Collin, and I say, and then a giggle escapes me.

James groans, threading his hands through his hair and staring up at the ceiling. "Not the giggles again."

Yep. The giggles. What can I say? For better or worse—oh, most definitely *worse*—they're a Pat trademark.

"Why don't you try to explain?" Collin asks with forced patience.

"Fine. We met my last semester of college. She planned to be a travel writer. I had the draft coming up. We said we'd keep it casual."

"Clearly, that worked well," James mutters, and Collin shoves him.

"We knew things would end, but it was a mistake. I should have taken her with me or asked her to come or—I don't know, *something*. Instead, I left town early and never told her goodbye. I've regretted that moment ever since. Yes, she lives in Sheet Cake. And yes, part of the reason I'm into this idea is because of her. But that's not the only reason."

"So, she didn't cheat or do something horrible to you?" James asks.

"Nope." Other than the lie about being in Europe. But

honestly, in the context of it all, I get why Lindy didn't tell me the truth.

"*You* were the idiot in the relationship," Collin says. "That makes way more sense."

I start to giggle again. I can't stop, not even when I bend over, my hands on my knees. The giggles become belly laughs until Collin and Chase join in.

James, of course, is immune to laughter. It's like he's become a grumpy old man a few decades too early. The thought of him with white hair, a cane, and that same irascible look on his face only makes me laugh harder.

"What are we laughing about?" Chase asks.

"All of this," I say through gasping breaths. "We're fighting over nothing, and Tank bought a town that could be the set of a horror movie."

"Wait," Collin says, his laughter coming to an abrupt halt. "What's this about a horror movie?"

"You said you saw potential," James says.

And just like that, my giggles are gone. "I do." I clear my throat. "It's just, well, there's a lot of work needed on the town itself. But I think Tank may be onto something."

Collin hops up on James's work bench a little too close to the table saw for my liking, but it's his butt, not mine. "Give me three reasons that don't involve The Woman," he says.

The garage goes quiet and I close my eyes for a moment, linking my fingers behind my sweaty neck. "I don't think I can explain. You'd have to go see it to know."

I think we're all shocked when Chase, whom we sometimes refer to as Boy Wonder because he's just too dang good, starts spinning his keys around his finger, a mischievous look on his face.

"Anyone up for a road trip?"

CHAPTER TEN

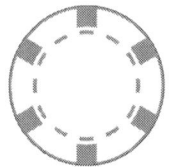

Pat

THERE'S VERY little chance I'll run into Lindy considering it's nearing ten p.m. when James pulls up to the center of Sheet Cake. Then again, I never thought I'd see her in the first place. I definitely don't know what she does with her nights. The idea of her being out now, maybe out with a guy or at a bar, makes my stomach dip. She did say she was single. I'll hold onto that.

I like thinking of her home with Jo. Only, I want to insert myself into the equation too.

I halfway considered having James drive by her house, but I'm not going to pull a Romeo at the balcony thing. Or even a John Cusack with a boom box. It's going to take something bigger. Lindy needs to see me as steady and serious—two things I'm not particularly known for. Which means I need to be a man who can stick around for the long haul. Not my strongest suit, but maybe I've just never had the right motivation.

Collin taps his window as we cross over the train tracks and into the town proper. "You were right, Patty."

"Thank you," I reply. Too quickly, as it turns out.

"This isn't a town; it's the start of a horror movie," he finishes.

"I can see the, uh, charm. It's got good bones," Chase says, trying and failing to sound like he believes this.

"Bones like a skeleton," Collin mutters. "As in, dead. Very, very dead."

James says nothing, but his jaw is clenched tighter than a fist. I'm hunched over here in the back seat, wondering what I was thinking. What was Tank thinking? My doubts about this idea are multiplying faster than a flu virus.

James stops in the middle of the main intersection and throws the truck in park. Turning to face me with an aggressive amount of force, he says, "This? This is where you think we should move a brewery that's in its infancy, just starting out?"

I can see his point.

But I can also see Tank's vision. Sure, my thoughts are a little clouded by Lindy haze, but I don't think that's all this is. I glance up and down the empty streets again, considering, remembering what it looked like during the day.

"You won an award," I say. "You're not exactly in your infancy."

James says nothing, still giving me that dark look.

Sighing, I point toward the hulking metal buildings at the end of the main drag. "Pull up there."

His eyes flash, but James does as I ask. A minute later he's parked at the curb, and we're all climbing out of the truck and I'm leading them through the unlocked chain link fence. I turn, walking backwards like a tour guide as I lead them through the cement courtyard strewn with litter and knee-high weeds.

"Picture this." I spread my arms wide. "Picnic tables. Lights strung overhead. A stage over there with live music."

They're tracking with me and not arguing, but only Chase is nodding along. Sometimes Boy Wonder comes in handy.

I tap one of the metal walls of the smaller warehouse structure. "There'd be a cutout here. A wooden counter for the bar. Dark Horse's latest selections on tap. Food trucks over there."

There's a gravel parking lot on the backside and a space between it and this courtyard with enough room for a few food trucks.

I walk them toward the biggest building with attached grain elevators rising above it. "Production for the brewery will be housed here. Plenty of space to start small and grow. Best of all—zero rent, because this property is part of the town proper, currently owned by our Dad."

Collin has his hands on his hips. "You think people will drive all the way out here from Austin for this? There are literally dozens of places in town they could go instead."

"Maybe if there were some other draw," Chase says hesitantly. "If there were something else here in town. Anything at all."

We all stare off past James's truck to the still deserted downtown. A stray cat slinking across the street is the only movement. Make that half a dozen stray cats. A few more, and I'll have to wonder if they're planning a coup.

I snap my fingers, because that's what you do when you have a sudden bolt of genius. "The Sheet Cake Festival!" I don't know why I didn't think of this before. "It's a huge event. Even the foodie magazines and blogs cover it. We have until then to get this place—this town—in a position to be a destination town."

"You really think *this* could be that?"

It's the first time James has spoken in minutes. His voice isn't what I'd call warm by any stretch. But there's no hostility. A small win. Hope rises like an air bubble in my chest, pressing against my sternum.

"The Sheet Cake Festival is massive. Thousands of people descend on this place. They'll come for the festival and see what the town has changed into. Shops, restaurants, Dark Horse Brewery. They stay for the town, or they make plans to come back. Above the stores downtown we'll build lofts. See the balconies? Historic, but with a modern aesthetic inside. Walking distance to the brewery."

"You're thinking we'd all move here to run things?" James asks. "We'd all leave Austin?"

"It's just a hop and a skip up the road," I say.

"I'm out," Collin says. "I've got the gym to run, and I need to be there. But you know I'll support Dark Horse, even if that's only financially. Here, there, wherever you think is best."

Chase doesn't say anything. He and Harper haven't even been married a year and just finished the renovation on their house. I don't see them moving anytime soon.

"And you're really all-in on this?" James asks, a tone of challenge in his voice.

I slide my hands into my pockets, rocking back on my heels. "Tank and I started demo on two lofts already."

This statement is followed by a stark silence. I don't mention I'm also paying the crew to expedite.

James gapes. "Even without all of us on board, you're moving forward with this? Like it's a done deal?"

"Tank already bought the town, remember? Dark Horse

would be an anchor, but we can't make that choice for you," I say. "Might as well start work on what we have. I'm giving it a chance."

"What happens when you change your mind about this, like you do everything else?" James demands.

Before, this might have hurt. But now, I just add this as fuel for my determination. Everyone loves a good underdog story, right? This will be the one about the guy who jumps from thing to thing finally settling down and committing to something—to someone—in his life.

"I won't. Not this time."

"I've heard that before," James says.

"There's a first time for everything," Chase says lightly.

"I think you're being a little harsh," Collin says, giving James a look. "It took us both some time to figure out what we wanted to do with our lives."

"I know what I want," I insist, meeting and holding James's gaze. "This is it. *She* is it."

Making a sound of disgust, James walks away, a shadowy figure in the dim light from the moon. I tell myself he can still change his mind. Tank and I could work on revitalizing the town with or without Dark Horse. But being here with Collin and James makes me long for *all* of it—the whole big plan. I want Tank's vision and also the woman and the happily ever after.

"When's the big festival?" Collin asks. "How long would we have to pull this off? Assuming we get Mr. Broody on board."

The *we* in his question has me internally cheering. "It's in January."

"Okay." He nods, then follows behind James, heading back to the truck without saying anything more. My stomach drops, and the cheering turns to booing.

Chase claps a hand over my shoulder. "Hey, man. I can see it. I really can. But the timeline is really tight. Even the renovations might take longer than that. And you'd need a bunch of businesses willing to start here. To take the risk to move all the way out here on what's essentially a hope and a prayer."

Chase was supposed to be my easy sell. And if he's not on board ...

I hear the truck door slam, and the engine rumbles to life. Without speaking, Chase and I head over. The air inside the cab is tense, and no one speaks as James starts back toward town.

As we're about to turn, three muddy pickups tear through the center of town almost t-boning us. James slams on the brakes and curses under his breath. My heart is thudding out an unsteady rhythm as I grip Collin's seat in front of me.

A few shouts ring out and the last truck honks its horn. Someone tosses a beer can out the window.

"Good reflexes, man," Chase says, and his voice is strained.

James shakes his head, and I don't like the glint in his eyes when they meet mine in the rearview mirror.

"I think it's time we go see what the residents of Sheet Cake do for fun."

CHAPTER ELEVEN

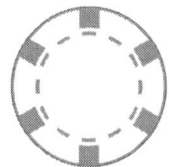

Pat

I'M NOT sure what everyone else was expecting, but I for one was not thinking those pickups would lead us to what amounts to a rundown, corrugated metal shed at the edge of the woods with rows of cars and trucks parked in a field next to it.

James followed the other trucks at a distance, and he has his lights off now as we watch a group of guys exit the three vehicles and head toward the open sliding doors. As James rolls down the window, we can hear country music blaring from speakers somewhere.

"This doesn't seem like the best idea, brother," Collin says.

But James guns it, pulling up next to one of the parked trucks that almost ran us down. "Might as well meet the locals," he says with a grin I do not like one bit. "Right,

Patty? I mean, if we're going to live here and set up shop. I'm sure they'll be happy to meet their new landlords."

Sometimes, I think my oldest brother has a death wish. James throws open his door and steps out while Chase, Collin, and I exchange uneasy glances from inside the cab of the truck.

"This does not bode well," Chase says as James takes long strides toward the building, not looking back.

"We probably shouldn't let him go in there alone." I unbuckle my seatbelt.

"If this goes south, I'm blaming you," Collin says.

I roll my eyes. "Clearly, I'm the family scapegoat."

By the time the three of us reach the shed, James has a can of beer he lifts in salute. He's standing at the bar, which is essentially a long board propped up by a few large metal barrels. A few white coolers are against the back wall, manned by a guy with a beard that's more Duck Dynasty than hipster.

"Beer?" James asks us, tipping his can at us. "I'm buying."

Chase shakes his head no, which isn't surprising, but Collin and I nod. James hands the guy behind the bar a twenty, and the man pulls two more dripping cans from the cooler, setting them on the makeshift counter. "Next time, you should try the moonshine. I'm Wolf."

"Of course you are," James mutters as he walks away.

"Thanks, Wolf." I tip my can his way, and he grins.

"Be careful out there, fellas," Wolf says, and I'm not sure if he's joking.

The room isn't as full as I expected based on the number of vehicles outside, but I can hear music and muffled conversation through another set of open doors. A couple of white-haired men in overalls pause their darts game to watch us.

I take a sip of the beer, which tastes more like sour water. The issue with having a brother who crafts microbrews is losing the ability to enjoy the cheap stuff.

"We came, we saw, and maybe it's time to head home?" I suggest.

"Don't give up yet," James says with a smile that looks more like a threat. "The night is young."

He heads out back and I follow on his heels, Chase and Collin close behind me. There is trouble in James's swagger and the set of his jaw. The sooner we can get him out of here, the better. But when he's like this, you can't force him to do anything.

This is where the party is. Though I don't get the impression it's a one-time party. Everything about this place screams homegrown bootleg bar. Not even close to legal but overlooked because all the locals know about it and don't care.

A few floodlights light the dirt clearing that leads to the edge of the woods. Small groups sit on hay bales and others in camping chairs or some wooden Adirondacks. Unlike Austin bars, which tend to cater to specific age groups, there's quite a cross section here. Old country music plays over a speaker duct-taped to the back wall, and several couples sway in a dirt area in the center. A fire truck is parked to one side of the clearing, though I see no men in uniform.

I scan the crowd for Lindy, just in case. I'm relieved and disappointed not to see her.

Just like in a movie, conversation halts as we step outside. Heads and bodies turn as the country singer wails about his lost love and spilled whiskey. The songwriter must not have loved his woman *that* much, because he seems more upset about the whiskey.

"Tough crowd," I mutter, taking another sip of my beer.

"Maybe we should go," Chase says.

"It's fine." James tips back his beer. "Don't be such worrywarts. Anyone up for a game of cornhole?"

I am definitely not in a game-playing mood. The last time I felt this level of hostility was on the football field lining up for the snap. I get the impression that people like us, non-Sheeters, are not welcome at this establishment. I think Chase has the right idea. We need to vamoose.

Before I can say as much, a booming voice calls out, "Hey! You're those guys!"

A man steps out from one of the small groups. He has an impressive thatch of dark chest hair climbing out of his button-down shirt. It doesn't match the bleached blond hair on his head.

"What *guys* do you mean?" Collin asks in a neutral tone.

My entire body tenses as Chest Hair crosses the distance to us. "You're those football players."

It's clear from the way his eyes bounce between the four of us he doesn't know exactly who we are but has enough of an idea to be mostly right. Guess word has gotten out about Tank's purchase. Phenomenal.

"Maybe we are," James says slowly. "Why? You want an autograph?"

Chest Hair steps far too close to my short-fused oldest brother. *Not a good choice, fella.*

I join James so we're standing shoulder to shoulder, and Collin, muttering a curse under his breath, joins us on the other side. Chase, the smartest of our little group by far, hangs back.

Chest Hair, clearly not possessing the kind of genes that play into survival of the fittest, only smiles wider. "I'd love an autograph. How about you sign my left butt cheek? Or my—"

"Or your chest hair?" I interrupt whatever untoward suggestion he was about to make. "That might be a little difficult, but maybe if we braid it first. Or we could shave our initials into it. What do you think, James?"

My eldest brother does not move, but he does rumble out something between an agreement and a growl.

Chest Hair steps closer. I hate to think this idiot is a representative of the town. But then, I realize nobody has stood up to watch his back. So he might be a party of one.

"You fancy rich boys think you can come in here and swindle the mayor out of the deed to this town? Not on my watch, son. Not on my watch."

"Is that what you think happened?" I ask, moving a little closer. Not because James needs backup, but I'd rather this guy take a swing at me than the one of us most likely to send Chest Hair to the hospital. "Because we've got a contract that says otherwise. All nice and legal. Sounds like you've got your stories mixed up. I can see how that would happen though. It's hard to be both smart and pretty."

That one takes him a minute, then he scowls and turns his full attention toward me, looking me up and down with a sneer. "Well, you're all pretty, so you must not be too smart."

"Guess not, since you and I understand each other so well. Now, do you mind if we enjoy ourselves a friendly game of cornhole?"

"Yeah, I do mind."

He spits on the ground, and I'm thankful he didn't hit my boots. Before we left on this little jaunt into dumb idea land, I took a quick shower and changed into fresh clothes at James's house. Just in case fate made my path cross Lindy's again. If this guy messes up my boots, this will go a whole lot less peacefully. Harper and the guys always give me a hard time about it, but I am a man who likes my clothes and shoes.

"Are you going to try and stop us?" James speaks, each syllable dropped with a deadly precision. Chest Hair whips his attention back to my dumb older brother.

"Yeah, I am."

I hear a noise behind me, and I'm pretty sure it's Chase, sighing heavily. Collin is glancing around discreetly, probably assessing the kind of lawsuit we might be looking at if things get ugly. He's always the kind to take stock of the practical side of situations.

Me? I'm just the mouth.

"After we're done here, can I shave a little bit of it? I need a new area rug in my bathroom, and this shade would go perfectly with my floors. I'm happy to pay you by the ounce." I sniff dramatically, then wrinkle my nose. "Though I might ask you to shower first. A little shampoo and conditioner would go a long way."

Chest Hair launches himself in my direction but before his body makes contact, out of nowhere, a powerful jet of water knocks him off his feet. Down he goes, and before I can react, the stream—which I have enough time to see is coming from the fire hose—aims our way.

Collin, Chase, and James go down like bowling pins. Last, but not least, a gush of water hits me square in the chest, taking my legs out from under me. I go down hard, getting the wind knocked out of me as I go.

We're a sopping wet tangle of legs and arms. Somehow, my face gets pressed right into the center of Chest Hair's most notable feature. He definitely needs a shampoo, and I need a bottle of mouthwash. I'll be coughing up hairballs for days. I get a solid yank in as I twist away from him, and he screeches.

The spray doesn't let up but isn't as bad when it's not hitting me directly. I don't know how they even got a water source out here for the truck. Surely, there's not a hydrant in the middle of the field? Either way, it doesn't matter. The damage is done. I guess I can at least be thankful we avoided a fight?

There's laughter, and a few catcalls as the spray comes to a stop. "The Devil Came Down to Georgia" starts playing over the speakers, which seems remarkably apropos somehow. The dirt has already become mud. Scrambling through the wet slop, my hands close around someone's shoe. It's impossible to even tell what color it is. When I tip it over, mud glops out.

"Well played," someone grumbles, and I realize it's James. I resist the urge to shove his face in a puddle, because somehow, this all feels like his fault.

He must feel the same about me—but with less restraint —because the next thing I know, we're rolling, swinging fists as we go. The mud dripping into my eyes makes it almost impossible to see. I'm pretty sure I land a blow somewhere, just before he nails me in the jaw.

Someone calls, "Soooie! Here piggy piggies!"

"HEY NOW!" a voice shouts, and it's the kind of voice that demands respect. The music even cuts out, and James and I pause.

I blink until I can make out a sturdy-looking fellow with a wide, friendly face. He's around our age, with a barrel chest and the build of a lineman. Maybe one who's a few years outside of training, based on the way his belly hangs slightly over his belt. He grins down at us, then clucks his tongue, glancing around at the crowd gathered to watch the show.

"What have I told y'all about pig jokes?" he asks, and it's then I see the badge on his belt. He's a cop. I groan and release James's shirt, rolling away.

"Well, now," the officer says, dimples flashing our way now. "How about y'all stand up for me."

Chest Hair lumbers to his feet. He starts to wipe his hands on his pants, then seems to realize they're just as muddy. "Sure thing, Chevy."

"Go on, now," Chevy says, inclining his head toward the parking lot. Chest Hair doesn't give us so much as a sideways look before slinking back and disappearing from the circle of lights.

"I'd offer you a hand," Chevy says, "but I think you'd slide right out of my grip."

The four of us get to our feet, looking like identical mud monsters. The very first thing I think about is how James is going to murder us over the interior of his truck if we have to ride home this way.

Chevy is still smiling, and it's an impressive feat how he can look so friendly yet carry a mild threat in his words. "I think it's about time to break up this party, don't you?"

"I wouldn't call it a party, exactly." I rub my chin. "Looks more like an establishment ducking pretty far underneath the liquor laws."

"Shut up, Pat," Collin mutters.

Chevy only grins wider, his dimples becoming even more pronounced. "Funny you should mention the law," he says. "That's why I'm here. And we're about to get to know each other a whole lot better. All four of you are under arrest."

"And they talk about small-town hospitality," James says.

"If you come quietly, I won't even put the cuffs on you. How's that for hospitality?"

"What are you even charging us with?" Collin sputters.

Chevy tilts his head, thinking. "For tonight, we'll go with disturbing the peace." He glances around the yard, then raises his already loud voice. "Is anyone here feeling their peace disturbed?"

Hands go up around the clearing, as well as shouts of affirmation.

"There you have it," Chevy says. "Now, let's find you a pickup with a big enough bed for y'all. I don't want all this mud dirtying up my cruiser." He grins at us again. I think in some other situation, he and I could laugh together over beers.

With a little bow, Chevy adds, "In case we've been remiss to say it, welcome to Sheet Cake, boys."

FROM THE NEIGHBORLY APP

Subject: Mayor scandal?

Cal_45

In case you've been living under a rock or underground (looking at you, Wolf Waters) and didn't hear, Mayor Whitehead sold Sheet Cake proper to some non-Sheeters. It's been nice knowing ya! If you need me, I'll be headed to Amarillo.

1BigBass

Mayor Whitehead is and always has been a total snake! Not that I blame him for leaving his shrew of a wife. No offense to shrews. Did he really buy an island? Who's in charge of the town?

TheRealBob

From what I understand, the Grahams purchased the town. I'll take football legacies over Mayor Whitehead any day of the week.

JB

I saw this coming years ago. No one listened during the last election but I bet you're listening now! Billy Waters for mayor!

BagelBytes

Let's not make this political.

JB

It literally IS political. The mayor is an elected official representing a particular party, therefore: political. I bet I can guess who YOU voted for.

1BigBass

Maybe we should just have Think Tank do it. He bought the town from the mayor! Tank Graham for mayor!!!

B_WatersJR

Howdy, folks! I see a lot of questions here and thought I'd step in as a representative of city council. We've called a special meeting and will hold a town hall next month to discuss and hear from Sheeters on our next steps in this unprecedented series of events. We encourage you to stay positive and not panic or spread baseless rumors. We'll sort this out and keep this town running! Thanks so much for your patience and your support.

-Billy Waters

JB

I don't know about anyone else but that sounded like a very mayoral post. My vote is with Billy. The whole Graham clan can [censored for language] a whole [censored for language] and a [censored for language] horse too!

Vanz

Billy and the Waters clan can go stick a [censored for language] in their big, white [censored for language] [censored for language]. They stole our land and I'll never forget their [censored for language] thievery and [censored for language].

Neighborly Mod

Users JB and Vanz have been temporarily muted for violating community standards. This thread is also being closed, and I'd urge all members to take note of the official post from city council. Find the link below. Please remember to be kind and above all, Neighborly!

[comments have been closed]

Subject: OFFICIAL RESPONSE FROM CITY COUNCIL RE: THE OFFICE OF MAYOR

City_Council_Official

As many of you may know, Mayor Whitehead did effectively terminate his contract with the city and resign the office of mayor. He cannot be reached for comment. City council is holding a special meeting to discuss the next steps, and we will hold a Town Hall as soon as possible.

Until the office of mayor is filled, city council will act as the ruling body of government, per the Sheet Cake ordinance 4.11.

We are also aware of the sale of the downtown area of Sheet Cake to one Theodore Graham. We are having our legal team check for the validity of the sale and will address this as well in the Town Hall meeting. Until then, city council will also be making sure all ordinances are followed and any necessary permits are obtained for any work done or changes made.

    City council takes very seriously the job you've tasked us with and we will make sure we preserve Sheet Cake.

    -your elected officials

[comments have been closed]

CHAPTER TWELVE

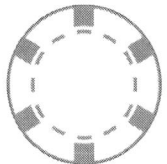

Lindy

"Do animals have souls?"

One second, I'm asleep. The next, a voice is right in my ear, and I'm screaming and rolling out of bed. Jo perches on the edge of the mattress, looking apologetic.

"Sorry. Do you need an ice pack?"

"No," I groan. The worst part isn't the pain in my knee or the dust bunnies I now have a perfect view of under the bed, but the SIZE of the dust bunnies. They're approaching real bunny size. Someone should really do something about that.

I drag myself to my feet, feeling seventy-two rather than twenty-seven. The dream I was dreaming—something involving a circus tent in the backyard, elephants, and a monkey swinging on a trapeze—slips away.

I should be used to Jo waking me up with questions or

prying open my eyelids with tiny fingers. But, no. Jo seems to find a way to startle me awake before my alarm almost every morning. Sometimes, on mornings like today, I also fall out of bed.

"Is it show-and-tell today?"

"No, it's not show-and-tell."

I don't think. What day is it, again?

Jo follows me as I limp to the bathroom, where I am reminded by the duct tape over the lid and Jo's hand-drawn sign that the toilet is out of order. It's too early to make decisions. Even small ones like: walk all the way downstairs or just go to the bathroom in the shower?

I turn on the shower and hazard a glance in the mirror. Yep, I look like I barely slept. Between worries about Jo and thoughts about Pat, I couldn't get my brain to stop doing its best impression of a jumping bean.

"You never answered—do animals have souls?"

"I'm not sure, Jojo. That's a big question for first thing in the morning," I tell her.

"What's for breakfast? We're out of cereal."

I think we're out of milk too. And almost everything else. "How about we stop for donuts on the way to school?"

"Yay! Donuts!"

"You'll have to eat a kolache first. For the protein."

I'm not sure how much protein she's really getting in what amounts to a pig in a blanket, but it counts. This is what I tell myself, anyway.

"I'll let the dogs out," Jo calls. "And I think they have souls."

Jo runs down the stairs, energized by the idea of donuts. I'll admit that it puts a little pep in my step too. But only a little.

I leave the bathroom door cracked before climbing into the shower. That's something I've gotten used to with Jo—no door is ever fully shut. Privacy is dead to me. Heaven forbid I lock something. The moment I do, Jo NEEDS me immediately and urgently.

The pipes groan and bang as the hot water finally kicks on, but they don't sound as bad as the noise the toilet started making last month. I wish I had a little more disposable income so I could call a plumber.

Maybe if I didn't also have a lawyer to pay for ... but it's always something. I can't remember a month going by that didn't have a surprise expense: worn-out tires, a dentist's appointment, the hot water heater flaking out, Jo getting an ear infection, or some random art fee. As long as there's one working toilet in the house, for now, we'll call it good. (Good-ish. To be clear, it's really not all that good.)

Ashlee's words about a stable home life flit through my mind. But having two toilets isn't required for that, right? Rumor has it Wolf Waters has three bathrooms in his bunker, so clearly stability isn't relative to number of toilets.

The moment the warm shower spray hits my face, my dream comes to me with alarming clarity. Pat, wearing a ringmaster's top hat and tails better than either Hugh Jackman or Zac Efron, grins at me from atop an elephant's back. Doing a neat flip, he lands in front of me, a thick-maned lion weaving around his legs like a house cat. And now Pat has a Doc Holliday mustache as he cracks Indiana Jones's whip, saying, "I'm your huckleberry."

Ringmaster Pat reminds me that Pat was actually here at my house, not in tails or with a mustache, but with cowboy boots and a sincere apology. I'm still processing how I feel about all of it.

I'm mad.

I miss him.

I'm glad he apologized.

I don't forgive him.

(Probably.)

I wish he'd come back.

I wish he'd leave for good.

I groan and lean over, pressing my forehead against the cold tile. "Can't you leave me alone, even when I'm sleeping?" I ask an invisible, imaginary Pat, who only winks, tipping his top hat to me.

Of course he can't leave me alone. Not even in my dreams.

And if I'm truly, deeply, frighteningly honest with myself, I don't want him to. Even if the fortune teller just outside my dream's big top would probably tell me she sees heartbreak in my future.

———

Thirty minutes later, I'm reaching back to wipe powdered sugar from Jo's nose as we wait in the drop-off line. Even with a donut-messy face, she still looks cuter than I do with her bright eyes and freckles. I look like I last saw good sleep half a decade ago, which is about right. I blow my bangs out of my eyes, wondering if I should keep growing them out or cut them again.

Does Pat like bangs on me?

Who cares!

But ... does he?

Clearly, I care. Even if I shouldn't. Now that I know Pat and his dad are investing in the town, I feel paranoid, like any moment, one of them is going to pop out from behind a cluster of bushes.

That may or may not be the reason I'm wearing eyeliner today.

"Have a great day, bug," I say as we near the drop-off area.

"I'm not a bug!"

The sound of her giggle brightens my mood instantly and helps the worry lift. "Have a great day, cupcake."

"I'm not a cupcake!"

We inch forward until we're finally at the drop-off spot, and I turn, kissing my hand and pressing it quickly to her knee as a volunteer mom opens the door.

I roll down my window, calling, "Love you, Jojo!"

"Be good!" Jo responds, making me chuckle.

I prepare to move the car into drive, but the door stays open. I almost jump when a head pops into the open passenger-side window.

It's Tabitha Waters-Graves, easily my least favorite of the PTO Mafia. Tabitha is the PTO Mafia queen. Or, I guess, the don. And, at least partly because of my bad history with her cousin, Billy Jr., Tabitha has made messing with me her favorite sport. She is living proof that mean girls never go out of style and aren't just relegated to movies or wearing pink on Wednesdays. It feels almost like coming full circle, being harassed by a Waters woman. But Tabitha's meanness makes Spring seem like my high school BFF.

"Hello, Linda," Tabitha says. Her unnaturally white smile reminds me of Jo's *Jaws* coloring book. I think I'd prefer to swim with sharks than converse with Tabitha.

"It's Lindy."

"Have you signed up to help with Galaxy Day? I don't think I saw your name on the volunteer list."

"I have to work." I also don't know what Galaxy Day is,

but I'm not going to mention that and add fuel to her dumpster fire.

The PTO Mafia doesn't seem to understand that even if I don't go to an actual office or have a specific boss, my writing is real work. It takes a lot more time than one might think to research posts like which items at the Dollar Tree actually save you money. I'm constantly getting passive aggressive emails from Tabitha or Melinda, the room mother and Tabby's BFF, disappointed I didn't show up for Muffin Day or Crazy Sock Day or Pretend It's Friday on a Wednesday Day. I swear, three to four times a month, there is another event requiring a sign-up and optional parent present.

Tabitha clucks her tongue, and I become mesmerized by her eyelash extensions. They almost touch her eyebrows. Isn't that uncomfortable? They have to be heavy. I wonder if her eyelids ever get sore. I'm hit with sudden inspiration to pen an article on the top dangers of eyelash extensions.

"Information has been coming home for weeks about Galaxy Day. It's a big event. But I know some parents—or *caretakers*—are too busy with their own lives."

I've got to give it to Tabitha—she's no dummy. That dart strikes exactly where she means it to, and I take a moment to breathe and count the No Parking signs along the fence ahead of me. I won't snap and give her the satisfaction of seeing me upset.

Maybe on paper, I'm Jo's legal guardian, her conservator. But that's just the official title, and anyway, it's *my* business. I've done the best I can by Jo, and I happen to think it's pretty darn good—broken toilets aside. We're happy. I love her to pieces, and she knows it.

"I can't help out with every activity, Tabby." She bristles at the nickname, which gives me a stupidly large sense of pleasure. Cars start passing me on the left, and I'm getting dirty looks. Like I have any choice in holding up the line. I can't move until Tabby closes the back door, which she doesn't seem to have any interest in doing.

"You mean *any* activity. I believe you are the only parent—sorry, caretaker—who hasn't volunteered in at least some capacity at the school. We make time for what's important, Linda."

"Did you get that line out of a fortune cookie?"

She glares. Tabby's husband is the sole doctor at Sheet Cake's family practice. Which means Tabitha has choices: work, not work, volunteer, get expensive eyelash extensions, harass other, lesser moms—excuse me, *caretakers*—in the carpool line.

I hope her extensions make all her natural lashes fall out. That makes me feel mean. Fine—I wish *half* of her natural lashes fall out.

Tabitha gives me a faux pitying look I'd like to remove from her face with the plastic ice scraper in my glove compartment. Considering it rarely freezes in Sheet Cake, it would be a great use for the thing.

"It must be hard to balance it all," Tabby says, and I can see her winding up her pitch. Looks like a fastball. "That's probably why your sister wants to take custody of Jo."

I was wrong. It's a curveball, and I swing wildly and miss.

"Rachel is not going to get custody of Jo."

"That's not what I hear. But it's a good thing. Babies belong with their mamas. You've done a good job; now it's time to let Jo's *real* mama step in."

I wonder if murdering Tabby would hurt my chances of keeping Jo. Nah, it would simply be considered a public service.

Then it hits me. Ashlee said I should try to be more involved with Jo's school. I grit my teeth, hoping I don't break a molar. I definitely can't afford a dentist this month. Or this year.

You can do this, Lindy. Just try not to look into her eyelashes, lest you be turned to stone.

"Actually, I'd love to help with Galaxy Day."

Tabby blinks in surprise, her giant lashes waving like antennae. "Really? Are you sure you can spare the time?"

I already regret this decision. She's liable to stick me with some kind of horrible duty like sharpening ten thousand pencils with a hand-held sharpener.

I heave an exaggerated sigh. "I just said I would help. Now, I need to go, Tabby. Do you mind letting go of my door?"

"Important journalistic pieces to write?"

That or today's article comparing the Jonas brothers to the Hanson brothers. "Yes. That whole pesky having a job thing. You wouldn't know."

I immediately regret making that dig. I love working. I'd probably do so even if money weren't an issue. But I definitely don't want to devalue women who stay home with a child. In theory, I'm all about choices. Sometimes it's hard to remember when I have so few of my own. And when I'm being made to feel guilty about the things I can't control by people like Tabby.

Tabitha's eyes narrow, making her eyelashes look even more spidery. Her smile turns sickly sweet. "I thought I'd heard something of you getting a big windfall. A winning lottery ticket of sorts."

"I think I'd be the first to know if I won any kind of lottery, Tab."

"I meant Patrick Graham. Isn't he your ex? Heard he's back in town, and I figured you might be cashing in on that."

The accusation that I'd ever use him for money burns. I'm

opening my mouth to snap something back when Tabby steps away from my car.

"I'll be in touch about Galaxy Day. Bye now!" She slams the door and walks away before I can say things that are undoubtedly true, but which I'm sure I'd regret.

I'm fuming as I wait for an opening to pull out. Another ten cars pass me before I can finally escape the line.

Back in college, Pat educated me on cleat chasers. "Or jersey chasers," I remember him saying with a bitter smile. "Take your pick on the name." Women threw themselves at him—and, he told me, at his dad and brother—because of their name, their fame, their bank accounts. He knew it would only get worse as the draft approached.

"Some guys start their careers only to find out a few months in that—*surprise!*—they're a baby daddy," he said. Which only made our no-sex rule make more sense for him.

I was never with Pat for fame or money or anything else. It was always and only about *him*. That hasn't changed. Not that I'm with him now, but I would *never* use him. I might be in desperate times, but they do not mean desperate measures. Not like Tabby implied.

Winnie calls when I'm halfway home and still hot with rage. I don't even say hello but instead launch into a Tabby tirade. "You won't believe what Tabitha—"

"I thought you'd want to know that your boyfriend is in jail."

I have not had nearly the amount of coffee I need for the kinds of things people are throwing my way this morning.

"I don't have a boyfriend."

"Sure, you don't. But your non-boyfriend and his brothers spent the night in the drunk tank, according to Chevy. I thought you might want to come by and gloat."

I have to pull over into a bank parking lot so I can focus on the conversation. "Chevy arrested Pat? Here? For what?"

Winnie laughs. "Disturbing the peace at Backwoods Bar."

I can only imagine the kind of trouble Pat would get up to at Backwoods Bar. The mouth on that man could incite war in Switzerland. Now that the whole town knows about the mayor selling to the Grahams, I bet it wasn't pretty. Winnie once took Dale, who's from Austin, to Backwoods with her, and the man barely made it out of there with his ironed polo shirt. Honestly, half the problem was that Dale is the kind of guy who *wears* ironed polo shirts. They say there's no accounting for taste, and it's definitely true in the case of Winnie and Dale, who is about as exciting as an unsalted Saltine cracker.

Is Pat okay? The errant thought is like a weed, needing to be yanked out by the root.

Pat is fine. He's in jail, not the hospital. And he's not your concern.

My worry quickly changes direction, and I settle back into the rage originally sparked by Tabby. Pat cannot keep showing up like this, making me *feel* things. Making me dream about him in a ringmaster's costume. I have to focus on Jo right now—and *only* Jo.

Seeing Pat again only whetted my appetite for more of him, and I can't have that. His apology doesn't change his character or his character flaws. Eventually, Pat will tire of Sheet Cake. A small town like this isn't big enough for his personality. Or his ego. He'll leave, but I need to help speed the process along. I won't let myself get attached only to be hurt again. And I definitely won't let him hurt Jo, who has been bringing him up daily, wondering when he and Mr. Tank will be back. The last thing Jo needs is another person leaving her.

"Chevy says their lawyer is on the way. They should be out within the hour," Winnie says.

I pull back out into traffic, headed toward downtown. "You know what? I'm on my way. Pat needs a little encouragement to leave town, and I'm happy to give him a reason. Text Val for me and tell her to meet us there. We've got some butt-kicking to do."

CHAPTER THIRTEEN

Lindy

BY THE TIME I park at the municipal building, I've listened to "Eye of the Tiger" no less than four times, and I am ready to rise up to the challenge of my rival. Who, in this case, is Patrick Graham.

"You've got this," I tell myself. "I've got this," I agree. Because it's totally normal to give yourself pep talks in your car. I'm going to count this as manifesting, and I need to manifest myself some strength right now.

Winnie and Val are waiting outside the building, looking like polar opposites—if we're talking opposite poles on two different planets. Win has on high-waisted jeans, a pink short-sleeved sweater, and a bandana as a headband. Val has on overalls today, no less paint-splattered than her coveralls, and is barefoot. Her hair is twisted into a knot with a paintbrush.

For a moment, the three of us grasp hands in a little circle, foreheads together. It's more group huddle than group hug. "We are such dorks," I say.

"Total dorks," Winnie agrees.

"Queens of Dorktonia," Val says. "But why are we here? Winnie said something about butts."

We pull back and I glare at Winnie. "That's what you told her?"

Win smiles, looking totally unrepentant. "I knew it would get her here."

The only butt Val's interested in is Chevy's. And I think he's the only one in town who doesn't know it.

"Plus, it *is* about butts. Lindy needs our help kicking some butts out of town."

Val looks confused.

"No actual butts will be kicked," I say.

"Figurative butt-kicking only." With Winnie, it's hard to know—it could go either way. Honestly, I'd kind of love to unleash Winnie's five-foot-two fury on Pat.

Val puts both hands on her hips. "Will someone please tell me what's going on?"

I let Winnie explain about the fight at Backwoods Bar as we walk up the steps to the municipal building. This is the only building besides the library not falling apart, solely because the Waters family pays to keep it up. They have a massive plaque out front. I suspect someone comes by to polish it every morning. As we walk by, I swear I can see my pores in the shiny reflection.

The metal detectors in the lobby are a stark contrast to the balusters and curved wooden railing for the grand staircase leading upstairs to the courthouse and mayor's office.

"I'm back, Burt!" Winnie calls. The security guard, who

also happens to be Judge Judie's husband, hops down from his stool and runs a hand over his mustache.

"Lindy, Val. What brings you two down this fine morning?"

"They're visiting inmates," Winnie says.

"Sounds like a good time," he says. Val sets her purse on the conveyor belt, and Burt sighs. "You don't still carry that knife in your boot, do you, Val?"

Val laughs and wiggles one bare foot at him. "Of course not. I upgraded to a taser."

Burt picks up her purse, shaking his head. "You can't bring a taser in here, Val."

"Don't worry. I left it in my car."

Too bad. It might have come in handy.

Burt clears us, and we walk straight ahead through the double doors leading to the sheriff's office. Like the mayor, our town sheriff is elected, and also like the mayor, the sheriff is totally worthless. We've been hoping Chevy will run for office one of these days, but so far, he doesn't seem so inclined. It's not that he's lazy, exactly, more that he seems very comfortable with the status quo.

Before we walk in, Val pulls me to a stop. "Are you sure you want to tell Pat to leave?"

"Yes," Winnie and I say at the same time.

"But why? Didn't he apologize?"

After the LLLS meeting, I filled my friends in on running into Pat and our conversation on my porch. Val, ever the romantic, thinks I should give him a second chance, while Winnie is more of the mind we should set fire to his car.

"Valentina," Winnie says, shaking her head. "An apology isn't enough."

Val heaves a frustrated sigh. "But if you gave him a chance—"

"No more chances." I shake my head. "I don't have time for that."

"I wish you'd stop feeling like you have to take on the whole world alone. Both of you." Val points between me and Winnie. "The two of you kill me sometimes. You are both strong women—good for you! But being strong doesn't mean you don't need other people. You can't hide away forever in your tall towers. At some point, people are going to stop showing up, asking you to let down your hair."

"I'm not doing that," I say. Am I?

Winnie only smirks. "I like my tower. I have a fantastic Wi-Fi signal. Plus, I've got you two. And Dale. What more do I need?"

Val and I carefully do not meet each other's eyes. Because, honestly? We're both more than a little mystified by Dale and Winnie. They've been together almost a year, and I know as much about him now as I did the night we met. Because … there's just not much to know. He's an accountant in Austin. Handsome. Nice. Gentlemanly. And a big ol' snoozefest. But he seems to make Winnie happy. Or—content? So, we do our best to be supportive.

"Lindy, you only ask for help when you're desperate. We would help more—if you let us."

"I asked for help today, didn't I?"

Val rolls her eyes. "Yes, but you also didn't tell us about Pat the moment you saw him."

"I was processing! Anyway, I'll do better asking for help, okay? Starting now. Help me kick my ex out of town?" When Val looks like she's going to argue again, I add, "If you won't do it for me, for Jo. She's already imprinting on the man like a little baby duck. Imagine how it will be if he leaves her." I mime being stabbed in the heart.

"Ugh. Fine," Val says. "But let the record show I disagree with this decision."

"Duly noted," Winnie says. "Now, let's move. We're burning daylight, people." She pushes through the doors leading us into the small sheriff's department.

Before I step inside, I do a quick mental check on the custom-made bulletproof vest I keep around my heart. I started its construction after dad left and then continued with Rachel. After Pat left me, I zipped that baby up tight. To get through today and the week after and probably the week after, I need this trusty vest firmly in place around my heart. I will tell Pat to go, leaving me one less problem. One less person who seems intent on breaking through my barriers, on breaking me.

"Ladies," Chevy greets us as we walk inside. He is the only one on duty in the open room, which has a few desks, a break room off to the side, and two holding cells at the very back which immediately try to grab my attention.

Don't look. Don't look. DO NOT LOOK.

It's like I can sense Pat's presence like an electromagnetic field around me. The room feels different because he's here. The air feels different. *I* feel different.

Which is ridiculous and also needs to stop NOW.

I force myself to keep my eyes fixed on Chevy. "Hello, Chev." Winnie greets him with a hip check that makes him stumble a few steps.

Narrowing his eyes, he takes her glasses and holds them out of reach while she grabs for them. I swear, the two of them never stopped treating each other the way they did in middle school. It's all teasing and pranks and insults. When she kicks him in the shin, he finally hands back the glasses.

Winnie is Chevy's total opposite in almost every way. Where Winnie is all cool snark, Chevy is warm humor.

Winnie is petite with lean muscle she works hard to keep, while Chevy is like a teddy bear with a big, broad body that's strong but also soft.

He gives the best hugs, and I didn't know how much I needed the one he gives me now until he wraps his arms around me. He is made of comfort, and I relax into his embrace.

"Hey! Get your paws off her!" a familiar voice calls.

The possessiveness in Pat's voice thrills and irritates me in equal measure. Pat does NOT get to comment on whom I hug or don't hug. That ship sailed when he left me without saying goodbye.

But his jealous display is like catnip for a very, very bad feral cat who apparently lives inside me along with the zombie butterflies. I need to have her spayed posthaste, because she is purring and asking to rub up against Pat's ankles.

Chevy chuckles as I squeeze him tighter. "Oh, is it like that?" he asks.

"It's like that."

Laughing a little louder now, Chevy picks me up and swings me around until I squeal.

"Police brutality!" Pat shouts, and several male voices tell him in various, colorful ways to shut up.

"Keep it down and don't make me show you police brutality," Chevy calls. His arms are starting to squeeze me like a sausage casing.

"I think ... that's ... enough," I gasp.

"You sure?"

"Positive. I ... can't ... breathe!"

Chevy gently sets me back down but leaves a wet smack of a kiss on my cheek before he steps away. I give him a dirty look, and he just shrugs.

"HEY!" Pat shouts, and I have a very hard time not looking toward what sounds like a scuffle in the cell. "Lips off!"

"Really, Chevy?" I mutter.

He shrugs unapologetically. "Might as well go all in."

Val tries to hide the lovestruck, hopeful look she always wears around Chevy. While I got the red carpet of greetings, he only gives Val a quick side hug. "Hey, kiddo," he says.

I've never been sure whether he knows about her unrequited crush or is actually oblivious, but it's getting painful to watch. Meanwhile, Val dates up a storm, trying to either make Chevy jealous or find someone to help her get over him. So far, she has accomplished neither.

When he steps away quickly, Val visibly shoves down her hurt and turns her attention to the cell at the back of the room. "Hel-lo, serious man candy."

I should have known this might happen. But there will be absolutely no shipping of anyone in that cell with my friends. This is a no-ship zone. Thankfully, Winnie's got my back.

"Ew, Val. No." She pokes Val in the arm. "Those are *not* guys you want to date."

Winnie is right, but neither of us want to date a Dale, either. And apparently there is no shortage of Dales, as Winnie has tried setting both of us up with multiple of his plain-cracker friends.

"Ow!" Val rubs the spot and gives Winnie a dirty look. "You and your bony fingers!"

"I'm with Winnie on this. They are definitely off limits," I tell her in a low voice. "They're not man candy. Think of them like an onion dipped in caramel. Looks like a caramel apple on the outside but—"

"Tastes like an armpit," Winnie finishes.

Chevy booms out a laugh. He was the one who played

that prank on us years ago at Halloween. We should have known, considering the way he always liked to prank us. But a caramel-covered onion looks surprisingly just like a caramel apple.

"Right," Val says, wrinkling her nose. "But just in case, should we call dibs?"

"No!" Winnie and I say at the same time.

Val begins counting on her fingers. She looks at me first. "Pat is obviously yours—"

"He's not mine," I snap, still managing to keep my eyes off the cell. I am a paragon of self-control.

"One can be for Winnie. Maybe the big, grumpy-looking one. I think he could probably handle her."

"I have a boyfriend," Winnie says. "Hel-lo."

"I keep forgetting," Val mutters. "He's just so—" I elbow her, and she changes course. "Right. Okay, and one is wearing a wedding ring, which leaves the super muscly one for me." Val gives Chevy a sideways glance to see if he's paying attention. He's scrolling through his phone.

"How do you even see a wedding band from here? Especially with all the mud?" Winnie asks.

Mud?

"It's a skill," Val says. "And why *are* they so filthy?"

Chevy chuckles. "They might have gotten hosed down at the Backwoods Bar."

I finally allow myself to glance to the cell, where my eyes have been begging to go since I walked in. I have to commend my self-control for lasting this long. My gaze lands immediately on Pat.

Are there even other guys in there with him? As far as I'm concerned, it's always only Pat. Regrettably so.

Pat is, in fact, covered in what looks like dried mud. From his hair to his boots, he is a light brown color, his hair and clothes stiff with it. Only his face and hands look like they've been cleaned at all. He should look worse for being filthy and for spending the night in a cell. But, this being my life—which is far from fair—even from here, Pat is still the best-looking man I've ever seen.

He flashes me his ridiculous smile, the one which would be cocky on someone else. Except Pat isn't puffed up or proud. On the surface, it might come across that way. He possesses a sense of confidence, a fearlessness, and an exuberance for life. But he's always been the kind of man willing to make a fool of himself, to let all his feelings hang out no matter the consequences. He's the kind to jump despite the risks.

Except when it came to me. To *us*. There, he was better at jumping ship. And I'm not going to give him a chance to do so again. Because it wouldn't be so hard to let me fall in love with Pat again. I'm not so sure I ever fully fell OUT of love with the man.

Remember—NO SHIPPING ZONE! Zero ships will be shipping from this port.

Val nudges me with her shoulder, finally breaking my gaze. Her smile is knowing, and it makes me feel a little stabby. "Are you totally sure we're here for butt-kicking?" she asks quietly.

"I'm sure."

Chevy crosses his arms. "Their lawyer should be here any minute. If you want a chance to talk while he's behind bars I'd do so quickly."

Why did talking to Pat seem like a good idea, again? Oh, right, because he and his family—a good portion of whom are also crowded in the cell and every bit as caked with mud—bought my freaking town. I cannot wake up every morning knowing at any moment I might run into the man who has that feral cat in me clawing up the furniture. Pat is simply too big of a risk.

I need to make sure he knows this—*us*—isn't ever going to happen again.

It can't. I've lost too much. I won't make the mistake of offering him my heart again. Because Pat isn't just offering me a second chance. He's holding out hope in a shiny, wrapped package with a bow. Hope is not a luxury I can afford right now.

I mentally check the zipper on my bulletproof heart vest.

Do bulletproof vests zip? ANYWAY.

I try to take a fortifying breath, but the air somehow tastes like stale coffee and pickles, and I end up coughing. Winnie pats my back ineffectually.

"I'm okay," I croak.

"Yeah, you are," Winnie says. "I wish I had popcorn for this. Chevy, is there any popcorn in the break room?"

"I'll check."

Ignoring them all, I draw in a steadying breath and stride toward the cell. My eyes stay fixed on Pat. His smile grows as I approach.

My heart tries to do some kind of flippy thing it definitely has no permission to do, and I tell it to stand down. The zombie butterflies try to stir, and I stomp them with the heel of my boot. The feral cat seems to be trying to figure out how to claw through the fabric of my bulletproof vest, and I kick her out of the way.

I'm vaguely aware of Val and Winnie flanking me a few steps behind. They're making sure I know they've got my back while giving me enough room to do my thing. Not sure what my thing is yet, but I've always been pretty good on the spot.

I stop short of the bars, just out of reach. Pat's touch has the power to undo me, so I can't give him that chance. I may be strong, but I'm not *that* strong. I point my finger toward the center of his chest. If I had a laser, it would blast right through his heart, making this a heck of a lot easier.

"You do *not* get to smile at me that way."

That's not what I meant to lead with, but I guess it's a start.

One corner of his mouth kicks up a little higher, and he flutters his lashes at me. Long, thick lashes people like Tabitha pay good money to poorly emulate.

"Whatever do you mean?"

I hate how well I know him. Because I immediately know Pat is quoting *Tombstone*, a movie we watched together at least half a dozen times. It is a Pat staple, for watching and for quoting. I haven't been able to sit through a Val Kilmer movie since. The man ruined Val Kilmer for me—just another thing to add to the list of his crimes.

"You can't keep showing up here, interrupting my life, buying my town, making trouble."

"Trouble? Me?" He puts a hand to his chest, mocking offense.

"Yes. You—the one in the cell. I'd call this trouble."

Pat grabs the bars in his strong hands. They are the kind of hands made for catching footballs. But I also remember the way those same hands cupped my cheeks tenderly or squeezed my waist with a possessive strength that always made my stomach tumble like an Olympic gymnast performing a floor routine.

Winnie puts a hand on my arm, and I regain some control over my wayward self, taking a big step back.

"What—is this town not big enough for the both of us?" Pat teases.

"Something like that."

Pat's eyes soften. And that's even worse. I can fight his big, confident personality. This tender side, though—it might undo me.

"It's good to see you, Lindybird. Let me introduce you to my family."

"You don't need to do that."

As if my words pinged harmlessly off his thick skull, Pat steps back, gesturing towards the other men in the cell. Whom, let's be honest, I haven't paid a lick of attention to, because they aren't Pat.

He points to the biggest and surliest looking man, who's leaning against the back wall looking bored. "That's James. He's my *least* least favorite."

I'm not sure if that's a good or bad thing. No one else seems to know either. Pat gestures to the one with the shortest hair and the broadest shoulders, his pecs practically bursting through his T-shirt. "The one who looks like he's on steroids—and just to be clear, he's all natural—is Collin."

Collin glares at Pat, then offers me a polite smile. "Nice to meet you, Lindy."

"And this is our newest brother, Chase." Pat throws his arm around the third man, who looks enough like them to be an actual brother. "He married my baby sister, Harper."

Chase holds up a hand. "I'd like to clarify that Harper is not literally a baby. She is an adult woman. Sorry for all the trouble, by the way. We probably should have stayed home."

"At least one of them has brains," Winnie mutters. "Not just muscles."

My head is spinning, and I need to get back on track. The goal was to get Pat gone, not become further entrenched in his life. "Okay, now that we've gotten introductions over with, it's time for you to—"

A crash followed by a cacophonous sound makes me jump. We all turn to the door, and my heart plummets.

It's Wolf Waters. With his shaggy beard, a whole lot of flowers, and … part of a drumline from the high school marching band?

"This should be good," Val says.

One of Pat's brothers says, "Hey, isn't that the guy from the bar?"

Wolf gives them an apologetic smile. "Hey, y'all. Sorry I turned the fire hose on you. Now, if you won't mind me. I've got a woman to propose to."

No. No he is not.

Wolf's proposals were usually light-hearted and in passing, like when he yelled, "Marry me!" out his truck window last week. I never thought they were serious or I would have shut him down for good a long time ago. It's hard to take the man seriously about anything when he lives in a self-built underground bunker and runs Backwoods Bar.

Chevy groans. "Wolf, you can't come in here and—"

Wolf gives some kind of signal, and the six boys and one girl with drums strapped to their chests begin drumming, drowning Chevy out. Wolf, with his classic Waters grin and none of their refinement, drops to one knee, holding out the flowers, which look like he clipped them off one of the bushes out front. He even has a ring, I realize, though it looks like he got it out of one of those machines for a quarter.

"Lindy Mae Darcy," Wolf shouts, his voice barely audible over the drums. "Will you do me the honor of being my wife?"

From the cell, I hear a sound that can only be described as a rumbling growl. The kind of sexy sound always described in books, one I've never had the pleasure of hearing. I like it more than I'll ever admit to a living soul.

The drummers do some kind of elaborate finish, which isn't quite synchronized, and then halt, all looking on with expectant, acne-dusted faces.

Suddenly, Ashlee's words echo in my mind. I would be a better candidate for keeping Jo if I were married. If I had a stable, two-parent household. This feels like the worst kind of joke. I swallow thickly, my fingers trembling as I glance at Wolf. My stomach is doing more churning than a washer set to spin cycle.

"I'm sorry, Wolf. I can't marry you."

He stands, totally unbothered by my refusal. "My bunker is big enough for you and Jo. Plus, I heard one of your toilets is broken. I have three working bathrooms. Three." He holds up three fingers, just to make this abundantly clear.

Three bathrooms is the best-sounding part of this proposal. Wolf slips a hand around my waist. "Come on, Lindy. Are you sure?"

Pat looks like he's about to start foaming at the mouth. "She said no, buddy. Step away from the woman."

Does it make me some kind of backwards, 15th century woman that his possessiveness makes me tremble?

Sorry, modern women. Sorry, feminism.

No, actually, I'm not at all sorry. Feminists should support my right to choose what I like, and I apparently like growly, overly possessive displays.

Wolf squeezes me, and I step out of his arms. "I'm sorry, but I can't."

He nods. "When I heard you needed to get married to help keep custody of Jo, I just wanted to offer. You know, to do my part."

It's such a cliché to say the world seems to stop spinning

on its axis, but that is exactly how the moment feels. Add in the sound of a record screeching to a halt and we've got a pair of perfectly overused descriptions.

"You heard *what?*" The words come out of me as a hiss.

First, Tabitha knows about the custody hearing. And now, Wolf has heard rumors I need to find a husband?

Kim. It has to be Kim. I remember how she was hovering right outside Ashlee's door. Kim must have been listening, and she told someone. Not Wolf, because they don't run in the same circles at all. She hasn't posted on Neighborly or Winnie would have removed it.

The point is: Kim told *someone.* And someone told Wolf.

I am standing inside a pressure cooker, and the lid's about to blow off. I'm not the only one, I realize. The visible tension in Pat's body matches what I'm feeling inside. His brothers seem like they're barely holding him in check.

One of the drummers—because yes, there's still a whole drumline of high school students witnessing this fiasco—drops a drumstick.

Chevy takes a shuffling step closer, as though he senses the rising tension.

"Who told you that?" I ask Wolf. I am deadly, deceptively calm, which fools him into thinking I am casual about this.

"Sorry, hon." Wolf winks. "I don't kiss and tell."

He couldn't have chosen a worse phrase to use.

It acts like a starter's pistol for Pat, who surges toward Wolf with a roar. Chevy steps between them saying, "Whoa, now, fellas," just as Pat's fist flies between the bars.

Chevy goes down hard.

He pitches forward into Wolf, Winnie screams, and the drum line, perhaps out of sheer nerves, launches into a song that sounds a little like a poor man's version of Taylor Swift's "Shake It Off."

Wolf and Chevy topple to the floor, taking a chair and a whole stack of folders with them. Papers flutter down like supersized confetti. Pat is still shouting threats at Wolf, and his brothers are holding him back.

And I—I am in the eye of the hurricane, watching the chaotic mess swirling around me. I don't know whether to laugh or cry.

At that moment, a dark-haired man walks into the room wearing a suit I can tell from here is expensive. No one but me seems to notice him until he sets down his briefcase and puts his fingers between his teeth.

The whistle he emits is so piercing that all movement stops. Dogs in Austin are probably howling.

The man surveys the state of the room and grins. "Looks like somebody needs a lawyer."

CHAPTER FOURTEEN

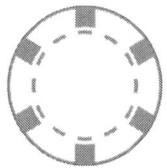

Pat

"Thanks to my lawyery magic, you are free to go, gentlemen," Thayden announces, waltzing into the small room where we've been waiting since Chevy unlocked our cell. The space seems to function as both an interrogation room and the break room, based on the burned coffee smell emanating from an ancient pot in the corner. Between our stiff, mud-crusted clothes and these metal folding chairs, we are all ready for a change of pace.

"About time," James mutters, shoving his chair back under the table with a loud screech.

But as I stand, Thayden grabs my shoulder, and his grin widens. "Oh, no no no. You, my dear Patrick, will be joining me in front of a judge today."

I swear our lawyer and friend is having way too good of a time with all this. He's on his way to being demoted to almost-friend. The amused smirk has not left his face since he walked into the fray thirty minutes ago, right after I accidentally assaulted a police officer.

Hitting Chevy was truly the cherry on top of my last twenty-four hours, in which my brothers came, saw, and dismissed Sheet Cake, we all got arrested for disturbing the peace at a local "bar," and I got to see Lindy proposed to and pawed at by a man named Wolf. I'd like to stuff him in a shipping container like in the movie *Madagascar*.

James, Collin, and Chase pause near the doorway, looking back at me.

"A court appearance?" Chase asks.

"Today?" Collin frowns. "Isn't that ... soon?"

"It's a small town. Not much on the docket." Thayden shrugs. "Judgement is swift when you assault a police officer."

I roll my eyes. "I didn't—"

"You did," James says, glowering at me. "Even if you meant to assault the other guy. And before you say this is my fault for bringing us here—"

"Wasn't going to say that. But now that you mention it ..."

James jabs a finger in my direction. "You started this when you joined forces with Tank and went behind our backs. Let's go."

And then, James is gone. Chase and Collin don't immediately follow.

I drop my hands on the table and slump in my chair. "They're really charging me?"

Thayden raises his eyebrows, like he's telling me to get with the program. "You hit a cop. And assaulted a private citizen. Wolf's lawyer, the illustrious Billy Waters, Esq., who is also his brother, has encouraged him to press charges."

"I never touched that guy!"

But I wanted to. From the moment he got down on one knee, it was like I was seeing through a pair of jealousy goggles. Not that I have any right or reason to feel so protective. When it comes to Lindy, reason takes a back seat.

I'm sure the fact we hardly slept last night didn't help. It was a shock seeing a proposal when Lindy told me the other day she was single. And what was all that about needing to get married to keep custody of Jo?

"And I'll argue your point before the judge," Thayden says. "But you struck the deputy, who then collided with Mr. Waters. You'll be lucky if his lawyer doesn't file a civil suit for damages. That's what lawyers do."

"You're a lawyer," Collin points out.

Thayden leans back in his chair, linking his fingers behind his head. "I am. But I'm not one of the undesirable ones. At least, not anymore. I've amended my smarmy lawyer ways. Now, I have your family to keep me in business. So, thank you for that. Delilah's been wanting to get a new rug. Why are rugs so expensive when you're just going to walk all over them?"

If I punch Thayden, will it look bad for me in court? Probably. Maybe I need to go at least a good twenty-four hours without engaging in fisticuffs. And I need to get out of here and ask Lindy about that custody stuff.

Collin rubs a hand over his jaw, then swings his gaze to me. "Do not do anything stupid."

"It's a little late for that, don't ya think?" Thayden asks.

"You know what I'm talking about," Collin says, looking remarkably like James at the moment.

I actually think I DO know what he's talking about, but I'm not going to admit it, so I only shrug. Thayden, realizing he's missing something, glances between us. Chase simply looks resigned to go along with whatever's happening here.

"Ooh! I want to know what stupid thing you think he's going to do," Thayden says. "As his lawyer, it's better I know up front."

"I thought it was better if you had deniability," I say.

"Depends on what you're thinking about doing. Murder— that, you should keep to yourself."

"It's worse," Collin says. "He's thinking about marrying The Woman."

He's not wrong. But I've been thinking about a future with Lindy since the moment I saw her again in the diner. It has nothing to do with Wolf and his stupid drumline. What kind of grand gesture was that, anyway?

If what Wolf said is true, though, and Lindy is having some kind of custody issue with Jo, I want to help. However I can. And yeah, that includes marriage. Everything is on the table.

Chase's face is priceless, like a perfect shock emoji. I wish I could take a picture, but the cops still have my phone and wallet. "Now *you* want to propose?" he asks.

I say nothing, because pleading the fifth seems like the smartest option right now. It's probably good practice for my case too.

Thayden studies me, amusement lighting his eyes. "Interesting plot twist."

"*Interesting* isn't the word I'd use," Collin says. "Impulsive, stupid—"

I lean back in my uncomfortable chair. "I never said a word about marriage."

"You didn't need to. It was all over your face the minute that Wolf guy said Lindy needs to get married. What kind of custody thing is she dealing with, anyway? Does she have a kid?" Collin asks.

"She's raising her niece," I explain. "And I don't know the whole story."

"Well, don't make a *Pat Decision* before you do."

"A Pat decision?" Thayden asks.

I lean his way. "He means it as an insult. A Pat Decision is one made quickly."

"Impulsively," Collin adds. "Stupidly. When you're thinking with your—"

Thayden holds up a hand. "I got it. Mind if I adopt the term? It has a nice ring to it."

"I mind," I mutter. "Not that anyone cares."

"Go right ahead. Just—keep a tight leash on him," Collin tells Thayden. "Whatever you do, make sure he comes back to Austin with you. I don't trust him not to get married otherwise."

"Has this been a problem before?" Thayden asks.

"Yes," Collin says, just as I say, "No."

"Google it." Collin gives me a last look I interpret to mean *don't screw up anything else and definitely don't get engaged.*

Chase clears his throat and looks my way. "Are you okay, man?"

"Finally, *someone* is concerned about my welfare. You are now upgraded to my favorite brother." I make the motion like I'm knighting him, then wave him off. "I'll be fine. Thayden can give me a ride home whenever he gets them to drop the charges."

Chase snorts. "Good luck with that. Sounds like you'll need it."

"I'm taking back my upgrade!"

He ignores me and shakes Thayden's hand. Then they do one of these bro-y back slap hugs. It should look dumb when a man in an expensive suit does that kind of thing, but Thayden is always smugly confident.

"You think this will stay on my record?" Chase asks.

Thayden waves a hand. "Nah. It was just a night in the drunk tank, unofficially."

"We weren't drunk!" he protests.

"And you weren't officially charged," Thayden says. "It's fine."

"You think Harper will be mad?" Chase asks me.

I chuckle. "At me and James and Collin? Yes. You, on the other hand, can do no wrong in her eyes."

"And if she is mad," Thayden drawls with a wicked gleam in his eye, "just leverage it into some good make-up—"

I slap my hands over my ears in case he's about to say the word I think he's about to say. I yell nonsense words until Thayden and Chase are laughing. Slowly, I uncover my ears, then shoot them both death stares.

"She's my sister! We don't discuss … whatever thing you weren't about to discuss because it doesn't exist!"

Thayden is still laughing after Chase leaves the room to join my brothers. I wait, arms crossed, until Thayden straightens his tie and turns to me, brows raised. "Well, well, well. You've dug yourself a nice, neat little hobbit hole, haven't you?"

"It's more of a dungeon."

Thayden lowers his voice. "Are you seriously considering getting married to help someone with a custody thing?"

Am I?

The reality is I have no idea what situation Lindy is in the middle of, only that she is in a tough spot even without what Wolf said. From her falling-down house to the thin veil of loneliness swirling around her, Lindy needs a leg up. I'm more than happy to be the leg in this particular situation.

Like I told her the other day, I want a second chance. We were so good together, and now we've been brought back together in the strangest way possible. I may not believe in signs, but I do believe in not ignoring what's right in front of you.

"Would it be ridiculous if I said yes?" I ask.

For a moment, Thayden studies my face, his eyes intense but curious. Then he breaks out in a grin and slaps me on the back. "Pat, I am the poster child for strange marriage scenarios. I'll tell you this—just because a marriage happens quickly or unconventionally doesn't make it a bad idea."

Not the answer I was expecting.

"I don't have time to tell you about my marriage," Thayden continues, "but ours was *not* the typical relationship. And Delilah is the best thing to ever happen to me. So, I'll support whatever, man. Just don't tell Collin I said so."

"Hey, lawyer-client confidentiality. It goes both ways. So, you and Delilah, huh?"

Thayden stands. "I'll give you the short version while we walk. Apparently, the courtroom is just upstairs. Gotta love small towns."

"I hate small towns," Thayden is saying an hour later as we exit the building.

I'm carrying my cowboy boots, which are almost unrecognizable with the mud caked over them. For the first time since I've known the man, Thayden looks flustered. I'll give the town of Sheet Cake this: they don't mess around.

I give him a few slaps on the back. "You'll be okay, man. Don't take the loss too hard."

He gives me a look. "Why are you smiling? You're wearing an ankle monitor. We both lost."

Thayden kicks at my ankle, which has indeed now been outfitted with a court-ordered tracking device of sorts. One that will confine me to Sheet Cake indefinitely. It also doesn't work with cowboy boots, which is the thing I'm most upset about. I don't mind being confined to this town. Actually, it couldn't be more perfect. Except for the fact that I don't have a place to stay. Or my truck. Or shoes. I'm also still covered in dried mud, which is causing chafing in several areas I'd rather not discuss.

"At least I wasn't slapped with a fine for being in contempt of court," I shoot back.

Thayden groans, shaking his head and muttering about small town judges.

"How'd you fare with Sheet Cake justice?" a voice calls.

We turn to see Chevy ambling toward us in street clothes, a wide smile on his face. Clearly, he's already heard the outcome.

I wiggle my ankle. "Is this y'all's way of inducting me as an official Sheeter?"

Chevy chuckles. "Hardly."

Thayden glances between us. "Well, fellas, it's been lovely. But I'm headed home."

"Hey—what am I paying you for? At least drive me to a hotel or to get some clean clothes and shoes."

Thayden raises his eyebrows. "You really want to pay my hourly rate to take you shopping?"

"Never mind."

"That's what I thought," Thayden says, then grins. "Plus, you've got a new friend! I'm sure Chevy here could be persuaded to take you. You might want to apologize for punching him first."

I look over at Chevy, otherwise known as the deputy I inadvertently assaulted and the reason I'm currently wearing a police-issued anklet. Chevy winks.

"Rrrrright." I clear my throat. "I'm sorry for hitting you, Chevy. I meant to hit the other guy."

He laughs. "You could have a future writing greeting cards. Best apology ever."

"Well done," Thayden says. "And good luck winning back your girl!" With that, he jogs off toward his car, leaving me with Chevy, whose eyes have narrowed considerably.

"Is your fancy lawyer talking about Lindy?"

I lean over to scratch my ankle. Dang if this thing isn't going to drive me up a wall. "Uh."

Chevy crosses his arms, and I stand back up to my full height so we're eye-to-eye. "What's that he said about you winning her back?"

I'm debating which answer is less likely to get me arrested again when Chevy's arm moves toward me. I flinch, then giggle. You know, like a real man does when faced with danger. Chevy barks out a laugh, and I realize he's holding out his hand for me to shake.

"What's this for?" I ask, clasping his hand. He squeezes uncomfortably tight, so I do the same until we're both gritting our teeth.

"We're shaking on a gentleman's agreement," Chevy says.

"What's the agreement?"

"We agree that if you hurt Lindy again, I will use everything in my power to make you suffer for as long as we both shall live."

I drop his hand, shaking mine out. He does the same. "That sounds a little like a wedding vow, Officer Chevy."

"And like a wedding vow, it's for life. Now, come on." Chevy starts off down the sidewalk at a good clip.

I follow more slowly, not sure of my alternative but not sure I like this option. "And where are we going?"

"My place," he says.

"Your place," I repeat. "Are you offering me a place to stay?"

Chevy turns, walking backward as he smiles at me. "You know what they say—keep your friends close and the people who may or may not be enemies closer. Either way, I think it's best for Sheet Cake if I keep both eyes on you."

CHAPTER FIFTEEN

Lindy

I AGREE to meet Pat for dinner entirely for selfish reasons: I haven't eaten out in a long time. That's the ONLY reason. Not because I've been thinking about the man nonstop for days now. I'm not here for the man; I'm here for the Tex-Mex. That's my theme song, folks.

I'm so desperate to prove this to myself that I inhale the first basket of chips in a record two minutes. I can't talk if my mouth's full. That's Manners 101. This single-minded focus on food also helps me ignore the almost-unignorable man across the table.

It helps. But only a little. Pat simply can't be ignored, the same way you can't miss the morning sun in a curtainless room. And he's got mass appeal; it's not just me. I've seen the way women keep eyeing him. Then they look at me, checking to see if I've got a ring on while I'm double-fisting chips.

Even as I'm licking salt off my fingers like some kind of heathen, a table of women are appraising Pat. They're awfully bold. I shoot them my best *hands-off, ladies* look. Not because I plan to have my hands ON. It's just rude to stare at a man when he's with another woman. Have they no common sense? Or self-preservation?

I can feel Pat's gaze searing into me. The heat of it is like the blast of hot air that hits you when you leave an air-conditioned building in summer. He clears his throat, and I fist my napkin in my hands, trying to draw strength from the cheap magenta cloth. I don't know how long I can keep up this charade of pretending Pat isn't there. Resisting is like opening the hatch in an airplane and trying not to get sucked out.

"More chips?" Pat asks, and my self-control snaps.

Fine! I'll look at him. Yes, he's still handsome. Yes, that's my favorite smirky smile. We've acknowledged it. Now, let's move on.

"You seem hungry," he continues, that smile rising just a fraction more.

Oh, we are, the feral cat purrs. *We arrrrrrre.*

I knew there was a reason I'm a dog person.

"I should save room for dinner," I say, taking a sip of water and sliding as far back as I can in the booth.

I fiddle with the salt shaker, but even in its rounded silver top, I can't escape Pat's face. Ugh! The man is a plague. *A plague of total hotness.*

"How did you get here?" I ask. "I heard you don't have a car, just an ankle monitor. And how'd you get my number, anyway?"

"Chevy. On both counts." He nods toward the bar.

My head snaps up, and Chevy waves from where he's

parked in front of the margarita machines and a TV showing some football game. *The traitor!* I hope my stare adequately conveys the ways in which he'll pay for this later. It must, because he ducks his head and turns back to the television.

"So," I say.

"A needle," Pat answers with a broad grin, and my stomach flutters.

This is a game. OUR game. I'm supposed to say *far* next, to which he'll add *a long, long way*. It's our shorthand version of the famous song from *The Sound of Music*.

Back when Pat and I dated, we spoke our own language peppered with movie quotes and song lyrics. And though we spent little time with friends and none with family—per our rules—anyone hanging out with us for more than a few minutes got seriously irritated.

"Which brings us back to *so*." My restrained smile has Pat practically wiggling with delight. The man is like an overgrown puppy sometimes. I wish it weren't so endearing.

"You remember," Pat says, his voice bright. I can only nod. His look turns assessing. "You just don't seem to want to."

I fumble for words, finally settling on the very lame, "It's hard, looking back."

Hard being with him. Hard not wanting to climb over the top of the booth to sit in his lap. Hard maintaining this emotional barrier, to keep the vest fastened tightly around my heart.

"I'm sorry," Pat says. "I know I said it, but I can keep saying it until you believe it—I'm so sorry I hurt you."

"You don't have to keep saying it."

What's different about Pat now? I can't quite put a name to it. Could it be—maturity?

Pat has maintained the same boyish charm, the effusive

and effervescent joy that drew me to him in the first place. His dark eyes always seemed to hold mischief, and that hasn't changed. There is the slightest crinkle now in their corners. Not laugh lines yet, but a hint of where they'll be one day. He still has the broad shoulders, the sheer power barely contained by his clothes. He looks like a slab of perfectly cut stone, aged to perfection.

I've been staring too long. My eyes snap to his, waiting for a teasing comment asking if I like what I see.

"Are you sure you don't want more chips?" Pat asks instead.

"Maybe just one more basket."

I need something to do with my hands other than grab this man by his shirt, something to do with my mouth so it doesn't get any ideas.

It would be so easy to stop fighting this.

I don't know where that thought came from, but I serve it up an eviction notice, effective immediately. Begone, ye trespasser!

Pat signals a waiter. We place our orders as another server brings fresh chips and salsa. Then, it's just me, Pat, and the chips again. Their crunch is carrying the conversation.

"So, your family bought Sheet Cake, huh?" I ask.

Pat gives me a wry grin. "Did I not mention that the other day?"

"You did not."

"It was Tank's idea. A family project of sorts. He roped me into it—which wasn't hard when I found out which town he bought. Now, we're just trying to get my brothers on board. What are the odds, right? My dad happens to buy *your* town."

"Don't tell me you think it's a sign," I say.

"I don't think it's *not* a sign. And now, thanks to this very stylish ankle monitor, I'll be here for the foreseeable future."

I heard about that hours ago from Winnie who heard from Chevy. Her brother clearly did not tell her all the details, like the fact he gave Pat my number and drove him to meet me for dinner.

"Thank you for agreeing to have dinner with me," Pat says.

"What can I say? I'm a sucker for Tex-Mex."

"I remember. You could almost out-eat me. But only in tacos. Remember that time we tried the—"

"Taco buffet," we say in unison.

I don't even try to hold back the goofy grin on my face. It feels slightly painful, like the muscles in my face aren't used to making such happy expressions. "I shouldn't have tried to keep up with you, plate for plate, taco for taco."

Pat chuckles. "It wasn't your best idea."

"One of my worst. But I didn't throw up!"

"No—you just had to lie very, very still on the couch for a few hours. And if I so much as touched you with a pinky finger, you screamed."

"You just couldn't keep your hands off me."

"No," he says, his eyes darkening. "I couldn't."

The heat in his gaze and the memory of his touch flips some kind of primal switch in me. The thing is, it's not just physical with me and Pat. It never was. He always reached some much deeper level in me, and he still does.

Now, I want to kick myself for tumbling face-first into his flirt-trap, leading us on a comfortable stroll down Memory Lane. It's a little overgrown and unkempt, but the views are still good. I need to reroute back to Heck No Highway.

I shoot Pat a narrow-eyed look and gesture between us. "This isn't happening."

Pat blinks with innocent Bambi eyes. *"This ...* as in dinner together? Sharing a basket of chips? Talking like normal people?"

"We aren't just any normal people. Not to each other."

The easy grin slides off Pat's face, replaced by something gut-clenchingly sincere.

Oh no! Bring back the flirt—I can handle that guy! The tender, vulnerable version of Pat ... not so much.

He reaches for me, and I tuck my hands under my thighs for safekeeping. His hand drops to the table, palm up, like he's keeping the offer open, just in case I change my mind.

I shift uncomfortably. "Why did you ask me to dinner? What's your agenda? And don't say you want to catch up for old times' sake."

"I wasn't going to say that. Though I do want to catch up." He bites his lip, studies my face, and sighs.

"Just spit it out. You're killing me with the suspense."

"I couldn't help but hear what Wolf said earlier." His lip curls a little at Wolf's name. "If what he's said is true, I want to help."

I shudder at his use of the h-word. Val may be right that I have an aversion to asking for and taking help. It takes me an extra beat to realize what Pat is saying. In a far less romantic way than Wolf did—which is saying something—I think Pat is offering to marry me.

Which *can't* be what he's saying.

Thankfully the waiter brings over our plates at that moment. "Very hot," he says, sliding a skillet of fajitas and all the fixings in front of me. I ordered fajitas because it requires assembly. Distraction for the win! And I definitely need it.

"No," I say, unrolling my silverware from the napkin.

"But I haven't even told you—"

"Still no."

Pat shifts in his seat, leaning forward with his elbows on the table, those nice forearms fully on display. His forearms are like an appetizer, a tease compared to the main course of his biceps and shoulders and pecs and abs and—

My skillet pops loudly, making me jump. Grease spatters right on the forearm I was just ogling. Pat hisses, jerking back. Before I can stop them, my hands are moving. I dunk my cloth napkin in ice water, holding Pat's arm in place while I press the cool napkin to the tiny red burns on his skin. Carefully, I draw us away from the danger zone of my sizzling skillet.

But now we're in a totally different danger zone, with another kind of heat sizzling between us. Our eyes lock, and awareness makes my skin feel heavy and tight. The years we've lost and the weight of my complicated feelings do nothing to stifle the electricity between us. Pat's thumb grazes the inside of my wrist, and I'm in danger of combusting on the spot, taking the whole restaurant with me in a blaze of glory.

And that just won't do.

I pull my hands away and hold out the napkin. "Here. Put this on the burns."

Pat shakes his head. "I'm all right. It's nothing."

"Good."

I focus on my food and take way more time than necessary to assemble a single fajita. This is the most carefully crafted fajita in the history of fajitas. Culinary schools could use it as an example for students. It still breaks apart in the middle when I take a bite. Juice runs down my arm, and before I think about it, I drag my tongue over the drip before it can reach my elbow.

When I look up, Pat is watching, open-mouthed, his

espresso eyes turning to a darker roast right in front of me. "You missed a bit," he says, shifting toward me.

Oh, no. I've seen this before in the movies. It starts with *You've got a little something right here,* and the guy goes to wipe whipped cream or some other sexy food (it's ALWAYS sexy food) from the corner of the heroine's mouth. Then, BAM! It's one of those kissing scenes with the swelling music and the heavy breathing.

I grab a napkin, practically scrubbing all my exposed skin from any hint of food. Those CSI guys and their little kit would find nothing on me.

Well. Nothing but napkin fibers.

"I've got it. See? Totally clean now. Like a newborn baby." I make a face. "Actually, newborns aren't very clean. They also don't sleep more than two to three hours at a time, so that whole sleeping like a baby thing is some kind of conspiracy theory."

Pat tilts his head, looking amused. "Did you think I was going to … lick your arm clean?"

Maybe. But it sounds ridiculous now that he's said it out loud. Also, Pat shouldn't be allowed to say the word *lick* ever again. It's way too visceral, too sensual.

"I was just going to offer you my napkin," he says. "The way you offered yours to me."

"I don't want to be your napkin buddy. I've got enough of those already."

Pat just stares, blinking in confusion, because what even is a napkin buddy? And what does it mean if I have a lot of them? Fantastic. Now I'm the napkin hussy of Sheet Cake.

Pat coughs, and I think he's hiding laughter behind his hand, because his shoulders are shaking. Whatever. Laugh away. See if I share napkins with you again.

I decide to save myself more embarrassing messes and eat

my fajita from a plate with a fork, which is just wrong. But it will require no tongues and no napkins and no use of the word *lick*.

Of course, just as I think this, I drop a caramelized onion in my lap.

"About what I said," Pat starts.

"We can pretend you didn't say anything," I tell him, stabbing a piece of beef with my fork. Perhaps a little more violently than necessary.

Pat sighs. "I know you don't like accepting help, or even admitting you need it—"

I set my fork down and curl my hands into fists in my lap. "After all this time, you can waltz in and think you know me?"

My words are harsh, but my tone is calm and cucumbers-on-ice cool. I could be talking about mathematical equations. All my eye contact is reserved for my tortilla, which is the kind of date I like: it keeps its mouth shut.

"I'd like to think I *do* know you."

"And I'd like to think I could pick the winning lotto numbers. Doesn't mean I can."

Pat frowns, and I realize he hasn't touched anything on his plate, while I've blown through two fajitas. Albeit with a fork, but they end up in the same place. Is the man even going to eat? Or is he planning on letting his enchiladas get cold while running his mouth? That's a waste, right there. In a show of protest, I pick up my fork and resume eating.

Pat clears his throat. "I loved you."

I drop my fork. It falls somewhere under the table on the Saltillo tile, probably never to be seen again.

"You couldn't have."

"I did," Pat says. "I did, and I realized this week I still do. I love you, Lindy."

I feel like I'm standing on an iceberg cracking into pieces. Only, the iceberg is my heart, and it's coming apart because it's thawing. I'm left on some tiny block of ice, floating away and watching the devastation.

Thawing is good. Not having a frozen heart is good, I try to tell myself.

But no—it's NOT good. Haven't we all seen the commercial? The one with the ice caps melting and that poor mama polar bear trying to find a space to live with her cubs? Thawing is definitely bad, at least when it comes to Pat.

He *loves* me? The nerve of him! I refuse to accept his words.

"You are not allowed," I tell him in the most reasonable tone possible.

His brows lift. "I'm not allowed to tell you I love you?"

"You're not allowed to tell me, and you aren't allowed to think you mean it."

"I don't think I mean it. I mean it."

"Absolutely not. You can't show up here, give me an apology one day, then say I love you a few days later. It's unacceptable."

We glare at each other across the table in what has to be one of the strangest arguments ever. Finally, Pat seems to concede, rubbing his jaw.

"What would be an acceptable number of days to wait, then?"

Not conceding. Apparently, he was just regrouping.

"None. No days." I wave my hand and the server passing by thinks I'm signaling him to clear my plate. When he tries to take my now-cool fajita platter, I grab it with both hands, hunching my body over it protectively like Gollum. I think I might have even hissed.

What is wrong with me?

"Sorry." The waiter mutters something else under his breath in Spanish that might be *I'm sorry* or maybe *Don't come between the woman and her fajitas.*

I realize Chevy is watching me with wide eyes from across the restaurant. My ridiculous display is at least partly his fault. When I tell Winnie that her brother helped Pat contact me, maybe she'll join me in exacting revenge. Chevy withers under my gaze and turns back to the bartender. I try to retain what tiny shred of dignity I have, uncurling my fingers from the platter and sitting up straight.

"You can have mine too if you want," Pat says, pushing his plate toward me. "I mean, if you're that hungry."

I'm not hungry. I'm *angry*. I'm also having some kind of adrenaline spike, whether I want to or not, whether I believe him or not because *Pat said he loves me*. Even thinking it again threatens to overload my system. Inside my brain, red lights are flashing, and one of those blaring alarms sounds. I imagine men in white coats running around, waving their arms ineffectually. A total reset is imminent.

"You don't want your enchiladas?" I ask, ignoring the complete pandemonium in my head.

Pat shakes his head slowly. "I want to marry you."

And … there goes the reset. An MRI of my brain would show only a blank computer screen with a blinking cursor.

Pat.

Wants.

To.

Marry.

Me.

With a whir and a hum, I'm back online, baby, and right back to angry. "That's even worse!"

"Why? Would it be so bad to marry me?"

Actually, no. I can imagine folding Pat right into my tiny life. Only, he wouldn't fit. He wouldn't last. I'm just another shiny object to him, another exciting new thing to try before he gets bored. I mean, supermodels and actresses couldn't keep Pat. How in the world would I?

And when he left, where would I be? Still here, alone with Jo, heart-broken for a second time.

Pat frowns. "And why is asking you to marry me worse than saying I love you?"

"People throw *love* around all the time. I *love* this fajita and I *love* my cowboy boots and I *love* the latest Adele album. Saying *marry me* is like putting your money where your mouth is."

Pat leans back, crossing his arms. "Then, that's what I'm doing. I love you, and I'm putting my money where my mouth is. Marry me, Lindy."

"You are ridiculous."

"I am, actually. But I'm also very, very serious about this. About you and Jo."

Pat leans forward now, steepling his fingers and giving me his best Very Serious Face. I've never seen him maintain this expression for more than ten seconds, tops. I count the seconds until more than half a minute has passed. He still hasn't cracked.

But I have. My response is to go back to my original plan: stuff food into my face. With my fingers now, since I lost my fork. I've eaten almost everything that came with my meal, even the parsley garnish and the little taco cup holding the sour cream.

"I can't change the mistakes I made," Pat says. "I know I gave you every reason not to trust me. I don't know if I can convince you how sincere I am. But I'm going to try."

I shake my head. *You don't need to do that* is what I want to say. My mouth is full, so what comes out is more like *Moofomeedtovovat.*

Pat seems versed in Lindy-mouth-full-speak, because he answers like he understood perfectly. "I know I don't *need* to convince you I mean it. But I'm going to. Whether you want me to or not."

I finally manage to swallow. "We are living in the age of consent. And I say no. I do not consent to this."

"I'm all for consent. But I won't ask your permission to prove I love you." His voice lowers. "Now, when it comes to kissing you, I'll wait until I'm sure you want it."

My thoughts catch on the word *kissing*, and I'm staring at Pat's lips when they start curving up in a smile.

"I will respect you," Pat says, and *why won't he stop talking? It just keeps getting worse!* "I *do* respect you. But I will keep coming after you like the Terminator."

I am a jittery mess. My brain is still trying to find its way around basic programming after the forced reset, which is the only way I can explain what comes out of my mouth next.

"Which version? The T-800 or the T-1000?"

Pat stares at me with surprise that morphs into awe and pure pleasure. I've gone back to speaking his language, *our* language. I'm horrified as my mouth keeps going.

"Because I think I could handle the T-800. But the T-1000 …" I shake my head. "That one, I'm not so sure about."

Who am I and what have I done with Lindy? The bitter, shriveled-up version of myself I've grown cozy with? I feel a strange warmth spreading in my chest. It feels a lot like waking up.

The warmth grows as Pat begins to laugh. It's the kind of laugh that makes heads turn and conversations cease. He has no shame, no pride, and no concern at all for what anyone in this room thinks of him. Except me. I command his full, rapt attention and, based on his expression, adoration.

Pat throws his head back, howling with laughter. I can see his pulse jumping, and when his Adam's apple moves, a cloud opens above, beaming down a ray of sunshine on his perfection. The throat is an underrated and unbelievably sexy part of a man, if you ask me.

"This is one of the things I love about you," Pat says, finally recovering. "You are *fire*."

I hold up a finger. "If you utter so much as *one* Backstreet Boys lyric, I will end you."

He puts a hand over his heart. "I'd never. You know I've always been Team NSYNC. I still hope Justin and Britney will find their way back to each other."

"You would."

This is the strangest, most intense conversation I've ever had, and I'm suddenly exhausted. I'm so worn down that I think if Pat were to ask me the marriage question again, a *yes* might pop out of my mouth. I don't think I could stop it.

When Pat grabs my hand, I'm not quick enough to move away. Or maybe I don't want to. His hand, warm and strong and instantly reminding me of a thousand and one good memories, envelops mine. He links our fingers, and I can't help the sigh that escapes me.

We are holding hands.

We. Are. Holding. Hands.

I want to pull away. I also want to climb over the table and kiss him until we get kicked out of the restaurant, then continue making out in the parking lot like a couple of teenagers.

I want to tell him off.

I want to forgive him.

I want—

My throat grows tight, not used to the swell of emotion. I keep things lake-calm in my life, a glassy waterfront on a warm, breezeless day.

Pat is a tempest, blowing a surging storm of waves and wind my way. I haven't felt anything this strongly in years. I haven't *allowed* myself to feel. It's simultaneously refreshing and terrifying.

I love it; I hate it.

But inarguably, I feel fully *alive*.

"Lindy, I want to marry you," Pat says, and that tempest becomes a tsunami.

I blink. Swallow. Remind myself to breathe. I tell my heart it needs to start back up and do its job so I don't drop dead in this vinyl booth, my hair forever smelling like grilled onions.

"This isn't how I wanted to ask you," Pat says, squeezing my fingers. "But Chevy told me about Jo and the custody hearing. I figured there was no point in waiting."

My stomach sinks. Chevy told Pat I *need* a husband. Pat wants to *help*. He wants to marry me because I need *help*.

I'm not an idiot—Pat isn't asking just because he's a nice guy and wants to help. Our chemistry is its own living thing. It has a zip code. He at least *thinks* he loves me. This proposal isn't just an offer of charity. But he also wouldn't be asking me right NOW if it weren't because of Jo. Of that, I'm certain.

His offer is like a mixed cocktail including five types of alcohol, the kind that tastes delicious and leaves you wishing you were dead the next morning.

I open my mouth to answer, though I have no idea what I'm going to say. Before I can speak a word, a mariachi band descends on us. Surrounding Pat, they begin a rousing version of happy birthday. There are at least ten people involved. One is playing guitar and another shakes maracas in a way that would make his mama proud. One guy's job seems to be just making celebratory noises which are all at ear-piercing decibels.

Our server plops an oversized sombrero on Pat's head and then smacks a dollop of whipped cream right on his nose. My side of the booth is momentarily clear, and I take advantage of the distraction to make my escape.

"Lindy, wait!" Pat calls. I ignore him.

Chevy, who is a dead man ten times over, is laughing and slapping his knees at the bar, while Pat, still in the sombrero and a face full of whipped cream, tries to fight his way through the band.

I bolt for the front doors before Pat and his terrible ideas that sound way, way too tempting can catch up to me.

CHAPTER SIXTEEN

Pat

WHEN WE CLIMB into his Mustang, Chevy is still laughing, and I'm still wiping whipped cream off my nose. I normally enjoy a good prank, but Chevy telling the waitstaff it was my birthday gave Lindy the chance to escape. Not that I can totally blame her. My proposal sucked. Hardcore. Even Wolf Waters with his drumline topped it.

The engine purrs to life, and I bend down to scratch at my skin under the ankle monitor. "Thanks for having my back in there, man. I kinda thought we had a whole bromance thing going on."

Chevy wipes the tears off his cheeks, still chuckling. "Too soon to tell on the bromance, but I appreciate the offer."

Honestly, other than the mariachi band, Chevy has been far kinder than I would be, if the roles were reversed. After he picked me up at the municipal building, Chevy took me to his place to shower, let me borrow some clothes, then to Walmart for toiletries and—*shudder*—a temporary wardrobe. For the foreseeable future, I'll be staying in his guest room.

I had the impression Chevy was a laid-back, stereotypical single guy. I would have expected him to drive a big truck and have the kind of bachelor pad where beer cans are the coffee table décor. But he restored the 1967 Ford Mustang we're currently riding in. He also renovated and decorated his farmhouse bungalow, which has all the charm Lindy's falling-apart house lacks. Apparently, Chevy is a small-town deputy who likes home improvement, restoring old cars, and could moonlight as an interior designer.

Oh, and he also likes pranks.

I just hope he can take as good as he gives, because it is ON. Maybe when I'm not dependent on his hospitality.

"Look, man," he says, his big hands flexing on the wheel, "I'm willing to give you a chance, even though this whole town knows you broke Lindy's heart once already."

He glances over to see how I'm reacting to his statement. I have no idea what emotion my face is showing because I have like seven different ones stirring up inside me. Usually I'm all about the words, but right now, silence seems like the best option.

"I get the sense you're a decent guy. Despite the past and that one time you punched me. I'd even go so far as to say I might support your efforts to win Lindy back."

"Really? Because I get the sense you and the town would love to throw me out." I shake my ankle monitor. "Except for this."

"And that is also interesting," Chevy says, nodding down at my ankle. "I've never known Judge Judie to hand out one of those. She generally leans toward the side of go to jail, go directly to jail, or pay super high fines. I've never seen her issue an ankle monitor. Especially to a non-Sheeter."

"Huh. So, what does that mean, you think?"

A slow grin overtakes his face. "I think," he says carefully, "it means some people in the town might actually be willing to give you a chance. They want you here for some reason. And it's not just because our team needs another win this year."

In addition to my anklet, the judge handed out a community service—a very specific kind of community service as an assistant coach to the high school football team. Chevy is the other assistant coach, and he's already warned me that the head coach is worthless and seems to have one foot out the door.

"Yeah? Why? Y'all barely know me. And I haven't made a good showing so far."

Chevy hums an agreement. "I can't speak for Judge Judie. But call it a hunch. I kinda like you. And I think Lindy does too, despite all her protests."

"Really? Because she just ran out on me when I proposed."

Chevy gives me a quick glance, his face shocked. "You were *proposing?*"

"Not well. But yeah. I think I bombed even before the mariachi band."

"Dude," Chevy says. "No one proposes over a fajita skillet. Even Wolf Waters and his drumline tops that."

Ain't that the truth. "Sometimes I can be ... impulsive. But the proposal was real."

For a few awkward beats, Chevy is silent, with just the roar of the engine cutting through the quiet. "Let me get this straight. You want to marry Lindy—after just now seeing her again for the first time in years?"

"I do."

"And you know you'd be getting Jo, like a package deal? I'm not saying anything about Jo—she's the best. Not every guy wants to raise some other guy's kid or is ready to be thrust into a dad role. Plus, all the legal drama—you want to propose knowing all that?"

Maybe Chevy's list of things should make me want to back down. I'm pretty sure he's testing me. It only makes me feel more determined, even more sure of my decision.

"Yeah. I do."

"Well, then. Maybe my hunch is correct." Chevy pulls the Mustang to a stop and leans against his door, eyeing me. "You know where we are?"

I glance out at the dark road ahead, lit only by the moon. The only things I can see are fields and fences in all directions. "A deserted stretch of road perfect for offing someone and hiding the body?"

He chuckles, leaning across to open my door. "A little dark, buddy. More like a good place to let you walk home and think about what you've done."

"Seriously?"

He nods. "My house is two miles straight ahead."

Grumbling, I climb out of his car, then lean down to meet his gaze. "If this is how it's gonna be, I might fully rescind my bromance offer."

"Fair enough. But lemme ask you—wouldn't your brothers do the same?"

I don't even have to think about that one. "They'd do worse."

Chevy chuckles and gives me a little wave. "See you at home, honey."

I close the door, listening to the purr of his engine fade as I start to walk, ankle monitor itching a little more with each step. If this town wants me to eat humble pie, I'll tie a plastic bib around my neck and put my face right in it. Whatever it takes.

I've had about ten minutes to walk and think about how stupid it was to propose to Lindy the way I did when my phone starts to buzz. I'm honestly shocked I get any reception out here.

"Hey, Pops."

Tank's voice is a little garbled. "How is it being stuck in Sheet Cake? What are you up to?"

I'm passing a broken-down shed and a few cows. "Just out for a stroll."

"You can do that?" he asks. "I thought you were under house arrest."

"More like *town* arrest. I can't leave Sheet Cake. Guess I'm here for a while, even if James never changes his mind about Dark Horse."

Dad hums and says something I can't hear through static. Only the last part is clear. "… stubborn brother. How are things with your girl?"

"I asked her to marry me."

Might as well drop that bomb now, let him get used to the idea before I try again. This time with a plan and a *real* proposal, one that will show Lindy how serious I am. Tank is quiet for a few moments, and I check to see if we're still connected. We are. "You still there? Did I cause a coronary?"

"I'm here," Tank says. "Just thinking. Do you know what you're doing, son?"

"It may not look like it, but for the first time in a long time, I really, really do."

He's quiet again, and I brace myself for a lecture on wise decisions—to which I'll argue the point that he's one to talk after purchasing a whole town. Instead, Dad is choked up when he speaks again. "If that's the case, then I want you to have your mother's ring."

I'm so shocked, I stop and lean on a nearby fence post, a wave of emotion hitting me. I grip the rough wood, closing my eyes and swaying slightly.

"Dad, I can't take that."

"Your mother and I had time to talk through this before she passed. She wanted the first of you boys to have it. We never told you, and honestly, I wasn't sure if I'd ever get the chance to pass it on. If this is the woman you want to spend your life with, it's yours."

"I—thank you. Wow."

Whatever he says next is lost to static, and our connection cuts out a moment later. I'm honestly relieved, because I'm standing by a deserted country road, crying like a little kid.

Lindy hasn't even said yes. She didn't say no, either, but that's hardly a shining endorsement. The thought of my mom's ring and having my parents' blessing only makes me want to prove myself to Lindy more.

I don't feel worthy of Lindy or of my mom's ring. But I will be. I will.

I hear a shuffle and look over to see a cow imposing on my private moment. I wipe my cheeks, making eye contact with the nosy bovine.

"What are you looking at?" I demand, and in answer, it lifts its tail and leaves a fresh pile of cow patties. "You're a real mood killer, Bessie. You know that?"

The cow does not seem particularly concerned with my insult and turns back to the herd. Sighing, I tuck my phone into my pocket and resume my walk, refusing to take Bessie's response as any kind of sign.

CHAPTER SEVENTEEN

Lindy

"Tell me you have some good news," I say to Ashlee, wedging the phone between my ear and shoulder as I grab my purse from the car and slam the door.

Honestly, the legal battle over Jo is the last thing I want to think about after bolting from the restaurant and from Pat. I sent the bat signal—AKA a 911 text—to Val and Winnie, so they're on their way. I'd love to shut off my brain until my friends arrive, but Ashlee's voicemail sounded ominous. I'd rather hear from her now rather than having to go to sleep tonight with a sense of unknown, impending doom.

Known impending doom is better by far.

Ashlee sighs, and the small sound makes my heart tumble. Maybe I was wrong, and unknown doom is better. "First, I want to apologize again for Kim. She's been fired, but I know the damage was done."

Turns out, Kim *was* eavesdropping, and not just on me. She's been dating Billy Waters on the down-low, so she let Billy know all kinds of confidential client information, including what Ashlee and I discussed. Though the brothers aren't on the best terms, somehow Wolf got the info out of Billy, leading to the second-weirdest proposal of my life.

Pat's Mexican restaurant proposal wins out, even without the drumline.

"I want to be honest with you," Ashlee says. "I think it's going to be more of a battle than we hoped it would be."

I lean against the car, needing its support, while Ashlee tells me what her private investigator discovered about Rachel. Which is … nothing. She actually seems to have turned her life around. At least, on paper. She did rehab, attends weekly AA meetings, holds several volunteer positions in the community, and, of course, has the wealthy tech bigwig husband to create the ideal two-parent household. They live in a big house zoned to a great school.

Rachel may be clean now, she may look great on paper, but I can't help but feel like her underlying issues are still, well, *issues*. At any point, she could have called me or come by the house. She could have initiated contact personally, rather than through legal channels. It doesn't seem like the priority is to be a mom to Jo, but more like Rachel simply doesn't want me to have her daughter. She doesn't want me to *win*.

But if we're stacking the odds and placing bets, my money might be on Rachel. She has three things I don't: the indisputable biological title of mother, money, and a husband.

But I could have a husband. One with money.

I feel ill even considering Pat's proposal in this context. It makes me feel like I'm no better than one of those cleat chasers. Tabitha's words come to mind, and I know what people would think of me if I married Pat. But he could provide me with two out of those three things Rachel has that I currently don't.

I bite the inside of my cheek. I don't want to use Pat. I *never* wanted to use Pat. Yet I am desperate to keep Jo. Not for selfish reasons, though it would kill me to lose her. I cannot imagine a world in which Rachel, a virtual stranger, is the best choice for *Jo*.

The thing is: I *want* to marry Pat for me too. The idea is so alluring. *Pat* is so alluring. My heart wants him. My body wants him. That deep soul-place only Pat has ever reached wants him. The feral cat most definitely wants him.

But I am terrified to let him in again. He seems more mature. He seems sincere. Whether Pat can truly remain in one place or a place like Sheet Cake long term is anyone's guess. And I can't allow myself or Jo to be hurt when he bails.

Maybe he won't bail. Maybe he really has changed.

Is he a risk I can bet on?

"Are you still with me?" Ashlee asks.

"Yep. Just processing."

"I am going to make the best case we can for you. You've raised Jo all these years. She's happy and healthy and has roots here with you. Abandonment isn't looked at kindly."

"Yeah, but Rachel is her biological mom. And like you said, Rachel has the stable life and the financial security I don't have."

"I wish I could say that's not true, but those things certainly are factors."

Ashlee goes quiet for a moment, and I tilt my head back, looking up at the pinprick stars punching through the deep velvet sky. Most nights, the starry sky soothes me and gives me perspective. Feeling small in the universe leaves me with a strange sense of peace, like my problems can't be SO huge.

Tonight, it's not working. A garbage truck has backed up to the curb of my life and emptied 30,000 pounds of trash onto my front lawn. Not even the stars can make my problems look small tonight.

"Thanks for everything, Ashlee."

"Don't sound like we've already lost, Lindy."

But it's hard to muster up any kind of hope.

After we hang up, I give myself a few minutes to just breathe. The early October air is crisp, not quite cool. Even so, I feel cold down to my bones.

When I unlock the door, I'm greeted with the sight of a sparklingly clean kitchen. I almost have to shade my eyes from the shine coming off the counters. Even the floor sparkles. This can mean only one thing: Deedee and her boyfriend must have broken up. Again.

The teenage babysitter in question has not only scrubbed every conceivable surface but dealt with the pile of dirty dishes that had been growing like a small, filthy city in my sink.

I wish when I was feeling sad, I took solace in something productive like cleaning. Usually, I keep it simple—wallowing in pints of ice cream or disappearing into a black hole of research online, like finding all the women George Clooney has been romantically linked to. That one distracted me for a good week.

I find Deedee in the first-floor bathroom scrubbing the grout with a toothbrush. Unfortunately, it looks like MY toothbrush. On the plus side, my grout has never looked better. It's apparently white underneath all the dirt. Who knew? I'm both disgusted and kind of amazed by this.

I lean on the door frame. "Huh. I always thought the grout was gray."

Deedee jumps up like she's been caught going through my underwear drawer rather than scrubbing my grimy tile. "Oh, my word! You scared the dickens out of me!"

Deedee talks like she stepped straight out of another decade, which I usually find amusing, but tonight I'm distracted by her red-rimmed eyes. Looks like my theory about a breakup with Mark is indeed correct. As if to illustrate the point, she wipes away a tear, and we both pretend not to notice.

"Sorry," I tell her. "I didn't mean to scare you."

"Want me to finish?"

I look down, seeing the clear line of how far she reached with the scrubbing. "Nah. I'll do it later."

Later, as in never.

Deedee tucks her honey-colored hair behind her ear and sets my ruined toothbrush on the counter. We reconvene in the kitchen, where she picks up her purse, playing nervously with the strap while I pay her through an app. I'm grateful for technology like this, because it allows me to pretend like money isn't real. If money isn't real, my money *problems* aren't real. Everyone wins!

"I hope it's okay I straightened up," Deedee says. With someone else, I'd think they were fishing for a compliment. But I can tell Deedee wonders if she overstepped a boundary.

"It looks great in here. I wish I could pay you double since you did the work of a babysitter and a housekeeper."

She waves me off. "That's okay, Ms. Darcy." I wince at the name. "Sorry. I mean, Miss Lindy."

I understand that parents want to teach their kids to be respectful. Deedee and her two younger sisters are the picture of manners. However, when you're in your twenties, being called Ms. is like hearing a trombone playing at your funeral.

"How were things with Jo?"

Deedee smiles big, and it's like someone tossed a match on to instant light charcoal in my heart. "We had a great time. She's so amazing."

Her compliment makes my heart swell with pride. Jo *is* amazing. Anyone who can see that is automatically on my good list for life.

I raise my eyebrows. "She didn't give you any trouble about going to bed?"

Deedee bites her lip and smiles. "Just a little. I had to read her a few chapters of *Harry Potter and the Sorcerer's Stone*, and then she was fine."

That's Jo. Colorer of *Jaws* pictures and reader of all things wizarding world. I love that girl. And Rachel would never understand or appreciate her uniqueness.

"And how are things with you?" I ask carefully.

Deedee is not just a crier, she's a hysterical crier once she gets going. Val and Winnie will be here any minute, and I need to be able to get Deedee out of the house. If Val sees Deedee crying, Val will start crying, and then it's all over.

The easy smile slides right off Deedee's face like ice cream from the top of a cone in summer. "Okay, I guess."

I'd like to set the dogs after Mark. Actually, the dogs would probably just lick him. I'd like to set feral hogs after him. That might be too violent. What comes between dogs and hogs? I have no idea.

Maybe the kid isn't so bad, though he is a Waters. It's hard to fight against bad genetics. They're misogynistic pigs, Wolf aside, and he has his own oddities. I'm sure there's a reason Deedee keeps falling for Mark (and I hope that reason isn't codependency). But they've broken up more times than

I can count, and he's usually the one doing the breaking. He doesn't deserve someone as sweet as Deedee. At all.

She looks like she's about to say more, but then we both see the headlights coming down the driveway. The dogs start barking, running to the back door. Deedee scrambles to gather her things, which include a giant purse with knitting needles poking out of the top. She truly is an old soul, and I wish she could find someone much better than Mark if he's not going to appreciate her.

"Let me know if you need me this weekend," Deedee says, fighting her way past the dogs to the door. "I should be free."

Her smile wavers and her eyes shine with unshed tears. If it weren't for the slamming of car doors outside, I'd make her sit down at the kitchen table and let her tell me all about the breakup. Then I'd warn her away from all men with the Waters last name—or any name with the letters A-Z.

Deedee slips out the side door just as Val and Winnie come in. Elvis almost makes it inside, but Winnie manages to shoo him out with her peep-toe pumps. Val comes straight to me, giving me a massive hug I feel down to my bones.

"Thanks, Valley Girl."

"Love ya, Linds." She pats me twice on the shoulder and then grabs a few bottles of water.

I eye the ingredients Winnie is pulling out of a paper bag: vodka, limes, and what looks like a big pile of herbs. "Wow. This looks serious," I say.

Winnie only snorts.

Val gives me an *are you for real?* face. "You got proposed to, chica. I'd say that's serious."

I stamp my foot. "How did y'all know?"

"Neighborly," they say at the same time.

"Winnie, your app is genius but also evil."

"Thank you," she says.

I wouldn't be shocked if people know what color underwear I'm wearing on any given day. Not that Winnie would let that kind of post stay up. She's told me and Val many times that we don't even want to know how many gross posts and photos she deletes on a weekly basis.

We move from the cramped kitchen to the cramped living room with waters and whatever drinks Winnie made. Val and I take the couch while Winnie perches on Jo's reading chair, the worn denim glider Mama and I purchased when Jo was an infant.

"Are you sure we won't wake Jo?" Val asks, glancing toward the door to Jo's room.

"Nope. She sleeps like the dead."

After she read the first Harry Potter book, Jo requested to move underneath the stairs. The tiny room was originally a canning room, extra pantry, or some kind of closet. It's narrow and has only one small window, plus the slanted ceiling. She's always liked little spaces, and there is barely enough room for her twin bed and all her books in there. You have to crawl in from the bottom of the mattress, which I do every night to snuggle her to sleep. I was supposed to install some bookshelves or have custom built-ins made, but it's on the long list of projects I can't afford. All the available space in the room has towers of books, organized by size and color.

"One post-proposal cocktail for you," Winnie says, handing me a glass.

I stare down at it, hoping it's not TOO much vodka. Even without Jo waking me up early, I'm not a big drinker. It's hard to be when I have a sister who's an addict. Alcohol was only her gateway to drugs, but still. Part of me worries I might start to like alcohol too much, and another part feels like I'm doing something wrong when I drink.

Tonight, though, I'm not going to argue.

"What is this?"

"I'm calling this a Dual Po-Pro," Winnie says, and when Val and I just stare at her, she rolls her eyes. "Po-Pro for post-proposal and Dual because you got proposed to twice today. And don't worry—it's not very strong."

Val takes a sip and gives an appreciative nod. "It should really be Duo or maybe Dos. Dual implies the proposals happened at the same time."

"Fine. Dos Po-Pro," Winnie says. "Happy now?"

"Yes."

I take a sip, and it's actually very refreshing. And a little … spicy? "What's in it? It looked like you brought a whole salad with you."

"Ew. Who would put salad in a drink? It's vodka, club soda, a little simple syrup, lime juice, mint, and some grated fresh ginger," Winnie says. "You like?"

"It's perfect. Light and fresh." Exactly the opposite of how I feel. If I were a drink flavor, I'd be heavy and hopeless with a garnish of pessimism.

Beast hops up into Val's lap, almost knocking over her drink. I close my eyes as I swing my feet up on the old trunk I use as a coffee table. Any minute now, the inquisition will begin.

As if on cue, Val nudges my foot with hers on the trunk. "Wanna start talking or are you going to make us drag it out of you?"

I sigh, looking down into my drink. "I don't know where to start."

"How about starting with Pat's proposal?" Val suggests. "Was it romantic?"

"It was over chips in a Mexican restaurant, so no. I wouldn't call it romantic."

"Two proposals in one day and I don't see you wearing a ring. Heartbreaker," Winnie says appreciatively, lifting her glass. "Good for you."

Val tosses a balled-up napkin at Winnie. "Let the woman talk. And who says it's automatically the right thing for her to say no?" She turns to me. "Wait—*did* you say no?"

"I didn't actually answer. I sort of just ran."

"But you *wanted* to say no, right?" Winnie presses.

It's not that Winnie is anti-man. But after helping scrape me up off the ground like a chewed-up piece of gum when Pat broke my heart, I understand why she's pretty firmly against the idea of us getting back together.

"Objection!" Val says. "Leading the witness."

Winnie grumbles. "What did you *want* to say?"

Val bounces up and down, shaking me and Beast with her. "Tell us everything! Every juicy detail."

So, I do. I share all the details, from how I ate everything not nailed down to Pat's confession of love (which made Val gasp) to me thinking he was going to lick my arm to his casual proposal. Winnie's eyes narrowed when I mentioned Chevy's involvement, and she laughed until she cried when I described running out of the restaurant while the mariachi band serenaded Pat.

When I'm done, all the ice has melted into my drink. Even watered down, it's still delicious. Val raises her hand.

"Yes, Val. You have a question?"

"What Wolf said this morning—is it true? You need to get married to keep Jo?"

I turn my glass around and around in my hands. "It's not so much that I *need* to get married. Ashlee didn't suggest I go nab a husband or something."

"I think that would be some kind of ethical violation," Winnie says.

"Probably. But being married does help Rachel's position. And being single might hurt my case."

Winnie makes a frustrated sound and leans forward. "That is so stupid and so backwards. You are the best parent for Jo. Single, married, whatever."

"Thanks." I agree, but it feels so nice to have support.

Val shifts, pulling her legs up to sit cross-legged on the couch, facing me. "So, marrying Pat would help your position?" When Winnie glares, Val throws up a hand. "What? It's a valid question."

Winnie shakes her head. "Saying yes to Pat would mean opening herself up to a world of hurt. Again. And getting married for a reason like that is a terrible idea."

"It's an *unconventional* idea," Val corrects. "Not terrible. It would help Lindy's case, and I think she would do anything for Jo. Just like we would in her position."

Hearing them go back and forth like I'm not here is oddly validating. Mostly because I've been having the same arguments in my own head.

"Plus," Val continues, "we all know Lindy still has feelings for Pat."

I hold up a hand. "Wait—we do?"

They ignore me.

"It's too complicated," Winnie insists. "The motives are mixed. Are they getting married to help Lindy keep Jo? Or because they want to get married?"

Val shrugs. "Why not both?"

The two of them finally remember I'm here. "Forget our thoughts," Winnie says. "This is your decision, Lindy. Think fast: do you want to marry Pat?"

"No." The answer is like a reflex, a leg twitch after being hit in the knee with the doctor's tiny mallet. But it's not the truth, or at least not the full truth. It's more like what I think I *should* say. "And yes."

I cover my face with my hands. Val squeals, and Winnie sighs. The feral cat purrs her approval loudly.

"Even if part of me wants to, marriage is huge. It's marriage. And Pat ... really hurt me." I swallow and look down, picking at the hem of my jeans. "He apologized, and he seems sincere about all this. But I don't know if I trust him not to hurt me again. And even though this would be to help Jo, if he left, it would be hurting her too."

"Do you really think he'd do that?" Val asks.

I shrug. "He's the kind of guy who jumps from thing to thing to thing."

And from woman to woman, I don't add. I still can't shut out the images of all those photos I saw on the gossip sites of Pat, *my* Pat, smiling and laughing with other women. He jumped into a marriage once already, then jumped out almost as fast. These thoughts make my stomach turn over.

"You're scared because you're still in love with him." Winnie's voice is dry, but surprisingly free from disapproval.

I'm already shaking my head. Another reflex. I'm full of reflexes tonight. Why does it seem like they're all doing the opposite of what they should?

"No, I'm—"

"Sorry, chica," Val interrupts. "It's true. You *never* got over him. And it seems clear he isn't over you. I mean, that whole jealousy thing when he was in that cell?" Val fans her face. "So hot."

"So very caveman. Typical male." Winnie rolls her eyes.

"Exactly," Val says with a sigh. "I want someone to go caveman over me."

I try to picture Chevy growling in jealousy over Val and ...

I just can't. Not for the first time, I wish she could find someone who could end the curse of her unrequited crush.

"I can't believe I'm even suggesting this," Winnie says, "but you could marry Pat for Jo's sake, while knowing you hope for more. See what develops. Hope for the best. Insert other optimistic catchphrases here."

I can't believe Winnie is the one saying this either. And what's more—I can't believe I'm actually considering it, even long after Winnie and Val have gone home.

Before I head up to bed, I open Jo's door and watch her sleeping, her brown hair a mess on the pillow. I used to do this more often, especially in the early days, tip-toeing in her room to make sure she was still breathing. I count her breaths for a few minutes, letting calm wash over me in the dim moonlight.

If the court grants Rachel custody, it will mean a new life in a new place. Jo will move to Austin. She'll have a new house. A new room. A new school. Rachel and her husband as her primary caregivers. Even in my mind, I can't think of calling them *parents*.

What if he's not a nice man? What if he's abusive? Or just doesn't care about Jo?

Will Rachel understand Jo's uniqueness? Will she encourage her reading? Will they laugh? Will Rachel give Jo affection? Attention? Love?

That last one trips me up, and I realize I'm clutching Jo's covers in tight fists. The only thing Rachel ever loved was herself.

I let go of the covers and flex my stiff fingers. Still watching Jo, I pull out my phone and open the text thread from earlier when Pat asked me to dinner. I haven't even added him as a contact in my phone yet, but I'm about to say yes to a marriage proposal.

For Jo.

Before I can change my mind, I tap out a completely unromantic answer to Pat's completely unromantic proposal: *Fine. I'll marry you. But only for Jo. Don't get any ideas.*

His answer comes back almost immediately and sends a whole-body shiver through me: *I hear you, and I respect you, but as for ideas—too late. I've already got PLENTY. I'll call you tomorrow, fiancée.*

When I finally fall asleep, it's with a smile on my face and a thin thread of worry weaving through my gut.

CHAPTER EIGHTEEN

Pat

WHEN I IMAGINED my wedding day—and yes, despite what people might think, some guys picture their wedding day—I wasn't wearing an ankle monitor under my suit. The ceremony also didn't take place in a courtroom whose décor was last updated in the 1970s. The people watching were considered guests not witnesses, and we had a string quartet instead of the bailiff humming a Blake Shelton song under his breath.

My imaginary wedding was always grand. No surprise there, right? A ceremony in a picturesque location with lovely weather—because in your dreams, the weather is always gentle sun and seventy-five degrees—or in some beautiful church chapel with wood accents, high ceilings, massive flower arrangements.

The reception to follow would be at night, with music and

dancing and wine—but not so much that we have sloppy drunks ruining the mood—and I would whisper in my bride's ear all the ways I planned to demonstrate my love as soon as we were alone.

The only thing my actual wedding has in common with my imagined one is the bride. Before I met Lindy, I didn't have an ideal woman in mind. I knew I wanted the woman walking down the aisle to be someone I could commit to for life and mean it, just like my dad did with my mom. After I met Lindy, it was always her I saw. Always.

So, even though she isn't in a white dress (it's a simple floral with a belt and boots) and she won't be walking down the aisle, I'm a happy man.

Today marks the start of my uphill battle to win over the woman about to become my wife.

Have I mentioned how much I love a good challenge?

And a challenge it will be. After shocking me by accepting my two-bit proposal, Lindy all but avoided me for the seventy-two-hour waiting period. She also flat-out shut down all my ideas to make today special. Lindy insisted that the ceremony should be as quick as possible. No rings. No vows. Just showing up and signing the certificate in front of the judge with our witnesses. I'm lucky she agreed to a reception, and I think her friends pressured her into it. I really like her friends.

At least Jo's excited. Sitting in the front row next to Mari and Val, Jo is beaming like it's Christmas and her birthday all wrapped up into one. The little wave she gives me warms my heart and sparks hope to life.

I will wear Lindy down. I'll prove to her that I am in this for the long haul. This may look on the outside like another Pat Decision, as Collin would say, but it's more. And that's exactly what I told my family when I told them over a group video call. There were protests and arguments and a whole lot of name-calling, but Tank finally shut it down when he told them about Mom's ring.

"I've already talked to Pat about this," Tank said in the voice we all know means arguing is futile. "He's serious about this, even if it's quick, and your mother and I agreed this is how we wanted to show our support."

I did not tell any of them that Lindy's just doing this for Jo. Only Thayden knows the details, and I invoked client confidentiality. Which meant he also charged me for the hour-long phone call where we discussed his marriage to Delilah, but whatever.

Their relationship started out because Thayden needed to fulfill his father's inheritance clause, and Delilah needed money. According to him, he wore her down and by their wedding, it was all real. Now, they're one of the most disgustingly in love couples I've seen—at last glance, kissing in the third row of the courtroom—so I'm crossing my fingers here.

"Give me just another minute," Judge Judie tells Lindy. There's some lawyer with an apparently urgent matter. He's been gesticulating wildly behind the bench for several minutes. Meanwhile the courtroom keeps getting louder. Half of Sheet Cake is here, plus my big family and a lot of friends.

"Take your time," Lindy says, all while looking as though she's about to bolt.

Just in case, I grab her hand. It's a little clammy. Bringing it up to my lips, I press a kiss to her knuckles. She blinks at me with those wide green eyes, and I can see her trying to retreat past the wall she's built.

Not on my watch, darlin'. Not on my watch.

I pull Mama's ring out of my pocket. "I'm supposed to give this to you later, but I feel like now's a good time."

Lindy's lips part as she stares down at the simple gold band and the single, albeit large, square diamond. She touches it with a single finger, the way you might poke a critter you find, unsure if it's alive or dead.

"It won't bite."

She glares at me. "Pat—I didn't think we were doing all this."

"This was my mom's ring," I tell her.

"Oh," she breathes.

I can feel her starting to tense, starting to pull back. Any second now, she'll say *it's too much* or *I just can't* or *it wouldn't be right*. And I just won't have it. Without giving her time to form an argument, I turn over the hand I'm holding and slide the ring in place, praying it fits.

It does. Like it was made for Lindy.

"It's beautiful," Lindy says. "Thank you."

"*You're* beautiful."

Suddenly, I am missing my mom. I always do. Missing her is a constant ache, like the faint stiffness in my bad ankle. But there are times even now when her absence is a runaway train, hurtling over my tracks. I wish she were here. I hate how many things she's missing. I know she'd want to be here. And this ring makes it so in a tiny way, she *is* here.

I feel like I'm about to burst with happiness and simultaneously melt into a puddle of tears.

Lindy looks alarmed. "Are you okay?"

I wipe my eyes with the sleeve of my suit. "Just thinking about my mom."

Her expression softens, and I almost fall down dead when Lindy takes my hand and squeezes. "I miss mine too," she confesses. "I couldn't invite her today because the doctors thought she might get upset and confused."

Her words catch on what sounds suspiciously like a sob, and without stopping to question it, I pull my seventy-two-hour fiancée into my arms. Lindy trembles against me.

She clings to me, and I lean in, speaking softly, my lips brushing her hair. "Do you want to call this thing off?" *Please say no.* "Do you want to pick up your mama? Or move the ceremony to her facility?" *Complicated, but doable.*

I try not to hold my breath, waiting for a response. Lindy sniffs. "I'm okay," she says, voice strong but quiet. "We're here, so we should do it."

I chuckle. "I didn't realize you were such a romantic."

"It's a well-kept secret. Don't tell, okay?"

"Never."

Judge Judie chooses that moment to rap her gavel on the bench, and Lindy and I jump apart. "Are we all ready to get started?" Judge Judie asks, looking down at us.

I give Lindy my most charming, hard-to-resist smile. "Last chance to run."

Lindy's eyes narrow. "Is that a challenge, Patty?"

"Nah. I just need to stretch if I'm going to have to chase you."

"We're ready," Lindy says to the judge. She gives Jo a quick wave. I grab Lindy's hand again. I take it as a good sign when she doesn't resist.

It's the most basic of basic ceremonies, like an off-brand wedding ordered from a sketchy site online. I try not to be disappointed we're not even reciting vows—I didn't even know it was possible to get married without them.

It feels disappointingly empty when Judge Judie says a few quick words and then asks for the certificate and our witnesses. The romantic part of me wants to wail. I ache for the pomp and circumstance, the drama and the magic. A wedding, in my mind, should be a capital-E Event. Not some kind of drive-thru, fast food thing like this.

But then Lindy looks up at me with a goofy smile that actually looks sincere. Romance, flowers, string quartets—who needs all that when I have *her*?

Tank joins me, beaming and clapping me on the back. A sniffling Val, wiping her eyes with an embroidered handkerchief, joins Lindy. I've signed a lot of legal contracts in my day, but I've never teared up while doing so before.

Tank leans in as I finish scrawling my name across the line. "There's no crying in baseball, son," he whispers, just loud enough for Lindy to hear.

She bites back a laugh and eyes Tank, then me. "So, this movie quoting thing—it's genetic?"

"Afraid so," Tank says. "Welcome to the family, Lindy."

She startles at his words, like she is just now realizing exactly what she's gotten into. Yep—you put your name on the line and now you get all the Grahams. For better or for worse.

Judge Judie adds her signature to the bottom of the license, and in the most anticlimactic ceremony in the history of the world, Lindy and I are married.

"Give this to the clerk on your way out," the judge says, handing the license back. Lindy hands it to Val, and before any of us can move, Judge Judie bangs her gavel again. I swear I see a tiny smirk before she steels her expression. "And now, you may kiss the bride."

Lindy's head snaps up, and her cheeks flush pink. "Wait—what?"

Maybe Chevy was right about a few people in Sheet Cake being on my side, because Lindy told me several times a kiss was not required.

Lindy leans closer to the bench as our guests begin murmuring. "I thought we agreed we would just sign papers. Not do all the, um, you know. Other wedding stuff," Lindy hisses.

Judge Judie raises her brows so high her forehead lifts her white tuft of hair too. "Are you trying to tell me you're not planning to kiss your husband?" She gestures toward me with the gavel. Her eyes narrow. "Are you making a mockery of marriage vows in my courtroom? Are you telling me this isn't a real marriage, but some kind of sham designed to—"

Before I can react, Lindy stretches up on her tiptoes and plants the quickest, most G-rated kiss on my lips I could ever imagine. I can tell she thinks she's about to get away with it too. But before she can escape, I cup her face in my palms and kiss her back.

I won't get too amorous in our current setting, but a closed-mouth kiss doesn't have to be cold and stiff. Or fast.

When Lindy doesn't resist, I keep on kissing her. My movements may be slight and restrained, but our chemistry makes even a chaste kiss light a fire. Lindy still smells of mint and strawberry, and her lips are pliant beneath mine. The curves of her cheeks are smooth under my rough palms. The ends of her hair tickle my wrists.

I'm aware of it all, drinking it in, memorizing it, taking as much as she'll let me right now.

We may not have said vows, but I let my lips hint at promises to come. *This is only the start*, they vow. *This could be so good if you let it. Be mine, Lindy. You are MINE.*

And just when I feel her start to melt against me, like she's forgotten the courtroom even exists, I pull back. Better to leave her wanting more than scare her off. From her parted lips and the glazed look in her eyes, I stopped right in the middle of wanting-more territory. Excellent.

Judge Judie grins her approval as she bangs her gavel. "I now present to you Mr. and Mrs. Patrick Graham."

The room erupts in cheers in stamping feet. The feeling is better than running out of a stadium tunnel onto the field. It's better than catching a touchdown pass. I drop my hands from Lindy's cheeks and circle one arm around her waist, pulling her into my side as we face our friends and family. I wave like a pageant queen, and when I glance at Lindy, she's got a stupid-happy grin on her face.

Pat, one. Marriage of convenience, zero.

Jo runs to us—to *me*—and without hesitation, I lift her up on my shoulders. Her skinny legs hang down my chest and her small hands tug on my hair. A little hard, if I'm being honest, but right now, she could make me bald and I'd be okay.

The celebration is cut short when Judge Judie brings out the gavel again, shouting, "Clear out! I've got another case coming in. Justice waits for no man!"

I take Lindy's hand, feeling my mom's ring there, and with Jo still on my shoulders, the three of us lead the way out of the courtroom. *We are married! Lindy is my wife!* And maybe it's the opposite of the typical order, but now it's time to woo her.

Not even a scowl from the man in handcuffs being led into the courtroom can dampen my mood.

CHAPTER NINETEEN

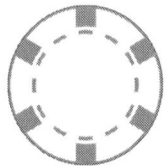

Lindy

I VERY FIRMLY TOLD EVERYONE IN my life today was Not A Big Deal. With capital letters and everything. *It's not supposed to be like* this, I think, watching from a back booth at Mari's. So celebratory. So ... happy.

I mean, technically, yes—weddings are supposed to be happy. The happiest day of your life, if we're getting technical. I wrote a post once on the best and worst days of your life, ranked in order. Your wedding day was right at the top, followed by having a baby.

But my marriage to Pat isn't real. I mean, on paper it is, and that's the only place it counts, where the courts can examine the document and somehow think I'm a more suitable guardian for Jo. Ridiculous.

Everywhere else, though, it's not supposed to be REAL. Which is why I'm sitting here, wishing our friends and family got the memo that we don't really need all the pomp and circumstance. We can all resume our normal Tuesday afternoon activities instead of all this dancing and drinking and laughing.

Wow, I sound like a real Grinch. A total buzzkill. I make the man yelling at kids to get off his lawn look like a cruise director.

Go join them, the feral cat is insisting. *You know you want to.*

I most certainly do not! I cross my arms as though to prove the point to myself, scanning the crowd of dancers like a true wallflower.

Sheeters decided to call truce on the whole hating the Grahams just for today. Terrifying Eula Martin actually smiled while dancing with Pat, who has shed his jacket, rolled up his shirtsleeves, and looks way too good. Collin is trying to keep up with Lynn Louise, who can really cut a rug. While I'm watching, she pulls a tissue from her coif to dab her forehead, then tucks it back in her hair.

Tank has one of Jo's hands and Ashlee has the other. I'm not sure I've *ever* seen Jo happier. Tank keeps sneaking admiring glances at Ashlee, a goofy smile on his face. I swear, he about fell over when he realized my lawyer is none other than Belle the supermodel. Apparently, he's a big fan.

Harper and Chase slow dance in a corner, despite the fast-paced music. Dale couldn't take off work mid-week, so Winnie and Val are shimmying in the midst of some friends of the Grahams. I met them all earlier, but it was a blur. Much like the whole day, which had the quality of a damaged video playing at varying speeds—some moments stretching long and slow like taffy and others only a blip. I'm left caught between an adrenaline high and a dizzying overwhelm.

My eyes skim back over to Pat like they can't help themselves. I'm blaming the kiss. Over the years, I hadn't forgotten Pat's skillful mouth and the raw power of our physical chemistry. But remembering and *experiencing* are two different things.

It wasn't a long kiss. Mouths stayed closed. And yet my skin flushes even now just thinking about the brush of his lips. My breath hitches as one corner of his mouth kicks up into a smile.

I'm going to dream about that kiss. And it will *only* be repeated in my dreams, because kisses are against the rules. Yes, I made rules. New rules. Because without them, I'm already lost in a sea of Patrick Graham.

Val and Winnie slide into the booth across from me. "Hey, chica! You're looking entirely too glum for a wedding reception. Especially your wedding reception."

"It's not a wedding reception. More like a party to celebrate a legally binding contract."

Winnie lowers her head to look at me over the top of her glasses. "Sheesh. We should call you Eeyore."

Big Mo appears at the end of the table, brandishing a tray with slices of tres leches cake, my very favorite. I give him a dirty look, but I'm not a monster. I also take a big piece.

"Thank you," I mutter as Winnie and Val grab slices of their own.

Mo rumbles out a laugh, beard shaking. "If you're trying to be thankful, you best mind your tone. And also, congratulations."

"Thank you." My tone is mildly better now. Maybe because it's been softened up by cake.

"I wish you a very long and happy marriage," Big Mo says, before wiping his hands on his apron and moving on. "Enjoy every day you get."

Our table is quiet for a moment, and I watch as he passes out cake like he's the bearded tres leches fairy. His simple words have special meaning. Big Mo came to Sheet Cake after his wife and daughter were killed by a drunk driver. He sold his house, quit his corporate job working for one of the big energy companies, and left Houston. Mari found him at the diner counter one day, red-eyed and limp with grief. She took him in like she had Val and her older sisters, letting him have the upstairs apartment. He's been here ever since.

If he's giving me marriage blessings, I should really take them.

"How's married life?" Val asks, licking frosting off her arm.

"Shut up, you." I take a bite of cake. It's delicious, of course, but I refuse to let the sugar soften my mood.

Winnie sets down her fork and leans across the table with a piercing look in her eyes. "I'm only going to say this once. Probably. You are allowed to enjoy this, you know. You are allowed to have happiness. To want things. To have things you want."

"I know."

"Do you?" Winnie asks. "Because from where I'm sitting, I've watched you live for other people for years now, forgetting that you're part of the equation. You like Pat."

"She loooooooves him," Val says.

I start to argue, but Winnie's on a roll. "You have feelings for Pat. Maybe you told yourself you're doing it for Jo, but that doesn't mean you can't be doing it for yourself too."

The cake is suddenly tasteless in my mouth. I take a sip of water before I answer. "Weren't you the one who said I should be wary of mixed motives?"

"Eh. When are motives ever pure anyway? You married Pat, so you might as well own it. Enjoy it."

Val waggles her eyebrows. "And we do mean *enjoy*."

Grumbling, I scrape my finger along the plate, getting the last bits of icing.

"Speaking of enjoyment, does that man have the superpower of sucking joy out of a ten-foot radius?" Winnie asks. She's pointing to James, who is standing in the corner, sipping a beer and looking like he's at a funeral.

"I'm guessing he disapproves," I say. "Or it might just be his default setting."

"Unless you want to turn into the female version of him, you should go dance," Val says. "It's your wedding day."

"Fake wedding day. And I'm fine right here. As long as Big Mo keeps bringing me cake."

"It's not fake," Winnie says. "You signed the papers. Legally, you are married to the hot man wearing the ankle monitor. It's very real."

"Not where it counts," I mutter. "It's just about Jo, about custody. Legal stuff. Pat's doing me a massive favor. That's all."

Val makes a loud buzzer sound at all my excuses, the things I've been telling myself over and over since I texted Pat my *yes*.

"You're just scared because the feelings are real," Winnie says.

"I'm not scared."

Val flaps her arms and makes chicken sounds. "Are too."

"Am not!"

Mari interrupts us by clapping her hands over the table. "Children, please! No fighting on this day of celebration." She turns to me, her dark eyes warm and crinkled at the corners as she smiles, stretching out a hand. "Mija, it's time for your first dance."

My eyes meet Pat's across the room. I expect pleading, his hands pressed together hopefully, and a teasing grin. Instead, his arms hang at his sides. The smile he had while doing the twist with Eula Martin is gone. He looks ... nervous.

Does he think I'll say no to dancing with him?

Probably so. After all, you've been avoiding him since the moment the ceremony ended, dummy. And for the three days leading up to the wedding. Not exactly inspiring confidence.

It's the vulnerability in Pat's eyes which makes me slide out of the booth and cross the room. I stop a foot away, and we just stand there as Ben Howard's "Only Love" starts to play.

"It's our song," I say. "Our old song."

"We can pick a new one if you want," Pat says.

At the look on his face, my heart sinks, a slow descent into the dark and silty bottom of a lake. I'm suddenly aware of how selfish I've been. I know Pat would have chosen a big wedding, and even with three days to plan, he would have made it happen. He told me as much, but he didn't need to. A giant wedding would be so very ... Pat.

Yet he went along with my insistence to strip it all down to only the bare basics. I didn't even want this reception, but Mari insisted. Maybe Eeyore is a perfect name for me today, because I've been raining all over everything. Especially Pat.

"May I have this dance?" I ask, holding out my hand. "I've only ever liked dancing with you."

Pat rewards me with the full force of his blinding smile and wastes no time dragging me against him. A cheer rises around us, and I don't even care, because I'm protected here, my cheek against Pat's chest, his arms around my waist, mine tangled in the hair at the nape of his neck. Here, it's just us.

This is not a slow song, but my feet find their rhythm as Pat leads us. My body always tuned right into his, as though we both run on some special frequency. Everything and everyone else is simply static.

"I need to cut it," Pat says.

"What?" I'm tempted to pull back and look at him, but I feel like it would break this spell. Plus, he smells delicious.

"My hair," he says. "It's getting to be mullet-level long."

My fingertips toy with the ends, and Pat shivers at my touch. I smile. "I heard mullets are back in style."

Pat scoffs. "They were never in style."

"Take it up with Buzzfeed. Anyway, I like your hair. Gives me something to grab onto."

He freezes for a beat, and I almost stumble, but he gathers me tighter and keeps us moving. My cheeks flame as I realize how that might have sounded.

"I don't mean—"

I can't finish my sentence because Pat pulls me tighter, making the air leave my chest in a quick burst. His mouth dips close, and I feel his hot breath on my ear.

"I know what you want from me, Lindy. But so help me, I'm going to convince you I can give you so much more. By the time my work is done, you will know it's okay for you to want things, to hope. And when you get them, they aren't always going to disappear on you. I won't disappear."

With that, he's suddenly spinning me out, his grip firm as he spins me back, dipping me low. There's more cheering, hooting and hollering. The room disappears. It's only me and Pat, as his face lowers to mine, our noses brushing.

I am terrified. But I also trust him.

His eyes are two burning chocolate coals, their heat searing through me. My body lights up, flushed with desire. Blood and bad ideas rush to my head.

Pat's gaze drops to my lips and my heart goes haywire.

Kiss me, I think. But I can't bring myself to say it. I'm not that brave. And he's right—I'm not used to asking for what I really want, or wanting anything at all.

Pat's eyes meet mine again and his expression is determined, like I am a challenge, a prize he won't rest until he claims.

When he presses a swift kiss to the corner of my mouth and pulls me upright, it's all I can do not to drag him to me and claim his lips with mine.

Walking through the lobby of Mama's facility, I'm greeted with congratulations from the nurses. Word doesn't stay quiet long in Sheet Cake. I guess I shouldn't have expected to fly under the radar, even with a quick courthouse wedding.

"We've left a wedding gift for you in your Mama's room," Neve says, giving my arm a squeeze. "We all chipped in."

"You didn't need to do that. Really."

Her smile is broad and kind, almost enough to bring back the tears I thought I exhausted on the drive from the diner. I asked Val and Winnie to watch Jo and keep Pat busy so I could slip away to see Mama.

"Nonsense," Neve says. "We're all so pleased. You deserve some happy in your life. And that is one fine hunk of man."

I can't argue there.

"Speaking of a hunk of man." Neve heaves a sigh and chases down the hall after a man dressed only in an argyle sweater vest and tighty-whities. Which, in this case, are more like gray baggy-saggies. I look away, but not before the sight burns an unwanted image onto my brain.

"Happy wedding day to me," I mutter, pushing open Mama's door. "Mama?"

She's in her favorite spot, the comfy chair by the window where she can watch the birds. Only then do I remember I promised to refill the feeders this week. With everything going on, I forgot.

An apology is on my lips, but I realize it's wholly unnecessary. Not only are the bird feeders full, several more have been added. Two stick to the window with suction cups, and three more hang from the oak outside the window. It's like a bird version of the dog party at the end of *Go, Dog, Go*, one of Jo's first favorite books. The birds are going to town, flitting and fighting and singing. A total bird party.

Mom beams at me, the smile so worn and familiar that it makes my stomach swoop. I kiss her soft cheek and sit down in the chair next to her. The birds on the window feeders scatter momentarily, then come right back.

"It's Lindy, Mama."

She waves a hand. Her nails are painted candy-apple red. "I know my own daughter, silly. It's fall break—I've been expecting you."

Okay, so it's my college years. I find that it's best if I play along. When I try to convince Mama of reality, it only agitates her, which in turn depresses me. If I just exist in her world, whatever that is for the day, we can have pleasant conversations. I can almost pretend things are fine.

It was the right decision not to have her at the wedding. But I was aware of her absence like a throbbing bruise. I can only imagine how today felt for Pat, not having his mom there. I turn her ring on my finger, feeling unworthy of wearing it.

I turn to the window. "Wow, Mama! You've expanded the aviary."

Since Mama got interested in birds, Jo and I have added feeders slowly, and the home put in a nice bird bath in view.

We've taken to calling it the aviary, though now it truly looks like one.

"Isn't it lovely? The nice new gardener I hired put them in."

What she likely means is the maintenance guy, Kevin. This is a few steps up from his normal duties. Maybe I have Lynn Louise to thank. We're already getting special treatment with Mama's discounted rate. This is a lovely facility, far out of my price range, and not like the ones constantly being written up in horrifying news articles. If Jo and I ever left Sheet Cake, we'd have to either leave Mama behind, or move her to somewhere with a much lower level of care. I'm not sure I could live with myself either way.

"He also brought me those," Mama says, pointing to a big bouquet of daisies on the dresser. Her favorite flowers.

"They're beautiful."

"He brings new ones every few days," Mama says. "Anyway. Enough about me! Catch me up on school. Any new boys to tell me about?"

If she only knew.

Well, Mama, I married a man I used to love and still maybe might love just a tiny huge amount, all so I could keep custody of Rachel's kid. Oh, right—and Rachel had a kid, then ran off and left her with us, and then you came here, and I had to take care of her, and now Rachel wants her back.

Which brings us back to the start: I got married today.

"Aw, sweetie. Come here. Don't cry."

I'm crying?

Mama pulls me to her, and I wind my arms around her waist, breathing in the familiar scent of her magnolia lotion. I'm aware of the tears leaking in a steady stream from my eyes, even if I don't know why they're falling. And now I'm full-on sobbing, with hiccups and everything.

Mama strokes my hair, and the birds sing and chatter just outside the glass as inside the small room, I allow myself to fall apart.

Why is it easier to do so with the one person who has no understanding of what's going on?

Or maybe it's because she's my mama and always will be my mama, whether she knows what year it is or not.

"There, there," she coos, "that's my strong, brave girl. Did someone break your heart?"

That's a question I can't answer. My heart feels surprisingly light and hopeful, but hope isn't something I trust anymore. The pattern of my life seems to be that the moment I find happiness, it gets yanked away. Though it's the worst possible thing to think about on my wedding day, I just keep wondering when it will end and leave me crushed and alone.

FROM THE NEIGHBORLY APP

Subject: Wedding of the Year?

The_Real_Shell-E
ICYMI Lindy Darcy got hitched in the courthouse. If anyone knows how she managed to snag one of the Graham brothers, please let me know. At least there are two more up for grabs! Also, what was she wearing?!?! So tacky.

BagelBytes
I think she looks beautiful. Good for them!

TheRealBob
Patrick Graham may be the best thing to happen to Sheet Cake football in years. Congrats to the happy couple. Go Sheet Cake!

DeltaDeltaDelta
Don't forget about their dad! He's old but not like THAT old. That's three Grahams left to choose from.

And what I've heard is Lindy dated Pat in college and he broke her heart. Maybe he knocked her up? She looks really puffy. Shotgun wedding?

The_Real_Shell-E

Are we sure Jo isn't really Lindy and Pat's baby? Has anyone even seen Rachel in years? I heard Pat has gotten in fights with both Billy and Wolf over her. I just don't get how someone so PLAIN has men falling all over her.

Kimmie
Jo is definitely not Pat and Lindy's baby. And I wouldn't say Lindy has men falling all over her. She and Billy dated YEARS ago. Someone told me the marriage with Pat isn't even real.

Vanz
What is VERY real is the danger of big pharma

BagelBytes
Sounds like we've got a lot of jealous people in this town with nothing better to do than spread rumors and gossip. I reported your comments. Hope you get blocked.

Neighborly Mod
[This thread has been closed and marked for deletion]

CHAPTER TWENTY

Lindy

PAT IS IN MY HOUSE. With bags and his truck parked out front. With the scent I know comes from a mix of cheap body products and eau de Patrick Graham. Jo and the dogs circle him with equal amounts of enthusiasm, making it difficult for him to even walk through the family room.

Pat is moving into my house, still wearing his wedding suit. The creak of my floor and thump of his footfalls assures me that *this is not a drill*. He could not look happier about the prospect of bringing in the bags his family dropped off after the reception. Meanwhile, I am hiding in the kitchen, with my hands manacled around a cup of coffee like it's my only anchor to sanity. I think maybe it is.

Now that I'm looking at Jo's and my life through Pat's eyes, it feels so small, so not good enough. I can't wait to hear what Pat says when I tell him he can't use the toilet upstairs. He'll realize when he sees the sign and the duct tape.

I tell myself this will be fine, that there's a happy ending in here somewhere. One where I get to keep Jo and Pat doesn't break my heart and the upstairs toilet starts working again.

I hear Jo jabbering as she drags the smallest of Pat's bags upstairs. "And did you know mama alligators hide their babies in their mouths when there's danger?"

"Is that right?" Pat asks.

There is not even a shred of annoyance in his voice, which makes me want to throw my arms around his neck. Even the people who love Jo sometimes tire of her seemingly endless repertoire of facts.

She's still going. "They can fit like twenty hatchlings in there."

Pat's voice carries down the stairs. "That's impressive. Did Lindy ever try that with you? Because I'm not sure you'd fit. Especially not now. But we should investigate. Come here, let me measure you."

I hear her squeal because the house is not even remotely soundproof. Which would be a real buzzkill if I hadn't told Pat we were sleeping in separate bedrooms. NON-NEGOTIABLE.

Other than my closet for crying, I haven't needed sound-proofing for the past five years, and I certainly don't now just because I'm …

I'm …

I'm … *married*.

The word doesn't feel real. Neither does the idea of Pat living across the hall for the foreseeable future. Even a hallway isn't enough space between us. He's already wearing an ankle monitor—maybe I could tack on one of those dog collars for an electric fence and set it up between our bedrooms. Just in case.

I've been adamant that this is a marriage in name only, though I saw the gleam in his eye, making me glad I wrote up a set of rules. The moment Jo is in bed, he and I will be going over those rules, and he will agree to them.

Then we will abide by them and everything will be FINE. And if, at some point down the road once the hearing is done, I want to consider the whole attraction and feelings thing and give this a real chance, we can toss the rules. But for now, they are my shield.

I lean back against the counter, closing my eyes. This is a mistake. Isn't it? Everything in my life feels so infinitely fragile. I'm like the little pig who's built a house of toothpicks and tissue paper, and Pat is the big bad wolf, here to blow it down with one breath.

"Why are you putting your things in the guest room?" Jo's wobbly voice carries to me. It's her about-to-cry voice.

I set down my mug and bolt for the stairs. When I reach Jo, it's just in time. Her lip is trembling, tears at the ready. Pat looks to me with huge eyes.

Jo's voice is breathless and wavering. "Are you getting divorced? Henry's parents got divorced, and he said they slept in different bedrooms. You just got *married*."

Like I could forget. Also, who's Henry?

A tiny sob follows Jo's words.

"Oh, Jojo. Don't cry."

I reach for her at the same time Pat does, and suddenly, we are three-way hugging. Because Pat and I are both kneeling, we're rocking unsteadily. Especially as Jo clutches at us with her scrawny arms.

Our heads end up behind Jo's back, our faces much closer than I want them to be. When our gazes hook and catch, a zip of something hot and electric moves through my body. Pat's dark eyes grow even darker.

It shouldn't be possible to think about kissing him when Jo is *right here*, crying, and yet, somehow it is. Kissing Pat is *all* I can think about until Jo gives a little sniff, dragging my focus back to where it needs to stay.

"We're not getting divorced, bear cub. Pat was just putting his things in the guest room because there's no room in my closet," I explain, my eyes still glued to Pat's.

This is true. My closet is full of the crying coats. But it is also true that he's not, no-way, no-how going to be sharing my double bed.

But he could, the feral cat whispers with a suggestive purr. *They don't call it a marriage bed for nothing.*

I can't seem to get rid of this stupid feral cat in my head. She's like a lipstick stain on a white T-shirt—near impossible to remove and just as difficult to ignore.

"Okay," Jo says.

I try to pull back, but Jo tightens her grip and I lose my balance. I never excelled at crouching. Maybe if I'd done more work on my leg strength...

We topple over, Pat taking the brunt of our weight with a loud *oof*. The three of us end up sprawled in the tiny hallway between the bedrooms and bathroom. When Pat chuckles, Jo bounces up and down, and his laugh vibrates through my cheek and chest, both of which are plastered to him.

Jo giggles, which makes my tension ease. Instead of jumping up the way I should, I relax into Pat, into Jo, into this kind of perfectly imperfect moment.

I lean in, letting Jo's laughter and Pat's familiar scent curl around me like smoke rising from a fledgling fire. His arm tightens around me, warm and strong, and just for a few seconds, I let myself sink into him, into the moment.

Family, I think. *This feels like family.*

The sensation is strange and new, yet as worn as the pair of jeans I can't bring myself to throw away, the ones with holes where my thighs brush as I walk. I'm shocked by the fierce fire of longing, exploding from wherever I've kept it locked away for years.

Longing, hoping, dreaming—they're liabilities I haven't been able to afford. Not even if there were some kind of no-limit, no-interest credit card could I consider these things. At least, not if I don't want to be buried alive under disappointment later. I swallow, my mouth feeling dry and papery. Can I possibly allow myself to feel these things now?

"I have an idea," Jo says brightly, sitting up suddenly. The beauty of the moment bursts like a soap bubble—delicate and beautiful, then gone.

I force myself to stand on wobbly legs, then hold out a hand to Pat before I can think better of it.

He rises slowly, much too close to my body, his eyes fixed on mine. Pat doesn't let go of my hand when he's on his feet. We are inches apart, the lack of distance feeling strangely obscene, even though we were just pressed together closer than this. I hold my breath, counting the number of boards in the wood paneled wall behind his head.

"You guys," Jo says, grabbing at us both, her whine a reminder that she's trying to tell us something. "My idea!"

Pat turns to her, but keeps my hand trapped in his. I'm a willing prisoner, not even pretending I want to escape.

He smiles at her. "What is it, Jojo?"

Hearing Pat use her nickname so easily is a pinprick to my heart.

"You can get rid of some of your coats," Jo says, turning to me. "Then Pat could fit his things in your closet."

I glance quickly at Pat, who's probably wondering why I

have so many coats in the first place. "Good idea, bear cub. We'll take it under consideration. For now, though, let's help Pat move his things to the guest room."

She obeys, bounding after Pat. I have a feeling I'm going to need those coats. Every. Single. One.

Whether I'll be screaming or crying in the closet, time will tell. I have a strong feeling it will be both in equal measure.

"Why do I feel as though I'm entering a cage fight to the death?" Pat asks, walking into the kitchen where I'm seated at the small table.

I tilt my head. "Not a bad idea. Maybe later."

He pulls out the chair across from me and sits, angling his long, jean-clad legs out to the side. His feet are bare, which makes the moment suddenly more intimate, and as I watch, he grabs a stray fork off the table and scratches underneath the ankle monitor.

"Do I smell coffee?" he asks.

I get up, refilling my mug and pouring him one. "Do you still take it black?"

"Like my heart."

I start to shake my head, then stop as the coffee sloshes over the rims of our mugs. Pat does not have a black heart. In fact, I think he might be the sweetest person I know.

My favorite kind of sweet too. He's not the cloying kind that makes your teeth ache, but more like the dark chocolate sprinkled with salt or with a hint of pepper to give it bite. There is always push and pull with Pat. So much friction, a delicious amount of tension.

I love it. I've always loved it.

"You have the furthest thing from a black heart." I set the coffee down in front of him.

Pat puts a hand over his chest. "Aw. And to think—I thought you hated me."

"You know I could never hate you. I married you, didn't I?"

That million-watt smile of his returns. I wish he'd shift to something more energy efficient, like the stupid forty-watt bulbs that keep my house perpetually dungeon-like.

"You did, *wife*." When I squirm, Pat's smile ups the wattage to blinding levels. "Marriage, sealed with a kiss."

At the word *kiss* my eyes skate down over his cheekbones, past the light brush of stubble to his full lips, curving in a grin. I clear my throat several times, dispelling the tension the way only a good, unnecessary throat clearing can.

"Mawwiage," I say, pushing a paper across the table, "is what bwings us togevah today."

Pat laughs at my *Princess Bride* quote until I hand him a pen. His smile dims as he actually reads the paper.

"'The New Rules'?" Pat groans. "What is this, Lindy?"

But he knows what it is. The flash of hurt now morphing to frustration in his eyes tells me that.

I lean back, telling my body to stop humming in awareness at Pat's nearness. Even when he's upset, there's a magnetism yanking me to him. Every room feels smaller with him in it, the air more dense, like he's surrounded by the atmosphere from some other planet.

I take another swallow of coffee. It's too hot and burns all the way down. "If this is going to work, we need ground rules."

His chuckle is humorless. "We tried that before, remember? How did the rules work out for us?"

Not well. We made rules and then I broke the most important one, falling in love. From what Pat says, he did too, though I'm still trying to wrap my mind around the idea.

"Consider it a prenup."

He shoves the paper back across the table. "We're past the *pre* part. We're already married."

"A post-nup then."

The less real this feels like an actual marriage, the better. For a few slivers of time today, I forgot the pretense, forgot the reason behind it all, and let myself enjoy the moment.

Which is a dangerous, dangerous thing. I need this flimsy piece of paper. It's all I have to guard my heart, to keep me from making the biggest mistake of my life twice.

Pat slides the paper back across the table. "There's no such thing as a post-nup."

There is, actually, but I'm not picking a fight about it right now. "Call it what you want, but I NEED THIS!"

There's a pause after I shout, one in which we both tilt our heads, listening to see if my shouting woke Jo. I don't know why I'm surprised Pat is already so attuned to her. She demanded that he put her to bed tonight. The sound of Pat reading to her, stumbling over the words a bit but making voices for each character, practically burned right through my protective heart vest.

Hearing nothing, Pat and I return to our battlefield on the worn table. Pat takes the paper between two fingers, spinning it so he can read. I know the whole thing by heart after writing like ten drafts. Ultimately, I kept it simple.

The Rules, Take Two

1. No unnecessary touching (if you aren't sure, it's probably unnecessary)

2. No kissing (if the situation calls for a kiss, it must be quick and closed-mouth)
3. No calling each other husband or wife in private or mentioning marriage
4. No shared bedrooms or beds
5. No sex
6. When in public, do as much as needed to validate the relationship, but no more
7. The marriage should be dissolved at a mutually agreed upon time so as to benefit both parties

After a moment, Pat looks up. "This is certainly thorough. Did you buy a manual on fake relationships or something? A template from Etsy?"

"I read the occasional romance novel. They're full of useful ideas."

Pat picks up the pen, twirling it in his fingers like a magician as he frowns down at the handwritten page. "You really want me to sign this?"

I just barely stop myself from saying, *I do*. "Yes. Please."

When he scrawls his name across the bottom of the page, the pen nearly ripping through the paper, I feel hollow. He pushes the paper back to me, but it catches air and slides off the table to the floor. Neither of us moves to pick it up.

Pat stands. He's so tall and broad, making the kitchen seem Lilliputian. Strangely, Pat never made *me* feel small, though in comparison to his height and bulk, I am. It always felt like together, we were more than what we were on our own—perfectly sized. At least, that's how I felt then. Now, I'm still not sure how or what I feel, other than twisted in a knot.

"You aren't going to haggle over the details?" I ask. "Argue the finer points?"

"Nope."

I didn't realize how much I was looking forward to the back and forth until he signed his name. I expected hours of verbal sparring over this. It's why I made a full pot of coffee earlier.

"No getting semantical with me?"

I'm baiting him, throwing out playful banter. I've sent my pawn forward, taunting his knight. But Pat only shakes his head.

"Nope."

"That's surprising," I tell him. "I expected more fight from you."

When Pat places both palms flat on the table and leans toward me, I almost pour hot coffee on my lap. He blinks, a smile slowly dawning on his face like a lazy sunrise.

"Oh, there will be a fight." His voice drops to a husky purr, one my feral cat responds to immediately. My stomach tightens. Not with fear, but with a soul-deep want.

Why am I fighting this again?

"Yeah?" It's the only thing I can choke out, and it's an embarrassing sound.

"You forget, Lindybird. I'm the king of bending all the rules."

He leans forward slightly, and I find myself doing the same. The zombie butterfly army is mobilized, though I think they've somehow turned themselves back into the real kind, fluttery and light and less interested in brains than they are lips and hands and other things.

Pat's going to kiss me. I know it from the way his breath hitches, how his lids are hooded over his espresso eyes, from the way he keeps inching toward me.

It will be a real kiss this time. Not a chaste kiss, a courtroom kiss.

We are engaged in the slowest head-on collision of all time, a game of chicken I know I'm going to lose. I'm tempted to end it, surging out of my seat to fuse my mouth to his, but I'm still aware enough of what's at stake to resist. That doesn't mean I back away, though, and we move closer still.

And closer.

And closer.

I can't focus on both of his eyes now because they've merged into a blur. I drop my gaze to his lips, barely parted. So tempting.

Just before our mouths meet, Pat inhales sharply and takes a step back. I almost groan in frustration. It's like a frigid wind has blown open the back door, swirling a winter storm in the room, strong enough to blow out the fire we'd been building.

I'm almost light-headed with want and with loss.

Pat knocks once against the wood, like he's decided something. "Goodnight, darlin'."

I toss a fork at him, the one he used to scratch his ankle, and I wish I had something heavier to throw, like an anvil. On his way out the door, he happens to notice my to-do list, which more accurately should be named a never-done list. It's written on the back of a lime-green takeout menu in three different colors of pen. Not for aesthetics. For lack of ever being able to locate the same pen.

Pat snatches it right off the wall. "What's this? 'Fix the screen door, get a new dryer, Jo's bookshelves'?"

I'm on my feet in an instant, trying to snatch the paper, which—fortunately or not so fortunately—means getting up close and personal with him. "Nothing you need to concern yourself with."

He holds it up above his head, craning his neck to read it

while swatting at me with his other hand. "Looks like a to-do list, which is very fortunate because I don't have anything *to do* right now. I think I'll take this."

"You will not!"

I grab Pat's shoulders and try to climb him like a tree. This is a common description that romance novels should stop using because not only is it physically challenging, it's not super romantic. What I end up doing is somewhere between a celebratory chest bump and mild assault.

"Ow!" Pat yelps. "That's my shin you just kicked. You realize you're breaking rule number one, right? Hardcore on the unnecessary touching."

I back off, embarrassed I'm panting like this was actually a strenuous workout. Clearly, I don't see the inside of a gym, like EVER. "Pat. Give me my list."

"It's my list now. And there's no rule against this, so you'll have to deal with it. Happy weeding day, weef."

And if I had any question about whether Pat would stick to my rules or do his very best to bend or break every single one, it's answered right there.

CHAPTER TWENTY-ONE

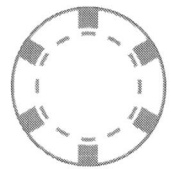

Pat

WHEN IT COMES to Texas and football, there are no excuses for missing practice. Even if you got married the day before. I'm exhausted but awake long before my alarm, with proverbial confetti still in my hair. *Lindy and I got married!*

I make a full pot of coffee and leave a note scrawled on a napkin after letting the dogs out: *Morning, darlin! Hope to see you later.* After a moment's thought, I grab another napkin and write, *Have an excellent day, Jojo! Stay away from sharks and alligators, even if they look like they need a friend.*

I feel strangely forlorn driving away from the dark house, imagining Lindy's dark hair spread over her pillow. If I play my cards right, maybe one day I'll get to see the real thing.

Morning practices have started to become routine even after almost a week in this town. It's like opening a strange portal back in time leading to the stink of sweat, the sound of pads crunching as bodies collide, and the feel of dewy grass dampening my shoes. There's insecure posturing, towels snapping on bare skin, and fierce competitiveness.

I love it.

I love it, and I had no idea how much I missed it. Football is king in Texas, but even more so in this small town. Practice might be six-forty-five, but three old timers are up in the bleachers watching practice every single morning. The two Black men and one white are all equally gray-haired and pot-bellied. They also share an intensely serious outlook about Sheet Cake football. I asked Chevy about them my first day, wondering whose parents or grandparents they were.

"Those are the Bobs," Chevy said, grinning. "The three of them played football for Sheet Cake back in their day."

"No kidding?" I'm not sure if I'm more surprised they're all named Bob or that these are former Sheet Cake players.

"Yep. They don't have any family on the team, just a lot of Sheet Cake pride."

Every morning, I've given the Bobs a friendly wave and smile. So far, I have yet to elicit anything but scowls.

Today, I stopped to pick up donuts. "Morning, fellas," I say, holding out the box. "I brought reinforcements."

Am I trying to buy the Bobs' affection with hot glazed?

Why, yes. Yes, I am.

Is it working? No. No, it is not.

The Bobs simply stare, and I set the box on the metal risers nearby before jogging down to the field. I've got plenty of days to keep wearing them down.

"Did you bring me one?" Chevy asks.

I hand him a paper bag filled with donut holes, still warm. In places, the white bag is almost transparent. "Of course. I'm not a barbarian."

"Remains to be seen," Chevy says around a mouthful of dough.

Not for the first time, the head coach is late. I'm not sure what Coach Bright's deal is, but he seems less invested in the team than his cell phone. Sometimes in the middle of practice, he'll take a call and head off the field. It's the kind of behavior that won't help him with job security, especially if the team keeps losing.

Chevy and I have fallen into a rhythm running warm-ups and drills. It's not until we're starting to scrimmage that Coach Bright emerges from the locker room. I notice the Bobs giving him the same dark looks they give me. I also notice that the top of the donut box is askew, and one of the guys is wiping his mouth. Score!

I turn my attention back to the players, clapping my hands. "Let's go! Y'all act like you didn't sleep last night. Pick it up and run the play again—this time like you've played football before!"

The guys scatter, and Chevy sidles up to me with a wink. "Speaking of no sleep—you don't look like you got any last night."

It's true. I got almost none. Definitely not for the reasons Chevy's smug grin seems to be implying. I keep my focus on the field.

"So, you had a good wedding night?" he presses.

Good is a relative term, but even on a sliding scale, my night was not *good*. Have you ever tried to sleep when the woman you love is just across the hallway? Even worse, in a house with walls so thin you can hear every movement? Lindy's sighs were *torture*.

My consolation was that it sounded like she tossed and turned just as much. I can only hope it's because she was thinking about me. To that end, I made sure to roll over a million times on what must be the squeakiest bed on the planet, sighing heavily each time.

When Lindy did finally settle to sleep, I loved hearing her soft, breathy sounds. They were a comfort to me. After so many years apart, so many years of thinking how I royally screwed this up, Lindy was right there. So close.

I'm living the dream! Well, almost the dream.

Lindy is my *wife*. Her rules don't cover my thought life, and I'm going to think of her that way as many times as I can until it feels true.

My wife. My wife. My wife, wife, WIFE.

Chevy clears his throat. I can tell he's still waiting for an answer, watching me with a sly smile. I take a sip of coffee and give him a hefty dose of side-eye, still trying to keep my attention on the field. A grunt seems like a better answer than confirming or denying anything. It's not my preferred method of communication, but I've learned to speak grunt fluently from James.

The play breaks up just as Coach Bright finally decides to do his job. I step back as he takes over the last few minutes of practice. Chevy is still watching me.

"What?" I demand.

He shrugs.

"Look, deputy, you didn't strike me as the kind of guy to want details, but if you do, I'm not the kind of guy who gives them out. Sorry."

Chevy looks horrified. "You think I want details about a woman who's like a sister to me? Gross. No, man. No. Keep it to yourself."

"Then why are you looking at me like that? Why ask?"

His mouth twitches, barely containing his smile. "I just wanted to see if you'd admit your wife made you sleep in separate bedrooms."

Does *everyone* know *everything* in this town?

If I had been thinking about where I am, I wouldn't have shoved Chevy—or at least, not so hard. I send him flying into the players making their way off the field. One or two are almost as tall, though not as broad, and yet they all scatter like bowling pins. Thankfully, none of them go down.

"Pull yourself together, Graham!" Coach Bright yells. It's hard to take the man seriously when his mustache covers half his mouth. It makes him look like a walrus. "This isn't Peewee football."

And you are not Tom Selleck, Alex Trebek, or Sam Elliot—the only three men who, in my mind, can pull off a mustache. I bite my lip to keep the words inside.

"Pick up the cones and hit the showers," Coach Bright calls, his face intent on his phone screen. "And I expect to see you bringing your A-game tomorrow or we'll spend the last half of practice running sprints."

Coach Bright disappears back into the locker room, and the players break. I overhear snatches of conversations reminding me how old I am. I'm not sure I know or want to know what a *yeet* is or what it means to be *cheugy*.

I can't help but notice one kid not picking up cones. It's number seventeen, the QB. His face is more memorable than the name—he's a kid who could grace the covers of magazines, and he knows it too. He also seems to think he's God's gift to football. As another player bends to pick up a cone, number seventeen kicks it out of his way. A couple of the other guys laugh when he kicks the cone even farther.

"HEY." I'm in front of Seventeen before I realize I've moved, blocking his way. "Everyone drop their cones. NOW."

The players exchange looks with each other before looking to Chevy. He nods. "You heard the coach."

Shifting uncomfortably, the guys all drop their cones where they stand. I haven't broken eye contact with Seventeen yet. We're having a regular old stare off. But I learned at the feet of Tank. I will not lose this battle. Especially not in front of the team.

"Seventeen is going to pick up all the cones."

He scoffs. "I am?"

"Yep. You are."

"I don't think you know who I am. I'm—"

"The QB. Which means you need to set the tone for the team. And I personally do not like the tone you're setting. Leaders don't just get to ride at the front of the parade, basking in all the glory. They *serve*."

His mouth flaps open, and I wonder if he's ever been made to serve in his life. No better time to start than the present.

"Get started, Seventeen. The rest of you, hit the showers. Now."

The moment stretches out, and I watch Seventeen's internal debate. I offer him a flash of my teeth, the kind with an edge. *Go on, boy. Try me.* I kind of hope he does. The rest of the team is frozen, a pack of wolves waiting to see who will be their new alpha.

Spoiler alert: it's gonna be me.

"Showers or sprints," I say to the rest of the guys, my eyes still on Seventeen. "Your choice."

That gets them moving. All but the one right in front of me. He's got more fight than I thought.

"What if I refuse?" Seventeen asks.

"You can," I say easily. "Just know that the backup QB has been looking really good. And he had no problem picking up cones."

"Are you threatening to bench me?"

"I'm trying to teach you a lesson, son. Haven't you seen *The Karate Kid?* Or *Kung Fu Panda?*"

"I ...what? Well, yeah."

"If I'm asking you to do something, it's not for fun or for my enjoyment. It's because I think it will make you better, on the field or off. Now are you going to learn the lessons fast or slow? Up to you."

I swear, I see a hint of something in his eyes that's not all bad. He might even be teachable under all his bluster. Time will tell. With a grumble, he drops his gaze and begins collecting cones.

When he's out of earshot, Chevy ambles over. "You know that's Billy and Wolf Waters's nephew?"

I groan. Can't I escape that family?

"I did not. But now the attitude makes sense. Hasn't anyone ever put him in his place?"

"People tend to let the Waters do what they want around here. I'm glad you said something. And I'm not the only one."

Chevy lifts his chin toward the bleachers where the Bobs are grinning and clapping.

"That's all it took? I would have skipped the donuts if I'd known. Now, what are you doing the rest of the day?"

I'm planning to pick up some supplies so I can fix Lindy's upstairs toilet. I have a long list of home improvements, but this one seems like a good place to start. I'm not keen on the three people to one toilet ratio and going downstairs to use the bathroom is pretty annoying. With Lindy and especially Jo in the house, urinating out the window feels more than a little inappropriate.

"Not much," Chevy says. "I'm not on duty until tomorrow."

"Good." I clap a hand on his shoulder. "You've just been

promoted to plumber's assistant. I've got a broken toilet with both our names on it."

———

A few hours later, I'm bent over the back of a toilet, sweaty and shirtless, a wrench in my hand. Chevy is a terrible assistant, especially for a man who renovated his own home. Instead of lifting a finger, he just watches me work, occasionally chuckling at my unsuccessful attempts to make any headway with the toilet.

I hope it's not a sign of things to come because there are a lot of things on Lindy's list. In addition to the toilet, there is no A/C, no dryer, and no television. Add in the temptation of sleeping across the hall from Lindy, and I'm living in a specially designed hell.

"How do you dry your clothes?" I'd asked, when Lindy gave me the grand tour yesterday. Not like I needed it. The house is more of a bungalow. The laundry room is a closet with bi-folding doors in the kitchen. The woman doesn't even own an *iron*.

Lindy had tapped the top of the washing machine, smiling in amusement. "I wash my clothes right here. And then I dry them on the line out back."

She'd pointed to a clothesline strung between two posts, where some shirts flapped in the breeze outside the kitchen door. I didn't even bother asking about the television in case Lindy has some kind of moral objection rather than a financial one. I've already ordered one to be delivered next week. I tried for two-day, expedited shipping, but Sheet Cake is too far from, well, everything.

"You're no help." I glower at Chevy. "I thought you renovated your whole house."

He takes a sip of his beer. "I did most of the work on my house, but I knew what was beyond my pay grade and hired it out. We should call a plumber."

We should. And I can't explain the stubbornness in me that won't allow me to do so. Am I trying to impress Lindy with my handyman prowess—which doesn't exist, by the way—or is it Tank's penny-pinching influence?

Tank was the kind of dad who made us all pitch in for yard work. "Just because we can afford to pay for something," I remember him saying more than once, "doesn't mean we *should*." We were quite literally the only family in our neighborhood who didn't hire a lawn service. Same with the pool, which we cleaned and maintained. He also taught us to cook and clean.

Unfortunately, his training did not extend to plumbing.

"There are easier ways to impress a woman," Chevy says.

I point the wrench at him. "Shut up."

"Did you, like, watch a YouTube video on fixing toilets or something?"

"TikTok," I mutter, removing the lid from the back of the toilet and staring down into it, as though it will answer my questions.

"TikTok? Aren't those videos, like, thirty seconds long?"

"I got the gist of it."

"Did you, now?" Chevy asks, laughing. "Because I'm not seeing a lot of results here."

I'm about to tell him to shut up again when I hear familiar footsteps padding up the stairs. Chevy straightens as Lindy appears in the doorway. She was gone when I got back from football practice and the store—probably working. She told me yesterday she often writes in a coffee shop, which I think is actually her way of avoiding me. She has an office upstairs. Small, but tidy and perfectly usable. Not that I've peeked. In any case, I was hoping to get this done by the time she came home.

Leaning on the door jamb, Lindy crosses her arms. "And what, pray tell, is happening to my toilet?"

I twist something inside the toilet with a wrench, unable to resist the urge to look like I'm doing SOMETHING important. Replacing the lid, I casually lean back against the wall. Perhaps I choose a pose I used in a sports drink endorsement. Maybe I flex my pecs unnecessarily. Lindy *definitely* notices. Faking a yawn, I stretch my arms above my head, which makes my jeans slip down my hips a half-inch. She notices that too.

Lindy rolls her eyes. Not the reaction I was hoping for, but it's a reaction.

Shaking his head, Chevy says, "Nothing is happening to your toilet, because Mario here doesn't know how to fix it."

"Mario?" Lindy and I ask at the same time.

Chevy grins. "Of Mario and Luigi fame. They were plumbers."

"You're such a dork," Lindy says.

"Never pretended otherwise," Chevy says. "Imma grab another beer while Mario here flexes a few more times for you."

I look for something to throw at him and settle on an empty water bottle, which bounces off his back and falls to the tile floor. Lindy grins and steps inside the small bathroom to let Chevy pass. I shuffle through the tools on the counter like I have a plan for the next step, when the next step is definitely to call the plumber.

Lindy picks up the hammer. "What are you going to do with this—hit the toilet if it's bad?"

"Not a terrible idea."

I turn to face her, leaning against the sink. The bathroom

is tiny, and we are toe to toe, our bodies only about a foot apart. I grab the countertop with both my hands, feeling it shift slightly as I do. This whole house seems like it's one screw from falling apart.

I hold out my palm. "Hand it over. The toilet's been very, very bad."

Lindy laughs, clutching the hammer to her chest. I'm drawn to the curve of her smile, the bright flash of her green eyes. My heart thuds at our closeness, at the way she seems to have lowered her guard temporarily.

"Better not," she says, setting the hammer on the floor out of my reach. "I don't trust you with this."

"Probably a good idea." I tug a strand of her hair lightly, and her cheeks flush pink. The temperature in the room seems to rise a few degrees and I catch Lindy's eyes moving over my bare chest and abs. I exhale, tightening up my stomach so the muscles pop.

"Stop that!" She pokes me in the chest, and I grab her hand, pulling her toward me. I noticed that she barely resists.

"Stop what?"

"Flexing."

"I can't do that." I shake my head. "It's an involuntary reaction."

"Right."

"It's true," I tell her, tugging her even closer until her chest is almost flush with my bare one. "You get in close proximity, and I react." I'm sweaty, but based on the way her pupils are dilating, she doesn't mind that a bit.

Look—I want more than a physical relationship with Lindy. But if attraction is the gateway drug to get her hooked on me, I'll work with what I've got.

I also know something about how Lindy operates. If I go too far too fast, she'll run away. But if I push her buttons then pull away first, she'll give chase. I saw it last night when I came *this* close to kissing her in the kitchen, after I signed her ridiculous rules. If I had kissed her, I know she would have kissed me back—and then immediately added some kind of extra rule to her list.

I have to be smart. We are dancing, Lindy and I, and I'm leading her toward what I hope is the realization that she loves me back.

I release Lindy's wrist, letting her go gently, though it's the last thing I want to do.

She looks flustered for a moment, then recovers, averting her eyes. "Come to any conclusions about the toilet?"

"Yeah. I've come to the conclusion it's broken."

Lindy laughs, eyes dancing. "I already told you that. It's just like a man not to believe me."

"Oh, I believed you. I also believed I could fix it."

"And now?"

"Now, I know better. Are you okay if I call a plumber?"

Mistake. I know it the moment I say the word. I should have done it first, then asked forgiveness later.

Lindy's eyes immediately narrow. "I can't afford a plumber right now. And I'm not letting you pay for one."

"It's not a big deal. I have the money."

She shakes her head, straightening up to her full height, which is still inches below mine but formidable. "I'm serious, Pat. I don't want you to pay for a bunch of things. I'm not using you for your money."

"I know that. I've always known that. Plus, helping with house stuff wasn't in the rules. I don't have a job right now, so consider me a house husb—" I catch myself just in time. "Your handyman."

"Just promise me you won't pay for a bunch of stuff. I mean it, Patrick."

We stare at each other across the small space, each as stubborn as the other. "Define a bunch of stuff."

"Pat—promise me!"

"I won't."

What I mean is, I won't *promise* her. But she takes it to mean what she wants to hear—I won't pay for a bunch of stuff. When I said I'm the king of bending the rules, I meant it.

"If it helps, think of it as me doing this for Jo."

That's right—I know your kryptonite. And it's a little girl who I think might end up being mine as well.

Lindy drops her head into her hands, but with so little space in the room, the top of her head grazes my chest. I slide my arms around her lower back, pulling her to me, then freeze when I remember I'm bare-chested and sweat-sticky. She doesn't fight, though, so I tug her fully against me. She drops her hands from her head and latches on to my belt loops as her cheek comes to rest on my chest.

"I'm sorry I'm all sweaty. Do I smell?" I wince, waiting for the answer.

"No, and it's infuriating. You should stink. You should be unattractive and a jerk, and you should smell worse when you sweat, not better."

I take a second to unpack all that. Those are sort of compliments ... right?

"I'm ... sorry?"

"You should be."

"Okay, then I am," I say.

"Fine, then."

"Fine." I pause, then add. "Are we having our first married fight?"

When Lindy laughs, I feel the vibration through my whole body. My fingers flex on her back and I steal a quick nuzzle in her hair. Hair smelling isn't listed in the rules, though I guess technically this all falls under rule number one—no unnecessary touching.

"I guess it is. The first fight of many, I'd wager," she says.

Leaning in even closer so my stubble lightly scrapes her cheek, I murmur, "Does this mean we get to make up now? I've heard making up is the best part of fighting."

She shoves me with one hand, while her other tightens in my belt loop. It's exactly symbolic of her state of mind—she's pushing me away and pulling me close at the same time.

She relaxes against me again, and my muscles bunch—this time involuntarily—as she traces her way up my side.

"What are we doing?" she murmurs, and I don't even know how to answer.

"It looks to me like you're preparing to consummate this marriage," Chevy says from the doorway.

He startles us both, and Lindy jumps back. Her fingers are still curled through my belt loops, so she yanks me with her. We tumble into the bathtub, taking the shower curtain and all her body products with us.

I do my best not to crush Lindy as we fall, cupping my hand around the back of her head and using my other arm to keep my full weight off her.

As our eyes meet, I'm suddenly aware of all the ways our bodies are pressed together, and of how close our mouths are. If I just leaned forward—

"Yep. Definitely about to consummate," Chevy says, his voice disappearing as he lumbers back down the stairs.

Lindy screams with frustration as I extricate myself and stand, pulling her up with me. The back of her shirt is soaked in her body wash, which is now forming a lake in the tub.

"You've got a little something right here," I say, tugging at her hem.

She cranes her neck to see, then makes a growling sound I shouldn't find sexy but do. "Will you be my alibi?" she asks.

"I'll be your everything, darlin'."

She blinks rapidly at this, her lips parting at my words. Tension cracks like a whip between us.

Then Chevy's deep voice carries from somewhere on the first floor. "Just kiss him already!"

With that, Lindy is gone, flying down the stairs. I hear Chevy's laughter fade as the back door slams.

"Lindy!" I call. "Your alibi for what?"

"Murder!"

The door slams again, and I catch my reflection in the mirror, smiling like I don't remember doing in years. When I glance out the window, I see Lindy closing in on Chevy, the dogs not far behind.

CHAPTER TWENTY-TWO

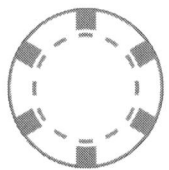

Lindy

ONE OF THE perks to marrying Pat is the fact that the man can *cook*. And I don't mean like mac-n-cheese from a box, cake from a box, or chicken nuggets from a bag in the freezer, which are my household staples. I'm talking FOOD food.

I'd almost forgotten how in college, Pat would don an apron and whip up some amazing meal for the two of us: risotto with goat cheese, grilled steaks and asparagus, or glazed chicken with roasted veggies. My stomach cramps just from the memory of it.

Tonight is the first time since the wedding he's been able to show off his prowess. And show it off, he is.

Jo and I are seated at the table, watching like this is Kitchen Stadium and Pat is the Iron Chef. She and I are not admiring him in quite the same way though. Jo is impressed because, aside from Big Mo and Mari, she hasn't had much exposure with actual food preparation. Evidenced by the fact she didn't know until five minutes ago we owned cutting boards.

Me? I'm watching Pat with an appreciation falling somewhere between the way you eye a delicious steak—what he's fixing—and a deliciously hot man in an apron. Is it normal for a man to look so good in an apron? Or while chopping vegetables? My stomach rumbles, and I'm not sure what it's hungrier for—the man or the dinner he's cooking.

Oh, you're sure, feral cat purrs. *It's definitely the man.*

I don't even bother mentally arguing with her this time. I'm beginning to concede that it's a lost cause and I should go ahead and give her a name, slap a collar on her, and let her sleep in my bed.

"What are you doing to the steaks?" Jo asks.

"I'm seasoning them. This is sea salt with dried garlic, cracked black pepper, and a little fresh rosemary. Smell this."

He leans closer to Jo, which brings him closer to me as well. She smells the sprig of rosemary. I smell Pat.

"Ooh, it's like Christmas," Jo says.

It certainly is.

She giggles as Pat tickles her nose with the rosemary. Then he turns back to the stove.

In addition to getting the toilet fixed this week, Pat went grocery shopping. We now own actual seasonings as well as a whole fridge stocked full of fresh foods. I'm still feeling uncomfortable with the expense of it all, but the man is like a freight train. Also, it's hard to complain about a second toilet and a dinner with actual food groups.

"Now we just need to put the steaks in the oven and— huh." Pat sets the pan of steaks back on the counter. "I swear I preheated this thing." He fiddles with the oven controls.

"We used it recently," I say, trying to think about the last time. "*Sort of* recently."

Within a few minutes, it's clear the oven is not working. Neither is the stovetop, where Pat had planned to sauté vegetables he's already chopped. My stomach growls again, though it sounds a little more like it's weeping now.

"We can get a new one tomorrow"—Pat anticipates my glare and shoots me a narrow-eyed gaze which says, *try and stop me*—"but that doesn't really help us now."

"We have a grill!" Jo says excitedly.

Pat holds out his hand and Jo gives him an animated high-five. "Yes! A grill will work. Great idea, sous chef. I'll just need to adjust a few things. Can you grab me a stick of butter and some foil?"

"On it!" Jo scurries to grab the supplies.

"I'm not sure the grill is in the best shape." If I haven't used the oven in a while, I *really* haven't used the grill in a long time. Maybe years.

"Is it gas or charcoal?" Pat asks. When I give him a blank stare, he smirks. "Do you turn it on with a button or add charcoal to the bottom?"

"It has buttons," I say.

"Perfect. Hopefully, you still have propane in the tank. Jojo, help me put these veggies in this foil and then I'm going to add some butter."

Pat makes a foil basket on the table, and Jo moves the vegetables from the pan into it. He lets her slice the butter and together, they distribute it over the vegetables. Meanwhile, I try to keep my heart from melting into total mush at the sight of them working together across from me. I could be offended Pat hasn't asked for my help, but honestly, I wouldn't ask for my help either. I am a happy spectator and will participate fully in the eating portion of the evening.

The three of us head outside, dogs in tow. Pat carries the steaks, Jo holds the foil packet, and I try to take discreet photos of the two of them with my phone. Because: *adorable*.

With one hand, Pat drags the grill away from the side of the house, where it's been functioning as ugly yard art. It's stainless steel, though it's a bit rusted over in places. More like—it's rust-colored with a little bit of stainless steel accents.

"It may or may not work," I warn. "We can always go to Mari's."

"Nonsense. It'll be great," Pat says, dodging the dogs, whose baser natures have been activated by the scent of raw beef. He pulls the grill to a stop. After examining the front for a second, he turns a knob and a hissing sound can be heard. Pat pushes a button. There are a few clicks and then a whoosh. He turns to me with a smile. "We're in business!"

Suddenly there is another noise—a kind of scrabbling, scratching sound from inside the grill. "Is that ... normal?" I ask.

Amber and Beast start barking, probably trying to hurry the steak-cooking process along. The scratching gets louder. And is that a squeak?

Pat stares at the grill. "Huh."

Holding the plate of steaks higher to avoid the dogs, Pat lifts the top of the grill, then immediately jumps back as not one but multiple squirrels leap out of the grill directly onto his body.

Three—count them, *three!*—squirrels, singed with tails still smoking, run up Pat's chest like it's a climbing wall.

I didn't know Pat had the ability to scream like a little girl, but he does. *Loudly*.

Amber leaps on Pat, going either for the squirrels or the

steaks, and Pat flings the whole plate, still screaming and pinwheeling his arms.

The squirrels use Pat's shoulders as a launchpad, leaping off and scampering away, thin wisps of smoke trailing behind their blackened tails. Beast and Amber sprint after them, pausing only long enough to grab the steaks. And there goes our dinner.

I still had my phone camera open and, in the confusion, somehow switched to video, recording the whole thing. I'll be really thankful for that later, but I probably won't mention it to Pat, who is still dancing around, aggressively brushing at his shirt. Which has tiny, soot-stained footprints up the front and on the shoulders.

"Are they gone? Are they gone?" Pat asks, his eyes wild.

"They are."

"Along with dinner," Jo says, and I realize in the confusion, she dropped the foil packet and now vegetables are scattered in the dirt along with the remnants of the broken steak plate.

"Maybe we should go out to dinner," I suggest as my stomach moans an agreement.

"Yes, *please*," Pat says, switching off the grill. "But first, I need to change. And then burn this shirt."

Before Pat takes two steps toward the house, Jo stops him where he stands, looking deadly serious. "You need to check first for cuts and scratches. Squirrels can carry rabies."

And that is how I end up in Pat's bedroom, examining his bare chest in close detail. Close, close detail. To make sure I was extra thorough, Jo gave me her magnifying glass.

Because the naked-eye visual of Pat's body wasn't enough. Nope. I needed the magnified version.

"I think you might have missed something over here," Pat says, grinning and pointing to his right pec. He flexes it up and down like it's waving hello.

"I hope you have rabies. I really do. It will totally serve you right."

His left pec joins in, and now it's like a two-ring pec circus. Lucky me—I'm getting a free show.

"For what? What am I doing, Lindy?"

You're taunting me with your glorious body. Trying to wear down my resolve at its weakest point.

But also: infusing laughter into my day. Making everything feel brighter and lighter. I hadn't realized how lonely I sometimes felt with just me and Jo. Or how utilitarian I had become, just focused on what each day's tasks were and what I *had* to do. Bringing Pat into my life was like turning up both the saturation settings and the volume. I feel almost like a new person—and this is after only a few days.

"Maybe you should check my back too," Pat suggests, turning around.

Though abs and chests tend to get the lion's share of attention when it comes to what women seem to like on a man, Pat's back is no less a work of art. And without his eyes on me, I can really *look*. Not for squirrel scratches. No, I'm looking the way I'd imagine an art dealer examines a new painting, trying to decide if they should sell it or keep it for their private collection.

He shifts, and the muscles bunch and ripple in an entrancing way. *Definitely the private collection.*

"See anything?" he asks.

Too much. Way too much. "No scratches. I guess we're done."

Pat turns back to me, and were we always standing this close? "You didn't check my shoulders."

"What? I did. With a magnifying glass."

He shakes his head, and I want to kiss that smirk right off his face. That would teach him!

"The tops of my shoulders. Those evil tree rats leaped off my shoulders. If they scratched me, it would be there."

I look up, and then up. I'm not short, but Pat is TALL. Tall enough that I definitely can't see the tops of his shoulders. He seems to already know this and looks way too smug about it. He's like a smug factory, producing smug at levels way above the government restrictions.

"I'll just sit on the bed, and you can get behind me and—"

"Nope. No beds. Rule number … whatever." My mind has gone blank, and I can't remember which of the rules addresses me and Pat and beds.

"I think you mean rule number four," Pat says. "But that one only refers to shared bedrooms and shared beds."

"It applies." I grab the wooden chair from the corner and drag it over. It's a little rickety, but it's better than me getting on a bed with Pat. I know Jo is downstairs and her presence would prevent any major mistakes, but I feel like all Pat needs is an inch and he's going to take a mile. If I break and kiss him, for example, I think it may all be over.

And that would be bad, why?

The reasons why are getting a little hazy, like I'm looking at them in the rearview mirror through thick fog. Which is why I need to stand on this chair rather than go near a bed with Pat.

"Whoa. You sure that's safe?" Pat asks as I climb up. His hands hover near my hips, poised to steady me, and I brush them away.

"Just stop talking and let me look at your shoulders so we can get this done."

The chair wobbles a little, and I curse the furniture that's been in this house since before I was born. It shakes a little more, and I grab Pat's shoulders for support just as his hands find my waist. Like this, I'm taller than he is. It should feel powerful up here, but with Pat's hands on me and mine on him, I'm totally weak. Boneless, spineless, resolveless.

Our faces are so close. Positioned like this, a kiss would have to be *my* choice. Totally my decision. My call.

Pat is a smart guy. He knows this, and he doesn't push, he doesn't make a comment, he doesn't even move. He's just right there, inches away, breathing in and out with lips slightly parted, waiting, hoping, letting me take control.

At that moment, my stomach makes a noise so incredibly loud and inhuman that my cheeks and chest immediately flame red. It sounds like a broken bagpipe playing a dirge.

I guess I should be thankful it broke the tension, but I'm disappointed instead.

Pat's eyebrows shoot up, and he bites his lip. "Was that ... your stomach?"

"I'm hungry, okay?"

"It sounded like a whale song," he says, and that's when I decide I'm TOTALLY uploading the video of Pat and the squirrels to Neighborly the first chance I get.

With a last glance at his shoulders—no one wants Pat to have rabies, after all—I jump down with as much pride as I still have and head for the door.

"It's your lucky day," I call over my shoulder. "After further review, you are totally rabies-free."

CHAPTER TWENTY-THREE

Pat

TANK'S FACE is lit up like this is Christmas morning and the big asphalt truck is the pile of presents under the tree. James, who I'm surprised is even here for this, looks as stony and unmoved as usual. I wish he had a ticklish spot. I would totally take advantage of that to get some kind of reaction out of him. But throughout our lives, we all searched for it like it was some kind of holy grail, and never managed to find one. My brother, the sole person in the world who isn't ticklish.

"Feels like we should have a red ribbon to cut," I say, looking out over the road.

"We really should," Tank says. "We'll have to plan a grand opening."

To my surprise, Tank has already lined up several businesses ready to take a gamble on this town: a bakery and coffee shop, a store selling unique gifts and art, and a clothing boutique. I nudged Tank to look in that direction after suffering through Walmart Junior's clothes before my family brought reinforcements.

"Who will get to cut the ribbon?" James asks.

I lean around Tank to give my brother a look. "Not you, Mr. Sourpuss."

"I'm here, aren't I?"

James *is* here. Which is progress. He still hasn't given the stamp of approval for Dark Horse. In fact, Collin told me just this week, James looked at several Austin properties. Technically, my dad's plan doesn't NEED James and Dark Horse. But it sure would feel better to have all of us on board, a united front.

"Are the cars okay, you think?" I ask dad. "I don't want my truck asphalted."

Tank chuckles. "Stop worrying about your truck. It's not *that* fancy. By the way, I've got the invoice from the dealer on the Aston."

He pulls a paper out of his back pocket and hands it to me. I try not to wince at the number. More than ever, I'm thankful for Tank's lessons in frugality and investing. At the moment, my bank account is like a sieve, pouring out money in a steady stream. Between fixing things at Lindy's place, getting the loft renovated, and now the Aston, it's a lot.

"When are we getting this thing started?" James asks. "I don't want to spend all day here."

Today, the asphalt will be laid over the crumbly concrete roads of downtown Sheet Cake. Right now, workers are prepping the area, removing any of the big, broken chunks of concrete. Next, they'll drive the truck slowly over the road, pouring the black asphalt right over top, then smoothing it out. The three of us are like a bunch of little boys, excited to watch some big trucks do big truck stuff.

Tank did his homework and found that pouring asphalt on top of the existing roads is a faster fix. Redoing concrete can take months: pulling up the old slabs and hauling them off, rebuilding the wood frames, and installing new rebar before the concrete is finally poured.

With asphalt, we'll be done in a day. I like that kind of timeline. I'm surprised how quickly things are starting to take shape. My loft is set to be done late next week—that is, if all the cabinets and appliances come in on time. The crew even finished installing built-in bookshelves in the second bedroom for Jo.

Not that Lindy wants to move out of the farmhouse, but I figure it's a good backup.

Despite her protests, I've been able to fix up a few things since I moved in last week. But little fixes aren't enough. I didn't like what I saw underneath there when I fixed the trellis under the porch the other day. The pier-and-beam foundation had a distinct lean to it and there are cracks in the support pillars. I didn't mention it to Lindy, who still gives me a dirty look every time she finds something new I've fixed. (Though I've also seen her enjoying the fruits of my labor.)

The whole thing needs a massive overhaul, from the foundation up. The house doesn't look to me as though it would pass inspection. If needed, the three of us could move to the loft temporarily while we get the house up to code. Or even build a new, bigger house on the property. But as I am wont to do, I'm getting ahead of myself.

"This looks like trouble," James mutters.

I see Billy Waters ambling over in a suit, looking as pleased as spiked punch at a high school dance, and I have to agree with my brother. He had the same look on his face when Judge Judie handed down my sentence in court.

"Who's the suit?" Tank asks.

"Like James said, trouble. Specifically, that's Billy Waters, a member of Sheet Cake's first family and a lawyer."

Billy must have hearing like a bat because he adds, "I also used to date your sudden wife. Congratulations are in order, I guess. Surprised to see you back from your honeymoon so soon. Oh, right. People don't take honeymoons for fake weddings."

Lindy dated Billy? I want to punch his smug face more than ever. James locks my arm in a tight grip, even though the ankle monitor is a great reminder I need to keep my cool. As if to prove the point, my ankle chooses that moment to start itching like mad.

"Thank you for the well wishes," I tell Billy, my grin a little bit more like baring of teeth. "Now, what brings you out here this fine morning?"

"I am also a member of city council. And it's on that authority I've got to stop you from any further work on the roads."

Billy offers us a breezy smile and a pink piece of paper. Pink slips are never good.

"I don't understand," Tank says, and James grabs the slip from him, squinting down at it with a frown. "I own the town. I can pave the roads."

"Ah," Billy says. "See that's where you're wrong. I know you've got permits for the construction inside the buildings, but roads constitute public works, and that's a whole other ball of wax." Billy winks at Tank, his voice changing to one that's even more patronizing. "I know it's probably complicated for someone like you. Put in the simplest words with the fewest syllables, you'll have to bring a proposal before the city council."

I can practically feel the anger coming off Tank in hot

waves. Based on the low growl I hear from James, the three of us are on the same page of this book.

"Where and how can I submit a proposal?" Tank asks, and though he's lost that Christmas morning smile, he's still got grit and determination.

Billy's smile widens, like a snake about to unhinge its jaw. "You have to do so in person at a city council meeting."

"When's the next meeting?" I ask.

Billy rubs his clean-shaven jaw. "Let's see ... I guess in about a month. The date is on the website." It's clear he knows the specific date but isn't going to make this easy on us.

Tank's jaw flexes. "Great. We'll be there with what paperwork we need."

"Good luck with that." Billy laughs and gives us a little jaunty wave.

But when Tank takes one step his way, Billy turns and heads back to his shiny Mercedes.

"I'd like to asphalt over his car," I mutter. *Especially now that I know he dated Lindy.*

Tank pulls out his phone and scrolls through before settling on a number.

"Who are you calling?" James asks. "And what are we going to do with all this asphalt?"

"I got the name of a developer from another retired player a while back. This guy is based out of Chicago, but his firm did some work on a town in East Texas. Maybe they'd be willing to do a consult. Clearly, I underestimated the complexity of this."

The foreman chooses that moment to approach Tank. The kicker of this whole thing is we can't just return the asphalt. It's hot and ready and needs to be used.

"What a waste," James mutters, running his hands over his face. "All of it is just a waste."

He stomps off, and Tank and I let him go. Honestly, when I see James heading toward the silos, my spark of hope at his involvement grows into a tiny flame. The circumstances are not the best, but I'm happy to see my eldest brother starting to get emotionally invested, even if the emotion he's feeling is despair.

That's step one: having feelings. Step two: total domination.

"I'm beginning to wonder if James is right," Tank says. "Maybe this is a waste. Of time, of money, of energy."

I put an arm around his shoulders. Well. As much of his shoulders I can get my arm around. An idea begins to take shape in my mind. "It doesn't have to be."

"The town or the asphalt?" he asks.

"Both. For today, we're just going to worry about today's problem. And I've actually got a very good idea of exactly where that asphalt can go."

CHAPTER TWENTY-FOUR

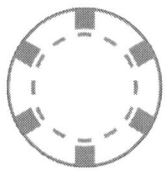

Lindy

WITH THE HEARING INCHING CLOSER, I find myself soaking up every second I can get with Jo. If some of this time also coincidentally keeps me out of the house and away from Pat's magnetic presence, so be it. Triple bonus if it includes shakes from Sonic.

Mari may think tacos solve life's problems—and they do—but milkshakes can brighten the darkest day. Sonic doesn't have the BEST shakes in the world, but they're more than acceptable, and if you're lucky, they'll be delivered to your car by someone on roller skates.

"You could always get a job here, Win," Val says, taking a long sip of her shake and eyeing the teenage boy skating away in skinny jeans.

City council informed Winnie after their special meeting this week that her services are no longer needed as secretary.

It makes sense, seeing as there's no mayor right now, but it also leaves her temporarily jobless.

Winnie's financials have been a little unsteady since college. She has a boatload of student loans, and when her dad died, he had run up bills of his own, which didn't leave much for her and Chevy. My friends and I are a really sad example of living the post-college dream, one thin paycheck at a time.

Winnie makes a face. "Thanks, but no thanks. I hung up my skates after college."

I glance at Jo in the back seat next to Winnie. She's never this quiet. Clearly she's just giving her peanut butter cup milkshake all her focus. Once the straw hits the bottom and the sugar hits her bloodstream, I'm sure that will change.

"Maybe you could work for Pat's dad or something," I suggest. "He's got all these big plans for downtown."

"Pass. I'll figure things out," Winnie says. "Worst-case scenario, I'll bunk with Chevy and work on building my business. Unless I get another offer."

And by offer, we all know she means a proposal. As much as Val and I aren't terribly enthusiastic about Dale, it's shocking he hasn't locked Winnie down. We expect it any day now. I think she said he wanted to make sure his savings account was at a certain place before taking the next step. Which only further illustrates my point about him. Responsible? Yes. Romantic? No.

"You and Chevy would kill each other," I tell her.

Winnie smiles. "Yeah, but then I'm the beneficiary of his house, so I just have to make sure I'm the last one standing."

"You can always move in with me," Val says. A lovely offer, except that her garage apartment at Mari's is one room. Plus, her tendency toward what she calls creative chaos is what Winnie calls a filthy mess no human should have to inhabit.

I'd offer my place, but the place is full with Pat there. Too full. Claustrophobia-inducing full.

"I'll figure it out," Winnie says, taking a long sip of her milkshake. "Don't you worry about me."

Val takes a loud sip and then gives me a pointed look. "So, are we going to head back to your house or what?"

"Why would you come by my house?"

"Why don't you *want us* to come by?" Val counters.

Ever since Pat and I did the thing at the courthouse—the whole *marriage* thing—my friends have been pestering me about all of it. I feel like a zoo animal they want to stare at through the bars. Forgive me for not wanting to be examined. I wouldn't like it under normal circumstances, and I definitely don't—not now that I have something to hide. Namely, the electric chemistry that ignites whenever Pat and I are together. It gets worse each day I have to share the house and my life with him.

Almost a week together, and I'm ready to crack.

"We could take a scenic drive?" I suggest. "Or ... go shopping? Get a car wash?"

"Maybe stop in CVS for a flu shot?" Val suggests. "Or an enema?"

"What's an enema?" Jo asks, slurping down the last of her shake.

I glare at Val. "Nothing you need to worry about, Jojo. But if the time ever comes, I'll be sure your Auntie Val explains it."

Val swivels in her seat and turns to face Winnie and Jo in the back seat. "What's the scoop, Jojo? How are things with Pat living there?"

"Val," I grumble.

But Jo is done with her shake, pumped full of sugar, and her mouth is already off and running. "Pat is the best. He's fixing a lot of stuff even though Lindy keeps yelling at him to stop. And he takes his shirt off a lot." She drops her voice to a whisper. "Aunt Lindy complains, but I know she likes it. I saw her watching him from the window."

I quietly die as the sound of Winnie and Val's laughter fills the car. "The two of you need to get out of my car," I tell them.

"Okay. But we'll meet you at your place," Val says. "Please?"

"Pretty please?" Winnie begs, and I glare.

"Come on, Aunt Lindy," Jo says. "Maybe Pat will make us all dinner!"

Val presses a hand over her heart. "He's cooking for you too?"

"I don't even know if he's there," I tell them.

"He's always there," Jo says, and she's right.

Pat is ALWAYS THERE. He's unavoidable. Most days, he feels inevitable. And dang it if I don't feel the slightest hop and skip in my heart thinking about going home right now to see him.

"Fine," I grumble. "You can come by."

Winnie and Val practically leap out of the car, anticipating that I might change my mind at any given second. Which I might.

"See you there!" Val calls as they hop into her car.

I don't bother with a reply.

We're approaching the driveway when I realize something is up. Cars—Pat's, Chevy's, and another I don't recognize—are parked along the road past the mailbox. But it's not until the driveway itself comes into view that I realize what has happened. Though, admittedly, it's a complete shock. One that has steam whistling through my ears like I'm a little teapot, about to be tipped over and poured out.

"Wow!" Jo says, pressing her face to the glass as I pull up and park in front of Chevy's Mustang. "Look at our new driveway!"

"I see it," I say through gritted teeth.

This morning there was only a pot-holed, mostly dirt stretch of driveway. Now there is a black ribbon of asphalt stretching all the way to the house. There's even a new, circular drive in front of the house, and it extends all the way back to the barn.

Pat and I are going to have words. Or more than words, whatever that would be. I told him not to do big stuff, and I've tried to ignore the little things he's done around the house, mostly because I'm so happy to have two toilets and a new oven. But a new driveway? This must have cost THOUSANDS.

I smell it when I get out of the car, the strangely pleasant scent of hot, fresh tar. Jo bounds across the lawn, where the dogs are frolicking with Pat and Tank. James and Chevy are sitting on the porch. Pat jogs our way, meeting Jo halfway. As Val and Winnie park behind me, Pat picks Jo up, swinging her around until she squeals with delight. I hope he shakes the milkshake loose and she pukes all over him.

"Whoa," Val says, clutching her hands to her chest. "He paved your driveway. That's so sweet!"

"It's not sweet," I say, slamming my door.

"It isn't?" Winnie asks.

"No. It's presumptuous. Among other things."

"Your driveway was a public safety hazard," Winnie says.

"I applaud this decision and think you're out of your mind if you're complaining about this."

"It was *my* safety hazard. And he shouldn't be spending money on me."

"Newsflash," Winnie says. "You married him. You are now sharing your life with him and that includes your driveway. Didn't you tell me he broke some fancy car in one of the potholes?"

That shuts me up.

"Incoming," Winnie says, and I see Pat approaching, his hands shoved deep in his pockets.

"We'll give you two a moment." Val hooks her arm through Winnie's, and they head toward the house. "Love the driveway!" she calls, and I stare machetes at her back, because staring daggers isn't enough.

I take a deep breath and head toward Pat. Though he's smiling, it's a sheepish grin. It's the same look Amber gets when I find her sleeping in my bed.

"I can explain," he says.

"Be my guest. Tell me why, when I've been explicitly clear about not wanting you to pay for big things, you do something that is by definition *very* big."

I don't realize we were both still moving forward until we stop at about the same time, our toes practically touching. The air vibrates with tension.

"Tank hired a crew to pave the downtown. Then Billy Waters showed up with some injunction from the city council saying we needed to have permits for the roads and blah blah, boring legal stuff. Tank already paid for the truck and the workers. So, we needed to pave *something*. I thought of you."

"How sweet," I say, my voice dripping with sarcasm even though ... it really *is* sweet. And thoughtful. Considering the situation, would I rather the asphalt go to waste? His explanation is totally reasonable. Yet I am personally feeling anything BUT reasonable.

My relationship with Pat is a life-sized game of Risk, and I cannot let him win this offensive. It's way too much ground to give up. Honestly, he has no idea how close I am to waving a white flag of surrender.

But every time I think I'm ready to lay down my arms, I remember the searing pain I felt losing Pat before. I remind myself how long I waited for him that last night for our final goodbye, how stupid I felt when I realized he left without saying goodbye.

I think about his quickie Vegas marriage to Booby McUnderpants, not all that different from his quickie marriage to me. Who's to say he won't change his mind about me in a few days or week?

But I feel like I'm having to work really hard to make these arguments convincing. My reasons to resist are becoming smaller and smaller the more time I spend with Pat. They are like a flimsy prop set for a movie, about to blow over with a strong wind.

Pat *has* changed. I see it in his patience with Jo, and even with the way he deals with my surly attitude. The special connection we had years ago is only stronger, deeper. Still, I've spent years building up my protective walls, not just for me but for Jo. It's my job to keep us safe behind these walls. They're sturdy. They're important. And here I am letting Pat bulldoze his way right inside.

Part of me wants to step back and just let him on through. But I can't rush my heart.

I'm completely overwhelmed with what's going on right now with Jo. I don't know if I have the emotional bandwidth to truly consider the relationship with Pat or make a rational decision I won't second-guess later. There's too much else at stake, too much on my mind. Until things with Jo are more certain, I can't even consider letting myself fall for my husband.

And so I put my hands on my hips and steel my voice. "No more big things, Pat. I mean it."

He totally ignores this. "I had an interesting conversation with Billy, by the way. He mentioned that you two dated?"

I narrow my eyes, feeling heat build in my chest. "You want to talk about past relationships right now? Maybe I have terrible taste in men."

Pat's voice lowers. Did he get closer somehow? I swear I can feel the heat of him burning into me.

"Could be. Maybe you should test that theory." His eyes drop to my mouth. "Want to see how I taste, Lindybird?"

And I totally do. I want nothing more than to grab this infuriating man and yank his mouth to mine and battle this out without words.

"Get a room!" Chevy calls, and Pat rocks back on his heels, groaning.

"One of these days, I'm going to pay that man back for all of this."

"I'll gladly help you," I say, stepping back. Pulling myself together, I manage to slow my heart to regular, human levels. "Thank you for the driveway. Even though you shouldn't have done it."

I stomp away from Pat before I can lose any more ground or think any more kissing thoughts.

Tank intercepts me as I reach the new circular drive in front of the house. His arms stretch out for a hug, and I can't refuse him. Tank hugs are starting to edge ahead of Chevy hugs, especially now that Winnie's brother is on my naughty list.

"Did Pat tell you about our mishap downtown?" he asks. "I hope it wasn't overstepping."

"It was," I tell him, "but it's also very kind. Thank you. What do I owe you?"

Tank waves me off. "Consider it a wedding gift."

Before I can respond, Jo bounds over. She drags Tank toward the house. "Come see what Patty did in my room!" she squeals.

"What did he do in your room?" I call. I'm sure whatever it is, Tank has already seen it, but he goes along willingly.

When she turns, looking over her shoulder, her face is full of glee. "He and Uncle James built me bookshelves!"

Pat and *Uncle* James built bookshelves. I'm so overcome with a mix of emotions I can't even respond. Winnie and Val come up on either side of me, wrapping their arms around my waist like I need them to hold me up. Maybe I do.

"Want to tell us why you're still resisting this man?" Val asks quietly. "He's like a dream."

"Exactly. A dream. And when I wake up, that's when it's going to hurt."

Winnie scoffs. "You know that's not what she meant. And if you really think Pat would leave you, you're not right in the head."

I'm definitely not right in the head.

Val leans her head on my shoulder. "You're only fighting yourself here, Lindy."

"Would you look at that," Winnie says. "The grumpy one might have a heart after all."

Jo has emerged from the house and is now sitting with James, a chessboard between them. Even out of hearing range, I can tell how carefully James is explaining the rules. Jo nods eagerly, her hands fluttering over the pieces.

"Ow!" Val suddenly bends over at the waist.

"You okay?" Winnie and I turn toward her with concern.

"I think my ovary just exploded."

It's Winnie, not me, who shoves Val. "Don't let yourself get sucked in. That one especially looks like total heartbreak material."

"Gorgeous heartbreak material," Val sighs.

This time, Winnie doesn't even argue. And when I catch Pat grinning at me, I totally know what Val means.

FOUR UNDERRATED PARTS OF THE MALE PHYSIQUE

by Birdie Graham

While popular culture screams from the rooftop about men's butts, abs, and even forearms, there are some gorgeous parts of men that need to have their day in the sun. This is a strictly PG-13 kind of list, folks, and (mostly) safe for family reading.

Caveat #1: Most of these features can be appreciated at different levels of fitness and hairiness, to taste.

Caveat #2: Objectification is not good! This list focuses on appreciating physical attributes, but we should all appreciate people as whole humans, not just for their looks.

And now, let's get to appreciating!

Four Underrated Parts of The Male Physique

1. The ankle. Ladies' ankles were at one time a scandal (and still are in some cultures), but men's ankles shouldn't be overlooked. Delicate but

strong, there is just something magnetic about this meeting of foot and leg.
2. The side of the ribs. Not sure what I'm talking about? Watch a shirtless man reach above his head. The muscles are more subtle and way less *look at me!* than the abdominals. But still very, very wonderful.
3. The nape of the neck. Sometimes people just refer to this as a nape, which freaks me out. Napes need to be attached to necks, thank you very much. Whether your man has long or short hair, there is something totally sexy about the place where hair ends and the soft, bare skin of the neck begins.
4. The lower back. So much time is spent ogling abs that we've missed the flip side, and it is a thing of beauty riding on top of that waistband.

Stay tuned for Part Two—Four Underrated Parts of the Female Physique!

CHAPTER TWENTY-FIVE

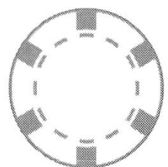

Lindy

BEFORE PAT, on a typical night, Jo and I would hang out in the family room with her reading and me doing a little writing or research. After Pat, all the relaxation and chill has been sucked out of our nighttime routine. Chill is impossible with a restless—and let's not forget, completely HOT—man in the house.

Pat has an aversion to stillness, and he doesn't seem to know what to do with himself. I'm pretty sure having no television is pushing the man to his limits. Even as I'm thinking about his restlessness, Pat shifts, sighing and wiggling as he scrolls through something on his phone. Is it bad I like to watch him squirm? And every time he shifts, I shift, because this couch is woefully small for two people, especially when one of them is Pat's size.

My poor, little house feels like a shirt we've grown out of.

Pat towers in every room and fills every doorway. And though I know it's small and Pat is a big guy, I can almost feel the intention in each touch, however quick. We can't pass each other in the hall or even in a room without some physical contact. Like when his fingers brush mine as we pass in the kitchen or when his hip lightly bumps mine in the upstairs hallway.

Each tiny touch is like a reminder: *Hey! I'm here! Hey! You can't resist me forever!*

I should remind him of the rule about necessary touching, but ... I don't.

What I did do was order a television for him. It feels like such a small thing—literally, it's a modest 36-inch TV, all I can afford—but the idea of giving Pat a gift makes me feel strangely vulnerable. It's silly to feel nervous about such a little gift. Pat gives so freely, so constantly, like he's a stream pouring down an endless supply of fresh mountain water.

Me? I'm a rusty spigot that's hard to turn. But I'm *trying* to loosen up without feeling like I'm totally losing control.

I glance down at my laptop, which is open to a page about narwhals, and slam it shut. Even the unicorn of the sea can't hold my attention tonight. Not with the warmth of Pat's body so close to mine and my thoughts a thorny tangle.

"What do you think about this one, Jojo?" Pat asks, turning his phone screen toward her.

It takes Jo a moment to climb out of whatever book she's fallen into. Her eyes light up almost immediately. "I love it."

"What are y'all looking at?" I ask, tilting the phone screen toward me and then going still when I see what's on it.

Hairstyles. Pat is searching up hairstyles for Jo. I'd tell my heart to be still, but it's no use. I'm pretty sure my heart has already vacated my chest cavity and is lying prostrate before Pat, crying, *Take me! Take me! I'm yours!*

Inwardly, I'm a weeping, wilting mess. Outwardly, I keep my voice steady as I say, "I like that one. It would look cute on you. I could always try it."

Jo tilts her head. "You want to wear double braids like that?"

"No, I mean I could try doing that to your hair."

She goes back to her book, and I try not to be offended when she says, "That's okay. Patty will do it. He's better at it than you."

Well, then. I raise my eyes at Pat, who looks like he's about to burst out laughing. "No need to rub it in. Where'd you get your beauty school certificate?"

Pat takes his phone back and gives me a crooked grin. "My brothers and I used to take turns doing Harper's hair."

That mental image is almost too much. Could the man be any more irresistible? It's like he's completely composed of the human equivalent of catnip. What would that even be called—man-nip? Ew. That sounds way too nipply. We'll stick to the human version of catnip. And Pat is practically leaking it from his pores.

"At least, we did until Harper punched James and told us all she didn't like us touching her hair and could fix her own ponytails, thank you very much." He chuckles.

Pat sets his phone down, and before I can stop him, he sweeps my feet up into his lap and begins rubbing them. I don't have an aversion to feet or anything, but I can't remember the last time anyone touched mine. It's way too intimate, especially when I'm feeling all squishy inside. I try to twist away, my protests quickly dissolving into giggles. He tightens his grip.

"Stop manhandling my feet!"

"I'm not *manhandling* them. I'm trying to *massage* them. You look like you need to relax."

I stop fighting him. Both because I *do* need to relax, and because he *noticed*. I'm beginning to feel like he notices everything. Pat is a star pupil, majoring in Lindy with a minor in Lindy studies. Which means he can sense my stress.

It's not that I had a bad day or anything, but the weight of things with Jo has hung heavily over me today in particular. Each day we inch toward the hearing feels like watching a doomsday timer. What will the courts decide? What will it be like to see Rachel again? What will happen if they take Jo away? I know I'm being too clingy with her, mostly because she's told me as much.

Pat sighs roughly and angles his big body toward me. The big body I can easily picture in high def, thanks to how often he is shirtless. Let's see, there was the toilet fixing incident which ended with him pressed up against me in the bathtub, then the squirrel examination, where I got up close and personal with his chest. Then there are his daily workouts. Sprints and push-ups and some kind of jumping things in the backyard. Not that I've watched him through the faded eyelet curtains in my room. Only creepy stalkers would do that.

Just this morning, I stepped out of my bedroom as Pat came out of the bathroom wearing only a towel. Steam swirled around him and the bathroom light caused a kind of halo effect. Beads of water ran slowly over the planes of his chest and the distinct ridges of his abs. The many, many ridges. Even all these years out from being in the pros, Pat's body is unreal. I feel like I need to hand someone a ticket stub just to view it. But he seems to enjoy giving me free shows.

I was mid-yawn, and I choked on my own spit at the sight of him. I bolted downstairs, locking myself in the bathroom until he left the house. He took his time getting ready too. What I didn't think about until later is that Pat probably assumed I was pooping for like half an hour.

Super sexy, Lindy. Super. Sexy.

"Does this feel good?" Pat asks, jarring me back into the moment. The one where he's almost putting me to sleep with this amazing foot rub. "Too hard? Too soft? Just right?" He grins, eyes glinting with mischief.

I lie back and put a pillow over my face. "It's good," I mumble through the fabric. "But massage at your own risk. I have hobbit feet."

I hear Jo set down her book and shift in her seat, probably pulled out of her story by hearing the word *hobbit*.

"You don't have hobbit feet," Pat scoffs.

"I do!" I wiggle them so he can get a good look. "See how wide they are? You have no idea how difficult it is for me to find shoes."

Pat lightly runs his fingers over the tops and sides of my feet. His touch sends a cascade of signals through my nervous system, from my toes all the way up to my scalp. Even my eyeballs suddenly feel hot. I take the pillow off and fan my face with it. Jo is leaning forward, elbows on her bent knees, watching us with interest.

After a moment, Pat says, "I've done a full examination. You are officially not a resident of the Shire."

Jo giggles, and Pat winks at her, which does something entirely different, though no less powerful, to my body. He's been so good with her, so warm and patient and perfect. And Jo has been soaking in his attention like a sponge.

There's that echo again, the word *family* carried on some invisible breeze, a whisper making my chest pinch with longing.

I settle a little as Pat begins rubbing my feet in earnest.

It's impossible not to—the man has good, strong hands. If I'm not careful, I'm going to be imagining his hands elsewhere.

"I'm going to bed," Jo announces.

"Who do you want to read to you tonight?" I ask, already guessing what the answer will be. Since he moved in, it's Pat. Always Pat.

Jo waves me off, looking like a mini adult more than ever, which is saying something. "It's okay. You can finish your mating ritual or whatever."

"Our *what*?" Pat's hands freeze on my feet, and he looks like he's having a heart attack.

"Did you say mating ritual?" I ask, attempting to keep my voice level. I've learned that's key: whatever shocking thing comes out of her mouth, I can internally freak out, but outwardly, I need to stay steady and calm.

Right now, steady and calm is a challenge. I'm not ready for this conversation. I should have years to prepare for any conversation around the topic of *mating*. And it will under no circumstances involve that term.

Jo shrugs. "It was in one of the animal books. When they want to mate, they puff up their feathers or do complicated dances to get the other one's attention. Then they mate. Which I guess is like being boyfriend-girlfriend or whatever."

Air comes back into my lungs, and Pat's hands start rubbing my feet again.

"Right," I say. "Yeah, mating rituals. I've heard of that."

"Can I have pancakes for breakfast?" Jo asks.

"Yep," Pat says. "I'll make some before I leave for practice. They'll be hot and ready when you get up."

"Cool. Goodnight!" Jo calls.

Her door closes, and it's on my lips to call out a reminder

to brush her teeth. Instead, Pat and I both sit statue still for another few moments, then sigh at almost the same time.

"I thought we were going to have to explain—" Pat starts just as I say, "That was close."

We both laugh nervously, and I turn, setting my feet on the scarred wooden floor.

"Want to help me with dishes?" I ask, not because I need the help, but more because I don't trust myself next to Pat on this little couch without Jo as a chaperone.

Pat gets up, holding out a hand to me. "I'll help with dishes only if you'll show me your complicated mating dance."

I get up without his help, shoving him lightly as I pass. "Wouldn't you like to see it."

He chuckles as he follows me, and his low voice is like a fingertip dragging lightly up my spine. "You have no idea how much."

"This is oddly domestic," I tell Pat, handing him the last plate to dry. Tonight's dinner was courtesy of Pat and the new stove he purchased and had installed while I was out today. I didn't even protest the expense because his homemade shrimp and grits was to die for. He even got Jo, who doesn't like seafood at all, EVER, to try it. She didn't like the grits, but she ate a dozen shrimp.

"Domestic—yes. Odd? No."

I glance his way without fully turning my head, letting my hair provide a curtain between us. "You don't find this a little strange?"

Pat stacks the dish on top of the others we've washed, then tosses the dish towel in the washing machine. He leans a hip against the counter, facing me. "What's strange about it?"

"This," I say, gesturing through the air. "You helped with dishes and just put a towel in the washing machine."

"Uh huh. I see your point," he says, rubbing his chin. "It's so weird when guys do helpful things, *domestic* things."

"Shut up. We aren't talking about stereotypical gender roles or the patriarchy. We're talking about me and you."

"Ah. Good. I much prefer that particular subject. Care to take this discussion outside? There's a swing with our names on it."

I hesitate. "I'm not sure it will hold us."

But Pat only grins, holding open the door to the porch. "It will now."

I hadn't noticed earlier, but Pat has replaced not only the rusted chains but also the swing itself. I can smell it before I really see it—the scent of fresh sawdust. I run my hand over the back of it, freezing when I see what's carved into the wood.

"Pat and Lindy," I whisper.

He sits first, hooking his arm over the back, careful not to cover up the words. "Told you it had our names on it. It's a wedding gift."

I sit down next to Pat. Not close enough, I guess, because he drags me closer, keeping an arm around my shoulders. "From whom?"

"James."

"James? The brother who spends all his waking hours glaring—*he* made us a wedding gift?"

"He's not so bad once you peel off the grumpy exterior," Pat says.

"I'll have to write him a thank-you note. So, he does beer-making *and* wood-working? Sounds like a regular Renaissance man."

Pat smirks a little at that, then pushes his toe gently against the porch, sending us in a gentle swing. "Yes. Both very good gifts for a man who seems to have a life goal of being a hermit."

We're quiet for a few seconds. But Pat doesn't do quiet well. "This is nice," he says.

"Nice but weird."

"Why do you keep saying that?" he asks, an edge of frustration creeping into his voice.

"It's weird because it's so *normal*. Think about it. You and I had a whirlwind romance in college, a rough goodbye where we both hurt each other, then, like a week after seeing each other for the first time in over five years, we're married and sharing a house. We're doing dishes together. You're cooking for us and tucking in Jo. Now we're swinging on a porch swing with our names on it."

I can't explain why the tears come. But they do. So hard and fast I can't keep them in. Thankfully, because my head is resting on Pat's shoulder, he can't see them. And I just keep going, like something inside me has been uncorked.

"You're paying for plumbers and installing a new driveway and fixing the broken porch step and replacing the screen door and rehanging the crooked shutters."

"You noticed all that?"

"It's hard not to. You've probably finished half the list by now."

"More like a third. It's a long list."

I groan. "Not to mention looking up hairstyles for Jo. I'm sorry I haven't said thank you. It's hard to know how when it's so … much." The emotion becomes too thick in my throat then, and I close my mouth, swallowing down a sob.

Pat leans in, pressing a kiss to my hair. His lips move, and I feel his breath on my cheek. "I don't expect that. I don't even want a thank you note."

"What *do* you want?" The words burst out of me, sounding like an angry accusation rather than a question.

The swing's gentle motion is soothing, even as I wait impatiently for Pat's answer. "I want *you*, Lindybird. Only ever you." He must feel me starting to protest because he gives my shoulder a firm squeeze. "Hold on, now. I want you, but I also want things for you. I want to see you get your shine back. You've shouldered a lot of burdens for a long time. You gave up your dreams and aren't even bitter about it. But I think in the process, you've lost the will to hope. The ability to let yourself dream. I want to help you get that back."

There's that h-word again. Only this time, help doesn't sound so bad. I can't argue with anything Pat said in his assessment of me. I haven't had room to hope or to dream. Having Pat around, having a partner, someone to shoulder the responsibilities with me has been life-changing. We feel like a team.

We feel like family.

As much as I want to fully embrace this, to stop fighting Pat and go full feral cat on him, I'm still so scared of what I might lose. Especially with the court case hanging over my head. Less than a week to go, and everything could change.

Pat seems so steady now beside me, but I've watched his pattern over the years, the jumping from thing to thing and person to person. He's told me himself how, after his injury, he hasn't found a job he liked or an apartment he kept for more than a year. How can I be sure he'll stay after the hearing? If Rachel wins custody of Jo, Pat doesn't have to stay. If I win custody of Jo, Pat doesn't need to stay. Any outcome, there's still a chance he could go.

But he's giving me every indication he will stay. He's steadier than he used to be, more settled. I can't believe I'm still harboring doubts when he is constantly bending over backward for me. I'm more than a little ashamed of doubting him. But that doesn't make the doubts disappear.

"You're doing so much, and I'm doing so little," I say. "It feels unfair."

"In a relationship, sometimes one person needs more help and support than the other. At another time, it may flip. And still other times, it might be totally equal give-and-take. For now, you need support and I'm freely giving it."

Relationship. He said relationship! I can totally hear Winnie scoffing in my head, because of COURSE he said relationship. We are married—that's, like the ultimate definition of a relationship. Still, hearing Pat describe us that way gives me a thrill. A thrill somewhere between terror and excitement, just like always when it comes to him.

I grip Pat's shirt with all the strength I can muster. Despite feeling weak and worn, I'd like to see someone try to pry me off him.

He speaks, his lips almost brushing the shell of my ear. "I cannot imagine anyone caring for and raising Jo better than you, Lindybird. You've also been caring for your mama. I'm sure that has been heart-breaking."

It really has. Anyone who has been through the deterioration of a parent's memory and brain function knows exactly how much.

"And while you've got a great support system here, you've done so much on your own. Through force of will and force of caring. You have the biggest heart."

I sniff, realizing the tears have regrouped and made an appearance again. They're a little more like happy tears now.

"I don't have a big heart. It's all wrinkled and shriveled up. Like a raisin. It's a raisin heart."

"Oh, I think it's bigger than a raisin, darlin'."

"A prune, then."

He snorts. "It's the most beautiful prune heart in the world."

I try not to let his compliments take root too deeply inside me. I'm not sure whether or not I'm successful. Pat's arms tighten around my waist and he rests his chin on the top of my head. A little breeze picks up, but it doesn't chill me. I've got my own Pat-heater right here.

"I do have a request," Pat says.

"Of course. What is it?"

"Come watch my football game."

This takes me aback. I hadn't thought about coming to the games, because it's not like Pat was playing. It just hadn't even occurred to me he might want my support as a coach. "You want me to come to your game?"

"You and Jo. It would really mean a lot. Coach Bright resigned this week."

"He did?" I feel bad that I didn't know, that I haven't even asked anything about football or Pat's life.

"Yep. Now, it's just me and Chevy." He pauses, and his next words sound like a confession. "I'm nervous."

"You, nervous?"

"I *always* got nervous. Playing or coaching, it's no different. Before every single game, even in the pros, I would freak out. Sometimes I'd throw up."

This is hard for me to imagine. Pat seems so unshakably confident at all times. "I watched you play in college."

"You did? Seriously? That was back before we dated." Pat

sounds so unbelievably pleased, like my words are the equivalent of giving the man a new car with a shiny red bow on top. "And you noticed me?"

Before we met, I was all too aware of Patrick Graham, and not just because of his exceptional playing or how good he looked in tight football pants. I might have harbored a tiny crush on him from a distance for years, one I never told him about. I never thought I'd meet a man who was famous on campus or that I'd snag his attention.

"You were unmissable," I tell him. "Except for the defense. They never could catch you." The part of my brain always seeking choice metaphors hopes there's not one in there for us.

"You watched me play. Huh." He shakes his head, looking awed and way too pleased with this information. "Why didn't you tell me back then?"

"And make that big head of yours any bigger? Nah."

"I still have my football pants, by the way." His fingertips find a ticklish spot on my neck. When I squeal and try to pull away, he stills his fingers but pulls me closer. "I could wear them sometime, if you'd like."

"Why would I like?"

I would very, VERY MUCH LIKE.

"Hm. Just seems like you've had your share of ogling my top half. It's hardly fair. My bottom half might be feeling jealous for the same attention." I shove him, and he chuckles, bouncing right back and curling his arm around me even tighter. "So, you'll come to my game?"

"We'll be there. Now, can I ask you something?"

"Anything," he says, and my heart shudders with excitement at the promise in that one word.

"Will you be wearing your football pants?"

CHAPTER TWENTY-SIX

Lindy

I HAVEN'T BEEN to a high school football game since, well, high school, but I promised Pat, so here we are. Even though we're just two days from the hearing, and all I want to do is hold Jo in a viselike grip in the comfort of home. But that's not really feasible or advisable, so getting out of the house is probably a good thing.

The stadium is the new and improved version of the one where I watched my high school games with Val and Winnie beside me in the bleachers. To anyone who hasn't grown up in small-town Texas, *Friday Night Lights* might have seemed like heavy fiction. A caricature of Texas football culture, whether you read the book, saw the movie, or watched the show. Ladies and gentlemen, I am here to tell you *Friday Night Lights* is not fiction. (Also, literally, the book is nonfiction.) Tonight, though, the game is going down on a Tuesday.

Unfortunately, Tuesday Night Lights just doesn't have the same ring to it.

Sorry, Tuesday. No offense. We can't all be Friday.

Because we're running late, Jo and I have to park in the grassy area next to the parking lot. An attendant with a flashlight directs us into a space. Most cars we pass have blue and white flags attached to their windows and sport Sheet Cake Football stickers on the back windshield. Many of the students' cars have messages written on the windows and windshields.

My car by comparison looks naked. But at least it's blue! (Other than the rust.) School spirit! Go team!

"Can I get a hot dog?" Jo asks as we make our way in the stadium.

"Ew. No." I steer Jo away from the concession stand, though I'll admit, the popcorn smells great. "I want you to live a long, long life."

"But isn't a kolache just bread wrapped around a hot dog? And I ate two of them this morning."

Touché.

"Lindy! Jo!" Tank's deep voice cuts through the noise of the announcers and the bands warming up. Not that we could miss him. The man is a solid wall in the middle of the crowd, which parts around him like a river on the bleacher steps. Most people stare in wonder as they pass, some of the older generations slapping him on the back or shoulders. I don't miss that even women twenty years his junior—or more—are eyeing him.

Jo takes off, and before I can even tell her to wait, Tank sweeps her up in his arms. He swings her around, his deep, booming laugh a perfect complement to Jo's high-pitched giggles.

"Hey, Mr. Tank!"

"Hello, Jojo. Looking mighty festive tonight, aren't you?"

She looks adorable. Pat brought home shirts for us both and pompom scrunchies in school colors. He wasn't home to help with her hair, but I managed two high ponytails with blue and white scrunchies. My hair is staying down. I draw the line at pompoms in the hair. Did I mention Pat thought a cowbell was also a good idea? Jo shakes it too close to Tank's ear and we both wince.

"Jo! Remember our discussion? No close-range cowbell," I tell her, mouthing an apology to Tank.

"Sorry, Mr. Tank," she says.

"It's all right, Jojo. I just might be a little hard of hearing on the left side tonight. No biggie." He turns his infectious smile on me, holding out his free arm to give me a hug. "Good to see you, Lindy."

Jo giggles as she's squeezed between us. I have to swallow down a massive lump in my throat as I pull back from Tank. He's still got Jo perched on his hip like he's been doing this forever. This feels like a tease, something I could almost claim as my own, almost real.

Get back down, you stupid throat lump!

"We're all up there," Tank says, pointing. "The rowdiest bunch in the stadium."

I look up, shocked when I see a full row of bleachers taken up by Pat's family and friends right alongside mine, united in a wall of hometown blue.

They are attracting stares already. I'm sure some because of the famous faces (Tank and Collin) and some because non-Sheeters aren't usually allowed on the hometown side. Then there's the whole thing about Sheeters feuding with the Grahams over the town. But Pat is a coach, and that carries a lot of weight. Tonight, as with our wedding reception, the pitchforks have been left at home. Except for the

Waters box above, where I'm sure a lot of people are glaring down.

But when are the Waters clan NOT looking down on the rest of us? Might as well let them do it from inside the box they paid for with their donations to the stadium. That way, we don't have to look at them.

I should crochet a pillow: *Football and Weddings Bring Us Together*. I don't crochet, so I'll have Val do it. I don't think she crochets either, but she'd probably take it as a creative challenge.

My heart constricts again as I scan the row. They're all here, even the grumpy James, who's standing next to an equally grumpy-looking Winnie. Dale was supposed to come and cancelled due to a last-minute accounting emergency. From the looks of it, Winnie is taking out her disappointment on James.

Val is talking to Harper, and even Thayden and Delilah are here. Judge Judie and Mari stand next to more of Harper's friends I don't remember meeting. The woman has dyed the bottom half of her hair Sheet Cake Blue. Now, THAT'S school spirit.

If the people in our row aren't holding posters, they've got pompoms, and even Ashlee stands at the end next to Collin, wearing a jersey and cutoffs. I blink. I catch Collin sneaking a look at her legs. Because how can you not???

This sight also has me fighting a steady rise of emotion, which I'm sure has as much to do with the impending hearing as it does my growing feelings for Pat and the instalife and instafamily he provides.

Could this be real? Could it be mine? Could I for once be lucky and have something good that doesn't turn to ash and blow away?

Tonight, amidst the excitement of the crowd, with the

smell of popcorn and the sound of whistles blowing and cowbells making people deaf, the idea of this new life feels both magical and very, very real.

"Follow me," Tank says, and I walk behind him, letting him cut a path through the throng.

Even as he keeps a steady pace, he also acknowledges the people who speak to him, giving out fist bumps, high fives, and waves with the arm not holding Jo. I can see his smile even from behind in the lift of his cheeks. He's a man who doesn't seem to have a public smile and a real smile. Everyone gets to experience the real one, and it's glorious. I want to slap people away, to stick a flag in him—in Pat's whole family, really—and declare them mine, *not* public property. Tank is a good man. And, as they say, the apples haven't fallen far from the tree.

"Lindybird!"

Pat's voice barely reaches me, but I am acutely attuned to the sound. I spin to see him, sprinting from the sideline. It may not be football pants, but Pat is wearing the HECK out of khakis and a blue polo with a matching Sheet Cake baseball cap.

"I've got Jo," Tank says, giving me a wink. "Go on."

He doesn't need to tell me twice. I'm already moving toward Pat, to the chain-link fence at the railing separating the raised bleachers from the field. The metal feels cold as I clutch it, waiting for my *husband*.

Like he's some kind of Marvel character, Pat leaps and grabs the metal bar, hoisting himself up so his grinning face is right in mine. I grin right back.

"Hey," he says.

"Hi."

A chorus of cheers and wolf whistles erupts behind us.

There is no shortage of cowbells clanging either, but I refuse to let more cowbell ruin this moment.

It's like I've been dropped right into the middle of a teen movie. Except usually it's the captain of the football team, finally confessing his feelings for the nerdy girl who instantly turned hot after removing her glasses. I'm not sure what roles Pat and I are playing right now, or if they're roles at all. But my heart is thudding in my chest like it's trying to break free.

"You came," Pat says.

"You asked."

His smile takes on a wicked tilt and his voice lowers. "In that case, what else can I ask for?"

"Don't press your luck, Coach."

The truth? Right now, Pat could ask for ANYTHING. Maybe it's the noise of the crowd and the collective excitement. Or it could just be the culmination of living with Pat for two weeks and trying to keep the feral cat at bay. Ultimately, it doesn't matter why. I'm a woman on the cusp.

The cusp of what? I'm not sure. All I know is in this moment, I'm as cuspy as cusp can get, the Queen of Cusptonia.

"Actually, now that you mention it ... how about a kiss for luck?" Pat taps his cheek, clean-shaven for the game. It's a good look on him, and I can't help but wonder how his skin would feel under my fingertips. Or my lips.

I'm momentarily distracted by the way Pat can keep himself hanging on this fence with just one arm. And how the muscles in that arm bunch and flex, straining against the sleeves of his blue polo. When I drag my eyes back up to Pat's face, his expression has dropped a little. Clearly, he misread my pause as hesitation and didn't realize it was because his biceps pulled me into their orbit.

"If you don't feel comfortable—" he starts to say.

"Stop talking."

And with that, I turn Pat's baseball cap backwards, grab his face in my hands, and proceed to make sure he can't say another word.

My intent was a PG, maybe PG-13 kiss, full of emotion but not so much passion. Because, you know, we're at a family event.

But I'm immediately lost to his warm, lush mouth. We always fit perfectly together, like his lips were designed as the complement to mine. I may have initiated the kiss, but Pat takes control immediately, or maybe I just gave mine up. I am completely lost to this man.

His lips move over mine like he's mapping every curve of my mouth. My hands slide from his face to the back of his neck, just inside the collar of his shirt where his skin is smooth and warm. I feel his muscles bunch and shift, and I long to trace every single one.

It's a kiss worthy of Kiss Cams—no, it belongs on *movie theater screens* with surround sound and those amazing reclining chairs.

The loudspeaker crackles to life, and an announcer clears his throat. Pat and I break apart, both breathing hard. Or maybe hardly breathing? Either way, this kiss took something out of us both.

"Just a reminder," the cheerful announcer says, "this is a family friendly event. Please save your public displays of affection for your homes ... after we win."

The crowd goes wild at that, and Pat presses his forehead to mine, his smile like a rush of dopamine.

"And that includes under the bleachers," the other announcer adds with a chuckle. "Come on out, you kids. Your mama is sitting right above your make-out spot."

The crowd laughs. I bet any kids making out under the bleachers have nothing on me and Pat, even with all their raging teenage hormones.

"Well, dang. There goes my plan to drag you under the bleachers later," Pat says, angling his head for another kiss.

Before his lips can do more than brush mine, he's being yanked down off the fence by Chevy, who shakes his head at me, then Pat.

"Don't make me arrest y'all for public indecency," Chevy says. "This time, you might spend more than a night in jail."

Pat holds up both hands, then winks at me, turning his hat back around.

"Come on, man," Chevy says. "Time to get your head in the game. We need a win. No pressure."

Pat's smile only widens. "I function best under pressure. Let's do this thing."

I stand at the railing for a minute, watching the two of them head for their spots on the sideline. Then, feeling a little like I'm doing a walk of shame amidst all the stares and catcalls, I make my way up the bleachers. It's more than a little awkward when I pass Kitty and the girls. Nothing like making out with someone in front of your teenage babysitter.

When I get to our row, most of the Grahams wear expressions of approval or amusement. James, of course, has a look of blank boredom. Or is that disdain? Jo is right next to Tank, who has wedged his way between Collin and Ashlee. He still has Jo in his arms, and I think even Ashlee seems to be falling under his spell.

"Can I sit with Mr. Tank?" Jo asks. "Please?"

"Of course, Jojo."

When I finally get to Winnie and Val, I roll my eyes at their knowing looks, but my skin flushes.

"Don't worry," Winnie says, "I distracted Jo during that kiss so she didn't get a sexual education."

I scoff, pulling the neck of my T-shirt out to fan myself. "It wasn't that bad."

Val laughs. "There was definitely nothing *bad* about that kiss. The question is—are you still trying to pretend like your marriage is just about Jo? Because, if so, you're doing a terrible job."

CHAPTER TWENTY-SEVEN

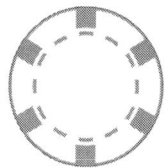

Pat

THE TEAM DIDN'T NEED to wait for the clock to run down on the final score to dump a cooler full of Gatorade over my head. I won the moment Lindy kissed me.

But I'm glad they did wait, because it would have been really uncomfortable to coach a whole game in sticky, soaked clothes.

"You sure do clean up good," Chevy says. "Trying to impress someone?"

"Maybe." I take a last look in the locker room mirror. Worn-in jeans, check. Tousled hair, check. Lucky shirt, check. At least, I'm hoping after tonight I can call this my lucky shirt. And no, I don't mean like a *getting* lucky shirt. I wouldn't expect to go from a kiss straight to Lindy's bed that quick. But I'd like to think my luck is changing, and that I'm finally starting to make some headway with my wife.

Also, I'd like to try that whole kissing thing again, but without the stadium of people.

Chevy leans against a bank of lockers. The room feels weirdly intimate now that the players have taken their amped up celebrations elsewhere. Only the scent of their body odor and body spray lingers behind.

"From what I saw earlier, I'd say you've already impressed her plenty," Chevy muses, a smile on his face. "Things going well there?"

How to answer that question?

Things are ... going. Some days, I think I'm getting through to Lindy. Other days, I feel a little bit like a live-in nanny, handyman, and cook all in one. I'm a regular old Mrs. Doubtfire, only with a Texas accent instead of a British one. I also wear Wranglers instead of a dress and am not pretending to be someone else.

Okay, so the Mrs. Doubtfire analogy only works in the sense that I'm doing acts of service in order to be close to someone I love.

Don't get me wrong—it's not like Lindy is forcing me to do this. Heck, half the time the woman is telling me to quit helping, quit fixing, and quit paying for stuff. I thought I was being sneaky with a lot of things, but as it turns out, Lindy is fairly observant. Could be that I make myself hard to miss by working shirtless as much as possible.

I'm starting to question the wisdom in what I'm doing. Not because Lindy isn't worth it—I'd do all this and more. Times a thousand. No, times TEN THOUSAND.

But the other night when we were on the porch swing, I hated hearing her say she feels unequal. I don't want her keeping some mental tally, feeling like she has to pay it back or pay it forward or pay it any old way. The last thing I want is her feeling like she isn't enough.

I've started to see a bit more of the old Lindy unfurling, but it also feels like she has one eye trained on the door, either waiting for me to leave or to kick me out herself. She doesn't trust this yet. She doesn't trust us. She doesn't trust ME. I know she just needs time. But every so often when she pushes me away, I start to get that low, heavy feeling in my gut, the same one I felt when I lost her the first time. I don't despair often, but when I do, I go at it hard, and I'm doing my best to kick that creeping feeling back down.

But she kissed you, I remind myself. *Tonight. She planted one on you in front of the whole town. So, maybe things are finally looking up.*

"I never quite know where I stand with Lindy." I straighten my collar, then unbutton one more button. "But I'll take every bit of forward progress I can. Every yard, every first down—"

"A word of advice?" Chevy says. "Leave the football analogies for the field."

"Noted." I walk over and tilt my hair toward his face. "Be honest. Do I still smell like Gatorade?"

Chevy shoves me. "You smell like a man who just spent an hour getting ready in a locker room infused with Axe body spray." He sniffs the air dramatically. "And like someone who is testing the limits of his fledgling bromance. Now, get on home to your wife."

———

On the drive back to the house, I let my mind replay the highlights of the day. I loved the earnest hope on the guys' faces in our pre-game huddle. Though I never relish pulling a player, it felt good replacing Mark Waters—aka Seventeen—the fourth time he tried to run the ball himself instead of passing. Watching his backup, an unassuming junior named Kyle, throw completed pass after completed pass with zero ego also felt phenomenal.

Not much beat the moment we came from behind to win the game—Sheet Cake's first of the season. It sure was nice having the Bobs nod their approval, even if they did also promise they'd be giving me their notes at practice tomorrow morning.

And those are just the *football* highlights. All of them paled in comparison to the moment Lindy grabbed my face and kissed me. My foot lands a little heavier on the gas pedal at the memory of her hands, her lips, her closeness ...

Unfortunately, I'm not fast enough. By the time I make it home, all the lights are off and everyone is asleep. Even Elvis, in a corner on the porch.

You only had one job, Lucky Shirt. ONE. JOB.

Disappointment floods me as I walk through the quiet house. It's not an easy crash coming down from the high of Lindy's kiss and our big win. I was really hoping to talk about what it meant. Or maybe just kiss some more, then talk. Kiss, then talk. Talk, then kiss. Kiss, talk, kiss. Talk, kiss, talk, kiss. The order doesn't matter, so long as there is talking and kissing. But I guess I won't be getting either tonight.

Why do I have the feeling that tomorrow she's going to pretend like the kiss never happened?

I glance at the TV Lindy bought me, a small sign—literally, the thing is tiny—that she cares. When my big flat-screen arrived, I hid it in the barn. Her gift means more than a screen size.

I climb the steps slowly, skipping the super creaky one near the top. Then again, maybe I could use it to my advantage ...

Backtracking, I put both feet on that step and shift my weight back and forth until it makes a screechy creak that could wake a mummy from its tomb. I pause to listen, but only hear Lindy's steady breathing. Does she HAVE to be such a sound sleeper? I give the creaky step a few more bounces until I hear Amber groan downstairs.

Fine. I give up. Lindy sleeps deeper than the dogs. Noted.

Changing into pajamas, I leave my not-so-lucky shirt on the closet floor so it can think about what it's done. Every night in this house has continued to be torture. Beautiful, exquisite, gut-wrenching torture. Tonight, though, I feel like Odysseus, needing my crew to tie me to the mast so I don't heed the sirens' call. Only, I don't have a crew, a rope, or a mast.

What I do have is a fully charged phone, a strong Wi-Fi signal, and the pen name Lindy has been writing under. I'm sure she never meant for me to find the printed-out article with her secret writing name, just like I never meant to snoop in her office when I left the mail on her desk.

I knew it was Lindy the minute I saw the byline. And boy, did it give me a thrill. I mean, Birdie Graham? Birdie, as in, Lindybird—the nickname I gave her. And, duh—Graham. As in ME.

Now, if I could only get her to change her actual last name …

I locate Birdie Graham's latest post and can't stop the grin spreading across my face. *Four Underrated Parts of a Man*, huh? Well, well, well. What a fascinating topic for some late-night reading.

Settling in for what's sure to be scintillating literature, I begin to read.

FROM THE NEIGHBORLY APP

Subject: Flaming Squirrels

LindyLouWho
For your viewing pleasure, I give you: Flaming Squirrels. Consider this video a cautionary tale about lack of grill maintenance.

1BigBass
This only gives me more reason to hate squirrels. Also, they're not so bad grilled. If he'd just left them in there for a while, you'd have had dinner.

BagelBytes
I hope you got rabies shots! I also hope you had permission to post this video.

DeltaDeltaDelta
Even when being attacked by squirrels, Patrick Graham is a total hottie. It had to be said.

Vanz
   Were the squirrels harmed during the making of this video

The_Real_Shell-E
   Oh my gosh this is so mean! Poor Pat! I'm reporting this video for bullying. He deserves so much better! Also, did he get tested for rabies? I'm concerned.

SaintValentine
   Can it, The_Real_Shell-E. He's a married man. Also, this is the best video I've ever seen in my life.

BobToo
   This video is hilarious, but I also have rabies concerns. We don't want to lose our coach.

WayneNGarthBrooks
   Speaking of rabies, I've got a possum living under my couch. I thought the feller was dead and brought him inside, and now he's hiding under there and won't come out. He's not the worst pet I've ever had, but I don't want rabies.

MaddieDVM
   I thought I'd weigh in with some rabies facts! Squirrels rarely pass rabies on to humans, but in cases of direct contact like in this video, it's possible, especially if the skin is broken through scratches or bites.
   Opossums—the correct name—almost never carry rabies. It's extremely rare. They're particularly helpful in ridding areas of other unwanted pests but do not make good house pets. Call animal control and do not attempt to pick it up

again! They may not carry rabies, but they have a wicked bite!!

DeltaDeltaDelta

I'd be happy to check Pat out just to make sure he wasn't scratched.

LindyLouWho

Don't worry—I've already given him a thorough examination. An EXTREMELY thorough examination. Happy to report there were no scratches. Pat is rabies free! No worries, BobToo. Your coach is happy and healthy and not going anywhere.

CHAPTER TWENTY-EIGHT

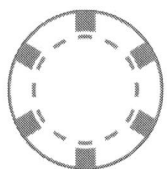

Lindy

I LOVE JO. And my love for her is not defined by how often I volunteer at her school. This is what I tell myself as I get dressed to help with Galaxy Day, trying on and discarding at least three outfits before deciding on my most comfortable skinny jeans, boots, and a simple striped sweater. I dropped Jo off at school earlier, then came home to change. Apparently, the school frowns on parents volunteering in their pajamas.

If I ran a school, everyone would wear pajamas all the time. Pajamas would be the required uniform. Pajama school: where everyone is comfortable learning. Great tagline, right?

"You're doing this for Jo," I tell myself, brushing powder over my cheeks.

This is my mantra lately, even though the hearing is tomorrow. TOMORROW. I can't see how anything I'm doing will have any impact. It feels like trying to sweep up feathers while in a wind tunnel.

But I cannot think about the hearing right now. I've been getting a PhD in avoidance lately. No need to skip out before I get my diploma. The other thing I'm avoiding this morning: thinking about that kiss. As a tactic, avoidance is only partially successful.

"LINDY! Where are you?"

Pat's voice booms up through the floorboards as the kitchen door slams. I jump, dropping my compact, which of course sends a fine dusting of powder all over my counter, shirt, and jeans.

"I'm up here!" I call. "Cleaning up the mess you made me make." I mutter the last part as Pat stomps his way up the stairs. One of these days, he's going to go right through the wood steps.

He's almost to the top when the memory of last night slams into me, along with the realization that we are in the house ALONE. Totally, totally alone. I freeze, the compact still in my hands, powder still everywhere. I'm supposed to be at the school in twenty minutes, but that leaves at least ten minutes to either replay that kiss or to pretend it didn't happen.

I fell asleep thinking about THE KISS. I woke up thinking about it. Heck, it played a starring role in all of my dreams. I planned to wait up for Pat last night, unsure whether I would tell him the kiss had been a one-time thing or—more likely—pick right back up at home where we left off at the stadium. Only slower. Longer. And without worrying about scaring small children or having announcers give a play-by-play.

But last night I fell asleep before he made it home. I'm sure they had all kinds of post-win celebrations, but I was more than a little disappointed.

What do I say now? Should we acknowledge it? Are we on kissing terms now? Make-out buddies? Husband and wife with benefits?

Or should we just pretend it never happened?

I'm so nervous, I drop the compact again. Pat's big form fills the doorway, but I keep my eyes on the powder I'm unsuccessfully trying to sweep back into the compact. The same way I'm trying to sweep my feelings for Pat back into a nice, safe container with a lid.

When you're looking for them, metaphors are *everywhere*.

"How was your first post-win practice?" I ask, trying to keep my voice totally neutral. But there is nothing neutral about Pat's voice as he shoves his phone in front of my face.

"How could you not tell me about this?" he demands.

Okay, then. Guess this answers my kissing questions. We're just going to go on like it never happened. Cool. I didn't think about it much either. Kiss? What kiss?

His phone is open to the Neighborly app. Specifically, to a thread rating the Graham brothers based on the way their butts look in jeans. There are even photos, some taken at the Backwoods Bar before their arrest and still more from the internet back when Pat, Collin, and even Tank played football.

I could say I haven't spent time looking at the photos, but I wouldn't swear to it in court.

It's a good thing Winnie deleted the thread that popped up last night about THE KISS. Apparently, that post had a lot of VERY strong opinions. I didn't ask Winnie if they were positive or negative because the last thing I need when I'm already questioning a decision is to have all of Sheet Cake weighing in.

"Oh," I say, infusing my voice with as much casualness as

possible—*look at me, cool and casual Lindy!* "Yeah, the Neighborly app. What about it?"

"*What about it?* That's my butt on there!"

It most certainly is. I try not to look like I'm ogling the photo of his posterior—though I totally am—as I elbow him out of my way. I wonder if he saw the—

"And you posted the flaming squirrel video? I didn't even know you *took* a video!"

"It just kind of happened."

Pat slides the phone in his pocket before crossing his arms over his chest. "Taking the video just kind of happened? Or posting it?"

"Taking the video. I meant to post it."

Plucking the compact from my fingers and setting it on the counter, Pat slides a hand around my waist and spins me toward him. He lets go far too soon. Which is probably a good thing. Because he wants to talk about Neighborly while I'm still thinking about THE KISS. Have our roles somehow been reversed? Now I'm the one obsessing over him while he's cooling things down.

"Lindy, you knew about this app?"

His face is so shocked, so incredulous that I have to bite back my laughter. "Neighborly is Winnie's app. It's her baby. She developed it and runs the whole thing. Every Sheeter knows about it. Well, *old* Sheeters. Maybe some new ones too."

"I didn't know."

"You're not a Sheeter."

"I married one. Seems like something you might have mentioned. Seeing as how I'm the subject of a number of posts."

"You mean, how your *butt* is the subject of a number of posts."

I turn back to the mirror. Putting on mascara is a great way to keep me from looking at Pat's face, which is only inches from my own. It's a little embarrassing to be the only one thinking about THE KISS.

Did the big win for the team overshadow it?

Was it just a game for Pat, and now that he's got me begging, he's going to change tactics?

I don't like any of these thoughts. Not even a little bit. Guess my lips should be prepared to winterize again. The feral cat yowls with displeasure.

"Where are you going?" Pat asks. "You look nice."

"I have to volunteer at Jo's school, helping the PTO Mafia."

"There's a ... mafia?"

I consider how to explain in Pat speak. "It's like ... the Plastics." Referencing *Mean Girls* always works. He maintains that Tina Fey's writing is simply brilliant. "And Tabitha Waters-Graves is Regina George."

"Huh." He rubs a hand over his jaw, and the sound of his palm over that unshaved skin makes me shiver. "Who does that make you?"

I think for a moment. "Kevin Gnapoor."

He chuckles, I guess already over the whole Neighborly thing. "Can I come? I love a little good Plastic sabotage."

It's tempting. Pat would provide a distraction, fabulous entertainment, and also be the best kind of buffer between me and the PTO Mafia. Then, I imagine Tabby in her flawless makeup and skintight leggings batting her heavy fake lashes at Pat. I mean, she's married, but I could see her wanting to upgrade from a Graves to a Graham. She wouldn't even need to change any of her monograms. Yeah ... no. Just no.

"I'll be fine. Oh—did you see the thread on Neighborly

about the game last night? They had good things to say about your coaching. Especially how you pulled Mark Waters."

Pat's eyes light up. "Yeah, most people seemed happy. Hard to be sad with a win, though. We'll see if we can pull it off again. I have a long list of notes from the Bobs."

He leans back against the counter, his shoulder brushing mine. Even in my periphery, Pat's presence is so distracting I almost stab my eyeball with the mascara wand. Instead I end up with a black streak on my face. Fabulous. I scrub it away and turn to face Pat, taking as much of a step back as I can in the small space.

"I've got to go."

I push my palms into his chest, shoving him lightly out of the way as I tell my hands not to linger. *Just keep moving, ladies. Nothing to feel here.* When I'm safely past him and out in the hall, I pause, turning back to face him.

"I voted for your butt, by the way."

Pat's expression morphs into pure pleasure. He looks like a puppy who's been released into a room full of shoes to chew on.

"You voted for my butt?"

His voice is rich and sweet, honey dripping straight from the comb. It brings to mind lazy mornings, long hours spent wrapped up in his arms, his mouth on mine. I keep moving for the stairs. If I'm late to help out, Tabby will probably send her minions to burn my house down.

I give Pat a quick, teasing smile. "I had to. It's the butt I married."

Pat makes a frustrated noise, and I don't tell him that, marriage aside, I'd vote his butt the best any day. Even if he's going to act like THE KISS never happened.

"Good of you to join us, Lisa!"

Tabby's voice is like the first sip of a Diet Coke, a rush of fake sugar and carbonation so strong it makes your eyes sting.

The classroom lights are off, but the room is well-lit by the big windows off to the side and a floor lamp by the teacher's desk, where Tabby is holding court. A handful of other PTO Mafia members are squeezed into the tiny plastic chairs around the room, looking every bit her loyal subjects. Just the way good old Tab likes it. They're all wearing the required Mafia uniform: athleisure. Based on their trim bodies, they all probably met at the gym beforehand for Hot Spin Yoga or whatever the newest trendy class is.

I don't own any athleisure wear because my life is devoid of both the *ath* and the *leisure*. Also, it's expensive as all get-out for clothing designed for sweating.

"It's Lindy," I remind her. "And I'm on time."

She waves a hand. "Oh, we always like to show up early. You know how it is—it's just such a joy to serve!"

You mean, a joy to make people your servants.

Ignoring the tiny chair Tabby points to, I stand near the window where I can glance out at the class on the playground. I locate Jo almost immediately, sitting underneath the slide, reading a book. No surprise there. But while I watch, she sets the book down—using a bookmark because I didn't raise a heathen—and joins in a round of tag.

Good for you, Jojo. Diversify those interests—reading AND playground games!

I turn back to Tabby, whose eyes narrow on me.

"You must be so tired after the big game last night," she says.

"I didn't actually play in the game, you know. Spectating isn't all that strenuous."

"I didn't mean the *spectating* part," Tabby says, and I know where this is going. Right to my VERY public display of affection. The one I need to forget, since Pat obviously has.

Before she can weigh in any more on the topic, I cut her off. "Yes, I'm tired. And I've got work to do, so if you could let me know how I can help, that'd be great."

Undeterred, Tabby taps her perfectly manicured nails against perfectly pink lips. "Let's see what's left. We've already done *so much* without you."

Each woman has a pile of perfectly cut-out stars. Lots and lots of stars. By the look of things, they've been cutting since before the sun came up. The woman closest to me glares while massaging her fingers, like it's MY fault Tabby is a ruthless dictator.

As if to further prove my estimation of her, Tabby's eyes narrow like a cartoon villain. "Actually, I do have something. A *very* important job I saved just for you."

Well, that sounds ominous. "Sounds great!" I try to infuse cheerleader levels of enthusiasm in my voice, but it sounds more like sarcasm. Okay, maybe it *is* sarcasm.

"I hope it's a two-person job," an all-too familiar voice calls from the doorway.

Pat saunters into the room looking even better than he did twenty minutes ago. Did he put on a tighter shirt? The gray tee he's sporting is basically like an anatomical diagram showing all his muscle groups. It would be highly educational for a unit on anatomy.

Pecs? Present and accounted for! Shoulders? Yes and yes! Abs? Here, here, here, here, here, and here!

Five pairs of eyes laser in on him as he crosses the room. I'd like to gouge them all out with the plastic safety scissors. Pat ignores every single one, moving purposefully to me. I can't seem to find my tongue or a thought in my brain as he wraps an arm around my waist and places a lingering kiss on my cheek.

"Hey, darlin'," he murmurs, stepping closer to whisper in my ear. "Your backup has arrived." His lips brush my earlobe in a way that makes my muscles lock up.

"I told you I was fine," I hiss in a low voice, trying to get my erratic pulse under control.

"Well, then, consider this me being a clingy, new hubby still in the honeymoon phase of our nuptials. Or maybe I just came to watch you take down the mafia."

I don't miss the way he skirts around the words the rules said not to use. *Hubby* instead of *husband*, *nuptials* instead of *marriage*. The man is infuriating.

Infuriatingly *wonderful*. I love his wordplay and wit almost as much as his abs. Maybe more. Together, they're a deadly package.

Pat turns his attention to Tabby, whose jaw is still on the floor. The man is and has always been larger than life, from his size to the way his presence fills any room. I'm so used to him that I can forget how overwhelming he can be to normal humans.

"You're here to help?" Tabby asks, finally managing to get her jaw working.

"I told Lindy I want to be wherever she is." He sneaks in another kiss, this one to my temple.

Tabby suddenly looks uncomfortable. "We were just finishing up, actually. I think everything is all done for the day."

"What were you telling Lindy when I walked in? Something about a very important job?" Pat asks. "Lay it on us. We can handle it together."

Tabby's face flushes and her hands clutch a cardboard box I hadn't noticed on the teacher's desk. "It's really nothing."

While I'd rather leave and get to work, I don't like the way Tabby is suddenly trying to backtrack. I cross the room because now I *must* know what's in the box. Scorpions? Moldy cheese? Used needles?

Worse—it's GLITTER.

I groan. "Really, Tabby?"

She steps back, crossing her arms. "Every star needs to be glittered." Grabbing her purse, she heads for the door. That must be the signal, because the rest of the mafia follows suit. "There are six hundred stars and a handful of comets and planets. I guess we'll leave you to it."

And with that, she leads her merry band of minions away in a sea of brightly colored fabric. It probably wicked away their souls along with their sweat.

"What's so bad about glitter?" Pat asks.

Everyone with a kid knows glitter is the butthole of crafts. I've heard it called worse, actually, but I'll stick with butthole.

I sigh and start arranging things on the table by the teacher's desk. "Oh, you poor, innocent man. You'll see. Grab those stars and we can get started. This is going to take a while."

Twenty minutes later, Pat and I are sitting side by side at the work table next to the teacher's desk, a regular assembly line of glitter and glue. He glues; I glitter. Then, repeat. We are both sticky and sparkling like a couple of *Twilight* vampires on the Summer Solstice.

"The couple that glitters together stays together?" Pat says, handing me another star.

He lets his fingers skate over the back of my hand as he does so, leaving a riot of goose bumps behind. I'm still feeling off-kilter, trying to decide if I should bring up THE

KISS or keep up this charade of pretending it never happened at all.

"What's the saying—sticks and stones will break my bones, but glitter lasts forever?" I ask.

"I thought it was more along the lines of the only certain things in life are death, taxes, and glitter."

I laugh and finish another star. I now have glitter underneath my nails. Earlier, I think I inhaled some. It's probably already embedded in my lungs.

"Sorry you got dragged into this with me." I take another star from him. "I did try to warn you."

"Glitter isn't so bad. Plus, I wanted to be here. I want to be anywhere you are."

Well, that's certainly sweet. But why hasn't he mentioned our kiss? Or tried to kiss me again? Usually I'm the one who's taking ten steps back for every two we take forward. Was the kiss bad? I mean, I know I'm a little rusty, but I didn't imagine the heat that practically left scorch marks on the stadium.

"Lindy?"

Pat's voice startles me, and I realize I've paused our glitter assembly line and have been staring at his lips for an undetermined amount of time.

"Sorry." I look away, reaching for the glitter.

Pat's fingers brush my jaw, a gentle urge for me to turn toward him. I resist, keeping my eyes on the star in my hand, making sure it gets all the glitter it needs. This job is very, very important and clearly needs my full and undivided attention.

"What's on your mind, Lindybird?"

Pat's fingers don't leave my skin. Instead, they skate along my jaw and trail down my neck, practically leaving a glowing trail of electricity in their wake. The little hairs on my arms rise.

"Just trying to do a good job."

"Mmm. Because this is very important work we're doing." His voice is low and husky, and it has me thinking about everything but glitter. Especially when he traces a single fingertip along my collarbone.

"The most important. Lives depend on these stars."

My eyes close as his finger slides back to my shoulder and down my arm until he finds my wrist and draws lazy circles on the sensitive skin there. I'm pretty sure he's hypnotizing me. Later, someone's going to say an innocuous phrase like *how was your weekend?* and I'm going to start barking like a dog.

"I owe you an apology," Pat says, and this sudden change of conversational course barely pulls me out of the mind-melting state of consciousness I'm in. I'd forgive anything in this moment.

"You do?"

"I do," he says firmly. "First, for not getting home quickly enough last night. I wanted to be there before you went to sleep."

I wanted you there before I went to sleep. Seems like these words are best kept to myself for now. Especially because I have no idea what would have happened if he had gotten home before I fell asleep.

"And then this morning. I came home and dove right into the whole Neighborly thing and didn't even mention our kiss. I'm sorry, Lindy. I didn't mean to make it seem like that kiss wasn't the highlight of my week."

Pat removes his hand from my wrist and cups my cheek, slowly urging me to face him. This time, I don't resist. We're only inches apart, and relief floods me when I see the same hunger in his eyes that I feel in mine.

"Sometimes with my ADHD I hyperfocus on something. This morning, that something was discovering all those posts on Neighborly."

Did Pat ever tell me he has ADHD? I can't remember him mentioning it when we were dating, but now doesn't seem like the right time to start asking a bunch of questions. He clearly still has things he wants to say.

"That kiss"—his eyes drop to my lips—"was much more important than some community-wide gossip site, and I'm sorry if I made it feel insignificant. Or made you feel insignificant. It was very, very meaningful."

Speaking of hyperfocus, I'm listening, but my eyes haven't left his mouth. It's such a beautiful mouth. And it is sweet relief to know he didn't forget about the kiss.

That means we can do it again, right?

"So, what I'm hearing you say is you don't regret the kiss?" I ask.

"Regret it? No. No! Is that what you thought?"

I drag my gaze away from Pat's lips to meet his espresso eyes. "Normally, I'd expect you to do a celebratory dance or maybe drag me into a supply closet."

His eyes spark. "Is there a supply closet in here?"

"I'm sure we could find one. But I draw the line at janitor's closets. The smell of chemicals is a real buzzkill."

"I don't think I'd be paying attention to the smell of chemicals, but as you wish."

Pat leans closer, his eyes now completely zeroed in on my mouth. Watching him watch me comes with a heady satisfaction. As he continues closing the distance between us, I catch a sparkle of glitter near the corner of his lips. Reaching up, I drag my finger over the spot. The glitter doesn't budge.

"You're going to get glitter all over me," I tell him in a voice that tells him I don't really mind.

Pat keeps inching forward, giving me plenty of time to resist or run, like he knows my two defaults well. "I hate to tell you, darlin', but you're already covered in glitter."

My eyes flutter closed just as his lips brush mine.

And, because I really do have the worst luck of all the luck that's ever been lucked, Jo's class chooses to return at this moment. We jump apart, but not before twenty-two small voices chorus, "Ewwww!"

We really need to stop kissing in public places. I'm not even able to maintain a proper level of embarrassment because there's a glint in Pat's eyes, a promise that he'll finish the kiss he started. Thankfully, when I catch Jo's eye, she looks delighted, not horrified.

We definitely shocked her teacher. "Oh, hello," Mrs. Stem says, and before I can even respond, she flicks the light switch.

As the overhead bulbs come to life, so does the big fan mounted in the corner pointed right at us, right at the open containers of glitter. And just like that, Pat and I are suddenly in the center of a glitter tornado.

CHAPTER TWENTY-NINE

Pat

WHEN I DIE, the mortician will still find glitter in some of my nooks and crannies. Probably even in my unmentionables.

The thought makes me chuckle as I'm scrubbing myself for the third time, watching blue and pink and purple glitter disappear down the drain. In the other shower downstairs, Lindy is probably finding the exact same thing.

But thinking of Lindy in the shower is probably not the wisest idea.

Not when we've just reentered kissing territory. I am not going to push too far too fast and then end up backtracking across the border. Nope. We are moving this journey in a forward direction. Onward!

I need to keep things moving slowly. I'm keenly aware of tomorrow's court date. There is no way to measure the emotional impact it will have and even is having now. Lindy and Jo might be mostly pretending it's not happening, but I can sense the underlying tension and worry. I've done my best to infuse whatever humor and lightness I can into this house, but in truth, I'm worried too.

I can't imagine Jo not being with Lindy. This is where she belongs. It would be wrong to move her to another city where she'd be living with strangers, even if it's a process that happens slowly. Sheet Cake is her home. Lindy is her home. And I want to be a part of that home too. I already am far more invested in this little girl than I have a right to be for this short stretch of time.

And though I don't want to be selfish, I can't stop wondering what this might mean for me and Lindy. If the courts keep Jo with her, I've basically outlived my usefulness to her. While we seem to have progressed, I'm also scared she's making decisions in a heightened emotional state.

I meant to have an actual discussion with her about where we stand before kissing her again. But I screwed up being a jerk with the whole Neighborly thing, and then I started to kiss her again in the classroom. I don't have a playbook for how to deal with my particular set of circumstances.

I turn the water to freezing cold for a few minutes, though my thoughts of the hearing have already significantly cooled me down. I shove all the worries into that dark cave of my mind where they belong.

Be gone, darkness! Head toward the light. That's better.

I get out and wrap a towel around my hips, examining my red-rimmed eyes in the mirror. I've never been so grateful for an eye-washing station. I can safely say having glitter blown into my eyeballs is one of the least pleasant things I've experienced. And having shattered my ankle, that's saying something.

Was it worth it though? Totally.

I step into the hallway and run right into Lindy. I grab her arms to keep her upright. Her skin is damp, and it takes me a minute to realize that like me, she's also in just a towel.

"Sorry," I say, telling my eyeballs they had better not stray from her face OR ELSE, despite their very strong urge to trace a path downward to see just where her towel starts and ends.

Her eyes are wide. "I forgot to bring a change of clothes downstairs with me."

"It's okay. Were you able to get all the glitter off?" Even as I ask this, I see a sparkle in her eyebrow. Best not to mention it.

"Probably not. I'm going to be covered in glitter forever. Just call me Sparkles McGee."

"Okay, Sparkles."

Her eyes drop down to my bare chest, and her eyes narrow. "You've got to stop walking around shirtless. I know why you're doing it."

"Why am I doing it, Sparkles?"

"To get a reaction out of me."

Lindy says this like we didn't share an epic kiss just last night. And that we didn't just get caught almost repeating it at the elementary school.

I keep my expression as innocent as a little baby lamb leaping through a spring meadow. "And why would me shirtless get a reaction out of you?"

Lindy sputters, and I can't help the lazy grin spreading across my face. "You know why," she says.

I cross my arms over my chest, not because it makes all my muscles flex. Just because it's comfortable, and I'm all about the comfort. "You realize I'm not the only one in a towel, right?"

Lindy's hands fly to the knot holding up her thin towel, and she backs toward her room. "Stop looking!"

"I'm not. But this is one area where I'm okay with double standards. You can look all you want, Lindybird."

I stretch my arms wide, hoping my towel stays in place. It does, and for a moment, Lindy does look. And look and look. Her eyes take a quick perusal of my abs and chest, a nice, little gazing tour of Patrick Graham.

Take your time, Lindybird. Make a map if you need too. All of this is yours, wife.

A little too soon for my taste, she slips inside her room and slams the door. "Put some clothes on!" she yells.

"You first!" I call back, just as thunder rumbles through the sky.

I noticed the dark clouds on the drive back from the elementary school, but I was too distracted by the pain in my eyes, and the reality that my truck will now be covered in glitter forever to pay much attention to the weather.

As I pull on jeans and a clean shirt, wind howls over the eaves. The whole house seems to creak and shudder. Thunder crashes again, this time followed by a flash of lightning and the sound of the first raindrops hitting the roof.

I hear Lindy's door slam open, and she yells, "Pat! The laundry!"

Her feet are already pounding down the stairs by the time I get with the program. We washed clothes yesterday and it's all hanging across the line to dry. Most notably, all the bed sheets. I've ordered a dryer Lindy doesn't know about, but the only model that will fit in the tiny laundry space is on back order.

By the time I make it out of the back door, the rain is falling in earnest. Big, fat, stinging drops pelt my bare arms and feet. The dogs, clearly not scared of storms, push outside with me and run in circles, barking at the sky before taking shelter in the barn.

"It's already soaked! Let's just leave it!" I yell over the storm, but Lindy only shakes her head.

I'm not about to leave her out here alone, so I join Lindy at the line, unable to miss the way her T-shirt is plastered to her, clinging to every curve. I know I just saw her in a towel, but there's something even more alluring about the wet shirt and the hints it gives.

Focus, Patty. I start tearing at the clothespins, keeping my eyes to the task at hand. But with the thunder crashing and lightning seeming to be all around us, the process is difficult. The wind whips the wet fabric around us. Have the sheets gotten bigger? It feels like acres of material, unwieldy and stubborn in the wind and rain.

The temperature is falling fast. Apparently, this is one of those fronts bringing a sudden temperature drop. Texas never does things small, including seasonal changes. Nope. At least in our area of the state, the weather prefers extreme change. A storm blows through and—BOOM! Twenty minutes later, it's forty degrees colder.

Lindy and I end up at the same spot, trying to wrangle the very last sheet. The wind tears through the backyard, and it's like we're on a stormy sea, trying to batten down the hatches or whatever you do with the sails.

The weight of the soaked cloth pulls at the line. The sheet smacks wetly against me, twisting around my legs and tripping me up. I stumble forward into Lindy, grabbing her waist. A wind gust whips the rest of the sheet around Lindy, and now we're plastered together like a soaked human burrito.

Rain drips steadily into my eyes, and my hair is plastered

over my face. Lindy wraps her arms around me and shivers. Then she begins to laugh.

"This is ridiculous!" she yells.

Thunder booms so loud she jumps, and I wrap my arms tighter around her, seeking her warmth, seeking connection, wanting to keep her protected.

She says something I can't hear over the wind and rain, so I bend down, my forehead pressing to hers. "What'd you say?"

Her eyes meet mine, but we're so close, they're out of focus. "I said, 'Kiss me!'"

It shouldn't shock me, not after our kiss last night and the almost-kiss at the school. And yet, shocked I am.

I don't even move, just blinking as cold rain runs down my face as I stare at her. "Kiss you?"

"KISS ME!"

When she yells the words at me this time, I don't hesitate. I don't question the wisdom of standing outside in the middle of a storm, or the fact that Lindy's whole body is shivering. I don't wonder if I should press pause on all forward motion until after the hearing or at least until after we're not in danger of being struck by lightning.

I simply haul Lindy against me and do as the woman says.

A flashing yellow light warns me to proceed slowly and with caution, but my self-control is a fraying piece of rope. The moment my lips touch hers, it snaps.

There is no stadium around us, no classroom full of elementary kids about to walk in on us. We are two married adults in our own backyard and there is no good reason to hold back.

This kiss is the explosion at the end of a mile-long fuse. Or maybe the fuse is measured in years not miles, and a tiny spark has been steadily traveling minute by minute, month by month, year by year toward this inevitable conclusion.

Her mouth is wet and hot in the now-cool air, her body pliant against me. The kiss feels like a battle, but it's really a surrender. We are laying our weapons down and throwing ourselves across the battle lines we've drawn.

I pick Lindy up, fumbling a little with the sheet still plastered to our bodies. My hands feel huge as they grasp her thighs. I've never felt so powerful. Kissing someone strong like Lindy, having this wild force of a woman in my arms makes me feel like the most powerful man in the world.

Her fingernails scrape lightly up the back of my neck and find their way into my wet hair. My senses are heightened, making me fully cognizant of each point of contact between us: each brush of her lips, the pad of every fingertip, the press of her torso inch by delicious inch against mine.

I kiss her like a man coming up to the surface after a dive, gasping for air. She is all I need, and I do *need* her. I was drowning without her, dark and cold and alone, not sure which way in my life was up.

I have no question. This is my life. She is my life. She and Jo and whatever else might come our way.

I am all in. And, at least for the moment, it seems that Lindy is calling my bet.

A loud crack of thunder makes us both jump. We break apart, but only just. Her hands still roam my chest, our lips still brush as we smile. Her breath is hot against my lips. I'm about to say something, probably something really stupid like, *I love you*, when there is another rumble, one louder and closer than thunder.

The whole yard lights up with a flash that feels way, way too close.

I've never heard a sound like the one that follows, a tearing, wrenching, terrible *craaaaack*.

I set Lindy down but keep my arms tightly banded around her as we turn toward the sound. As we watch, the dead oak tree falls right toward the other side of the house. There is a crash and the sound of glass shattering.

I feel the thudding boom in the bare soles of my feet.

Grasping Lindy's hand, I tug her with me, discarding the wet sheet on the muddy ground. As suddenly and violently as it came, the storm begins to let up, and the angry rumble of thunder recedes.

We reach the other side of the house, and Lindy gasps. The house is still standing, but all the windows on that side are broken. Some branches are fully inside the house. Wet curtains flap through the openings in the wind, which is dying down along with the storm. In places, the wood siding has been ripped away, splintered wood everywhere.

I let go of Lindy's hand to wrap my arm around her shoulder. It could have been worse, especially if Jo were home and we were all inside. But this is her childhood home, and the damage is significant.

Lindy turns to me with wide eyes, her lashes spiky and wet. I can't read the emotion in her face. "My *house*."

I press a kiss to her temple. "I'm so sorry. We'll take care of this, Lindybird. You and Jo are safe. The dogs are safe."

"Pat, the unflinching optimist," Lindy says, lightly pinching my side. "Next, you're going to tell me you have an extra house just lying around."

I shift on my feet, bending to scratch my ankle monitor, which is even more uncomfortable when wet. Lindy stops laughing and stares up at me with narrowed eyes.

"Pat—I know that look. What?"

"Actually, I have a surprise I was saving for a rainy day." I look around with exaggerated surprise. "I guess that ends up being today."

Lindy brushes her wet bangs out of her eyes. "Cut the suspense! What is it?"

If Lindy protested the things I've done around the house, I have no idea how she'll respond to THIS. Go big or go home, right?

"I've been restoring a loft downtown for us. It's not quite finished, but it's definitely habitable. Especially compared to this. So, um, surprise?"

The look on Lindy's face says she's either thinking of kissing or killing me. When she goes up on her toes, pulling my lips down to hers, I get my answer.

CHAPTER THIRTY

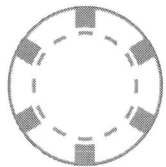

Lindy

I MAY REGRET THIS LATER, but for the moment, all I can think about is how good it feels to give in to Pat. I've waved my white flag, invited him in to storm my castle, and am loving every moment of being vanquished. The weird part is, I may have surrendered, but it somehow feels like I've won. I gave up everything, lost nothing, and gained even MORE.

Is this what love is like?

I lean closer to Pat, trying to ignore the way the center console of his truck is digging into my ribs. We need to replace his truck with one that doesn't have this annoying thing in the middle of the front seats. It's really cramping my style. Who needs cup holders or storage? Not I!

I'm honestly thankful right now just to have dry clothes on my back. Pat felt like the house was too dangerous to even go inside, so we took the dogs to Val's, where I borrowed some clothes, and Pat changed into some extras he kept in his car. Val had a lot of questions, which I promised to answer later. I'll probably need to figure out the answers first.

"You okay?" Pat asks, grinning as I lean my head on his shoulder. "Looks like you're having a battle with my truck."

"And losing. How much would it be to remove this console?"

Pat laughs. "Is this where we're at, now? We've gone from you not wanting me to spend money on things for you to you requesting we trick out my vehicle?"

"You don't have to change it. You could just buy a new one."

I'm joking—mostly—and I hope Pat knows it. Maybe I need to make *sure* he knows. Otherwise he might show up tomorrow with a new vehicle. But he seems totally delighted by this new side of me, even if I've caught a few flashes of wariness in his eyes. Totally warranted considering my quick flip. And it is quick. I've gone from pumping the brakes on everything to going full throttle.

Right now, I am too overwhelmed to question the wisdom in this. My house is basically totaled, and tomorrow is the hearing. My life has all but imploded. Forgive me if I'm putting off all the mental gymnastics and self-examination I should probably be doing. I'm just going to enjoy the moment. Carpe diem and all that jazz. Except I'm choosing to have selective memory about my diem—ignoring the looming issues and seizing Pat's mouth on mine whenever I can get it. He is a perfect distraction.

Speaking of—my perfect distraction pulls the car up in front of a building downtown and presses a quick kiss to my cheek. "If I'd planned this out, we'd have a dramatic reveal."

"The last thing I need right now is more drama."

Pat jogs around the front of the truck to open my door. I start to climb out, but he scoops me up like I weigh no more than a sheet of printer paper. I settle into his arms, wrapping mine around his neck.

"Planning to carry me over the threshold, husband?"

Pat freezes on the sidewalk, then tilts his head to study me. I expect a smile, but he's gone all serious on me. "You've decided to break all the rules today, huh?"

"I thought you'd be thrilled," I say lightly.

"Don't get me wrong," Pat says. "I am. You're just going through a lot, and I don't want to take advantage."

"You aren't taking advantage of me," I protest.

"And I also don't want to get my hopes up. I don't want to push, but it would be helpful to know where things stand. Where *I* stand. If this is …"

He trails off, looking away. I cup his cheek, loving the bite of his stubble there. It's already started to fill in from yesterday's clean shave.

"I'd like to have that talk. But could we temporarily table the conversation?"

I can't even say the word *hearing* right now, but Pat seems to understand me perfectly. Per the usual.

"Of course." The concerned look slides off his face, replaced by a huge grin. "Get ready. You're going to love this place."

He fumbles with a set of keys, finally managing to open a door next to an empty storefront. Once inside, he starts up a creaky set of stairs. I press my cheek to his chest, not minding the bump of his collarbone against my forehead as he climbs. I kind of wish this was a taller building, as I'm enjoying the ride. It would make a fantastic addition to a theme park.

Not that I'd let anyone else have a turn. Nope! Private attraction. Special ticket-holders only.

At the top of the stairs, Pat unlocks another door, then pauses. I give him my very best drumroll, which admittedly isn't very good. But it's enough to light up his eyes and put my favorite grin on his face.

Pat throws open the door, and I simply stare. "I give you casa de ... uh, to be named later. Welcome to Casa TBD!"

My first thought: This is nothing like Big Mo's cramped apartment above the diner.

My second thought is a very eloquent *WOW*.

Pat starts to set me down and I cling to him like I'm a sloth and he's my very favorite tree.

"Do you want a carrying tour?" he asks, chuckling. "Because that can be arranged."

"Tempting," I say, and his smile widens. "But no. Just give me a minute. I'm taking it all in."

Pat steps inside and nudges the door closed. I feast my eyes on the space, not believing how perfect it is. It has high ceilings with exposed ducts and beams. The walls are a color that falls somewhere between dark gray and navy. Huge windows along the front flood the space with natural light. The floors are a refinished wood, somehow retaining their worn history while also looking smooth and fresh.

Furnishings are sparse, though there is a sectional sofa and massive TV. I can see where a big table will go, right under a modern iron light fixture. The massive kitchen island looks like it's just waiting for stools.

Only two things hang on the walls, and both make my throat swell with emotion. The first is Jo's *Jaws* coloring page, which Pat has framed. The other is a painting I haven't seen but immediately recognize.

"You can put me down now."

Obediently, Pat carefully sets me down, and steps back, shoving his hands in the pockets of his jeans. I walk over to the painting, an abstract in varying shades of blue. A bright yellow bit of yarn works through the thick paint, part of Val's signature style. I see her actual signature in the bottom corner, a big sweeping V.

"You bought one of Val's paintings."

"I did. She's really talented."

"She is." I turn to look at him. "Do she and Winnie know about this place?"

Pat shakes his head. "Just my family. I started the renovation after the first day I saw you. Then I kept it going just in case."

"Just in case what?"

"Just in case a tree fell through your house," he says lightly. When I raise my eyebrows, he glances away. "I've been a little worried about the structural integrity of your house. Even before the tree. I thought if needed, we could move here while we fix it up or ... I don't know."

His thoughtfulness threatens to capsize me completely. Just when I think I know the extent of this Pat's kindness, he goes and *renovates a gorgeous apartment for us*. He looks uncharacteristically unsure, which is entirely too many UNs. I walk closer, then stand on my toes to kiss his jaw. I can't reach his lips without a stepstool. Maybe I'll start walking around with stilts for easy access.

"This is amazing, Pat. The place is gorgeous."

He grins, bending to press a warm kiss to my lips. "The place is gorgeous? How about the man behind the place?"

"He's not so bad either."

"I can work with *not so bad either*. What do you think about this exposed brick wall?" he asks.

I glance back at the wall in question. "I love it."

"Really? Let's make sure."

His big hands find my hips and urge me back until I'm flush with the wall. He slides his fingers up to my shoulders and then places them on either side of my head, caging me in. "How about now? Still like it?"

"I *think* so ... but maybe I need some convincing."

Pat needs no more convincing, fusing his mouth to mine. I grip his shirt, pulling him closer, letting my hands glide up his broad chest. The loft is forgotten as we pause for a minute—or an hour? Pat's kisses have a way of bending time. When we come up for air, I'm feeling languid and kiss-drunk.

But Pat's energy only seems heightened. He gives me a broad smile and then tugs on my hand.

"Time for the full tour," he says, his boyish excitement returning in full force. "I have so much more to show you."

"I think I might need to think about the wall a bit more," I tell him, but he only laughs, dragging me onward.

The kitchen is fully functional, even though a few things are still missing, like stools for the island and the hood over the stove. Pat already has dishes and all the necessities in the drawers and on the shelves. Everything is gorgeous, a mix of modern and classic—the best of both worlds. It's very Pat, but it also is the style I would have chosen. It feels like US.

Pat leads me to the giant windows along the front. An electric saw and some other tools sit near a puddle from the storm, and a new metal railing is in place but unsecured. "The balcony isn't quite done, but you can walk out to it here and from your office."

"My ... office?"

Pat grins and throws open a door. Inside is a small room flooded with light. There are bookshelves waiting to be filled, a chair, and a desk facing the window and balcony door.

Another big window on the side wall overlooks the library down the street.

I run my palms over the surface of the desk, then sit down. The small wingback is so much more comfortable than the cheap office chair I suffer in when I work at home.

"I know you don't use your home office much, but I thought it was because you were avoiding me."

It was, actually, and guilt floods me. I stand up and wrap my arms around him. "This is perfect. I will love working here."

If my office got me all emotional, Jo's room pushes me over the edge. The room is at least three times the size of her little closet room at the farmhouse, but still maintains the same cozy aesthetic. Curtains hang around the bed, which will give Jo the ability to close herself in. There is a built-in window seat with a cushion and storage underneath. One entire wall is bookshelves, half-filled already with many of her favorites. There is even a ladder that slides along the bookshelves, every book lover's dream.

"Jo will never leave this room," I say. "Speaking of which, I need to pick her up from school soon. She's going to totally flip out."

"One more room first," Pat says, dragging me by the hand. We barely glance into the bathroom next to Jo's room, and then Pat pauses in front of the last door, which is back by the kitchen.

"What?" I ask, suspicious of the guilty look on his face. "Is this like Bluebeard's secret closet?"

Pat doesn't immediately say no, which is not the best sign. He bites his lip, then puts a hand on the doorknob. "In my defense, I designed this place with hope in mind. I didn't think we'd be moving in so soon."

"Hope for what?"

The door swings open. I'm so distracted by the gorgeous master bedroom that it takes me a moment to see exactly why he's hedging: the king-sized bed in the room.

The ONLY bed in the room.

CHAPTER THIRTY-ONE

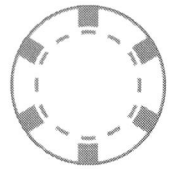

Pat

AFTER LINDY LEAVES in my truck to pick up Jo, I head out, feeling a restless tension building in my body. Maybe it's all the pent-up feelings left after twenty-four hours of being in the kissing zone with Lindy. Or perhaps I've been clubbed over the head with the same emotional overwhelm Lindy has.

I mean, sure—the house that just got eaten by a tree isn't MY childhood home. Jo isn't MY niece I've raised since infancy. But I don't halfway invest in things. I leap before I look, or maybe *as* I'm looking. I'm fully in this thing, and it feels a little like I've jumped off a high dive platform. As I watch the water coming closer and closer, I'm not sure whether I'm going to execute a perfect ten or a big ol' belly flop.

I consider heading to Mari's for something to eat—I can

always eat—but then I spot James's truck parked by the silos. Well, isn't that interesting!

I find him wandering around the open space outside the silos. "Well, look what the storm dragged in," I say, making him jump.

He spins to face me and quickly smooths his expression, but not before I see a flash of panic, like a kid caught elbow-deep in the cookie jar. He nods. "Patty."

"Whatcha doing, big brother?"

James clenches his jaw and looks away. "I'm just …"

"Just considering how this place would look as a thriving brewery? Don't worry, your secret's safe with me." I mime locking my lips and toss the invisible key over my shoulder.

"You couldn't keep a secret if you had your jaw wired shut." He steps closer and squints, brushing a hand over my hair. "Is that glitter in your hair?"

I bat his hand away, ignoring the glitter comment. "Since neither of us have our jaws wired shut, how about some lunch on me?"

A few minutes later, we're tucked into a back booth at Mari's, the one where Jo sat the first day we met. Mari brings us both menus and me a kiss on the cheek. "Good to see you boys. How are Jo and Lindy?"

I explain the events of the morning and let Mari know the dogs are at her place with Val. James's expression doesn't change much, but Mari coos and pats me on the head.

"We'll keep the dogs for however long. Whatever you need, necio."

I put a hand over my heart. "After all this, am I still a pest?"

"Always." I hear her laughter even after she heads into the kitchen with our orders. The Bobs are settling up their check, then the three of them amble over to our table.

"Did you read over our notes, Coach?" the first Bob asks.

Not even a little bit. This morning at practice, they handed me six single-spaced, typewritten pages. Even without the glitter tornado and the tree falling, I doubt I could have read their thesis. "Working on it. Thank you."

The second Bob shakes his head. "The best thing you did was bench the Waters kid."

"If he can get his ego in check, he'll make a fine QB," the third Bob says.

"Can any Waters keep their ego in check?" Bob number one scoffs.

"Hey!" someone calls. "I take offense to that."

I somehow missed seeing Wolf Waters reading a book at one of the tables. He sets down his book—an unauthorized biography of Dolly Parton—and joins us. James gives me a look, silently asking if I'm going to need him to hold me back. But the whole proposal thing feels like a lifetime ago. Wolf's easy expression makes it clear he isn't holding a grudge about me trying to punch him OR about me getting the girl. He shakes the Bobs' hands.

"Sorry about that, Wolf. Didn't mean to toss the Wolf out with the bath waters," the first Bob says, chuckling a little too hard at his own joke.

Wolf only smiles, running a hand over his beard. "No problem. Good game the other night, Coach."

"Thank you."

"And congratulations on your wedding." He shakes his head sheepishly. "I didn't mean to move in on your territory or anything. I didn't know you were Lindy's beau when I proposed."

"Oh, uh, no worries. Things were a little complicated."

Wolf nods. "Love always is." He pins his gaze on James. "Heard you're thinking of opening a brewery here."

James's eyes bore into mine. "Did you, now?"

"You know small towns and rumors. Anyway, if I can be of any assistance, let me know. I've got some experience in that area, as you know."

I'd hardly call Backwoods Bar experience, but hey. It's a peace offering of sorts. "I thought Sheeters were against the Grahams," I say.

Wolf rocks back on his heels, grinning. "I guess I like defying expectations. Y'all have a good day, now."

The Bobs leave not long after, and James raises one eyebrow.

"Those are the Bobs," I explain.

James snorts. "Of course they are. And that was the guy from the bar and jail. His brother is the suit who keeps trying to shut things down."

"You know your Sheeters! Ten points for you, James." He spins his knife on the table, watching me closely. "What?" I ask.

"You've really set down roots here. I wasn't sure how much of this was for real."

I can't help but bristle at his tone. Or maybe I'm being defensive because I wasn't fully honest with my family about the marriage to Lindy. "I got married, Jamie. I'm here to stay." Or until Lindy kicks me out if she decides she doesn't need or want me.

"And it wasn't the first time. With your other marriage, you jumped out just as quickly as you jumped in. Forgive me for seeing a pattern."

"This is different."

"So you've said."

James adds nothing, just giving me a typical James look. Could be disinterested. Could be bored. Could be constipated.

I sigh. "Look. I know how y'all feel about me. Pat, the flake. Pat, the guy who makes quick decisions he can't stick with, then jumps to the next thing."

"That's not how I see you," James says, and when I scoff, he holds up both hands. "Fine—some of it is how I *saw* you. And now you do seem different. Like maybe you were only restless because you hadn't found the right place or the right person. I guess my question is—does Lindy feel the same way?"

I go stock-still. Like I'm a baby fawn hiding in the grass and a big, bad wolf just walked into my clearing, sniffing around. "Why would you ask that?"

"Call it a gut hunch. She didn't look happy on your wedding day. She didn't have on a real dress. What woman excited about her wedding can't rustle up some kind of fancy, memorable dress?"

"We only had a few days to plan," I protest.

"Women are resourceful. I'm not saying she would have found her *Say Yes to the Dress* perfect wedding dress or whatever, just that it didn't seem like a priority. None of it did. Also, I know you. A courthouse wedding? That smells like …" He shakes his head. "I don't know. It just doesn't seem right. Something's up."

This is just like that night in his garage where James stared me into telling the truth about Lindy. His piercing gaze chips away at my resolve not to tell him everything. This time, I won't crack. I'm relieved when Mari drops off our plates, giving me a moment to regroup.

"You're not telling me everything." James takes a bite of his breakfast taco and groans, his eyes rolling back, taking his grumpiness with them. "This is—wow."

I butter my waffle, making sure to hit every square. "Just

think—if you move Dark Horse to Sheet Cake, you can eat here every day."

"Don't change the subject," James says through a mouth half full of tacos. "What's the story with you and Lindy? The *real* story."

I'm going to hold out. I'm not going to confess anything to James, the one brother sure to think all of this is a terrible idea. But I need someone to talk to. I need an outside perspective on what I'm dealing with, because it's too murky where I stand.

I can feel the truth bubbling up out of me. "She kissed me last night."

"I think the whole town is aware." James rolls his eyes. "Also, I should hope so."

I set down my utensils, giving my waffle a silent apology for making it wait. "Here's the thing about my marriage."

And, lowering my voice so this doesn't end up on Neighborly, I tell James how I've been trying to win over my wife. When I'm done, his elbows are on the table, his hands clasped together. His eyes look a lot like the sky just before the storm earlier today.

"Why didn't you tell us all this?"

I give him a pointed stare. "Would *you* have told you?"

"No. But I also don't tell anyone anything. You, on the other hand, tell everyone everything."

"I told Thayden."

"You told our *lawyer*?"

"And friend," I add. "Friend with built-in confidentiality. Turns out, his marriage had a similarly unconventional start."

"Unconventional? Is that what you're calling it?" James rubs a hand over his jaw. "Good for Thayden. I'm still more interested in why you felt like you had to hide this from your family. She's wearing Mom's ring, Patrick. That means something."

His eyes flash, and I feel my heart trip a little before picking up speed. "I know it does. Trust me, I know." Leaning back in the booth, I drag a hand through my hair, which still needs a trim. "Y'all didn't have the best impression of Lindy before—with the whole The Woman thing. I thought this might paint her in a worse light."

"Might?" James shakes his head and keeps going before I can cut in and defend her. "Pat, she's using you."

"She isn't. Or—I guess in some ways she is, but only in ways I've agreed to. I suggested this. It was *my* idea." That really, REALLY doesn't make this sound better. For a guy known for his way around words, they all seem to be on strike at the moment.

James looks like he's going to argue, so I just keep talking. "I knew what I was getting into. I meant my wedding vows."

"You didn't make any vows," James remind me. "Your courthouse wedding took four minutes and fifty-seven seconds."

Leave it to James to time my wedding. "Well, I made vows in my head. Silent promises. And I intend to fulfill them."

"What about her? What promises did Lindy make you?"

A sudden mental image of Lindy's rules comes to mind. Especially rule number seven—the one about dissolving the marriage at a mutually agreed-upon time. My gut churns.

Is that still what she's thinking?

If Lindy keeps Jo, will she keep me too? If she loses custody, will she let me go too?

Each question leaves a sour taste in my mouth and the sensation of a brick being shoved into my belly. I'm being dragged down into the kinds of worries and dark thoughts I've been hiding in my mental cave for days. James's words have rolled away the stone blocking them in, and now they're all swirling around me, weighing me down.

"What makes all this worse is Jo," James continues. "That little girl worships you."

"The feeling is mutual."

James leans forward, his gaze intense. "What happens to her when this all goes south? Did you think about that?"

"Of course I have."

But maybe not enough. What's seemed like a game at times with Lindy is suddenly all too real. Not like chess, where we're moving pieces around the board, but something a little more deadly and with possible casualties outside of the two of us.

Groaning, James leans back, running a hand over his face. "I'm sorry. I just unloaded on you."

I want to tell him it's okay, but I'm teetering on an edge here. Instead, I find myself shredding the paper napkin in my lap. When I realize Mari will probably be the one to have to sweep this up, I feel even worse and try to gather up all the pieces of the mess I made.

"Look, just make sure, okay? Don't settle," James says. "The timing is bad with all of this, so wait until after the hearing. Then talk to Lindy. Actual words, not flirting and wordplay. A serious conversation. Make sure it's you she wants."

In a rare show of brotherly affection, James slaps my shoulder. "You'll be okay, Pat. You always land on your feet."

Not this time, I think. *This time, I'm not sure if I'll land at all.*

But I swallow down the rising panic and force a smile, because it's what he expects. It's what everyone ALWAYS expects from me. "Of course I do."

CHAPTER THIRTY-TWO

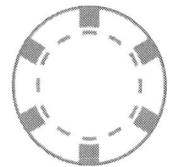

Lindy

As expected, the loft is a huge hit with Jo.

"Can we stay forever?" she asks from the very top of her sliding ladder.

She's been channeling her very best Belle, complete with singing "This Provincial Life" for the past five minutes. Which was cute and all, but five full minutes of it is a LOT of minutes.

I glance at Pat, grinning, expecting some kind of witty response from him. But he's staring out the window, his hands in his pockets. I'm not even sure he heard Jo. Ever since I got back with Jo, he's been strangely subdued. Very un-Pat-like.

When he doesn't answer, I give Jo the best answer I can, given the circumstances. "We've got a lot to talk about."

After tomorrow, I don't add. We're all thinking it. That's probably what's wrong with Pat. I know he's grown incredibly attached to Jo. The man usually hides his worry behind layers of cheer and optimism, so maybe this is the version of Pat with all those layers peeled back. Ashlee said only in the most extreme circumstance would we come home tomorrow without Jo. But this certainly is a kind of final night, and it's all I can do not to duct-tape Jo to my body. Pat's probably feeling the same.

I link my fingers through his, and he blinks a few times, like he's just waking up.

"Did you ask me something?" he says, his voice rough.

I shake my head. "Everything okay?"

He's silent for too long, and when I give his fingers a squeeze, it's again like he's just waking up. "Sure. Fine."

Aside from how he looks—where it most definitely applies—*fine* is not a word that belongs to Patrick Graham. It's way too middle of the road, not superlative enough to encapsulate the grandness of him.

He seems to have shrunk down into someone I don't recognize. As the evening goes on, our last evening together, I find myself filling up the space he's left vacant. I sing silly songs off-key. I play loud music through the speakers he's had installed through the loft.

We pick up food from Mari's since the fridge is empty, and after we've finished and cleaned up, Jo asks us both to tuck her in. "Patty can read, and you can scratch my back," she says in a tone that doesn't allow for questions. I'd do just about anything she asks tonight.

The bed in her new room is bigger than her closet room at the farmhouse, but that's not saying much when it's all three of us. We manage to squeeze in together, Jo giggling at the tight fit.

"I like being the jelly in this sandwich," she says. "We should do this every night."

Pat meets my eyes over Jo's head. An aching wound opens up way down deep. I want to choose hope. I *want* to. But despair and fear are right there, elbowing for dominance. And Pat, who has quickly become my solid ground, seems slippery himself right now.

"We should," I say, my voice catching a little toward the end.

Pat's eyes shine, but he blinks and then picks up the book Jo has chosen for tonight. It's one of the Lemony Snicket series, but I can't manage to grasp the plot or the characters. Pat does a valiant job with the voices, and Jo giggles while I scratch her back, trying to memorize every second of what feels like the most luxurious kind of tease.

I can smell Jo—the watermelon shampoo and the smell of outside that clings to active kids. But Pat's scent also rises around me, the two combining into the most perfect smell of home. The name of this scented candle would be *Family*, and I would hoard them until they were out of stock.

Will we have nights like this again? If so, how many?

I refuse to think about this as our last night. I can't. I won't. I invoke the power of positive thinking. This needs to be the start of forever—a lifetime of nights tucking Jo in together, Pat and I the bread in this little family sandwich.

Did you hear me? I INVOKE IT. The invocation has been invoked and shall be as such, forever and ever! Amen.

I must fall asleep shortly after my ridiculous invoking, and when my eyes open sometime later, it takes a moment to realize where I am. Jo is nestled into me, and Pat's arm stretches above her, his hand resting on top of my head. I'm toasty warm but have a crick in my neck from the odd angle of my head.

Pat watches me with a tender, quiet expression. It's one that I've never seen, and it makes my breath hitch. He's so still, so perfect. So very MINE.

I know I said we should table the discussion about us, but part of me wants to drag him from the room and confess that I love him. I want to beg him to stay, no matter what happens tomorrow. I want to find lighter fluid and make a Molotov cocktail out of my stupid rules. Just like the rules before, they did NOTHING to guard me against the full-scale assault of Patrick Graham. His intent was to win me and win me, he did.

He tilts his head toward the door and I nod. I manage to extricate myself from Jo's limbs without waking her. Pat offers me a hand to help me up the rest of the way. He doesn't let go, keeping my hand curled securely in his. The touch is comforting, but every touch from Pat also lights a fire.

As I quietly close Jo's door, Pat lets my hand fall from his. In the silence of this new space, he and I enter what can only be described as The Awkward Zone, *The Twilight Zone's* much dorkier cousin. We move to stand near the kitchen counter, but I think our minds are both focused on the master bedroom door ten feet away.

OUR bedroom. With the ONE BED.

"So?" The single word comes out of my mouth like a massive, existential question. Not even a little bit rhetorical.

"So," Pat says, scuffing his foot along the floor, then bending to scratch his ankle monitor.

"You're going to get an infection," I scold, not for the first time.

"Maybe I just want to have an excuse for you to nurse my wounds." His grin appears, then recedes too quickly.

I bite back a flirty response about playing nurse. After the weird overwhelm of today, it seems like a bad idea. Or an idea for what I can hope will be a later date. My eyes flick to the master bedroom door as a yawn overtakes me.

"Tired?" Pat asks.

"Dead on my feet. You?"

He nods, his eyes intense on mine, and then he chuckles, dropping his chin and running a hand through his hair. "Look, Lindy. I can make this easier and just sleep on the couch."

"Jo would know."

Because of Pat's early football mornings, Jo never realized Pat and I were sleeping in separate bedrooms. On the weekends, whenever Jo and I rolled out of bed, coffee and breakfast were already made, and Pat was already blazing like the morning sun. He is never more annoying than he is first thing in the morning. Annoying and also more than a little endearing.

Ever since I kissed Pat at the game, I've been debating with myself, feeling like I was plucking petals from a daisy. Only, instead of asking if he loves me or loves me not, I'm going back and forth about myself and mitigating my risks.

I risk it all; I run away. I risk it all; I run away. I risk it all; I run away.

I'm still plucking a never-ending stream of petals, no closer to an answer even now.

Risk it all; run away.

Pat's deep brown eyes meet mine, and the last petal falls. *Risk it all.*

I step closer to Pat, close enough to feel an electric charge in the air between us. "We can be adults about this."

Pat's eyebrows slowly climb up, and his smile erases the worry that's been hanging in his eyes all day. "You want to be … *adult* with me, Lindybird?"

I feel more than a flutter in my belly; it's more like a seismic shift. A blush starts creeping up my chest and neck, finally reaching my cheeks. It's utterly ridiculous that I'm having this reaction. Pat and I are, in fact, adults. And even if we're talking about the figurative sense of being *adult*, we are married. We can be allllll the kinds of adult we want to be. We are free to do any adulting we'd like.

My face isn't the only part of me that's hot. "I'm saying we can safely share a bed like two mature people. For sleeping purposes."

Even though we never shared a bed. Or slept together—in the literal or figurative sense. A few accidental naps on the couch in college were as close to sleeping together as we came.

Pat's eyes darken into deep wells, and I'd happily throw myself into them any day of the week. "You don't think that's … risky?" he asks.

Risk it all. Risk it all. Risk it all. It's now like a chant in my head, not so different from the cheers in the stadium the night before.

I don't want to simply share a bed with this man. I want to share it *all*. I could lose everything tomorrow—but I could have e*verything* tonight.

Pat and I are married. Even the Hallmark Channel would approve of whatever happens behind that closed door. We've made our vows—okay, maybe we skipped the vows, but our signatures on the marriage certificate are legally binding and fully official. The agreement we made out of desperation and in haste, has felt more real every day. We've been growing into silent promises we made. We're *living* this marriage into existence.

I think of our public kiss at the stadium and then our private one in the rain, wrapped in a wet bed sheet. I eye the brick wall where he gently pressed me earlier, making me lose time.

I remember watching Pat braid Jo's hair, coming home to see what new thing he fixed in the house. The way his eyes met mine first thing after the team won the game, just before a cooler of icy Gatorade was dumped over his head. I think of his bare chest, fresh and dripping from the shower, and the way he pulled me into his chest on the porch swing. Meeting his eyes over Jo's head just now, snuggled in her bed.

Pat and I have made a montage of memories in such a short time, and I want more.

More, more, MORE.

Desire floods through me. Now that the idea is there, I'm electrified, almost desperate for the need to have Pat completely, in all the ways I can.

Our eyes meet and lock.

"Maybe I'm in the mood for a little risk," I whisper.

But for some reason, this remark doesn't land where intended. Instead of throwing me over his shoulder and sprinting to the bedroom—which would be a totally Pat move—he clears his throat and shifts awkwardly. Not meeting my eyes.

My stomach drops, desire instantly shriveling up in the face of humiliation. So much for being risky. Never mind about that whole adulting thing!

"Could we just, um, forget I said anything?" I cover my face with my hands. "Please?"

Pat sighs. "Lindy, it's not that I don't want to—don't want *you.*"

"You don't need to explain."

I wave my hands awkwardly, like one of the people who directs planes on the landing strip. Only I want to direct traffic far, far away from me. I'd like to shut down my airspace altogether. Nothing is landing at my airport tonight! All flights are grounded. Maybe forever.

In a few quick strides, Pat comes to me and wraps his arms around my back. I struggle to get free for about three seconds before I realize I don't want to resist him. Also, he's way too strong. It's a dumb battle to even attempt.

I shouldn't want to be held by him, not now that I'm good and humiliated. After suffering the most embarrassing rejection of my life BY HIM. But I can't resist the comfort of his solid body. Sagging against his chest, I let my arms snake around his waist and keep my red face buried in his shirt.

"I *need* to explain," Pat says, his breath ruffling my hair. "There is nothing I want more than you, Lindy. But I don't just want you in my bed. I want your heart. I want everything. Every. Single. Thing." He clears his throat again. "But right now, there's a lot on the line. This has been a big week. Tomorrow is a big day. My emotions are all over the map, and I suspect yours are too."

He is so right—I know he is. I try to swallow down the feeling of rejection. It's hard to shake, even with Pat's sensible words.

He cups my cheeks, slowly tilting my face to his. "Look at me, Lindybird."

I do, though it takes effort to meet his eyes. But the love there, the kindness, the concern—it's so clear, so rich and full, that for a moment, I feel as though my heart stops, held perfectly still in Pat's capable hands.

His lips find mine, the kiss sweet and soft, easing the sting.

"I have a counter-offer," Pat says, his mouth moving against mine as he speaks.

"I'm listening."

"I'll take you to bed, to *our* bed, but only to sleep. For now. Believe me, I really, really want more."

He kisses me again, lingering in a way that gets my body even more electrified. His lips find my ear, and I shiver as his voice drops to a husky whisper.

"But when we're together for the first time, I don't want there to be any questions. I don't want it to be in the middle of emotional overwhelm. I want both of us to be sure. I want it to be a celebration, not an escape. Do you understand what I'm saying?"

I nod, words temporarily lost to my feelings. Warmth curls like a ribbon in my chest at his words.

Without warning, Pat sweeps me up in his arms, bridal style. I squeal, and he chuckles, the rumble of his laughter moving through me. He moves with purposeful strides to the bedroom and kicks the door closed behind us.

It is a really, really hot move, and now I'm wishing we could forget everything we just agreed to. Emotional overwhelm—what emotional overwhelm? I don't see any of that here.

Pat sets me down and I straighten my top, feeling suddenly shy. I'm still wearing Val's ill-fitting clothes, baggy jeans a little too short for me and a T-shirt. "I don't have anything to sleep in."

I took Jo to Walmart after I picked her up from school to grab some clothes and toiletries. It seems obvious that I should have gotten some things for myself, but my mind has been a hazy mess all day long.

Pat grins, as close to full-wattage as I've seen since I brought Jo home. "Check the built-in dresser in the closet."

I make my way to the walk-in closet, and to a row of built-in drawers I hadn't paid much attention to when Pat first showed me the loft. I find an array of pajamas in one of the drawers. Pat has bought me everything from flannel to soft cotton to—

I hold up a lacy black negligee, one eyebrow raised. Pat only shrugs, his cheeks flushing an adorable pink.

"I figured I'd cover all the bases," he says.

I bark out a laugh. "Yeah, *all* the bases. First base, second base, third base ..."

"Touchdown?" He gives me an adorably boyish grin.

"I think you're mixing your metaphors, Mr. Graham." I tuck the negligee back into the drawer, wishing it were that easy to set aside my desire. "Another night?"

His voice is low and husky, but he keeps his distance. "I certainly hope so."

Though the giant tub is calling my name, I'm too exhausted even for a bath. I choose one of the pajama sets in a deep blue in a soft material with long pants and a short-sleeved top. Even though it's almost as full coverage as I can get, Pat's eyes darken as I join him in the bedroom. He's already in bed, propped up against the pillows and—surprise, surprise—shirtless.

"That's not really playing fair," I tell him, pointing to his bare chest, still standing by the edge of the bed.

"What? This old thing? You've seen this dozens of times," he teases.

But I haven't spent the night snuggled up against his warm, bare skin, and that is completely different. I haven't kissed him while he's not wearing a shirt either, and it's a totally different experience when Pat pulls me into bed and brushes his lips over mine. What starts soft and teasing quickly turns into something spinning out of control.

Pat pulls away when my hands start to explore his skin, my fingernails scraping over the big, square muscles in his chest. A soft groan falls from his lips. Before I can even protest, he picks me up, turning me away from him and spooning me.

"This might be safer," he says, practically a growl.

"You don't trust me?"

"I don't trust either of us."

"Thank you," I say, running my hands over his arms, feeling the muscles flex there.

"For what?"

"Where do I start? For chasing after me, even when I tried to chase you away. For marrying me. For all the things you fixed. For all the surprises, like this one. For loving Jo. For loving me so well, even when I don't deserve it."

"You do," he insists, nuzzling his face into my hair. "You deserve so many good things, Lindy. You are my solid ground. My place of rest. My forever home."

"That sounds a little like a description of a grave."

Pat laughs, my whole body shaking with his. Then he shifts, reaching back to click off the lamp beside the bed, and the room plunges into darkness. Though I didn't think it was possible given the worries in my mind and the tumult of my day, I start to drift into sleep. Pat's breaths rise and fall in perfect rhythm with my own.

The last thing I hear is Pat whispering, "I love you," against my hair.

I love you too, I think, and then I tumble into the dark curtain of sleep.

CHAPTER THIRTY-THREE

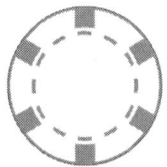

Lindy

I WAKE UP TO PAT, a solid furnace against my back. I'm damp and maybe a little sticky. His arm is banded tightly around my stomach, skin on skin where my shirt has ridden up. Our legs are tangled together, his hair brushing my smooth legs. His breath stirs my hair, and now that I'm awake, each puff of air tickles, making me want to squirm closer. A lazy smile spreads across my face.

"Cinnamon Toast Crunch," he mutters, dragging me even closer, his lips feathering over my neck.

I bite my lip, holding back a laugh. It does not surprise me at all to know Pat's sleep-talk includes food.

I could live and die right here. Even with the whole sweat situation going on. Pat's warmth is like a tropical beach without the possibility of sunburn or sand getting stuck in uncomfortable places.

He's also the man you propositioned last night.

I freeze as the memories come back with painful clarity. I squeeze my eyes closed.

Oh. No. I. Did. Not.

Oh, yes. Yes, I did.

My entire body goes rigid as I trace back my memories of the night before. I practically begged Pat to take me to bed.

It shouldn't be a big deal—I mean, we're married. We've kissed. He's told me he loves me, and I know I love him, even if I haven't said the words.

But all those facts do nothing to ease the sharp sting of humiliation.

I know Pat was right to say no. I can only imagine how I'd feel if I had woken up in this same position right now, but *naked*.

Remembering, I *feel* naked. Is Pat getting hotter? Does he have a fever? Am I melting into a puddle of sweat or embarrassment?

I don't know how I'll face him when he wakes, or what I'll say. *Hey, remember that time I tried to proposition you and you turned me down like a gentleman? No? Me neither! That definitely NEVER happened.*

This is bad. This is so bad. My shame burns with the intensity of a thousand suns.

I hear soft footsteps outside the room. Jo must be up. *Jo.*

The hearing.

A second wave of gut-wrenching realization washes over me. What started out so pleasant is now officially the worst morning ever!

I feel like I've been tossed into an industrial kitchen mixer that's turning me end over end over end. Drawing in a deep breath, I start to count bricks in the wall. One row then two and three until my breathing slows to a manageable rate.

I'm going to get through today. I will. I WILL.

But in order to do that, I need to channel the Lindy who did this life on her own for the last five years. I need her to be strong today for me, for Jo. I need to zip that bulletproof vest back in place and kick the feral cat back to the curb. I can't think about what happened with Pat last night, or about what my future with him will be.

One big, emotional thing at a time.

Pat smacks his lips, mumbling something about llamas and first downs. I love this man, despite my utter humiliation. I love him, and I *will* tell him, but first, there is a horrible, terrible, rotten day to get through.

As slowly and quietly as I can, I slip out of bed. Pat doesn't even stir.

I can't tell you a single thing about the drive to Austin for the hearing. We might have time traveled or flown in a shoe for all I remember. Too soon, I'm sitting at a table in the courtroom next to Ashlee wondering how I got here. Not just physically, but how my life brought me to this point.

Jo is in a secure room with Mari, and I already feel this small separation like a soul-deep paper cut. Because I'm the only one named as conservator, Pat is seated with his family behind us. Judge Judie agreed to grant permission for Pat to be here today, and in the end, removed the ankle monitor altogether, winking and telling him to stay close.

I'm hyper aware of things like the squeak of Ashlee's chair and the faint smell of wet dog. I'm not sure where the wet dog smell is coming from, but after a discreet sniff of myself, I'm about eighty percent sure it's not me.

Though some details are strikingly clear, I also feel like

I'm suspended underwater. Everything around me is slow and muted. Nothing can quite touch me down here. Even the harsh lights in the courtroom seem be filtered through a soft, watery blue.

Which, I KNOW, makes it sound like I've opened the bag and let all my marbles roll away. I'm sure it's a defense mechanism of some kind. I'll take all the defense mechanisms. As far as mechanisms go, they're pretty good.

"What does it mean if Rachel doesn't show?" I whisper to Ashlee. "Is it an automatic forfeit?"

"Unfortunately, this won't work like a football game. But she should be here. I'm not sure what the judge will say if she doesn't show, but it's good for you. I wish I could tell you something for sure. I just don't know," Ashlee says.

We've discussed so many scenarios in the last few weeks, and Ashlee went over them briefly again when we sat down today. More than likely, any changes will be implemented slowly, and a final decision might come after more time has passed. There could be court-ordered visitations or evaluations. If Rachel is awarded custody, there will probably be a transition period.

Yeah, yeah, yeah. Got it. A stranger who doesn't know me or Jo or Rachel will make a decision that will change all of our lives. Sounds like justice to me.

Rachel still isn't here when the judge arrives. This shouldn't surprise me, given my sister's lifetime track record, and yet, color me surprised. She went through the trouble of retaining a lawyer, having someone pose as a pizza delivery guy to serve me with papers, and now she doesn't show up?

I can't stop watching her lawyer. Above the collar of his expensive suit, his neck is bright red. Anger? Sunburn? Body paint?

When the judge, a shrew-faced man with a patchy beard,

asks Rachel's lawyer where his client is, he stands. The room seems to hold its breath.

No—it actually DOES hold its breath, audibly. I feel like I'm not just holding the air in my lungs, but my soul itself. I hear what sounds like the start of a giggle behind me—Pat's nervous tic. Then some shuffling that I imagine is Tank or James slapping a hand over his mouth.

"Your honor," Rachel's lawyer says, his neck somehow growing even redder. "My client could not be present today." He pauses. "She has asked me to dismiss the request for custody."

Ashlee grabs my hand, and I feel Pat's fingertips brush my shoulder. I don't lean into him, but neither do I pull away. I'm not sure I can move. Rachel is dismissing her case?

Rachel's lawyer shuffles his papers, opening and closing the same folder several times. I want to grab him by the lapels of his suit and shake more information out of him.

He glances our way, just once, then looks back to the judge. "Mrs. Davis has made the decision to terminate her parental rights."

Terminate her parental rights? Rachel?

Of all the possibilities we talked through, this was not one. I didn't even allow myself to hope for it.

Relief rushes over me and rushes through me as I sink down in my chair, head in my hands. It's over. The courtroom erupts into cheering and crying, and I swear I hear a cowbell in there somewhere.

The judge has more to say when he finally quiets the room, but I don't hear a word. Hopefully Ashlee can fill me in later. A few minutes later, we are dismissed. It's over. It's OVER.

Ashlee hugs me, and Val and Winnie practically knock me down with a group hug, but all I need in the chaos is Jo.

I head for the courtroom doors because JO IS OUT THERE SOMEWHERE but I'm being overwhelmed with hugs and congratulations, all the while dimly aware of Pat's presence somewhere nearby but just out of reach. I need his arm, his touch, but first I have to get to Jo. I suspect he's got the same idea I do.

Mari enters the courtroom with a bailiff and Jo beside her. Jo breaks away, running toward me with a face like the only sun I'll ever need.

I crush her to me, much too tightly, but she doesn't so much as complain. I'm tempted to locate duct tape so I can attach her to my person.

"You smell so good," I tell her, and why this is the thing I say right now, I'll never know.

"Can we stop for frozen custard?" Jo asks.

"Of course."

Someone shouts for us all to clear the courtroom, but don't they know WE ARE HAVING A MOMENT? I pick up Jo, being jostled from all sides as I carry her out. I need to find Pat, but I catch sight of his dark hair and broad shoulders somewhere behind me in the throng. He's coming. He'll find us.

The hallway is hardly better than the courtroom. As much as I love my best friends and Big Mo and Mari and Eula Martin and whoever that random dude was who just hugged me, I need to breathe.

I also need to work out or something, because my arms are exhausted from carrying Jo for more than two minutes. But there is no world in which I'm putting her down until she asks.

Where is Pat?

His is the one face I haven't seen, and he should really be right up in here, a part of this hug, a part of this moment.

The three of us, together. I've lost him in the throng of people.

"Where's Patty?" Jo asks.

"I don't know, baby."

"I'm here."

The two of us melt into Pat, and now—NOW—everything is right in my world. I wish the moment didn't happen just outside a men's restroom. It would have been so much more poignant without catching a glimpse of a man standing at the urinals. It's also strange—Pat's arms are like overcooked spaghetti. It's not a real Pat hug.

When he pulls away and Tank steps in with a crushing hug, it only highlights how weak Pat's embrace was. I can't take my eyes off his face, which is strangely blank. Pat is never blank. He's never on mute. It's like he was yesterday, only worse.

I like my Pat dialed all the way up. He is best enjoyed at top volume and full strength. I'm not sure what's happening here. We won—shouldn't he be doing a dance worthy of an excessive celebration flag? Or tossing Jo up into the air? Maybe releasing doves or shooting off a confetti cannon? Pat is a grand gesture kind of guy. Not one to stand back, shove his hands in his pockets, and look distant.

Except that's what he's doing.

Ashlee stands before me suddenly, an envelope in her hand. "This is from the other attorney. Rachel wrote it for you. Do you want me to read it first? He said it's personal, not legal."

"No. I don't care. Just shove it in my purse, will you?"

I'll read it later. I don't even care. Rachel, in typical Rachel fashion, created an enormous amount of drama, dragged all of this out only to make us drive down here for something we could have had our lawyers discuss on the phone.

I'll be angry later when I'm not so bowled over with relief.

"My place isn't far from here," Tank is saying, and I don't miss the way he eyes Ashlee. "I'd love to invite everyone over to celebrate. Lunch or drinks or—"

I'm already shaking my head no. I feel short of breath, suffocated by all the touching and the emotions. I need space from the crush of people bottlenecking and rubbernecking and that one couple I don't know who is *actually* necking quite amorously just a few feet away.

"Could I take a rain check? All this is just ... so much," I say weakly, and of course, Tank understands. Something crosses Pat's face and then is gone. Is he mad? Disappointed? I cannot get a read on him.

"You don't need to explain," Tank says. "Of course. Another day. Anytime, really. We would love to have you both."

Tank glances between me and Pat, his brow furrowed. So, I am definitely not imagining this strangeness. An uncomfortable prickling sensation starts in my fingertips and works its way up until it reaches my heart.

"Congratulations again," Tank says. "I'm going to head on, I guess." He grabs Pat's shoulder, giving it a good shake, like he's trying to reset him.

"I'm going to stop by," Pat says. Tank's mouth pulls down, but he doesn't say anything else before walking away to join Pat's siblings.

"You're going to your dad's?" I ask. "You're staying here?"

Pat's eyes dart away. More like slink away. There is definitely some slinking going on. "I think I'm going to stay in Austin for a bit. It's the first time I've been home since, you know, all this went down."

All this being his arrest and our marriage, I guess? I'm

practically melting into a puddle of emotional overwhelm, the likes of which cannot handle whatever is happening here.

James appears like a grumpy specter. "Can I borrow Jo for a few?"

Winnie and Val swoop in from the other side, clearly feeling their best friend emergency beacon activating. "We've got her," Winnie says. "Jojo, come with us." She and James exchange glares over Jo's head.

"I saw an ice cream vending machine down the hall." Val waggles her brows, but she had Jo at ice cream vending machine. James steps back, and my friends whisk Jo away, leaving Pat and me to deal with whatever this is.

He's apparently not so eager to talk, and we just stand there in the middle of the busy lobby, saying nothing for a good minute. I'm not sure I've ever known such an awkward pause. If someone handed out awards for awkward pauses, this one would be giving a teary acceptance speech right about now.

Can't we just be super, super happy and then drive home and fall asleep for ten hours, wake up and stuff our faces with pizza, be happy some more, maybe have a DTR and then some celebratory making out? Or more than making out?

Pat's face all but assures me I'm aiming the bar too high.

I know I've been weird all day—with good reason. I was cool with Pat this morning, not really meeting his eyes or saying much. In the car, I rode in back with Jo, and I may have shrugged out of his touch when we walked into the courthouse. None of this is really about *him*. I'm embarrassed I made an idiot of myself last night, and today has been emotionally exhausting, even though the outcome was better than I could have dreamed. I'm running on the fumes of fumes here. I just needed to get through the day, thinking of Jo before I could deal with Pat.

Was my weirdness contagious, like a flu? Or did he read more into how I've been acting today?

"Congratulations," Pat says, and the word feels like a slap.

It's what you say to someone else who's won, not when you're on the same team, celebrating a victory together. We should be doing chest bumps, hugging for REAL, making out like bandits.

I press a hand to my temple. "What exactly is happening here? Because this feels like a breakup. Will you just tell me if it is? I am hanging on by a thread here, Pat."

He makes a face. "It's not a breakup."

"It's *something*." He shuffles, and I cross my arms over my chest, trying to still my quaking heart. "I know I've been weird all morning, and I'm sorry. I felt really stupid about last night, and then totally overwhelmed with today. I just needed to focus on Jo."

Pat nods, then bends to scratch his ankle. I can see the moment he remembers there's no monitor covering it. In a few days it will be like the monitor was never there at all.

I swallow.

Pat is free now, free to unfasten his seatbelt and move around the cabin. The only thing tying him officially to Sheet Cake is our marriage license. That piece of paper has never felt so thin. I'm not even sure where it is. But it still counts in the state of Texas, even if I lost it. Right?

"You're not breaking up with me, but you're also not coming home with me and Jo."

Pat touches my shoulder, once, briefly, then drops his hand. "Lindy, I love you."

So, why does this sound like an apology? Or a goodbye? I swallow down what feels like a mouthful of sawdust while he continues.

"Like I've said from the beginning, I want a second

chance. I've wanted nothing more than to convince you this could be real. It could be so good."

I sort of thought it WAS good.

There is a ride at the Sheet Cake Festival every year called the Scrambler. I begged Mama to let me ride it once, and once was enough. The jerking, spinning, twisting car left me heaving up my dinner behind the ticket booth. I feel like I'm on that ride now, being yanked into one whiplash after another.

"But? I can feel the *but*. Just say it, whatever it is. Please. Put me out of my misery here."

"I am all in, Lindy."

He meets and holds my eyes, his expression sincere and intense, like a laser searing going straight to my soul. And I'm frowning in confusion, because he sounds anything but all in. His mouth is saying one thing while his body language says something totally different.

"I don't know where *you* are," he continues. "And I can't keep doing this until I know it's what you really want. Now that you don't need me for something, I have to know you still want me, just for me."

Of course I still want you! I want to shout. *I want you and I need you not for legal reasons but because you're like my oxygen! You're the sun! You're everything to me!*

The words are all jockeying for position until there's just a lot of noise and confusion in my head. I say nothing. I just stare at Pat, willing him to know the things I'm feeling, willing him to not do this right now.

Pat waits, like he hopes with a tiny shred of himself I'm going to answer right here, to declare my love for him.

And I *do* love him. I know it now more than ever before.

I am also a fifty-car pile-up of emotional overwhelm. I know—I KNOW—Pat has given me so much these past few weeks. More than I asked for and probably deserved. But today, I just need one more thing. I need *time*.

A day to process, a night to sleep—even in his arms, feeling safe and a few degrees too hot when I wake up.

"Do we have to do this now?" I ask, hating myself even as I do. I know Pat deserves all of me. He deserves an answer. I want to give him that. Just not RIGHT NOW. Not standing in the crowded, too-noisy, hard-to-breathe hallway after the most emotional day of my life.

"I need to know," he says. "But I'm giving you time to decide. That's why I'm going to stay here for now."

For how long?

Pat takes a step back. Then another. He's really leaving, going to his dad's house. *It's not a breakup*, I tell myself. *He said he loves me.* Maybe it's unfair of me or maybe it's totally fair—and I just don't KNOW because my brain is a fried egg—but I just cannot handle this conversation the way I want to.

Pat may feel like he's giving me time and space, but what it feels like is him leaving me, just the way I always feared he would.

CHAPTER THIRTY-FOUR

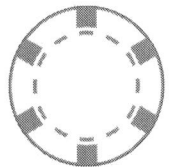

Pat

A PERSISTENT NUDGE to my ribs starts to bring me into consciousness. I groan and roll over. My face itches—what is this fabric? These aren't my sheets. The nudge turns into a poke, then more of a kick. Definitely a kick. I shove away the offending foot.

"Come back later," I groan. "I'm closed."

There's a snort, but I'm too busy falling back into sleep to pay much attention. At least, until a wet, smelly dog tongue assaults my face. Swatting at whatever dog is bathing me, I end up rolling right off the couch. And now I'm awake.

This is Tank's rug, and that is Tank's couch, where I apparently fell asleep last night in my clothes. Smoky is still enthusiastically licking whatever he can reach, while Harper watches me with narrowed eyes from a chair she's pulled up.

The television is playing reruns of house-flipping shows. Tank must be asleep.

"It's still dark," I protest, rubbing my eyes. "What time is it?"

"Time for you to snap out of it. Why are you still here?"

I yawn, pushing Smoky back with the other. "Why are you?"

"I'm here to prevent one of my idiot brothers from making a dumb decision. Or, since you've made several dumb decisions lately, I'm here to stop the bleeding. And I have to train someone in half an hour, so you better start talking."

I climb back up on the couch, running a hand through my hair. A sour taste fills my mouth as I remember yesterday's events.

"Everything's fine," I lie. "You don't need to worry about me."

Harper arches a brow. "So, you didn't try to tell your emotionally overwhelmed wife she needed to make a final decision about your relationship? Because according to the rumor I heard, you did that right in the lobby of the courthouse. Not ten minutes after the hearing."

I scratch my ankle. I'm not used to it being bare, and it still itches like the ghost of that monitor is still there. "Um. I might have done something like that. But you're making it sound so—"

"Selfish? Careless? Inconsiderate?" She nods. "Yeah, I guess I am making it sound that way. Because putting all those things on Lindy at that exact moment was all of those things. And then some. Like I said, dumb decisions."

I already know Harper's right, and my stomach drops at the thought. I've done what I always do best. I made an impulsive choice. I ran my mouth when I should have shut up. I can hear Collin in my head, scoffing at another classic Pat Decision.

Crossing my arms, I stare out the back window, where pinks and purples are just starting to wash over the edge of the dark sky. I wonder if Lindy is waking up alone in the bed we shared the night before. Or maybe she slept curled around Jo. I would have. It physically hurt to walk away from them at the courthouse. This is the last place I want to be.

And yet, thanks to me being dumb, I guess, here I am.

Harper leans forward and touches my knee. Her voice softens. "Talk to me, Patty. What was going through your head?"

I shrug. "Hard to explain."

"Try me," Harper says.

Much like I'd done with James a few days ago, I tell my sister everything, from the way I screwed up way back when to Lindy's rules and my attempts to win her over—which seemed to be working. Harper seems surprised by nothing, but maybe she had more of an idea what was going on than James.

I don't realize I've paused until Harper touches my knee again. "What happened?"

What DID happen? It all seems so messy now, my thoughts like briars and weeds sprouting up everywhere in a messy, overgrown garden. I hate the heaviness pressing down on me right now, like I'm wearing a weighted blanket as a cape.

"I'm not sure. I wanted to talk about where we stood, but Lindy asked to wait until after the hearing. Which made sense. I mean, it's been weighing on her, you know?"

"I can imagine," Harper says.

"Then we had this moment while putting Jo to bed, and

Lindy wanted to ... take things further, but I asked her to wait."

"That also makes sense. Especially if you wanted to make things clear."

I nod. "But she was so weird yesterday, and I know it was a crazy day, but she hardly spoke to me all morning. Like, it seemed like she regretted what happened—even though *nothing* happened. Maybe she regretted asking me or was embarrassed? I don't know. She wouldn't touch me, wouldn't talk to me. She barely looked at me. Then the court stuff happened."

"And this is where I get confused," Harper says. "What happened to prompt you to have a DTR talk right in the heat of the moment?"

Sinking deeper on the couch, I let my head fall back and close my eyes. I'd been elated to hear that Rachel dropped her petition and terminated her rights. I may be an optimist, but even I hadn't hoped for that outcome. I almost vaulted over the little barrier separating my row from where Lindy sat. But I managed to keep myself under control, counting down the seconds until I could wrap Lindy up in a hug.

You did it, I wanted to tell her. *We did it. Let's go home!*

And then ... Lindy seemed to forget all about me. It's understandable that she sought out Jo. But I watched the two of them embrace, feeling like an outsider. They weren't thinking of me or missing me. It was like Lindy and Jo reverted right back to the duo they'd been before Lindy needed my help. James's words echoed in my head about being used, about needing to know where I stand.

I'd seen the sum of all my fears realized in that moment. I'm not needed. Heck, I didn't even feel *wanted* in that moment. It's like I didn't exist.

"It's like she didn't even remember I was there," I admit.

"Tell me why you think that."

I lean forward again, dropping my hands between my knees so I can scratch my ankle again. "Maybe it sounds dumb, but I didn't feel like part of the celebration. I know I haven't been in their lives long, but I feel tied to them." I thump my chest. "They're here, you know? I thought we were becoming a family. It's what I've always wanted, and in that courtroom, I was just watching on the outside."

Harper nods. Smoky nudges me, and I scratch his belly until he rolls over in a most unbecoming manner. The heaviness has eased a little, but now I just feel thin and empty.

"I kept thinking about what James said, and I knew he was right—"

"Let me stop you right there." Harper shoots me a questioning gaze. "Where does James fit into this picture?"

"We had lunch the day before the hearing. I talked to him about Lindy, and he said it sounded like she was using me." Harper starts to say something, but I keep going. "I told him he was wrong about that, but he was right about one thing—I need Lindy to make a decision. I've put myself out there again and again. I need to know where she stands."

Harper gives me a long look, one that I think is intended to make me think about what I've done. But I'm tired of thinking. My mind is just running in circles, and each thought seems to be making the ruts in the road deeper. I'm sinking. And I'm just so tired.

Suddenly, Harper stands and holds out her hand. Smoky is already on his feet, tongue lolling. "Come on, big brother."

I put my hand in hers and let her pull me up. I don't make it easy, but my sister is no lightweight. "Where are we going?"

"Outside."

There's a chill in the air, but it's refreshing, and a little of the mess in my head starts to clear. Smoky takes off for the yard, where he chases off some birds and finds trees needing his proverbial name on them. Harper walks to the edge of the patio, where steam rises off the heated pool. The water looks ethereal, pink and orange reflecting on the surface. Harper and I stand shoulder to shoulder, looking out over the water and the brightening sky.

"Permission to speak freely?" my sister asks.

"Granted."

"You tend to operate in one of two speeds. There's typical Pat, which is high speed, high happy, and extremely high energy."

"Okay ..."

"For the record, I love that about you. As someone who is not built that way, it's refreshing. Maybe even a little endearing." Harper bumps me with her shoulder. I bump back a little harder, and she smiles. "Your other speed isn't really a speed at all. When you hit something hard, you crash. There is no slowing down, just a sudden stop, and then it's like you exist in this dark pit."

"Would you call it a pit of despair?"

"I would. And it even comes equipped with the Machine, designed to suck years from your lifespan."

I can't help but smile. "Look at you with the *Princess Bride* references. It's depressing as all get-out, but I appreciate the effort." I pause, watching Smoky chase his own tail before rolling around in the dewy grass. "Do you really think I do that?"

"Do *you* think you do that?"

I'd love to say no. Only ... I can't. I've been in that pit since yesterday, so it's very hard to argue with Harper's assessment.

"Maybe. Yeah, okay. Sure."

"I've done some basic research about ADHD, and sometimes it can bring with it very high highs and very low lows. They talk about it like being flooded with emotions. I think yesterday was intensely emotional for you and for Lindy. You got flooded, and you couldn't hold it back. Does that sound at all like your experience?"

When did my baby sister get so smart? That's what I want to know. And she's researching ADHD? For me?

I'll admit—I only did a tiny bit of googling when she told us about being autistic and her sensory processing stuff. My sister is just Harper. Completely herself. And after the third webpage trying to define her for me, I gave it up. I didn't need a manual to understand her. Knowing what a diagnosis said didn't change who she was. Other than being a little more sensitive when she tells me things (like about hating the smell of cigars), I didn't see the need to overanalyze.

So, why would I do that for myself? Every third person these days seems to have some kind of ADHD. It's something I can know about myself, but as an adult, it doesn't have an impact on my daily life.

Does it?

"Flooding is a good description," I confess. "But it's not because of the ADHD. It's just me."

Harper rolls her eyes. "Fine then. It's because of you."

I lift my hands, trying to maintain a serious face. "Hey—don't blame me. It's the ADHD."

Grinning, Harper looks up at me. "You're impossible."

"I'm not impossible. My ADHD, on the other hand, is—"

"Don't say it." She laughs, shaking her head. "You know it doesn't really matter, right? And you'll never be able to separate the two things? You are you. You have ADHD. Personality, brain function—who knows. It might help to look up some of this stuff, just to see what you might struggle with or what some workarounds are." She waves a hand. "Whatever the reason, the result is the same. If you get emotionally overwhelmed, those feelings build up and spill over. Then, you crash. You did that yesterday. You're doing it now."

My sister is so right. About all the things. And just talking about this, recognizing it, I feel lighter. As the sun crests over the trees and houses in the distance, hope emerges in my chest. I've messed up, but this isn't the end. I'm not going to stay in this pit.

"I was an idiot," I say.

"You were. But it's not too late to fix that. I'm not always great at reading people, but Lindy and Jo love you. It's clear, even to me. And I think you need to be with them, not here with me."

I nod, already itching to get moving, to get back home.

I'm turning to thank Harper, when she gives me a hard shove. I go straight into the pool, arms flapping.

It may be heated, but it's still a shock, and I emerge soaking wet.

Harper, clearly anticipating retaliation, has retreated to the door leading into the house. I see Tank behind her, blinking sleepily and squinting out at me.

"What was that for?" I ask, climbing up the steps and wringing out my shirt.

"That," Harper says, "is for going to James—of all people, *James*—for relationship advice instead of me."

When she puts it that way, I can't even argue. Plus, I don't have time to argue; I've got things to do. I have an apology to make, and not a single second to waste.

CHAPTER THIRTY-FIVE

Lindy

I'VE REALIZED something about the loft. It's only the perfect space if Pat is here. Without him, even with Jo in the other room, it's like a coffin.

Okay, okay—that's dramatic. It's like a stone tomb that holds coffins. A slightly less maudlin and morose comparison but only SLIGHTLY. The emptiness I feel in the loft only echoes the one in my chest cavity, which feels as though it's been scooped out with a spoon and left gaping.

I could totally bust out some Edgar Allen Poe style prose right now, but since that's not what's trending on Buzzfeed, I can't even try to lose myself in my work this morning. It was still dark when I woke up, and the sun is just starting to tint the sky a lighter blue. Coffee, usually my morning BFF, tastes the way cigarette butts smell.

When there's a soft knock, I practically sprint to the door. Pat came back! Pat's here! He's—

"Hey, chica." Val and Winnie stand in the doorway.

"Don't look so happy to see us," Win says.

I sag. "Sorry. I thought you were—never mind." They push past me inside. "Come on in. Welcome to my sort of home."

"Whoa. This place is killer," Winnie says. "He's still not back?"

"Nope."

"Is Jo asleep still?" Val asks.

"Yeah. She crashed when we got home, then woke up at like six and we watched a movie until late. I bet she'll sleep for a few more hours."

Val sets a bag down on the kitchen island. I didn't even realize she was carrying it. "Breakfast tacos from Big Mo. And donuts. Not from Daylight Donuts, just in case they really are trying to poison us."

Normally, the smell of either of those things would be enough to add some spring to my step, but my olfactory system seems to have shut down. I can only smell the ghost of Pat lingering in the air. I eat a donut anyway, just in case the sugar will do anything to drag me out of this depressing little rut I'm in. It tastes like nothing, so I give up after two bites and flop down on the couch, which has no right being this comfortable when I'm having a crisis.

Val and Winnie join me after taking a self-guided tour of all the rooms but Jo's, oohing and aahing over it all.

I roll my eyes. "Yeah, yeah, yeah. The place is amazing. Pat is amazing. Blah blah blah—ugh."

"We left you alone last night because you asked," Winnie says. "Now, spill. What the heck happened and why isn't Pat here?"

"How are the dogs?" I ask, and they both stare at me like I'm an alien wearing a human suit.

Val heaves a sigh. "I'm feeding your dogs, and they're chasing squirrels and taking lazy naps. I even stopped by yesterday to scatter some food around for Elvis. Can we talk about real stuff now?"

"Sheesh. Forgive me for caring about the welfare of my animals."

"Lindy!" Winnie groans. "Stop it! What is happening with you and Pat?"

Starting with our conversation in the courthouse yesterday, I work backwards. Mostly because I knew they'd completely freak when I tell them I tried to get Pat to sleep with me, and he said no. And, of course, they do. I have to put a pillow over my face when I tell them this part.

"That's nothing to be embarrassed about," Winnie says. "You're married. He's a hottie. You've got literally years of sexual tension built up between you. It would be super weird if you weren't interested in sleeping with him."

Val shrugs. "I'd have thrown myself at him on the wedding night, but that's me. I applaud your self-control."

"Thank you? Anyway, that's the story. Now I'm just wallowing."

Winnie picks up my partially eaten donut. "Clearly."

"The question is—are you ready for a little friend intervention?" Val asks. "Frientervention. I like the sound of that. Patent pending."

"You can't patent phrases," I tell her. "That's a trademark."

Winnie waves a hand. "Back on topic. Frientervention—yay or nay?"

I hug the pillow to my chest. My empty, cavernous, heartless chest. "Yes. Please save me from myself. Even if it's not what I want to hear. Even if you don't agree with each other—because y'all almost never agree."

"I'll go first." Winnie takes a deep breath, then says, "I think Pat is right."

Val gasps and smacks Winnie's knee. "You're breaking girl code!"

"How am I breaking girl code? Also, it should be woman code. Or women code."

"It doesn't have the same ring to it," Val argues. "Girl code just rolls off the tongue. Like girls' night. Women's night sounds lame, like a hangout where you'd crochet doilies or fold napkins."

"Who folds napkins these days?" Winnie asks, and Val throws her hands up.

"Guys, usually I'm all about not being the center of attention," I say, "but right now, I'm kind of having a crisis. Could we please focus? I need help here."

They both stare at me. Then just keep staring.

"Y'all. I hope you heard me—I'm *asking for help*," I repeat.

"Oh, we heard you," Winnie says. "We're just committing this moment to memory. That way we can hold it over your head later."

I toss my pillow at her. Val gets up from her corner of the couch and invades my space, hugging me with the kind of force that could derail a train. "Despite what I said about girl code, I think maybe Winnie is right. Half right," she amends.

"Go on." Speaking is difficult with the softball lodged in my throat. Huh. How'd that get there?

"Pat's timing was the absolute worst," Val says. "It was. I think you were both emotionally frayed and overwhelmed, and he threw something at you when he should have waited. But Linds, you've been pushing him away since the moment he came back."

"And, you said yourself, you were being kind of distant yesterday," Winnie adds. "I happened to see his face right after everything ended. He was so excited—and then you breezed right by him to hug Jo." I start to protest, and Winnie holds up a hand. "I get it! I do. Jo was the most important part of everything. But Pat looked crushed, like he wanted to be part of the moment and wasn't."

I swallow. "I didn't mean to leave him out. It was all just so chaotic and overwhelming. I wanted him to be with us. I did."

"Do you think he knows that?" Val asks gently.

"I don't know."

"He said he loved you," Winnie says. "Did you say it back?"

I shake my head. "I thought it. I *wanted* to say it."

"But you didn't." Val strokes my hair. "And that's okay—you were overwhelmed. We get it. It's not such a big deal. Now that things with Jo are settled, you can work this out. You have time to tell him."

"But he left." My lip trembles. "What if he doesn't come back?"

"Which is like your Kryptonite," Val says. "But I have a feeling Pat is like a boomerang. He's coming back. He is. And you're going to be ready when he does."

"Look, sometimes it takes two to be dumb," Winnie says. "You were both dumb back in the day, and you're both being dumb now."

"Um, thanks?"

"The point is, this is fixable," Winnie says. "So, let's fix it."

Val claps her hands. "Yes! We're moving on to the action plan. Action is good."

I feel like I'm coming out of a fog, and the more the air

clears, the more I realize my friends are so right. I've been thinking about my own hurt, focusing on the fact that Pat left me. Which—yeah, okay. He did. But Pat's actions have spoken loudly over the past weeks, confirming the words he said. He loves me. He's all in.

Now, it's my turn to show him that I'm all in too. "I don't even know what to do."

"Yes, you do," Val says, giving me a little shake. "It's Pat. Think big."

"We need a grand gesture," Winnie says, and both of our heads swivel her way. "What? I'm not a monster. I've read a romance novel or two."

"You *have?*" I ask. This is somehow more mind-blowing than my realization about Pat.

"Just for the witty banter." Winnie pauses, then smooths back her ponytail. "And maybe for the fictional men. But women don't do the big romantic thing nearly enough. And I think they should. So, let's figure out a way for you to do something for Mr. Grand Gesture himself."

THE TOP SEVEN ROMANTIC GRAND GESTURES FROM MOVIES

By Birdie Graham

Who doesn't love a grand gesture? In real life, you should consider yourself lucky if you are on the receiving end of a grand gesture, but they are EVERYWHERE in the movies. Here are my top seven grand gestures from movies in no particular order (because I couldn't decide on my favorite).

7. Heath Ledger serenading Julia Stiles in *10 Things I Hate about You*. (Oh, Heath. How we miss you!)

6. Meg Ryan and Tom Hanks meeting at the top of the Empire State Building in *Sleepless in Seattle*.

5. Adam Sandler's airplane proposal to Drew Barrymore in *The Wedding Singer*.

4. Billy Crystal finding Meg Ryan at a party for the perfect New Year's Eve kiss in *When Harry Met Sally*.

3. John Cusack holding up the boombox outside Ione Skye's window in *Say Anything*. (I feel like Peter Gabriel should get a mention here too for being instrumental. The moment wouldn't have worked with, say, Phil Collins. Love ya, Phil.)

2. Beast giving Belle the library in the cartoon *Beauty and the Beast*. (Tell me I'm not the only one who preferred the Beast to the man he became???)

1. Mr. Darcy's final proposal to Elizabeth. (You can't make me choose between the miniseries and the movie. Sorry. And while the rest are not in order, this is by far my number one.)

Did I miss any? Leave your favorite grand gestures in the comments below!

CHAPTER THIRTY-SIX

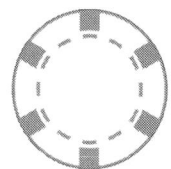

Lindy

SOMETIMES, you just need your mama. And this, I decide, is one of those times.

Once Jo woke up, cutting off our fruitless but hilarious brainstorming session of grand gestures, I headed out. Val, Winnie, and Jojo were happily watching cat fail videos on YouTube.

My car ride didn't inspire any ideas better than Winnie's suggestion involving a group of peacocks (technically called a muster) or Val's idea to have Chevy fake lock Pat up. I think she just likes that one because it involves seeing Chevy. I kinda like it too because it would be fun to see Pat behind bars again. But ultimately, none of the ideas are quite right.

I may not know how—yet—but I will come up with something. I will. And then, I'm going to grand gesture him so hard, he won't know what hit him.

Before I head inside the facility, I finally dig Rachel's letter out of my purse. It feels like a door I need to close, even if I'm a little nervous about its contents.

The letter is so very *Rachel*.

Apparently, she wrote the letter from rehab, where she returned after a week of bingeing. Sad, but not really a surprise. The rest of her letter alternates between passive aggressive and just straight-up aggressive. While acknowledging I'm "probably" the best person to care for Jo, Rachel also made sure to mention how much she hates letting me "win" and hopes I'm happy now.

Yes, Rachel. I *am* happy now.

Or, I will be, once I resolve things with Pat and restore the family of three we've been building.

I hope Rachel can find healing, I really do. But I don't feel the tiniest bit bad throwing her letter away.

When I reach Mama's room, she smiles, eyes lighting up. "Hello, my Lindy Lou Who!"

I haven't heard her use that nickname in *years*. I sit down, pulling my chair close to hers, noting the fresh flowers and a few extra bird feeders.

"Hey, Mama. What's new?" I ask, hoping to get my bearings on what year we're in today.

Mama looks down at her wrist, then frowns, rubbing the place where a watch used to be. "Have you heard from Rachel? She left for the library earlier and should have been back by now."

I cannot seem to escape my sister. "Haven't seen her."

The library is not a place she ever set foot, but I can see her using it as a cover when she was sneaking off somewhere else in middle or high school. Which would make me college age, maybe late high school?

Mama reaches out, taking my hand. "Would you mind

driving up there, looking for Rachel? I just don't like the people she's been hanging around with lately. They're ... not the best."

No, they hadn't been the best. They helped my sister take the leap from bad to worse, from struggling with addiction to going fully off the rails. Though I think even if Rachel had friends like Winnie and Val, she would have chosen the same path. It seems inevitable.

I think of Rachel's letter, of the venom and bitterness she still holds all these years, and I'm just sad for her. I don't think anything Mama or I did could have made a difference, but I wish she could escape her own demons. Throwing away the letter has left me with a sense of closure I didn't know I needed. Even talking and thinking about Rachel now, I feel somehow more free.

"Is everything with you okay?" Mama asks. "You seem sad. Talk to me. I've been so worried about Rach I've probably been distracted. I'm sorry."

Tears roll down my face, despite me squeezing my eyes shut as much as possible. They're terrible at security, my eyes. Just letting all the tears roll right through like tiny escaping bandits. No concern at all.

"Oh, Lindy Lou." Mama envelops me in the kind of hug that only loosens up everything inside me. She's like an expert lock-picker, her kindness just one of the tools in her kit.

"There's a guy, Mama."

Might as well let it all hang out. Allllll my secrets. Even if they don't fit into the timeline she's living on.

"Tell me all about him, baby. But first—spare me the tension. Should I hate him or tell you to forgive him?"

I laugh and sob at the same time, clutching to Mama like she's all I have. Because, at this moment, that's how it feels.

"He isn't the one who needs to be forgiven. Maybe a little, but not really. I messed up, Mama. A lot."

Oh, how I miss being able to talk to her like this! And maybe she doesn't know what year it is, or where she is, but she is always the one person I can trust with anything, and at this moment, I need her more than she knows.

"Oh, I doubt you messed up that badly." She waves a hand in the air, and a few birds scatter away from the feeders.

"You'd be surprised. I know how to sink a ship."

"Nonsense. Tell me about it," she says. "I'll give you my honest assessment."

"I love him." It feels so, so good to say it out loud. "I really, really love him."

Her smile is wide and warm. "Well, that's good to hear. But are you keeping him at arm's length the way you always do?"

Was I doing that, even back then?

Mama continues. "I know my girl. And as wonderful as you are, you seem determined to make yourself like Fort Knox and keep everyone locked out. Don't push this man away, Lindy Lou. Not if you love him."

"I already pushed him away, but not because I don't want him. I was just ... scared. And overwhelmed. Things have been hard lately. I haven't had a lot to give, and I feel like I've taken too much from him without giving enough back."

"I know your father and I didn't have the best relationship."

Understatement of the decade.

"But before he left, he was different. We had a good thing for a time."

This is all news to me. Mama almost never talked about my father, and we kind of drew our own conclusions. I mean, a man who leaves his wife and two daughters without writing or calling, barely paying child support—it's kind of a no-brainer to assume the man is a loser. I'm having a difficult time wrapping my brain around the idea of him and Mama having anything good, ever.

"With a relationship, you aren't always on the same page," she continues. "The important thing is to make sure in the grand scheme of things, the give-and-take is mutual. If you had a hard time and he was there for you, that's a sign of love. Now, you just need to give that love right back."

She makes it sound so simple. Could it be that simple?

"Have you told this young man you love him?" she asks. I shake my head, and she brightens. "Well, then, start there."

"That's just it, though. Telling him I love him doesn't seem like enough. He loves big things, drama. After all that he's done for me, I want to make some kind of grand gesture. I need to show him I love him, not just tell him."

"I don't need a grand gesture."

My head snaps to the door, not believing what—or, rather, who—I see. Pat stands there, holding a big bouquet of flowers. He looks rumpled and sleepless and like he needs a good shave. Though day-old stubble is a great look on him.

"What?" I whisper.

"I don't need a grand gesture," he repeats, shaking his head for emphasis. "I just need you."

Pat's smile goes crooked and his espresso eyes soften, even though he doesn't move. We're just staring across the room that smells like baby powder and faintly like the disinfecting solution they use to clean everything. As far as romantic moments go, this one smells the worst.

Mama interrupts our staring. "Oh, wonderful! Patrick, come meet my daughter. Lindy, this is Patrick. He's the one who's been brightening up my life with the flowers and the birds."

It takes my groggy, overworked brain a moment to catch up. The man Mama called her gardener is my Pat. He's the one who's been bringing Mama flowers and adding bird feeders. Not someone on staff here at the facility.

This is exactly the kind of man he is—the man I love. Always thinking of others—giving, giving, giving. Even when it's in secret.

The sweetness makes me tear up yet again, and I am so sick of tears, I'd like to close down my ducts for the rest of the year. They can reopen after January first, or maybe next summer sometime.

Pat may have just said he doesn't need a grand gesture, but I vow right then and there to keep finding ways to show him I love him. Large, small, medium. All the gestures in all the shapes and sizes will be coming his way. It will be a lifetime of Gesturepalooza.

That is, if he wants me.

Shut up, Lindy. He wants you.

I'm going to listen to the bossy voice in my head which sounds a lot like Winnie right now. I stand, and Pat meets me halfway between Mama and the door. With zero hesitation, he wraps me in his arms, crushing the flowers between us.

"You're here," I say, my mouth against his neck. "You've been coming here, doing all this for Mama?"

"You love me." He says the words like they're a precious treasure he's holding. There's awe in his voice and happiness too. "I heard you say it, didn't I?"

"You did, and I do. I love you, Pat."

"I think I might need you to pinch me."

I do, right at one of his ticklish spots, and when he giggles, a tear drips right into the corner of my smile. "I'm sorry for pushing you away, and for not telling you sooner. I don't know why you're still here."

"I'll always be here for you. Always, Lindybird. And I'm sorry for putting everything on you yesterday. It was terrible timing. I should have waited."

"It was the worst timing. The absolute worst."

Pat pulls back enough to look at me. "I'm so sorry."

"I forgive you."

He presses a kiss to my cheek then another, tracing a seemingly random path over my skin with his lips. It takes me a moment to realize he's kissing away my tears.

"Just like before, we both made some missteps. Do you think we can forget about the mistakes and move on toward the good part?"

His lips curve, and his eyes gleam. "And what, pray tell, is the good part?"

I capture his lips in mine, showing him exactly what the good part will entail. Mouths, lips, hands—all the closeness, all the connection. The kiss is flame and sugar, hot and sweet. I'm starving, and Pat is delicious.

And finally, finally I feel the wall of my resolve for distance come crumbling down. It more than crumbles. Pat's love is like a wave of water, slamming into that wall and obliterating any resistance.

Letting go feels like love. Giving in feels like freedom.

I want Pat. In all the ways I can have him. My husband. My friend. My lover. My family, my forever.

The spark of desire returns, burning brighter and hotter than two nights ago when I begged Pat to take me to bed. Now, the desperate need for closeness, to feel his skin on mine, is pure, and it's about cementing the commitment we made to each other, in that courtroom and again, today. I'd happily make vows to Pat every morning and renew them again at night.

Because this? This is everything.

We'll probably make a lot of mistakes together. But together, we're better than we are apart. We're *more*.

A throat clearing has us jerking apart, both breathing heavy. The flowers Pat held in his hand, probably meant for Mama's vase, are crushed between us. This is ... totally awkward.

Mama raises one white brow, her expression both mischievous and disapproving. "As happy as I am for you two, I'd prefer a little distance from the full show."

Pat and I mutter apologies, exchanging sheepish glances as we pull apart.

"Do we need to have *the talk* again?" Mama continues, and I remind myself she thinks I'm years younger than I am.

"Nope. No talk necessary," I tell her, my cheeks flaming. Pat chuckles, and I shove him.

"I might need the talk," Pat says to Mama. "I'm not sure if I've ever had it."

I go to shove him again, and he darts out of the way, giggling. Mama eyes him like she's totally got his number.

"Boy, with the way you kiss, it looks like you're well versed."

"Mama!" I hide my face behind my hands, because I don't want to have any more of this conversation.

Pat does his best to revive the flowers, which is pretty much a lost cause. Petals litter the floor and I kneel to pick them up, counting each one as I try to cool down the raging heat flooding my bloodstream. We set what's left of the daisies in a vase, wave goodbye to Mama, and practically sprint down the hallway. We don't stop until we reach his truck, which is parked beside my car.

"Can I take you home?" Pat asks. "To *our* home?"

"Where exactly is our home?" I ask. "We're weird sort of

nomads right now. Like, are we going to stay permanently at the loft? Fix the house?"

Pat rubs a hand down my back. "Slow down, darlin'. We'll figure out the long-term plans as we go. The location of our home isn't the most important part. The person—the people involved—are. Where's Jo, speaking of?"

"She's with Val and Winnie at the loft." I pull my phone out, realizing I haven't checked it since I left. "But, it looks like they've taken her to Val's to see the dogs." I clear my throat. "That means we have some time."

It doesn't take him more than a second to catch my meaning and my heated gaze. "Then it seems like we best get home. And quickly." He leans closer, his lips tracing over my ear and sending shivers in a straight path up my spine. "I might need a *lot* of time."

I clutch his shirt, holding him close and speaking into his neck. "How's the soundproofing in the loft? Asking purely as a rhetorical question. For later tonight. And the night after that."

Pat pulls back, and the look he gives me makes my knees tremble. "I made sure the soundproofing is excellent, wife."

"Let's give it a test run later, husband. But first, I think I need to do one thing."

I pull a piece of paper out of my purse, one I've kept there for weeks. Pat grins when he recognizes the rules he signed, before doing his very best to skirt around each one. I start to tear it apart, but his hand stops me.

"Can I keep it?"

"Why would you want to?" I ask.

Pat shrugs, grabbing the paper and folding it up before shoving it into his pocket. "Posterity. Also, just in case I need to remind you how I made you want to break them all."

"That's the kind of gloating I can handle."

Pulling me close, Pat's lips find mine. He kisses me through my smile, through the words he speaks next. "Those rules may be void, but the piece of paper saying we're married still stands. Are you okay with that? Are you okay being mine, so long as we both shall live, for real?"

"More than okay," I tell him, pulling back enough to meet his eyes. "Now, stop standing here talking and take me home, husband."

EPILOGUE

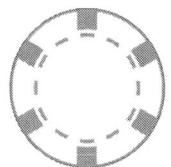

Pat

THEY SAY the third time's the charm and for me, at least in terms of standing before Judge Judie's bench, that is absolutely true.

The first time, I received an ankle monitor. The second, I gave a ring. And this third time, I'm gaining a daughter.

The courtroom is just as packed—no, maybe more—than on my wedding day. And I dare you to find a dry eye in the place. Actually, I take that back. Jo isn't crying. She is smiling so big someone could trip and fall right into her dimple. It could be me.

I wipe my eyes, and Lindy hands me a tissue over the top of Jo's head. It's already a little damp, but I'm not a picky man. My wife and I can share a tear-stained tissue. After all, we're about to share everything else.

"Last question," Judge Judie says, and I swear even her voice warbles a bit.

Has she been asking questions? Have I been answering them? This whole day is like a wild dream come true.

"Lindy and Patrick Graham, is it your intention to provide Jo Darcy with a loving home?"

"Yes," Lindy says, just as I say, "And then some."

There are a few chuckles in the back, and Jo squeezes both of our hands. Judge Judie nods, then turns her fierce eyes on Jo.

"And Jojo—just to be sure, you want to proceed with this adoption?"

"Absolutely. Let's *official* this."

I'm not sure if I imagine or actually hear Tank's groan at the way Jo just verbed a noun. He doesn't need to worry though. I know it was for my ears. Most of the time, Jo corrects what she calls my abuse of the English language. I give her hand an extra squeeze and wink when she turns that smile up on me.

"Well, then." Judge Judie shifts, and I realize she's holding out the gavel to Jo. "You want to *gavel* us to a close, Jojo?"

I definitely hear Tank groan this time. Sue me if I'm an influencer. I can't help the gifts I've been born with, and starting trends seems to be one.

I hoist Jo up on my hip so she can reach. Lindy steps closer, winding her arm around my waist and putting a hand on Jo's shoulder. This is how we've spent the last few weeks: together.

Like, so together that I think other people are sick of our togetherness. Too bad for them, because we aren't sick of it. We're just getting started.

Leaning forward, Jo raises the gavel, then pauses, thinking. Clearing her throat, she says, "By the power vested in me, I now pronounce us ... FAMILY."

Not even a little bit legal, but hey. It's ridiculously adorable. And as Jo bangs the gavel down perhaps harder than necessary to claps, cheers, and hollers, no one cares. The judge signs the decree of adoption, and we are officially OFFICIAL.

Judge Judie stands, taking off her robe to reveal a worn pair of overalls underneath. "I missed the wedding celebration due to work, but I'm not missing another one. Let's party, y'all!"

I'm still carrying Jo, who somehow managed to steal the judge's gavel. But Lindy pulls me to a stop before we're swallowed in the throng of well-wishers. She wraps her arms around us both in a quick hug, then kisses Jo's cheek and plants a longer kiss on my lips.

"You promised," Jo warns.

Biting her lip, Lindy steps back, her eyes aglow. "Sorry, Jojo. We'll keep the PDA to a minimum."

It's not easy. Not when we have those five lost years to make up for. I give Lindy a look that says *I'll give you some PDA later*, and she laughs. Not sure the exact meaning got across, but I'll just have to show her.

The newly renovated town square is already decorated with lights for Christmas. A LOT of lights. Because Tank has always loved Christmas, he wants downtown Sheet Cake to officially open Thanksgiving weekend boasting more lights per square foot than any other city in the world. It would mean attention by way of the *Guinness World Records* people, and it also means it practically looks like daylight in the waning November afternoon.

This is the first time I've seen it all lit, and it is nothing short of magical. Tank's smile is the only thing brighter out here.

"Wait here for a sec," Lindy says, "I've got to go speak to Val."

She disappears into the crowd, which consists of my family and friends, just about all of the old Sheeters, and even a few faces I don't recognize. Probably people from new Sheet Cake or even Austin who just happened to come see what all the buzz is about. Now they'll all probably stay for the party, not even realizing what they're celebrating.

Hey—the more, the merrier.

"Can I steal my granddaughter?" Tank barely has the sentence out before Jo has launched herself at him.

"I think you have your answer," I say, but Tank and Jo are already off, admiring the lights strung over the square and across the streets and on top of every single building. We're going to need some blackout curtains for the loft for the remainder of the season, since the new house won't be done for several months.

Turns out, Lindy wasn't emotionally attached to the little farmhouse, which upon inspection, was condemned. "It's got too many sad memories," she said, and we sat in camping chairs and watched bulldozers take it down.

I would have loved the drama of a wrecking ball, but it turns out they're expensive and make more of a mess. Also, Miley Cyrus pretty much ruined wrecking balls for everyone, so bulldozers worked just fine. The new foundation has been poured, and this week, they'll start to frame it up. The dogs are still with Val and Mari, but I caught sight of Elvis watching over the place.

"Hey, brother. Congratulations again," Collin says, giving me a hearty slap on the back. "This place looks great. I couldn't have pictured it when you first brought us out here."

"Tank is doing well."

"You're both doing well," Collin says. "Heck, even James. Still can't believe you got him in on this."

Me neither. And I'm still not sure what pushed him to say yes, but he's starting to make progress on the warehouse and silos, sometimes crashing at Tank's place, which is now done. Dad splits his time between here and the house in Austin. I have to say, it's been great having him just across the street. Not only does Jo get the benefit of more family, but he's a great babysitter when Lindy and I need some alone time. Which we do. Frequently.

"There's a whole empty part of the warehouse that would be perfect for a gym," I remind Collin.

He sniffs. "A very rudimentary gym, maybe."

"Nothing wrong with humble roots. Fitness is fitness, right? It doesn't have to be fancy."

And Collin's gym certainly has gotten fancy. His clientele of elite athletes has attracted a whole host of wealthy Austinites who care more about meeting those athletes and taking a photo of the latest trendy green smoothie for Instagram than they do actual fitness. They are everything Collin loathes, but it's great for business. I'm just not sure that his business is great for him any longer.

"Pat, we need you." Mari emerges from the crowd, grabbing my hand with urgency.

"Is Jo okay? Lindy?"

"They're fine, necio. Don't worry your pretty face about it. Right over ... here."

She leads me to the gazebo, where Judge Judie is standing at the top of the steps, back in her official robes. Suddenly, all the lights go out.

There's a collective groan, whispered questions, and then, a light. It starts with the judge, who has a large candlestick, now lit. She touches the wick of Lynn Louise's candle to her right, then Kitty's on her left.

"What's happening?"

"Shh!" Mari says. "Just watch."

I couldn't stop if I tried. The whole town, it seems, has candles and is passing the light from person to person until the whole square is bathed in warm, flickering light. It's beautiful, but it's a moment I should be appreciating with Lindy and Jo.

As if reading my thoughts, Mari says, "They're here. Go on, up you go."

She gives me a nudge that's more like a shove toward the gazebo steps. Judge Judie rolls her eyes and waves me up. "Hurry it up, then. We don't have all night."

I climb the steps, glancing around as I do so, seeing the faces of just about every person I know and love—and some I know and tolerate—holding up candles. But where are Jo and Lindy?

Judge Judie grabs my arm and wrangles me into place on the step just below her. "Open your eyes, boy."

She turns my head toward the sidewalk and ... OH. There are Lindy and Jo, at the end of the sidewalk, hand in hand. But they've both changed, and this is what finally clues me in to what's happening here.

Lindy is wearing a white dress. A WEDDING dress. Shorter in the front, showing off her legs and cowboy boots, but with a long train in the back. It's covered in crystal beading, and as they walk toward me, she shimmers in the glowing candlelight, a beautiful, ethereal dream.

I can't speak. I can't move. I don't even breathe until they reach me.

I'm probably supposed to wait, but I can't. When they're at the bottom of the steps, I leap down, taking Lindy's free hand.

"You are so beautiful," I whisper. "Lindy, what is this?"

"It's the wedding you wanted," she says. "Technically, a vow renewal, but whatever. Who has time to worry about technicalities?"

"Not me."

"I know you said you didn't need a grand gesture, but I wanted to give one anyway."

Oh, the irony. She's got her own grand gesture coming her way at the end of this party, and I love that we've both been unknowingly grand gesturing the other. I didn't need a ceremony, or a big thing. But I absolutely love that Lindy planned this for me.

Judge Judie clears her throat. "Can we get this show on the road? These candles aren't going to last forever. Who gives this woman to be wed?"

Jo lifts her chin, and I get a glimpse of the strong, brilliant woman she will one day become. "I give my mama to marry my daddy."

At her words, both Lindy and I suck in a breath. Jo gives us a mischievous grin. "I didn't check with you about the new names," she whispers, "but I've learned it's better to ask forgiveness than permission."

She definitely learned that from me, and Lindy will give me an earful later. For now, we're both still caught on her words.

"It's official now," Jo continues. "But even without a piece of paper declaring it, I want to call you what you are—my mom and dad."

We're probably supposed to wait for the end to hug and

kiss and cry like babies but who cares? If you can't throw things off a little at your second wedding, when can you?

We finally get to the actual ceremony, and I fumble my way through impromptu vows, say *I do* to my already bride, and everyone blows out the candle as we kiss. Which is a good thing because this is NOT a chaste courthouse kiss.

Lights explode above us as someone sets off fireworks. I catch sight of James and Chase up on a nearby rooftop, lighting the fuses.

My heart swells with joy and pride and a sense of rightness as I look around this square. It's Tank's vision starting to come to life, only bigger, grander, better. *It's my dream too*, I think, looking at Lindy, then Jo. My dream and then one bigger than I ever could have imagined.

And until an apologetic Chevy shows up with the sheriff to shut the whole thing down due to an ordinance from city council about public gatherings and fireworks in the town proper, I'd say it's the best wedding in the world.

Winnie

"Don't fret. They're going to love it," I say, smoothing the wrinkle of worry from Val's forehead with my fingertip. We're sitting in Mari's at the counter after my dumb brother shut down the party. I mean, fine—it's not his fault. It's probably Billy Waters using city council as his own personal playpen again, but whatever. I can still blame my brother some.

"But if we'd had more time to plan—"

"You would have found more things to add to the itinerary, and it *still* would be perfect. Stop worrying."

While Lindy was secretly planning tonight's wedding as a surprise for Pat, he's had our help planning a secret European honeymoon. The two of them are disgustingly, adorably in love. Val and I helped with tonight as well as the travel plans, and it was hard as heck not to slip up and tell one person what we were doing for the other. We somehow managed that and the caretaking schedule for Jo while they're gone.

Val sighs and takes a bite of pumpkin pecan pie. "Fine. Ooh, this is good, Big Mo."

"Thank you. I think it's the bourbon," he says, passing by with a wink and a grin.

"There's bourbon in there?" I perk up. Because if I weren't primarily into app development, I'd want to be a mixologist. "I want a slice!"

"Coming right up," Big Mo says, ducking—literally, he has to duck—into the back.

"So," Val says, wiping the corner of her mouth. She's finished her pie and swiped up every last crumb with her fingertip. "Dale was a no-show again?"

"I don't want to talk about it."

"Maybe he's really in the CIA. So when he says he has an accounting emergency, what he really means is he's off catching an assassin or pulling out someone's fingernails in an interrogation."

Big Mo chooses that moment to set the pie down in front of me, now that I'm imagining straight-arrow Dale yanking out someone's fingernail. Gross. And impossible. He'd more likely pull out a manicure kit and push back their cuticles.

"He might still come," I say. "And anyway, I wouldn't be

dating him if he gave off CIA vibes. The last thing I want is that."

"You wouldn't find it the least bit exciting and romantic?" Val asks.

"Nope. My idea of romance is …"

I can't finish that sentence, because my idea of romance is a guy who simply shows up when he's supposed to. Which is starting to feel like a very low bar. While I keep pretending things are fine with me and Dale, he's not even able to handle my very low bar.

I'm getting tired of this long-distance thing and being the one who always drives to Austin to see him. Maybe Dale is right, and I should just move. But something keeps me anchored here in Sheet Cake. I'm not sure if it's just the fact that Dale hasn't given me a ring, which would be a real reason to relocate, or if it's the Sheet Cake roots I wish I could pull up. But so far, I don't want to leave. And I'm getting tired of driving for Dale when he can't do the same for me.

Anyway, leaving Sheet Cake isn't on the table considering the new job I start tomorrow. I'll be doing everything from web design to … I don't actually know what. Because I have no idea what it takes to run a brewery. But I'm more than a little excited to find out.

Excited about everything but my boss, that is.

As if on cue, a voice cuts through the noise. A voice that is like a spear straight into my soul.

"Shouldn't you be getting a good night's sleep before your first day tomorrow?"

Does James Graham have to stand so close when he talks? And does he have to smell so good? It's really unfortunate when the kind of man who is a total jerk is hotter than a pizza oven and smells just as good.

"Sleep is for the weak," I say. "Plus, it's only nine. I'll be okay, but you should probably be in bed, grandpa."

His scowl, which was already like a crater, deepens. Fascinating. I wonder just how deep it could go. Maybe that will be my new game—finding out just how much I can tick off my new boss.

James stares at me with that dead-eye look of his. Sometimes I really do question if the man has a soul. Right then, I get my answer because Jo runs up, flinging herself around James's big, muscular legs. He definitely has at least a partial soul, and the man's body is something else.

"Speaking of people who should be in bed—why are you still up, Jojo?" I ask, trying not to stare open-mouthed at the smile James aims Jo's way. When the man smiles, he could almost be human.

"I'm going to Tank's now," she says, passing hugs on to me and Val. "Just wanted to say goodnight."

"Night, little one," James says.

He has his own nickname for her now? Ugh.

I try not to look like I'm watching, but it's fascinating to me every time he cracks a smile. It only seems to happen with Jo. Otherwise, he seems to hate all people, especially women. And most especially me in particular, which is going to make working alongside him interesting.

Tank waves to Jo from the door, and she follows him out. I turn back to my pie and away from the man who is currently taking up too much of my brain power. Big Mo has really outdone himself with this pie. It's incredible.

"What kind of bourbon did you use?" I ask, but before he can answer, a hand skates up my back.

And maybe it's because I'm on high alert because of James, but I react quickly and violently. I haven't taken self-defense classes, but after playing roller derby, I've got a few hits that can take out someone unprepared. The shoulder I throw back into the person standing behind me—who I assume is James—knocks him off his feet.

But when I spin around, ready to start yelling, James is still standing, his eyebrows almost at his hairline and his lip curved up in a smile. It's *Dale* on the floor, eyes wide and mouth gasping. Looks like I knocked the wind out of him as well as taking him out.

"Dale!" I'm on the floor beside him in an instant, only thinking for a minute about the fact that I'm probably ruining my pantyhose—and they were a new pair too, with a cute little seam up the back. "I'm so sorry! Are you okay?"

"Fine," he gasps a moment later, when he finally catches his breath. "Wow. That was some hit."

"Yeah, it was," James says.

I jerk my head up and glare at the infernal grouch, who only shrugs, whispering, "What? It was."

"Do you need water? What can I get you?" I ask Dale.

He shakes his head and starts getting to his feet. I stand first and offer him my hand, but he uses a chair for leverage instead. He's still blinking fast, with one hand pressed to his chest. "I'll just use the restroom. Be right back." And with that, he high-tails it to the bathroom.

I slump back down on my stool, jabbing my fork into the pie. But it seems to have lost all taste.

Val leans into me. "Your boyfriend is definitely not in the CIA."

"That guy is your *boyfriend*?"

I don't even know what James means by the tone in his voice, but it's offensive any way you look at it. I spin on the stool and give him my fiercest look. While it would wither most people, he's unaffected, still just looking shocked. "Yes, that's my boyfriend."

"Almost a fiancé," Val adds, and I really wish she wouldn't have, because honestly, it's been a while since Dale and I have talked about the whole marriage thing.

Being an accountant, Dale is slightly obsessed with being fiscally responsible. Which has meant putting off even discussing the next step in our relationship again and again. I tried telling him once I'd happily live on ramen, and he looked so horrified, I didn't bring it up again.

"What is an almost fiancé?" James scoffs.

"He's not—whatever." I wave my fork. "He's my boyfriend. It's serious."

"That guy? The boring, buttoned-up one you just took out with one little hit?"

It's the *little hit* comment that does it. I'm really not a violent person. I mean, not unless a situation calls for it. Even when I played derby, I was a jammer—more about speed and agility than big hits and blocking. Still, I know how to hit, and no one expects it coming from little ol' me. When I stand and launch a hip hit into James's thigh, I give it all I got.

Which leaves him on the floor exactly where Dale was just moments ago. Instead of getting down to help him, I stand over him, hands on my hips. He clutches his thigh, groaning.

"You gave me a charley horse!"

"You deserve worse." I lift my chin. "And I regret nothing."

"I'm your boss," James groans, giving me an incredulous look.

Dale chooses that moment to come out of the bathroom. He's glancing down at his phone. When he looks up and sees me standing over James, Dale drops the phone and it goes clattering across the floor.

I give James one last, withering look. "You're not my boss until tomorrow."

With that, I step over James's prone body to collect my boyfriend.

I have a feeling I'm really, REALLY going to regret my new job.

THE END

A NOTE FROM EMMA

I joked with someone that I needed to get a T-shirt after finishing this book saying, "I finished writing *The Buy-In!*" I have been wanting to write this book since I wrote *Falling for Your Best Friend* (Harper's story), and yet, when I started ... it just took forever. Some books do. I'm so happy with how this one turned out, but also SO GLAD to have it done.

I LOVE the Graham family. Tank, James, Collin, and Pat just came alive to me when I wrote *Falling for Your Best Friend*. I've been WAITING to write their story. I can't wait to get to each book!

You might also get some other Sheeters' stories in this series. When I started planning this series, I had a pretty strict idea of where it would go, but even in this book, I was surprised by some things—and that is how I like it. My BEST writing often comes with the things I don't expect and plan. So, buckle up, buttercups! We'll see where this ride takes us.

One other character I've been planning for a LONG time: Chevy. I held an Instagram giveaway last year where the winners could choose a character name in the book. A

Brooke and Her Book won and wanted to use her brother's name. Her brother, Chevy, passed away in an accident ten years ago. I felt like Chevy needed to be a BIG part of a story to honor his memory. He's one of my favorite side characters in this book, and I love his bromance with Pat.

A quick note about the situation with Jo—holy moly, legal situations are a hot mess to write. It's incredibly convoluted. Laws vary by state, and there are so many contingencies and factors that may weigh in. After talking to lawyers, researching, and speaking with moms who have been through custody situations and hearings, I did my best to write a realistic situation that worked for the story. A big thanks to Lorie for talking to me about your family story! So glad we're neighbors.

I really want to create books with depth, quirky characters, witty banter, and some over-the-top humor. That's what I want to bring. As I was editing, I felt like I needed one more funny scene. I originally thought this book would be like *Money Pit*, but thinking about it being Lindy's childhood home and about safety, I just couldn't make the bathtub fall through the floor or the oven explode.

I told my husband, Rob, I needed a funny grill incident. He said: squirrels. And off we went. (I love the flaming squirrels. So much.) While these humorous scenes may seem TOTALLY ridiculous (and they are), the squirrel part had real-life inspiration.

My friend, Eric, unknowingly had a squirrel build a nest in his car engine. When they opened the hood to see why it wouldn't run, a squirrel leaped out onto the mechanic. And Rob's friend Thomas had a squirrel get electrocuted in a transformer, jump (while flaming) into Thomas's shed, and burn the whole shed down.

So, yeah, my stories sometimes have wild humor ... but it's not THAT far off from real life.

The name Lindy comes from Bookstagrammer @Reading-Lindy, who has been so supportive and happened to message me the day I needed a name. Ashlee's name comes from @bookswithnopictures, a fellow friend in snark and great supporter. You just never know when you might have a character named after you ...

Thanks so much for waiting so long for this story! I've got more books to come in this series, and I can't wait to give you more of Sheet Cake and the Grahams.

Emma St. Clair is a *USA Today* bestselling author of over twenty books. She loves sweet love stories and characters with a lot of sass. Her stories range from rom-com to women's fiction and all will have humor, heart, and nothing that's going to make you need to hide your Kindle from the kids. ;)

Sign up for emails to get recommendations and book news: http://emmastclair.com/romcomemail

You can join her reader group at https://www.facebook.com/groups/emmastclair/

ACKNOWLEDGMENTS

Thanks to Jenny Proctor for talking me down off the ledge and for all the feedback on the first draft. Love you! A big thanks to reader Krista White for coming up with the name Sheet Cake for this town.

I want to give a giant thank you to all of the early readers and also to the Bookstagrammers who support me. You guys and your shares and kind words make my job even more of a joy. THANK YOU!!!

Thanks also to Amy L, Jody, Devon, Jill, Marsha, Sunny, Lindsay, Nicole, Catherine, Makayla, Ruth, and anyone else I missed who helped with missed things and typos!

Printed in Great Britain
by Amazon